Philip K. Dick:
The Dream Connection

Philip K. Dick:
The Dream Connection

Edited by D. Scott Apel

 **Atomic Drop Press**

Copyright © 1987, 1999, 2014 by D. Scott Apel
Originally published by The Impermanent Press

ISBN 978-1-8864041-0-6
Published by Atomic Drop Press
www.atomicdroppress.com

For my parents

Contents

ACKNOWLEDGMENTS

A book of this nature could not be produced without the cooperation and resources of a great number of people. I would like to take this opportunity to thank them all.

First and foremost, I owe a great debt to my girlfriend during this time period, Margie Bowers, for her understanding and unfailing emotional support, among other virtues.

Secondly, I wish to thank in equal measure the triumvirate of Paul Williams, Russell Galen and Andy Watson. As founder and head of the PKD Society and executor of the Philip Dick estate, Paul proved invaluable in eagerly assisting me in obtaining information, material, addresses and publicity. Russ, too, gave freely of his time and expertise as agent for the estate for similar assistance, permission to quote, and encouragement. Andy, editor of the PKDS Newsletter, provided the initial inspiration of publishing the interview portion of this book. All three communicated quickly, freely and in a very friendly manner. Their help and interest is truly appreciated.

Third, I owe major thank-yous to others who assisted me without thought of personal reward, specifically Kevin C. Briggs, Alan Vaughan, Ray Faraday Nelson and Robert Anton Wilson.

All of these people proved that talk is indeed *not* cheap: it is their word.

Finally, my deepest appreciation must go to Philip K. Dick, for his time, his guidance and his caring friendship. He is missed.

Preface

In this intimate volume, I am aiming at the reader already familiar with much of Philip K. Dick's work and odd life experiences. I do not intend to clutter up the flow of the conversation or narrative with scholarly footnotes explaining things the reader is hopefully already familiar with. I am assuming at least a nodding acquaintance with such things as the *I Ching, VALIS, Locus* magazine, synchronicity, and the part these played in Philip Dick's life.

Most of the information about PKD's life in my essay "Phil As I Knew Him" is based on researchless memory, and should not be taken as gospel. For a more complete, detailed and researched account of Phil's life during his final years, I can recommend Paul Williams' *Only Apparently Real* (Arbor House, 1986), or Larry Sutin's excellent biography, *Divine Invasions: A Life of Philip K. Dick* (Harmony Books, 1989). The material in my essay is, however, how I remember the man.

Some information from the essays is repeated in the introductions to the various pieces on the (understandable) assumption that readers will be more interested in the Phil Dick sections than in the rest, or may turn to them first. The book has been organized, however, so that the maximum effect is obtained by reading the material in the order in which it is presented.

Enjoy!

Preface

To the Second Edition (1999)

A quarter of a century has now passed since Philip K. Dick's "mystical experiences"; twenty-two years have passed since our interview; seventeen since Phil's death; and a dozen since the initial publication of this book.

And yet, with each passing year, interest in the life and work of Philip K. Dick grows. It is this continuing interest that inspired the reprint of this modest volume. Whatever one's reaction to my own essays, the importance of the interview with Philip Dick cannot be denied, and his thoughts and philosophy certainly deserve to be kept alive.

Advances in desktop publishing over the last decade have made it possible and practical to upgrade the layout of the book (which was always desirable), as well as to correct some typographical errors in the text of the original edition. Aside from these and a very few other very minor changes—hopefully improvements—this volume is a "99.99% exact" reprint of the original.

My thanks once again to the key contributors for allowing this reprint of their material, and particularly to Russ Galen for allowing the reprint of the PKD story which made its debut in the first edition. Thanks this time around are also due to the readers of the first edition who have written me describing their own experiences with Phil Dick.

A dozen years later, is there anything to be added to the "Dream Connection" essay? Nothing of great importance—and still no definite conclusions. Alan Vaughan, on the other hand, thought highly enough of the evidential material to reprint, with my blessing, a large portion of the story and my analytical musings in a chapter entitled "Do We Live After We Die?" in his 1998 book *Doorways to Higher Consciousness* (Celest Press).

In closing, I can only reiterate and reinforce the final line of the Acknowledgements to the first edition: Even after nearly two decades of absence, Phil Dick is still missed.

Phil as I Knew Him

D. Scott Apel

My first contact with Philip K. Dick was indicative of several aspects of the man, and prophetic of several more.

It was the summer of 1977. I was between apartments, staying in my parents' house in Los Gatos, California. One afternoon when I arrived home, I found a message waiting for me

"Your friend Phil called," my mother said as I walked in.

"I don't have any friend named Phil," I said.

"Well, I don't know about that," she said, handing me a note with a phone number. "He just left this number and said to tell you your friend Phil Dick called."

Phil Dick! My friend? My God...

I knew what the call was about, though. Since 1973, my friend, college buddy and ex-roommate Kevin C. Briggs and I had been at work—and I use the term loosely—on a history of science fiction. In late 1976, due to flagging interest and changing circumstances, we hit upon the grand plan of salvaging what we could from that project and changing directions. We would now produce the world's first book of in-depth interviews with a few bright stars in the science fiction universe. We'd call it *Approaching Science Fiction Writers,* a three-level pun: an approach to their work; the stories of how we physically approached them for the interviews; and...*us*, two new science fiction writers approaching the horizon of the field. We'd use this book as a springboard for our fiction. We'd be rich and famous.

We'd never see it published.

(Note to the 2014 edition: This book, retitled Science Fiction: An Oral History, *is now available as an ebook through most major ebook outlets and will soon be available in print from Atomic Drop Press.)*

In mid-1977, though, everything was going great guns. We had early on made a list of the people we wished to include; writers who fit our criteria: science fiction writers we admired, who wrote exceptional science fiction relating to the themes of our book, and who were capable of analyzing their own work intelligently. We had already accomplished two-hour interviews with Norman Spinrad, Roger Zelazny, Robert Anton Wilson and Fritz Leiber. Yet to go were Theodore Sturgeon, Leigh Brackett, C.L. Moore and Philip K. Dick. Fortunately for us, every one of these eight writers either lived in or passed through the San Francisco Bay Area during the period we were working on the book.

Every one of them, that is, except Phil Dick. We were in the midst of planning an expedition to Los Angeles only to discover that Dick had recently moved to Sonoma—a mere ninety-minute drive north of our home base. We sent him a letter outlining our project and requesting his participation. His answer was the phone call.

I called back immediately and set up a meeting. In like Flynn.

Or so we thought. A day or two later, I got another call. This one came from Joan Simpson, the woman with whom Phil was living in Sonoma.

"Phil changed his mind," she said apologetically. "He doesn't want to do the interview. I'm really sorry. He feels bad about it, too; he made me call you because he didn't want to face you."

She sounded genuinely apologetic when I expressed my disappointment. This book and this interview meant so much to us, but if that's the way he wanted it...

"Well, hold on," Joan said, perking up. "I read your letter too, and I think it sounds like a great book. Phil should be in it. The only reason he's backed out is because he's been depressed lately, and not writing. He's afraid he's lost it, you know, and that he'll come across sounding stupid or crazy in a long interview.

"But we know better," she whispered conspiratorially. "This interview would be good for him. It might be just what he needs to stop him moping around and restore his confidence. Let me talk to him and see what I can do. Don't give up hope."

Joan worked on him and kept me posted with regular phone calls. Eventually she convinced him. A date and time was agreed upon.

On the day of the interview, I packed the tape recorder and a few blank tapes, picked up Briggs, and we were off. We spent the long drive through San Francisco and Marin going over our notes, reviewing our themes, talking ourselves up for the hard-won interview. In about two hours we were parked in front of Joan's house.

Memory fades, but I remember it as a white, wooden two-story house. It looked old, but well-kept and comfortable.

Joan greeted us at the door. She was slim, dark-haired and very cute, with an engaging voice and manner. She welcomed us and took us in to meet Phil.

He was not what I expected. Photos do not do him justice. He was large, physically imposing and hairy. He was wearing slacks and an open shirt, as if his hairy barrel chest and barrel belly couldn't stand being confined.

We stood around chatting for a few minutes, unpacking equipment, looking each other over. Phil took us on a tour of their house. He had a framed copy of Paul Williams' *Rolling Stone* article on the wall of the kitchen. I stopped to admire a bookcase full of his books in the living room.

"Those are Joan's," he drawled. "If it were up to me, I wouldn't even have them in the house. They make me nervous." He scowled again at the forty-odd paperbacks. "She made me autograph *every one of them*," he said wearily.

He took us out front, too, to show off their untended yard. "This is my dead lawn," he deadpanned. "And this is my dead rose bush, and that's my dead lemon tree. I have a black thumb."

Eventually we settled in to begin. We sat in the living room, Phil perched on the edge of a bed-like couch, us on pillows on the floor, the all-important tape machine between us.

Next to Phil was an end table, and on the end table were several boxes. Each box contained a dozen or more little yellow canisters, about the size of 35mm film cans. And in the canisters was Phil's snuff; a variety of flavors from the Dean Swift Company of San Francisco. He was overjoyed when Briggs began talking about "the subtle lavender scent of Inchkenneth."

"Hey, honey!" he called to Joan. "Kevin knows Inchkenneth!" We each tried a couple flavors—"the beginner's stuff," he chided, adding darkly, "You're probably not ready for the hard stuff yet." (Today I'm up to an ounce a week, and order it by the case. The hard stuff. Thanks, Phil.)

Throughout the interview he sat near his snuff, regularly choosing one can or another, tapping out a hefty pinch onto the back of his hand and quietly "taking" it. He was a pro; nowhere on our tapes can one detect the sound of sniffing—the ultimate snuff *faux pas*.

And we talked. Phil listened to our questions with an attention that seemed almost a physical presence. Each question we presented him with was intercepted by an intent, thoughtful glare...almost as if each simple question or statement was the most profound and serious revelation he had yet encountered. His very attitude and presence inspired us to seek questions more profound than the itinerary we had agreed upon.

I had never seen—and have still never seen—anyone so in charge of an interview. He took us through his topics, at his pace, to his own level of depth...and then let us know he was finished: "What do you want to talk about now?" And yet this guidance was subtle; nearly invisible. I had, during those days, the impression of Phil that he knew he was so physically intimidating—so large and intense—that he had made a conscious decision to be just as gentle as he was strong. This attitude appeared to carry over into his intellectual life as well: the control of the conversation was there, but so subtle that we were barely aware of it. The bottom line is that even the subtlest coercion on his part was unnecessary; he was such a treasure chest of ideas, opinions and stories we were more than willing to let him rap on for hours.

We spent two full days with Phil and Joan during that hot summer. Every moment was nonstop conversation: before the interview, during the interview, during breaks from the interview, through our carry-in dinners eaten on the floor like picnics.

While the tape machine was rolling, we tried to stick to the topics at hand. When it was off, we felt freer to ramble. We discussed everything from *Finnegans Wake* to our favorite crank theories; from Beethoven to Kiki Dee.

Mostly Phil wanted us to listen to music. "You guys wanna listen to my Kiki Dee tapes?" was his frequent question. "No, Phil," we'd reply in exasperation; "we want to talk." "Oh," he'd sigh, crestfallen. "OK, whattaya wanna talk about *now?*" (We found out, years later, that he wanted to point out to us the "secret messages" embedded in bubblegum rock he'd been theorizing in his uncompleted novel *VALIS* (originally *Valisystem A,* later published as *Radio Free Albemuth*—complicated, isn't it?); messages which later resurfaced in galactic songstress Linda Fox's songs in *The Divine Invasion.*

One funny thing about Phil's personal habits I've yet to see mentioned concerns his telephone etiquette. Next to his phone he kept a Rolodex—a circular card file; the type usually filled with names, addresses and phone numbers. But Phil—in addition to these items—kept a running log of notes on his conversations. At least half a dozen times during our days of taping he'd get a phone call, let the caller identify him or herself, and then beg off the phone on some trumped up excuse while he fiddled with the file and reviewed his relationship with the caller. When he came back on the line, it was always with some personal comment, like, "How'd the surgery go on your cat?" or "How come you haven't called in six months?"

After ringing off, he'd make a note of the conversation on the caller's card, and then continue with the interview. In later days when I'd call, I always felt a little proud that he didn't have to "turn the stereo down" or "take the tea kettle off" after I identified myself.

Following our time together, I went back to the solitary work of transcribing and editing the eight hours of tape and typing the final book draft. I discarded half the transcript, on topics that wandered beyond the artificial boundaries of the themes of *Approaching Science Fiction Writers*. Even so, Philip Dick's section of the book was twice the length of any other interview we had done. We sent him a copy and he seemed pleased.

The next time we saw him was about three months later at the Octocon, a science fiction convention held in Santa Rosa, California, just north of San Francisco. Briggs and I were there to work; we had arranged an interview with Ted Sturgeon, and took advantage of the guest list to seek out and corner—"approach"— Leigh Brackett and Catherine Moore. Phil was there to play; he lived only a short distance away and stopped in to see us and to make an unscheduled cameo appearance.

The weekend was marvelous. Three Phil Dick anecdotes emerged.

Phil wanted to go get a drink one afternoon, for instance. We told him we couldn't go because we were off to interview Leigh Brackett. His eyebrows furrowed and his lips puckered.

"Ya know," he drawled, "I've never met Leigh Brackett. People think that when you work in a small community like science fiction writing that everybody knows everybody. But I never met her, and I've always admired her work. Do you guys think...uh, would you mind if I tagged along? I mean, I won't get in your way or anything, I just want to meet her and then I'll go get my drink. I'll behave myself; I promise. I won't go rushing around the room drinking up all the booze and gibbering like an idiot and telling her the truth about you guys..."

A lot of thoughts went through my head: this big guy, afraid to introduce himself to a little woman; the image of a puppy wanting to follow you home; a major figure in the field begging favors like a fan; the deadpan parody of his own reputation; the perverse urge to say, "No. Go away. You'll just embarrass us."

But how could we say no? The situation was just too outrageous. The guy who'd done us so many favors was now giving us a chance to repay a small portion of our debt. So off we went. Phil behaved himself, exactly as he'd promised. We introduced him to Leigh, they exchanged a few words of mutual admiration, and then he bowed out gracefully. Philip K. Dick's first novel, *Solar Lottery,* was originally published as an Ace Double, back to back with Brackett's *The Big Jump.* Twenty-three years later, we closed the circle by introducing them.

We also had the pleasure of introducing Phil to our old friend Robert Anton Wilson. Bob Wilson and his beautiful wife Arlen had become like family to Briggs and me over the previous two years. We visited them in Berkeley about once a week, went to dinner, went on picnics, read our newest masterpieces to one another for amusement and review. *Oh, boy,* we snickered in glee; *we get to introduce these two geniuses*—our friends!—*to one another. This is gonna be* great! I carried the tape recorder to preserve for posterity this meeting of like minds.

We took Phil up to Bob Wilson's room and found Bob on the balcony overlooking the motel's central court. A bellydancing exhibition was in progress below. Phil joined Bob on the veranda and we introduced them. Their attention immediately went back to the dancers. They both stood there silently, watching bellies and listening to the music. Briggs and I sat down at the small table in the room, exchanging glances. "This is *it?*" he whispered. I shrugged. They'd have to stop dancing sometime.

After maybe five minutes of this, Phil turned to Wilson. My finger hovered over the "record" button.

"Like your stuff, man," Phil said.

"Thanks," Bob replied. "I like your stuff, too."

And they both turned back to the dancers.

"Well," Phil sighed eventually; "I gotta go. Some people are waiting for me."

"Nice to meet you," Wilson said.

"Nice to meet you, too," Phil replied. He bid us all goodbye and left.

Yeah, that was it. The great meeting of the minds. Ah, well. Sometimes the magic works, and sometimes the bellydancers work. (Curiously enough, a bellydancer plays a major role in the Dick story "The Eye of the Sibyl" included in this volume. Paul Williams says the story was "written I think in 1978"; maybe this incident played some role in sparking Phil's memory, or inspired him more than we realized. Another circle is thus closed, as his story is published here for the first time...)

Later, we popped up to a small party in the room of an English teacher friend of Ted Sturgeon's and mine. Paul Williams was there, sitting on the couch with a couple of the teacher's students; Ted and his lovely wife Jayne sat on the bed. A few minutes later the door burst open and Phil stormed into the room, followed by an entourage of people he had arrived with and picked up along the way. He was massive; impressively conspicuous. All talk stopped; all eyes were on Phil. The scene was similar to those old Westerns where the stranger enters through the swinging saloon doors...

Phil eyed the room from behind his sunglasses, then boomed to no one in particular, "D'j'ya ever notice how much a dead frog in the road looks like money?" His makeshift audience roared. After Phil said his hellos all around, Ted Sturgeon cornered him. "I've been waiting fifteen years to have this discussion with you..." was all I heard Ted announce, and then they talked intently for over half an hour.

While preparing this volume, I wrote repeatedly to Sturgeon asking him if he would detail their philosophical conversation. But he never replied. Later, I found out why: he was just too ill to take on an assignment like this. Now he and Phil can share their secrets once again.

One final story concerns the mysterious manila envelope which was an appendage of Phil throughout the weekend. We'd see him corner writers, editors, convention personnel—even fans—to display to them the contents of the envelope. What was he up to? we wondered. Trying to sell a story? To fans? Passing out "documented evidence" of his contact with aliens?

Curiosity finally got the better of us. We cornered him and confronted him. "What's in the envelope, Phil?" we asked pleasantly. "How come you're showing it to everyone but us?"

He grinned sheepishly and removed a sheaf of papers from the envelope.

It was a copy of our interview.

After the Octocon, time passed, as it has a peculiar fondness for doing. Phil and I exchanged regular phone calls and irregular letters, but they were mostly status reports, or vague plans to do a book-length interview, based on his agent's praise for the existing piece. A sample letter from Phil, typical in its contents, is enclosed in this volume.

The next milestone occurred with the publication of *VALIS*.

Briggs called to tell me it was out, it was great…and we were in it. I rushed out and grabbed a copy, and damn if he wasn't right! There we were—Kevin as "Kevin," and David Scott Apel as "David"—wandering around Sonoma, talking about the things we had talked about.

I was thrilled: I had become a character in literature. Surely Fame and Fortune were not far behind! I called Phil to let him know what a masterpiece I thought *VALIS* was…and to confirm this new fame. After all, much of David and Kevin's role was played out in Los Angeles. "I know from experience that any fictional character is bound to be an amalgamation of many people the writer knows," I told him; "but I detect a strong connection between 'David and Kevin' and me and Briggs. Did you really base your characters on us...at least partially?"

"Sure did," he chuckled.

(A few months later, I attempted to return the favor. I was doing a major rewrite on my first detective novel, *The Coincidence Caper*. Already it had characters based wholly on Briggs, Robert Anton Wilson and Robert Heinlein. To this rewrite I added "Richard K. Philips" as a central figure. This novel, retitled *The Uncertainty Principle*, is available as an ebook and will soon be available in print from Atomic Drop Press.)

It wasn't until late 1984 that I learned the whole truth about "David and Kevin." The fourth issue of the Philip K. Dick Society Newsletter ran an article by Tim Powers which contained these shocking lines: "The character 'David' in *VALIS* is based on me, and 'Kevin' is K.W. Jeter—virtually everything that Kevin, David and Horselover Fat do and say, at least until they go to see the movie, Jeter, Phil and I really did do and say."

His story made sense. He and Jeter were close to Phil for a long time during that period; they were obviously bigger "Dick"-heads than we were. And Jeter's dead cat story matched the one in *VALIS* more closely than Briggs' dead cat story.

But we recognized our conversations, too. And Phil himself had validated that Briggs and I were—at least in part—these characters. But he was dead and couldn't settle the argument.

What to do? I could write the PKDS Newsletter and start a controversy. But who would I believe if I were a reader? A successful, award-winning author; a known friend of Phil's...or some unknown, unpublished, glory-seeking, argumentative graverobber? The question contained its own answer. Fucked again. I couldn't even take solace in hating Powers...I had already read and loved *The Anubis Gates*.

The answer to my dilemma, though, was contained in Powers' next, parenthetical, sentence: "(I'm tempted to say we flew up to Sonoma, too, and met the Savior, but I'll stick to the facts)."

That was the clue I needed. We—Powers and I—were *both* correct in assuming we were "David": Powers was David in the L.A. chapters of *VALIS;* I was David in the Sonoma sections. Phil's writer's mind had fused us into one composite character...as Powers mentioned Phil had done with others in the book. And this is precisely the theory Phil had validated for me years earlier: not that Briggs and I "were" the characters, but that we were *elements of an alloy.* Whatever resentment I might have felt over my "loss of status" was quickly replaced with pride at being combined so closely in Phil's mind with a fine writer like Powers.

(Another thing Powers and I share is that neither of us wants to take responsibility for the "pious and credulous" personality of "David." But this description is easily explained if *VALIS* is seen as a parallel world or mirror-world book, where the negative traits of the characters' real-world counterparts are dominant. This is obvious in the split between Phil and Horselover Fat, and can also be seen by perusing Powers' work...no piousness or credulousness there.)

The frustration of not being able to do anything with this knowledge was lightened somewhat by the amusing thought that I was the only one who knew the whole truth...or at least as much of the "whole truth" as could be pieced together without direct consultation with Philip K. Dick.

Out of our communication during Phil's final years, three phone calls stand out in my memory.

Late one evening in August of 1981, he called from Santa Ana. He had moved back to L.A. after breaking up with Joan Simpson. We chatted for a few minutes, then he came to the point.

"You know," he said, "that Ridley Scott, the director *Alien,* has been filming the movie *Blade Runner,* based on my book *Do Androids Dream of Electric Sheep...*"

"Yeah," I said, "I've been keeping up on that."

"Well, Ridley Scott called me recently and wants me to come up to Northern California to meet him and Harrison Ford, who's starring in the film..."

"That's great," I said.

"Well...I was wondering if maybe I could talk you and Briggs into going along with me..."

"'Talk us into'...Phil, we'd love to go. What do you want, an entourage?"

"Well...it's more like moral support."

"What?"

"I'm...I'm scared to meet these guys, you know? I mean Ridley Scott is a big Hollywood director, and Harrison Ford is a major talent...I'm afraid I'd be out of my league with people like that. So if I have some friends around to stop me from saying anything stupid..."

"'Out of your league'?" I said. "Jesus, Phil! These are guys who admire *your* work enough to sink several million dollars and several months of their lives into it. And now *they* want to meet *you*. They'll probably treat you like a Hollywood star yourself."

"Oh. shit..." he mumbled.

"OK, OK...Look at it this way: they'll probably treat you like an equal and feel they're elevating themselves in the process. Listen: If my opinion means anything to you, I say: Do this thing."

Eventually, he went. Alone. We had to read about it in *Locus*. I guess my sales pitch was just too damned effective.

Soon after that, he called again; this time depressed. Sure, he was selling stuff, working hard, making money. But he missed Joan.

"I now see that breaking up with her was the biggest mistake in my life," he said dully. "I was really very happy with her, and I keep fondly remembering all the good times we had together." He wanted me to act as a go-between: to call her and tell her how much he missed her. I promised I'd do what I could to mend the split. It was the least I could do; she'd done as much for me, talking Phil into granting our interview, after all. If he'd just provide me with her phone number, I'd do my best. He never did.

His final phone call to me came soon after that; only a couple months before he died. He sounded much happier. He was now in love with actress Margot Kidder, and convinced that his goal in life was to meet and marry her.

"You're in love with her," I said slowly, treading that fine Phil Dick line between deadpan hyperbole and innocent sincerity, "and you want to marry her...but you haven't even met her yet?"

"Well, I saw her in *Superman*," he said, "and she just blew me away. And I got—I actually got a phone call from her. A friend of a friend gave her one of my stories, and she was interested in doing it as a movie."

So there was some logical—if tenuous—basis to his fantasy. One thing I learned about Phil: For all the talk of his wild imagination—or latent craziness—every one of his high-flown fantasies had some basis in reality...if one looked hard enough.

We chatted some more about his latest publishing coups. And my last words from Phil ended on a note as curiously prophetic as his first.

"So I guess I'm a big success now," he chuckled. "The only thing left for me to do is die."

We both got a big laugh out of that.

Phil K. Dick in Interview

D. Scott Apel and Kevin C. Briggs

INTRODUCTION

The following interview was conducted in two parts, on June 20 and July 23, 1977, at the Sonoma home of Joan Simpson, with whom Philip Dick was living at the time. It constitutes a total of nearly eight hours of conversation conducted during those two days.

Every effort has been made to preserve Philip Dick's speech patterns, however, some "false starts" have been eliminated and some questions rephrased for the sake of clarity. A very few editorial liberties have been taken in the arrangement of the material, notably combining the two parts of the interview into one, then breaking out the *VALIS*-related material into a separate segment.

Aside from these minor conventions, this is Philip K. Dick speaking: a slice of (larger than) life from the beginning of the final creative phase of his career.

Now: read, and enjoy the genius of Philip K. Dick.

PART I

Apel: We're in interview today with noted science fiction author Philip K. Dick. I guess the first order of business is to thank you for consenting to this interview.

Dick: My pleasure.

Apel: We've been starting out most of these interviews with a simple, basic question that allows us and the readers to grasp some kind of reality before we go on to talk about themes and opinions; the question which is foremost, therefore, would be: What are your working habits? Are there definite guidelines you've given yourself as a writer for getting a book produced?

Dick: My working habits fall into two distinct groups. The first group was when if I didn't write three or four novels a year I'd starve to death, and so I wrote three or four novels a year. Mark Hurst, my Bantam editor, says I wrote something like 16 novels in five years. I don't know if that's true.

Apel: You didn't keep count?

Dick: Well, I just wrote all the time. I remember typing the words "The End," pulling that page out, and putting in another page which said "Chapter One." I calculated I had typed...well, two drafts on a book would be 600 pages—and I do two drafts minimum—that's 1,200 pages in three weeks. I was beginning to show real signs of wear. I had an electric typewriter, of course; everything to facilitate a large output.

Then there came a point where there were two factors involved that changed. One, the simple factor of fatigue. You just cannot go on forever doing that much, even if you have the ideas. The physical condition that you find yourself in prohibits it. This was all around 1964, after I won the Hugo for *The Man in the High Castle.* I said to myself, " Strike while the iron is hot," and I wrote. I was a writing fool. Sixteen novels in five years. Now how long a life span would you want to give a person that tried to make that a professional working schedule? I didn't run out of ideas; I just ran out of energy. I was depleting myself.

Then another thing happened. Terry Carr said to me, "All your novels are exactly the same." Boy, do I remember this; this really got put in my long-term memory banks. He said, "Whenever you pick up a Poul Anderson novel, it's completely different from all other Poul Anderson novels." (I'm not willing to concede that that's correct, but that's what he said.) "Whenever you pick up a Bob Silverberg novel, it's different from all other Bob Silverberg novels. But pick up one of your novels, and they're all the same. And the fans are grumbling," he says. "Why don't you stop trying to figure out what reality is and asking what reality is, as you continually do, *and say what it is."* And I thought: *Golly!* That is pro*found!* I *have* written that theme perpetually: What is reality? And now They—and by "They," you know who I mean...those giant figures that surround you all the time.

Briggs: *Them.*

Dick: *Them.* Yes. *They* say I have to say what reality is, and I never had any intention of doing that. And the reason I never had any intention of doing that is that *I don't know*—I have no knowledge at all of what reality is. All I can do is plaintively inquire, "Hey, gang, what is really real?" And then here is Terry Carr—the great anthologizer—and a major figure in the field—and he says, "All right!" and he blows on his little whistle, like the Recreation Director at camp has... "All right! Time to write about what reality is!"

Apel: "Everybody outta the pool! Honeymoons's over!"

Dick: "You have asked the question, now you have to answer it."

Apel: You're duty-bound.

Dick: Yes. Right. I had a moral obligation. He got me from my Protestant, moral obligation side.

Briggs: Crept up on your blind side, eh?

Dick: So I discovered—as amazing as it may sound—that it was a lot harder to *say* what it was than to ask what it was.

Apel: What was it?

Dick: Damned if I know! *(general roar of laughter)* But I thought: *I'll fake it.* So in 1970 I started working on *Flow My Tears, The Policeman Said.* And it was my intention to resolve the problem by the discovery of what reality really was. So that meant there was a three-year ellipsis in my writing…

Apel: When you had to go out and find out what it was?

Dick: Yeah. Well, I just sort of sat there at the typewriter. I did eleven drafts of that novel. I mean literally; I'm not using that as hyperbole. I had a complicated code system worked out so I wouldn't start feeding the old drafts back in, in which case I guess I'd still be there today.

I decided the thing that was really real was *love.* Then I thought, *Y'know, somebody else said this. Now who the hell was it that said this?* Well, actually, a lot of people have said it. My revelation which I'm about to lay on the world is not going to come as a complete surprise.

Apel: St. Augustine said it, and Aleister Crowley…

Dick: St. Paul said, "If I have not love then I am jack shit"…or something like that. So anyway, I worked for three years on *Flow My Tears,* then when Terry Carr wasn't looking, I began to go back to the question of what is real. But another thing happened then—because your question had to do with working habits. Working all those years on *Flow My Tears,* doing all those drafts, changed my working habits. I'd never done more than a rough draft and a final on a novel before. And there were *eleven drafts.* God—I was reshaping it word by word. Once in, never out; I couldn't go back to doing *a* rough draft and *a* final draft, just like that. So the next novel was *A Scanner Darkly,* and it took *years* to write *Scanner;* it just took *years.* The idea came to me in the early part of 1972, and it wasn't until '76 that I sent the manuscript off to Doubleday. And I wasn't trying to say what was real; I was just no longer able to dash stuff off at the rate I had done before.

The novel I'm working on now for Bantam, which is called *VALIS*…They gave me a 45 day deadline to go from the rough draft to the final draft. And I didn't read my contract. I signed the contract when I got the first payment from Bantam. And I was prepared to work a couple of years between the rough draft and the final. Then I looked and saw I had 45 days—that would have just given me time to do the physical job of typing, really. I couldn't believe that my agent would pass that contract on to me, then I read his letter, and he said, "You'd better read this contract." Jesus Christ, I've been in this business 27 years and I still have to be reminded that I should read these things before I sign them. I couldn't produce a final draft under those circumstances. It would have just been a correct typing; a polished form of the first draft.

So I began to play a very complicated game with Bantam. They then gave me a few extra weeks, but at that point it might as well have been 24 hours, because what I discovered in *Scanner* was that when the final draft was completed, after several years from the rough, it was much better than the first draft. The book was *so* much better. The difference was incredible. And so once that fact had been correlated in the processing center of my brain—that if you work on it a couple years you get a much better book—I could hardly reject this and go back to the old system. So I said to Bantam, "Do you want the fastest possible book or the best possible book?" Now of course the answer is contained in the phrasing of the question. They can't very well say, "No, we don't care if it's rotten. What the hell do we care? We're just a word factory." *(laughter)* Of course they said they wanted the best possible book, sensing as they did that they were falling into a trap. I says, "Fine. I'll have it for you when it's finished," or some such tautology. I'm still working on it. I did a rough draft last October, and this is now June. I've got like two years of work left to do on that damn book before I'll be satisfied with it. I've had to get people in the business to go into Bantam and assure them that I'm really working on it.

This happened with *Scanner;* it was so funny. I sent off an outline of the first four chapters, and then I didn't come up with the final book for several years. Even my agent was saying, privately, to people he doubted if there really was a completed manuscript.

Apel: *The Maltese Scanner.*

Dick: Yeah. When Paul Williams came out to interview me for

Rolling Stone, he said, "Uh, Phil...Do you have the rough draft of *Scanner?"* I says, "Sure. Why?" He says, "Well, I want to settle a bet I have with your agent and your publisher. They don't believe there is a complete draft." But of course I did have one. So naturally I hauled it out, and he said, "I am amazed. There really is one."

So my work habits now are: I work *very* slowly and I do a lot of research—and I'm speaking of several years of research—and then proceed at a snail's pace. The only way I can be secure economically under these circumstances is my foreign royalties. If I wasn't getting money from abroad, I would be doomed.

Apel: Where do you sell best, France?

Dick: France, yeah. I've been told that I'm the most popular American science fiction author in France. I used to say it's because they have very good translators in France...really hip. But the real reason is very simple: I'm feeding back to the French public their own novels.

The novels that influenced my writing, when I was in my late teens and early twenties, were the French realistic novels. Flaubert, Stendhal, Balzac, *et al*...and the Russian novelists who were influenced by them, like Turgenev, and so on. I even read the Japanese novelists who were influenced by them. That was what I really liked, that slice-of-life stuff.

Apel: Was that part of your search to find out what reality was?

Dick: Well, in those days, I didn't know I didn't know. I hadn't even formulated the question yet. I read them because I liked them; I enjoyed them. I thought Stendhal's *The Red and the Black* was maybe the finest novel I'd ever read. And *Madame Bovary* was a close second.

I wasn't writing novels when I started out, I was writing stories. But the second I switched to novels, this inner template based on the French realistic novels just fired like a circuit board. You can see that *Solar Lottery,* my first novel, is literally like the French novels in that respect: all manner of people in all walks of life...portrayed as best I could. It never occurred to me when I did this that these books would be published abroad. That was not a factor that entered my mind. It wasn't until 1964 that I was approached by a French publisher...and I had been writing since 1951, and writing novels since 1955. It wasn't until 1964, when *Editions Opta* of Paris approached me with the extraordinary proposition that they would publish every novel I had written. They have a fancy book club edition that they put out, and for this they got a picture of me for the back cover, and an article about me by John Brunner. They sent me a copy of the first book—*The Man in the High Castle* and *Counter-Clock World*—and they had a complete bibliography of my stuff. They had everything, and it was *beautiful*. Oh, my God! In comparison to, like, Ace Books...*(laughter)* I used to hold the French edition in one hand and an Ace edition in the other...*Clans of the Alphane Moon* is the one I used.

Apel: *(sarcastically)* Yeah...great cover for that book...the guy with the gun...

Dick: *(also sarcastically)* Yeah, right...it's a book about guns... *(laughter)* So I said, "Holy smoke! I can see a tremendous difference in the physical qualities of the two books. This is great. And they say they're going to publish all my novels." Well, they did not publish all my novels, because other French publishers bid on them and outbid them for a large number of novels. So *Opta* just republishes the ones they acquired title to. Somebody told me I have like 26 to 29 novels *in print* in France.

So it's really very simple as to why my stuff is more popular in France than it is in America.

Apel: You learned the art from them...

Dick: ...and then I fed it back to them. So I don't take any credit; if I had thoroughly mastered the English novel, I'd probably be terribly popular in England. But it's France's royalties that keep me alive...United Kingdom royalties, for instance, come in in hundreds of dollars, but France's come in in thousands of dollars.

I guess that was one of the smartest things I ever did. I had meant to say this sometime in an interview. I think the most important thing for me in writing was before I wrote novels I very thoroughly read and studied a very large number of what we generally agree on as the "Great Novels."

Apel: You educated yourself as to how you should behave as a writer of novels.

Dick: Yes. In other words, I was not raised on science fiction novels. It wasn't like I read Hal Clement's *Mission of Gravity.* I remember reading a synopsis of Part One of *Mission of Gravity* in a magazine, and it went something like this *(affecting a dimwitted narrator's voice):* "For the first time, Man was in a position to measure three gravitational fields at one time." So I got up one time at the WorldCon to make this short speech, and I said, "Here's an idea for a book: There's an alternate world where nobody has thought of the collapsible measuring tape. They only have large, solid rulers, ninety to a hundred feet long. Somebody invents the measuring tape, so he can go around measuring things. This book will be all about how this guy goes around measuring things. It would be very interesting, because he would define reality in terms of its physical dimensions. Like his girlfriend he would call "Five-Four," because she was five foot, four inches. And his cat he'd call "Two-and-a-half-One." I never got to the point I was trying to make during the speech because then I got to talking about the Phone Company and how they were taking over the world and I got deflected from my purpose.

And that purpose was to point out that one of the saddest things that's happened in our field, and has been happening for a long time, is people coming in to write who are just science fiction fans *per se*—that is, they read science fiction, then feed back an eviscerated form of what they've read. It's almost like Gresham's Law—making copies of copies of copies.

Apel: You lose something with each generation.

Briggs: Each one becomes more blurry and less distinct.

Dick: I'm really lucky; I grew up in Berkeley, where it was absolutely natural to read people like Proust. You really couldn't get into a party—you couldn't get in through the door—if you hadn't read things like Proust, and Henry Miller, and...shit, I forget what else. It was really a burden. All these damn books were real long. *War and Peace* is an example. You really didn't dare go to a party unless you'd read *War and Peace*, because somebody'd start talking about the scene where she gives birth to the child and dies, and you'd say *(in a cowboy accent)* "Ah've never read *War and Peace*...and not only thet, Ah've never read *The Brothers Karamazov.*" Then you'd go right out the door you came in; you're just heaved right out into the street.

So I'm really lucky; if I'd grown up in Turloc, or someplace like that, I don't think the pressure would have been on me. I mean, I even got to read *Finnegans Wake,* which we were discussing earlier. Reading *Ulysses* was *super*obligatory; reading *Finnegans Wake* was *almost* optional, but it was important that you tried to read it, and could say something more about it than, "Man, he was crazy when he wrote that! It's utter gibberish!" That wasn't sufficient. You could say, "Well, I think the whole thing is a dream, told from the standpoint of the dreaming mind, which is remembering reality, and that Earwicker is waking up," which was always my theory on it. You have to come up with some theory on it, so you have to have some familiarity with it.

But it didn't enter my mind when I read those books that I was going to be able to make use of this knowledge of those novels myself, because I didn't plan to write novels, I planned to write short stories. When I broke into the field there were—oh, God, I don't know how many—maybe 16 magazines.

Briggs: You published a lot of stuff in those days, too.

Dick: Yeah. Like, I remember in June of 1953 I went to... to... wherever it was I bought my SF...and there were seven magazines which were carrying stories of mine simultaneously. So I was doing nothing but writing stories. Then in 1954, I met an editor at the '54 WorldCon, and he said, "Novels." I said, "Huh?" He said, "Novels. Write novels." I said, "How come?" He said, "You'll make more money." I said, *"How come?"* He said, "Well, *Astounding* will print them as a serial, and then you can sell it later in book form. So you can sell it twice." I said, "That's terrific. I never thought of that. I'll write a novel!" So I went home and wrote *Solar Lottery.* And it didn't work out the way the editor had said. Nothing that I wrote for any of my early novels got bought by any magazine. They just went into Ace Books, and the revenue was not any greater than if I had written a whole lot of stories. Ace Books paid $1,000.

Briggs: Do you have a Donald Wollheim story?

Dick: Matter of fact, I have. When I was preparing the Ballentine collection, Donald Wollheim wrote to me and said, "I'd like to do a collection of your stories." I said, "I'm sorry, Don, but I'm going through my stories to sell to Ballentine right now." He wrote back and said, "Well, Betty"—Betty Ballentine was still editor—"Betty and I have different tastes. Give me what Betty doesn't want." And that's exactly what he got. Wollheim read them over and became hysterical. He said, "These are Betty Ballentine rejects!" I says, "Don, that's what we contracted for." He says, "Well, the stories aren't very good." And I said, "Yeah, and the price ain't very good, either." He published them, but he was grumpy about it. That's my Wollheim story.

Briggs: For my ever-growing collection.

Dick: Oh, I'll tell you another story. He was late in paying me for *We Can Build You.* I was really broke; matter of fact, I was starving to death. My wife and I were living in Southern California, sharing one can of Chunky Chicken soup a day; that was all we could afford. So I wrote Wollheim this piteous letter: "Dear Don: I must tell you that I have been forced to give up writing science fiction and am going to work at Disneyland as one of the janitors who sweeps things up. The reason is because you have not sent me the money due me on *We Can Build You.* " And you know what his answer was? "Why don't you come to New York and go on Welfare?" *(general hilarity)* He said that! Talk about your heart of stone! Shit!

Apel: Speaking of *We Can Build You* and Disneyland in the same sentence, I've wondered for years how many times you went to the Lincoln exhibit on some foreign substance and wondered how you could write a book about it.

Dick: Well, you know—maybe you didn't know this—but my book was written long before Disney proposed building the Mr. Lincoln robot. That book was written in the '50s.

Apel: That book is great; it's one of my favorites of your books. It shows great subtlety and amazing depth in its characters. And the humor is magnificent. Like that scene where the splinter group introduces their answer to the Lincoln robot... God, I just roared. So logical, and still a complete surprise.

Dick: I wrote that novel before Disney even proposed to build the Lincoln simulacrum. I couldn't sell it for years and years and years and years. I wrote it while I was trying to fuse my mainstream stuff with my science fiction stuff, so it's not *quite* science fiction, in the usual sense of the word. Finally Ted White, who knew of the existence of the manuscript, asked for it so he could publish it in a magazine. Ted added a final chapter to it, because—as is well known—writers are incapable of writing their own books. *(explosive laughter on our part; Phil deadpans the whole routine with perfect sincerity)* If it wasn't for kindly editors, who are your best friends, who'll help you out by adding another chapter, or removing one here or there, or turning one inside out, or changing all the names, or whatever, you'd never have gotten off the ground. Naturally I was very indebted to Ted White, and I let him know. The way I let him know was that when Wollheim published the book, I told Wollheim to remove the final chapter. So one day I ran into Ted White, and he said, "Do you know what they did to *our book?*" I says, "I know exactly what they did to *'our'* book, Ted. They took the *'our'* out of *'our' book!"*

I have seen the Lincoln simulacrum down there. I cut out the notice in the newspaper that Disney planned to build the Lincoln simulacrum and pasted it up on the wall of my study. I remember doing that because the novel had already been written. So he built it and I went down to Disneyland and looked at the goddam thing...

You talk about synchronicity that governs the universe— coincidence which is meaningful... I rented an apartment in a building where one of the ladies living in the building worked at Disneyland. I said to her, "What do you do there?" She says, "I reapply the makeup to the Lincoln every night, so the next morning when the park is open, it looks real."

Apel: It has a vinyl skin which actually secretes oil, so they have to wipe it off and put powder and makeup on it. It's very close to human skin in its chemical composition. It can bruise, for instance.

Dick: Can you imagine how I felt, finding I lived in a building with a woman who added a touch of verisimilitude to the damn thing? "Well, let me ask you a question," I said. "You see this thing after the park is closed. How *real* does that thing seem to you to be?" And she says, "Well, I'll tell you exactly how real it seems to be to me." Now it's important to remember that every part of all the rides are continually scanned by closed circuit television—to make sure no *hippies* will leap out of the ship and steal the jewels from the pirate treasure, or rape one of the women the pirates are trying to catch up with...

Apel: If you try to blast a reefer on the water rides they catch you at the end and take you to the Disney police.

Briggs: Guys dressed like the Beagle Boys will beat you up.

Dick: So anyway, she says, "One time I was painting the Lincoln thing and one of the monitors was still on. The guy on the screen saw me and reached over and pressed the controls. And the thing stood up."

"And what did you do, miss," I asked.

"I peed my pants."

"I take it," says I, "that you found a high degree of verisimilitude in this simulacrum."

"Sure scared the shit out of me."

Apel: There are dozens of stories like that about the Lincoln audio-animatronic device. The first time they tried to animate it, it threw a fit, thrashing out with its arms, smashing its chair.

Dick: Well, you know what got me thinking was that when it's sitting down, it's supposed to put its arms on the arms of the chair, and it'd put its arms down an inch above and would sit there like that.

I really sympathize with the Disney people, though, because in my book 1 foresaw... That's another example of precognition in my writing, the Lincoln robot, or... what did you call it?

Apel: Audio-animatronics. That's what they call it. Down in Disney World, they have a Hall of Presidents—all the presidents done as audio-animatronic figures. More robots in that one room than in the whole rest of the world; more simulacra in that one room than in all your novels put together, I think.

At any rate...onward and upward, from the ridiculous to the sublime. We've spent quite a bit of time talking about one of your main themes, which is "What is reality?" I thought we might go into some of the other major themes that run like threads weaving through the fabric of your work. Since we've been talking about *We Can Build You,* this might be a good time to go into the one you yourself refer to as your "Grand Theme," the question "Who is really human, and who is merely masquerading as human?"

You seem to have established that the dividing line between the two categories is *kindness:* an act of kindness separates real humans from android humans. When we put this together with the results of your search for reality with the conclusion that *love* is the true reality, it seems to me almost as if you are echoing or perhaps rediscovering the early Christian concepts of *karitas,* or kindness, and *agape,* or love. Do you want to comment on this?

Dick: The way you put it, it certainly sounds as if we're talking about the same thing. I had never really thought of it that way before. You've articulated it very concisely, and the articulation appeals to me. It sounds consistent and coherent... which for me is a big relief, when something of mine sounds consistent and coherent.

There was another quality that I felt distinguished the human being, that being the tendency to *balk* at things which were wrong. I developed quite a strong inner image of this happening.

Taking the worst possible social situation imaginable, which would be Nazi Germany, you can imagine, say, in those days, the ordinary police—not the SS police, the Gestapo, but the civil police—were given lists of Jewish people in their precincts to pick up, and they weren't told what would be done with these Jewish people; they were just told to go get them and bring them to a central point. It's very important to understand that these were not the Gestapo, who had a very good idea of what they were doing; these were the municipal police.

A Quaker, Milton Meyer, wrote a book in which he interviewed five different Germans who had either been Nazis or had lived under them—there was no clear distinction; it was a way of life during those years, and party membership was more of a technicality than anything else, because nothing else was permitted. Meyer talked to a man who had been a civil policeman, and the man described how he had been given a list of names of Jews to go and bring downtown... "downtown," like in all the old detective movies you see...that's where the police always threaten to bring you: "downtown." And Meyer asked him, "Did you know what would be done to the Jews when they were brought there?" And he said, "No." And Meyer said, "Did you have any idea that they were to be taken to extermination camps and killed?" The policeman said, "It never entered my mind that there was anything more than relocation involved."

That made a big impression on me, and I got to thinking about this. Suppose you have a job as a civil servant and somebody hands you a list and says, "Go get these people and bring them downtown." Now the mechanical, the android, element takes place when the person simply takes the list, goes to the door of these people, and says, "Come with me." And then this same android quality shows up tragically—and incredibly—among the very victims, who come along docilely, who don't say, "Well, what are they going to *do* downtown?"

Meyer said it was quite different than what we had been told in most cases, where the Gestapo supposedly bashes down the door in the middle of the night and grabs them and flings them in the backs of trucks, and kicks and beats and humiliates them. It was more a procedural thing where the local constabulary would knock politely and would say, "Would you get your possessions and come with me."

The idea occurred to me that the human element would come in where the policeman would say, "Wait a minute. I want to know what you're going to *do* with these people." I got this idea of *balking;* this very vivid picture of a human being suddenly stopping in his tracks, just literally physically stopping, and turning around, and then I had a vivid image of this person saying, "No, I won't do this. I won't go get these people. I don't really know why I won't get them, because I don't know what's going to happen to them...maybe that's why I won't go get them." Or the victim saying, "No, I won't come with you." This is exactly what did *not* happen. Except for the uprising of the Warsaw ghetto, the Jewish people came along. Meyer discovered this, too: everybody just simply did what they were told.

So I got this vivid picture of the human element...somebody, anywhere along the line, balking. Some secretary, for instance, who has to type up the list. All of a sudden she could say to herself, "No, I'm going to leave a name out...or I'm going to leave two names out...or I'm going to give the addresses wrong," or something like that. I got to thinking about this as one of the fundamental constituents of the human being. W. H. Auden put it this way: "There is some shit up with which I will not put." But that requires that you know it's shit you're putting up with, whether it's some humiliating thing or some hostile thing, or some degrading or unjust thing. If you know that these people are going to be murdered and you perform your duty, you round them up, then you are a clear collaborator and conspirator in murder. A court would agree. And you are as guilty as anybody else along the line.

The point is that all five of the people that Meyer talked to really didn't know, and all that really would have been required would have been some balking along the line by people here and there, and the structure would have begun to become unglued.

Apel: This balking, then, is more than just a sense of guilt, correct? It would involve taking action on that moral decision that something is wrong.

Dick: Right. Actually, I got the idea clearly from a book written by Martin Buber's wife, who was in an extermination camp. There were Jehovah's Witnesses there; they're taught to "obey Caesar," but not salute the flag, and so on, and that's how they wound up in the camps: they would not accept the national political authority. Since allegiance is directly to God, they wound up in the camps with the Jews, the Gypsies and the Communists, marked for extermination. At the same time, they were taught to "obey Caesar" whenever Caesar's edict did not conflict directly with God's. And typing up lists of people who were to be gassed that day did not directly conflict with the Bible. So Buber's wife would see these Jehovah's Witnesses carrying lists of people who were to be taken from their bunkers and exterminated, and she'd say, "Why don't you just lose the list?" And they'd answer, "Oh, no, we couldn't lose the list—we were told to take it to Officer So-and-so." She'd say, "All right; I agree that Officer So-and-so is expecting a list, and if you don't show up with a list *you'll* be immediately killed. But you *know* those people are going to be killed. Couldn't you leave a name off?" And they'd say, "No, we were told to type up twenty names today, so we put on twenty names."

And I got to thinking that this is the essence of the unhuman. That is it, right there. Frau Buber had put her finger on the core of what is not human. These Jehovah's Witnesses knew the situation; they knew that they and other people were going to be gassed. And yet they were typing lists, and emptying wastebaskets, whatever, as long as it didn't break some damn ordinance in the Bible like "Thou shalt not salute the flag." They'd go to their deaths rather than salute the flag, and yet they'd type up and carry lists of people who were to be exterminated!

Apel: Do you think they would have left their own names off the list?

Dick: No. I really don't. I think we're talking about the android which has passed over into complete insanity.

This raises the other issue of the relationship between being human and being sane, and requires us to define sanity. There is really something *insane* about this behavior. The android—and of course, we're not really speaking about "androids" in the strict scientific sense of "a human being created in a laboratory"; we're talking about a form of unhuman behavior, with an element of pathology.

Apel: We're using "android" specifically as you use the term in your novels: a parable of a human; a pseudo-human, or a "Xerox copy"; a person that has all the outward appearances of a human being, but is lacking some or all of the psychic components that distinguish humankind from animals or machines.

Dick: Right. Exactly.

Briggs: Gurdjieff would call them "sleepwalkers."

Dick: Yes. One of the things I've noticed is that many people equate insanity with extravagant behavior—shouting, impassioned violence, and so on. But if something is done very calmly and dispassionately, this is rational. "Rational" and "dispassionate" are somehow synonymous, and a person who speaks in a calm, modulated voice is, *ipso facto,* a rational person. This is a typical Anglo-Saxon fallacy; you won't find this confusion in Greece or Italy or Spain.

This is beautifully illustrated by the Gestapo. Himmler once delivered a very important speech, a major policy speech, to the Gestapo and SS, cautioning them that they must never *enjoy* the death of the Jews in the camps. They must never get emotionally excited by it, but must view it all calmly and without feeling.

Briggs: A small-known fact about the SS—specifically the Totenkamp branch of the Waffen SS—is that they ran a training camp for people who were going to be extermination camp commandants; who were going to be physically responsible for carrying out the death orders. At this camp, they took German citizens of perfect Aryan stock and no particularly harmful political opinions and had them executed, under the theory that if a Gestapo man could kill a right-thinking German he'd have no trouble with the Poles, and Russians, and Jews, and Gypsies and other wrong-thinking types.

Dick: What Himmler was really saying was this all must be done *as if* it were rational: scientifically, not as the result of hate or passion. Therefore, I'm sure that to the people who did it, it seemed a rational thing they were doing. But they were making the same error. It's not sane at all. If you remember the film *Zorba the Greek,* there was a great deal of behavior which, from the conventional standpoint, would be called pathological: people dancing around crazily, swilling wine, breaking things. The book was even more that way: he cut the widow's head off, for instance. It was all extravagant, grotesque, hysterical, bombastic—it was not *crazy.* Being crazy very commonly can be typing up a list of names and turning them over to the officer at the end of the hall. And this can be even *more* crazy because it is done in such a dispassionate way. This is what first led me to the thought of the *machine-like* quality of pathology and of the "inhuman." What's lacking is a *sense of perspective,* a sense of proportion. If you pick up your instructions that morning when you go to work and it says "Twenty people will be gassed today," and this is typed out, and it's all spelled right, and it's on the right order form, and this seems fine to you, then what we have here is not just an insidious pathology, but almost, in a way, the very heart of true pathology. What we have here is a lack of an emotional grasping of a situation. We have here a purely mechanical mind; a metal sphere rotating without any contact with the earth or other humans.

I remember one time I went down to the Department of Motor Vehicles to renew my license. This is always very traumatic for me, because I don't want to take the driving test. I know what I'll do when I take the driving test. I know how many people I'll run over. So I *must* pass the written test so I don't have to take the driving test, and I get very frightened by the written test. You can make five errors and still pass. So I went up to the girl with my answers, and I handed the sheet to her, and she was grading it, and I said to her, "If I do not pass this test, I am going to kill myself." And she turned absolutely ashen, and she said, "Oh, no, you've passed; I swear to God you've passed. Look, look here—two mistakes—you've passed." And I thought: *Here's a real human being.*

Another time I went into the bank carrying the largest sum of money that I'd ever had in my possession at one time: $7,800. I said to the clerk, "Every cent of this money has to go to the IRS. What do you think of that?" And she didn't say a goddamn thing. I thought to myself, I see a correlation between insanity, lack of a sense of proportion, and something that we encounter very often in the bureaucratic mind, which processes people as *things.*

Apel: You weren't a human to that clerk, just an account number. That type of insanity seems to me to be an emphasis on form to the exclusion of all content or meaning. Like you mentioned earlier...if the typed form is correct, everything is fine. It doesn't matter or register that the meaning of the form is the termination of human lives.

Dick: Exactly right. The key word is *significance:* what's lacking is an insight into the *authentic significance* of things. If the list says, "These twenty people will be mailed a $20 utility bill refund," you then mail it to them; if it says, "These twenty people will be exterminated," you *balk,* you see. But the true insane person will calmly, very calmly, process both the same way. And this is what I regard as insanity, rather than regarding extravagant behavior—ripping off clothes, screaming, carrying on—as insane. In fact, you get this dispassionate insanity at times where great emotions are appropriate: when someone has died, when some terrible calamity has happened, the insane one will proceed as if nothing of great importance has occurred.

I remember when I was living in the country, my wife and I had a little baby, so we were up at 6:00 for the early feeding. And one morning I looked out the window, and wild dogs were killing our sheep—they were tearing their legs off. Now, the sheriff had told us whenever we saw this to call him immediately and he'd come and shoot the dogs. They were killing thousands of dollars worth of sheep—or to put it more along the lines of the way I would view it—hundreds and hundreds of innocent animals. Those dogs were being sought by every sheep owner in that part of Marin County. So I said to my wife, "Call the sheriff." And she said, "I'm busy." She was warming the bottle. The thing was, she had planned to feed the baby at 6:00. If I had said, "Look, a giant tidal wave is washing toward us, carrying all the houses with it, and we're next. Get out the rowboat!" she would have said, "I'm busy." There was a failure to respond to the gravity of the situation.

We're talking about the inhuman as an inadequacy; inhumanity is the *absence* of something, rather than the presence. We're always looking for the presence of something. Clinically, we're speaking of the schizoid personality, which technically has lack of adequate affect. I have a lot of trust in schizophrenics, for instance. They have an overabundance of affect. They have frantic crying jags, frantic depressions, frantic manias...

Apel: They are the ones most often pointed out as "crazy," because of their extravagant behavior.

Briggs: Your "baseline crazy" is generally a schizophrenic... although paranoia has been gaining in the last 15 years or so.

Dick: Right. I remember in a Gilbert and Sullivan libretto the directions, "Mad Meg comes out, the picture of theatrical madness."

Apel: Clothes in disarray; large wild smile.

Dick: Yeah. Eyes bugged out. I thought: That's very interesting... *theatrical madness.* Gilbert was such an astute human being that he didn't say she's the picture of madness; he says she's the picture of *theatrical* madness.

In a way, your schizophrenic is theatrically mad. I had one poor schizophrenic wife who used to paint herself all over with lipstick—circles, designs and so forth—but she was just a sweetie-pie; she'd kiss you and hug you and all that. But she heard the Virgin Mary talking to her, and at Easter she'd lie on the floor with a lily clutched over her stomach until 3:00, then she'd say, "I'm rising now from the tomb; I'm immortal." And I would say, "Yes, dear; I know it's Easter." Obviously she was crazy. Yet I would prefer this any day to the schizoid.

I'll give you an example of *that.* The woman who told me this was working at the Bevatron...a qualified scientist; educated, intelligent, calm and rational. She had this beautiful orange cat, and I came over one time and he was missing, so I asked what happened to him. She said, "Well, we didn't want him anymore, so we drove him seven miles out into the country and dumped him off. Y'know, a month later he showed up with all his pads worn off his feet, having trudged seven miles, and had come back." And I said, "Well, where is he now?" She said, "Oh, we took him and gassed him."

Apel: I learned a lot about sanity from Scientology; they equate sanity with *survival*. Basically the position is that the better you are surviving—and helping those around you survive—the more sane you are. This agrees with something Robert Anton Wilson's beautiful wife Arlen once said while we were discussing this same point: her criterion for sanity was how valuable you are in an emergency.

Dick: The schizophrenic is not sane because he overreacts to an emergency; the schizoid is not sane because he underreacts. If the house catches fire, the schizophrenic's immediate response might be, "It is God's will that we all perish, for we are all evil!" This is inappropriate...and doesn't help put out the fire.

Apel: Or he says, "Oh, gee, isn't this a beautiful flame..."

Dick: ...and walks into it.

Apel: While a schizoid reaction to the same fire might be something like, "I have to save my library," when his wife and family are asleep upstairs. Another form of choice that's wrong, that's insane, that's anti-survival.

Dick: I'm not worried about the theatrical madness of the schizophrenic, because it's self-evident that the person has disengaged himself from everyday reality. He wears a very bold badge that says, "I am completely crazy."

Apel: What intrigues me about these people is the dream logic that they seem to use...the same sort of rationality you find in dreams, where the most outrageous events are accepted as perfectly natural. I've worked in several asylums, and in one, we admitted a fellow who went around his first week there telling everyone he was a woman. His second week there, he was not only a woman, but he had been raped, and by his third week the rape had made him pregnant. When he didn't mention his pregnancy during the fourth week, I asked him how it was coming along. "Oh, I got an abortion," he said. A perfectly logical, step-by-step fantasy which bore no relation to reality.

Dick: I remember when I worked in a record store, there was a lady who used to come in wearing man's clothes, with her face painted purple, her hair shaved, and her body rubbed all over with garlic. Harmless enough, I suppose, although it could lead to the Charlie Manson thing.

Briggs: Even Manson, to a certain extent, exhibited the cold, schizoid personality. He would have made a first class SS officer—he never got emotionally involved. You're right; those are the guys that are really dangerous.

Apel: The insidious ones.

Dick: Viewing from a global standpoint, from the standpoint of most cultures, the Anglo-Saxon is a pretty cold fish. Your Englishman is a better example than your American, perhaps. The dangerous madness of the Anglo-Saxon is not that he'll go raving mad, in the theatrical sense, and run down the street painted purple with garlic cloves sticking out his ears—the bizarre sort of things—it's this insidious thing which I feel is an absence of the passions of the heart. They're not literally in the heart, of course—they're literally in the thalamus.

So divide it this way: you've got the person with an overabundance of the thalamus, who goes into emotional spasms sometimes, and we treat him with the phenalthiazines, which suppress the thalamus; but the really inhuman person for our culture is the overtrained cerebral person. What I'm saying now exactly conforms to Jung's concept of schizophrenia; that schizophrenia is a failure of adequate affect and an overdevelopment of the thinking function, until the thinking function breaks down by an onrush of contents from the unconscious, which are attempting to compensate for the exaggerated use of a single function, the thinking function.

Apel: It's like pulling yourself up by your own bootstraps—the "bootstraps" being the major differentiated function—to a certain height, and when you lose control you fall that same distance, or deeper, into the unconscious. I really like Jung's idea of the psyche as a self-regulating system, where concentrating too much on the major function of consciousness and ignoring the other three vital functions always leads to an attempt at compensation by the unconscious. So that any function overextended too far becomes its own opposite. There's a word for that...what'd he call it? *Enantiodromia?*

Dick: Like Jung said, you cannot think your way through life, you have to feel your way through life.

Apel: He was a thinking type; that may explain why he said that. He'd have to differentiate his opposite function, his least developed function, the feeling function, as much as possible, then constantly use it, so it didn't slip back into the unconscious. It's still good advice, though...especially for us cold fish.

Dick: In relationships, especially, the thinking function is inadequate. And the thinking function is overly utilized by the Anglo-Saxon. We have far too great a regard for it. I was interested in this business about I.Q. tests, because the ones I've seen are a deformed culture's way of ratifying the adequacy of its deformity; of certifying its own deformity as being adequate. They feed back their own deformity to themselves as a positive value. There ought to be tests with questions like this: If your cat is sick, do you: a.) take it to the vet, or b.) kill it?

Apel: Or c.) chant over it to make it well. I agree with you 100 percent.

Dick: This goes back to the authentic human displaying kindness. Kindness is a very complex act and emotion. It's involved, for instance, with making exceptions. You can imagine this very simply in the paradigm of the Hall of Misery—from which we have *all* come—which is high school. It's Purgatory.

Apel: Junior high school is the concentration camp of the American school system, then they send you to high school, which is purgatory, but which looks better by comparison.

Dick: I was going to say junior high school originally; I was thinking that my traumas all came from junior high. But gym class is usually where this all happens. *(peals of laughter)*

Apel: What never failed to outrage and embarrass me was watching the coaches up in their glass booth above the locker room watching the boys take their showers after every class.

Dick: That's why *Carrie* was such a great film. You take your junior high school gym class and you have some kid who's too fat to climb the rope, all that's going to happen is the kid is going to suffer terribly, and be humiliated. The gym teacher who out of kindness "accidentally" skips that kid's name and doesn't require him or her to climb the rope is exhibiting true humanity. This is almost where it begins.

Briggs: I never ever met a kind gym teacher.

Apel: Well, in all fairness to my old gym teachers, I did have a couple who had their shining moments. One guy in my class got out of swimming once by telling the coach it was "that time of the month." But you really had to work at looking pitiful enough so that it registered with them.

Dick: But you can see it in a simple situation like that. The willingness to make an exception is somehow intimately connected with the act of kindness, which is also connected with the act of balking. A person will do what he's told to do, and all of a sudden he will *balk,* and this is an exception. So you've got the common theme of knowing when an exception is to be made. And an emergency is an exceptional situation, where exceptional behavior of some type is required. There is no formula for this behavior; you can't post rules for it, because by definition, exceptional behavior is something other than formula behavior. Therefore the total brain, on all levels, must be brought to bear; all its functions *and* faculties.

I remember one time I had ten acres of land, and I was way out in a pasture, and one of my little girls was heating paraffin to make a paraffin puppet. And the troll who was in charge of the class had not told the children that paraffin has a flash point. When that is reached, it becomes a flamethrower. It's incredible. So I'm standing out in the pasture hoeing weeds, when all of a sudden I see this column of flame in the house that goes from the stove all the way up to the twelve-foot high ceiling. Just this jet of flame in which my little girl was standing. I run across the pasture, leap over the fence, run into the house, right past the child, without even stopping, and grab the fire extinguisher, yank it down, turn around, and just confront her with it. She was OK; she had stepped back and the flame had singed her eyebrows off completely, but she was not on fire. The point is, there was no time for me to say, "Let's see now... should I wrap her in a rug?" like going through the list of rules, or a formula: "When someone is on fire, you wrap them in a rug." My cerebral cortex never got involved in the situation.

Later, I worked back to what my sub-cortical reasoning had been: If she was on fire, there was no use running and grabbing her and putting her head in the sink; it would probably take the fire extinguisher to put her out. I did the right thing, but never did I think, in the usual sense of the word "think."

I have a great respect for the older, more primitive parts of the brain. I think these are the things that are going to save our lives when the chips are down. Korzybski always talked about that ten-second cortical-thalamic pause. There are so many situations when ten seconds later, when the cerebral cortex cuts in, it's all over; it's all happened. Anybody who drives a car knows that. If you wait the ten seconds to respond—

Apel: —you're dead, about nine and a half seconds earlier.

Dick: The interesting thing is that schizoids are often very good in emergencies, because they don't lose their cool. They stay calm. I used to think that was really neat. But this goes back to the whole Anglo-Saxon idea that sanity and calmness are somehow the same, and that to get very upset is to be crazy. The schizoid calmness in an emergency: that's the one where you save the book instead of the child. This is where calmness goes astray.

I remember this one girl I knew walked into a plate glass window and the window just burst, and all these goddam huge giant shards of glass were falling. She just ricocheted off it, and was standing away from it, but her face was bleeding from the impact. I rushed over and took hold of her by the shoulders, and said, "I want you to sit down," because she was stunned. And she said, "If you don't let go of me, I'm going to kick you in the balls." And I thought, *Well, fuck it. If she's got a concussion, she can just handle it herself.*

What had happened was she was *mad...* She was mad because she had misjudged regarding whether the sliding glass door was open or not. She was very angry that she had fucked up...there was company there, and so on. Then later she gave me a complicated explanation about why it was completely insane for me to suggest that she sit down. I won't even give it. It just seemed to me that that summed up your inappropriate response.

There's always a counter-incident. I remember when I rolled my VW and my passenger fell out unconscious, and was lying there beside the road. I thought she was dead, and I was badly hurt. These people stopped and a woman came over to me and said, "Look, she's not dead; she's breathing. But *you're* badly damaged," she said. "I can see your entire shoulder is hurt. You've got to stop moving your arm; you've got to lie down." And she took hold of my good hand and clasped it as hard as she could, and just held onto it. My passenger was unhurt, but I was in a full torso cast for many months afterward, and had extensive surgery. But here's this complete stranger, just out for a Saturday drive, you know, and she got a blanket from her car and covered the girl, and all that.

The bottom line about all this is that for every nut who offers to kick you in the balls when you're trying to render aid, there is this helpful figure.

The other side of those instinctual reactions are the times when you feel almost preternaturally guided by a higher destiny rather than motivated by primitive survival patterns. There is a figure that occurs quite often in my novels, a figure which I regard as very real; not a metaphoric thing, but a very real thing. And that is the kind stranger who intervenes and then disappears immediately afterwards. You never know who it was, but whoever it was knew exactly what to say and do. It's a mysterious *figure* who just seems to be there.

I played that role once in a situation, and having played that role even once, I know it from the other side, too. It's been done for me so many times that I have the feeling that there is something of a supernatural quality in this kindly stranger, that this is more than just an ordinary person.

One time—this was in the summer of '74—I was in a car, and

we came up to a stop sign alongside this convertible full of jocks, with one girl in the back. And the girl was screaming, "Somebody help me; I'm being kidnapped! Help me! Help me!" She was struggling and trying to get out of the car. I turned to the guy driving our car and said, "Do you have a hammer?" He said, "Don't mess with it." But I got out—this was when I was in that torso cast; all I had was my left arm—and went over. I reached over two of these big jocks, wrapped my arm around the girl's waist, and lifted her right out of the car and onto the pavement. Then I took her by the hand over to a large group of people at a bus stop...none of whom were doing a goddamn thing except standing there watching. One guy was writing the license plate number down. And I took hold of the girl's hands and started talking to her. I have no idea what I said to her; just talk talk talk talk. The guys got out of the car and I said, "What happened?" They said, "She's dropped acid; she's freaking out." I said, "Well, all right, you'll have to take her to a hospital. But I want you all to stay away from her right now. Don't come near her; she's afraid of you." And I went on in that vein.

I didn't let go of her hands until she was calmed a little. "Look at these people around you," I told her. "None of these people is going to hurt you. Look at their faces...they all want to help you. Is there any of these people you feel calm with, that you want to be next to?" And she picked out a lady and I told her to go stand with that lady.

One of the guys says, "I'm her husband." "You stay away from her; don't even come near her," I told him. And I did that until the police came. Then the police arrived, and I told them which hospital to take her to... *I did all that stuff?* Then I got back in the car with my friends and we went on.

And I supposed that in that situation I was the stranger that intervened. I knew what to do and what to say and got her calmed down. This was in the early days of acid, when people didn't know you could go completely *crazy* on acid, which she had done. Her friends were scared; they didn't know what to do. When somebody freaks out on acid... Norman Spinrad told me one time he looked out of his window one night and there was this guy rolling around in the street. Just rolling around; just screaming and shrieking and rolling around. *(general laughter)* Norman watched for a while; finally the cops came and took the guy away.

Anyway... For all I knew, the girl *was* being kidnapped. That's what she said. I had the very strong impression that what I did did not emanate from the part of my brain that I call "myself"...the "self-system," or the ego, or *me*. It came from a supra-personal level, which everyone has access to. If the spirit had struck either of you at that time, that spirit might have animated those levels and you might have said equivalent things.

The human brain has areas in it of grandeur, beauty and appropriate knowledge. Wisdom—incredible wisdom—which is not going to show up on those I.Q. tests which test whether or not you've read *David Copperfield.* I sometimes have the feeling that we really contain superconsciousness in other parts of the brain that are not the personality, that we draw on from time to time. I don't care to be the one to make a definitive statement about this.

Apel: You can always refer people to Jung, who says much the same thing. The ego is just a constellation of these contents that remains conscious for relatively long periods of time compared with those relatively unconscious supra-or sub-personality constellations. Jung often used the metaphor of the ego as an island surrounded by a sea of unconsciousness. And a great deal of his work dealt with delineating those other archetypal personalities that sometimes overwhelm consciousness.

Dick: I sometimes have the feeling that if the conscious ego were to dissolve... something we very much fear—

Apel: *"I'll lose control!"*

Dick: Yes...I'll paint myself purple and run around naked. But we might possibly exhibit an incredible ancestral or primordial wisdom that might then be free to come forth; a wisdom based on thousands of years of reality-testing and problem-solving and coping, and things like that.

We guard our individual egos we build up during our individual lifetimes so carefully, as if it's the total repository of all skills, all knowledge, all experience. It's really a very limited and ignorant creation, very short in duration. What it has acquired in the way of knowledge and skills is very little. There are really fantastic layers that can be tapped. Unfortunately, we don't have reliable techniques for readily tapping them.

Apel: I'm glad you brought up the whole subject of insanity without being asked, because one of the things I wanted to mention was something that I just recently realized. About the same time you were writing several books—*We Can Build You, Clans of the Alphane Moon,* and others—with the theme of situational behavior versus chronic psychiatric categories, there was a revolution occurring along these same lines in the field of psychiatry. R.D. Laing was asking if it is insane to be insane in an insane society; Thomas Szasz was writing about how society manufactures madness and pointed out that single instances of extravagant behavior were not enough to justify the label of insanity; that the situational context needed to be considered as well; E. Fuller Torrey was comparing psychiatrists to primitive shamans and labeling them labelers of behavior. What makes your books more inherently interesting, at least to me, and even perhaps more valuable than those others was the fact that while these psychiatrists *explained* what they thought about "madnesses" which are situationally appropriate, you *illustrated* these same basic themes and conclusions—societal madness versus individual sanity; appropriate situational behavior verses apparent psychiatric pathology—which left the meaning not as a reader's agreement with the author, but as a reader's discovery or revelation.

Dick: The only thing I could add to that is a redundant thing: Since I am not satisfied that there is *one single* reality—I have this feeling we live in a pluraverse rather than a universe—any critique as to which divergent view is correct must be suspended until we can settle certain epistemological questions about the nature of reality. Since we have *not* settled such questions as Kant brought up—and before him, Spinoza, or the Pre-Socratics—we are *not* in a position to state categorically that Person A sees reality properly and that Person B does not. The most reputable philosophers have strongly indicted simplistic views of what constitutes reality; I would include among them people like Heinrich Zimmer, and Jung, and David Hume, for example, who doubted causality. *(laughter)*

Apel: Jung tried that, too, and came up with synchronicity, causality's equal opposite.

Dick: Yeah. He and Pauli. Since it is an actual fact that some of the finest minds of the different cultures, including our own, have not come to an agreement on a.) whether there is a single reality or several, and b.) what that single or those several realities are, I don't see how we can at this point in all fairness to people give guidelines for insanity. I read some Szasz, and he said somebody who talks to God is considered praying, and somebody who has God talk to him is considered schizophrenic.

Apel: They tell you all your life, "God answers your prayers," but as soon as you start to get answers, they lock you up.

Dick: This to me is the crucial question. I'm not satisfied that we know *what* we are living within. We call it "the cosmos," but what this "cosmos" is we've really not established, to the extent that we can prove what it is. Until that day comes, when we can epistemologically, empirically demonstrate what the nature of this cosmos *is,* it is not fit or proper that we categorically label Person A's view of reality "rational" and Person B's view "psychotic." Those labels really presume that we know what reality is. This is really the underlying postulate of just about everything I write, I think. I tackle this one over and over again.

The psychiatrist is forever talking about people being in contact with reality... The most charitable thing that you could say about him is that he's incredibly naive. I remember I was in my *teens* and I saw a psychiatrist—I was having trouble in school—and I told him that I had begun to wonder if our value system—what was right and what was wrong—were absolutely true or whether they were not merely culturally relativistic. And he said, "That's a symptom of your neurosis, that you doubt the values of what is right and what is wrong." So I got hold of a copy of the British scientific journal *Nature,* which is the most reputable scientific journal in the world. And there was an article in which it said virtually all our values are derived essentially from the Bible and cannot be empirically verified, therefore must fall into the category of the untestable and the unprovable. I showed it to him, and he got very angry and said, "I consider this nothing but horseshit. *Horseshit,* I say!" Here I was, a teenager in the '40s, and here he was, a psychiatrist; now I look back and see that this man was cemented into a simplistic mold. I mean his brain was *dead* as far as I could determine. Somewhere along his life-track, his brain had ossified. He thought certain things were absolutely right, empirically right. Like I say, "That box over there is blue," and I say, "Balling sheep is bad"...to him, those were similar statements. Thinking of that kind is rarely encountered in such a blatant form; people usually show a little more sophistication. Maybe he thought that since he was talking to a teenager, he was free to "announce." They don't say that to me now. They don't say, "How *dare* you question these values, these absolute verities." I'm too old for them to say that to me now. But psychiatrists are philosophically naive. Most of them, except people like Laing and so forth.

I tackled the reality problem from the standpoint of having read Hume, Kant, Plato and the Pre-Socratics. And *that* is what bothers me. We have to solve *that* problem first: What reality is. Or what realities are. And that point may never come. I mentioned my wife, who said the Virgin Mary talked to her... All we can say is that it is *unlikely* that the Virgin Mary talked to her.

Apel: Right—a low statistical order of probability.

Dick: I've always had a lot of sympathy toward people who saw different realities than we do. Maybe because I'm one of those people.

I remember when I was a kid I worked in a record store that had front two doors. And one day I said to one of the other clerks, "Let's walk out one door and in the other." And he looked at me and he started laughing, and he says to me, "I want to tell you something. No one who's ever worked here has thought of walking out one of the front doors and walking back in through the other. You're gonna go far in this world." So I was already off in my own orbit. *(laughter)*

Apel: In response to the question of reality, I found a quote in the

Talmud that I really liked: "We do not see things as they are, we see them as *we* are."

Dick: One of the Pre-Socratics said—I should know which one it is, but it doesn't matter: "If elephants believed in God, they would assume that God was an elephant." Even before Plato, there at the origins of philosophy, we have this awareness.

So now do you want to proceed to another subject?

Apel: Well, let's just change directions slightly and talk a bit about paranoia, since we've been talking about the nature of reality and psychiatric categories.

Dick: Let me say, before you proceed any further, that I promise I'll take my medication...and I won't mix it with alcohol. *(laughter)*

Apel: Oh, now, we weren't going to *accuse* you of anything...

Dick: *Oh yes you were!* I know what you were gonna do! *(laughter)*

Briggs: We were talking about it behind your back.

Dick: You were planning the whole time—I knew you were working up to this question!

Apel: A great many of the protagonists of your books either are or appear to be—

Dick: *It's a lie!* It's something that's *said about them* by their enemies! *(laughter) Really!* On behalf of my protagonists, I *resent* that. They're misunderstood. They're...they're...*ahead of their time!*

Apel: They're the only ones who *really* know what's going on, eh?

Dick: That's right! I remember I wrote a letter once, saying that I thought it was the government that hit my house, when my files were blown up and all my papers were taken. And Dr. *(name unintelligible)* read the letter I wrote Dick Geiss about that, which was the first time I'd ever said publicly what happened, and he said, "Well, I understand that paranoia is total awareness. And I looked at him—sourly, I think is what I'd say if I were writing a description of it—and I thought, *Oh, shit. I can see where this is all going to lead.* I always know where it's gonna lead.

Apel: Do you think the *Rolling Stone* piece [by Paul Williams, 6 November 1975] concentrated too much on the break-in? I thought so for a long time, but when I reread it recently, I think he might have been trying to get across the point that even in your life, as in your fiction, alternate realities were the rule. He was using the break-in as a metaphor for multiple realities.

Dick: The first thing I ever read of Paul's that he wrote about me, years ago, was a review of *Game Players of Titan*. It was the first serious notice that had ever been taken of my writing. And it started out, "There's this paranoid guy..." *(laughter) That* was the way critical attention directed at me began. I do remember that.

There was an article on paranoia in *Harper's* a few years ago, and they said that the word "paranoia" has become an essential word in the counter-culture.

Apel: An essential *lifestyle* in the counter-culture.

Briggs: Yeah—how many hundreds of times have friends of ours or yours said, "I'm getting a little paranoid"?

Dick: That was the point of the article...the word has lost its pejorative context. I regard it as a pejorative term. I mean, I don't like paranoia, I don't like paranoids.

Briggs: They don't like you either. And they're all gonna get together and do something about it.

Dick: They've tried, but I've foiled them.

To be really serious about the subject, if there's one thing I don't want to be, it's a paranoid. If I thought I was, I'd really throw in the sponge. All anybody has to do to stop a line of argument I'm pursuing is to say that it's paranoid.

I remember one time I was talking to Kris Neville, I said, "Kris! You know what happened to me? They blew up my files and they took all my cancelled checks..." And he says, "You're paranoid." I says, "No, they really did, Kris; honest to God!" And he says, "No, you're just being paranoid." And I says, "Well, what do you mean? They *didn't* do that? Is that what you mean?" And my wife got really just *furious* at him. She says, "Listen: Phil is just describing what *happened*. I mean, this is a simple, factual description of what *happened*. Somebody *did* blow up the files; somebody *did* take the papers. Now where in this is the paranoia?" She was really very eloquent. She says, "Look. The files didn't self-destruct; the papers didn't vanish into thin air. Phil has no theory as to who did it, why they did it or what they were looking for. Paranoia consists of a coherent system of identifying certain people as your enemies, and they're doing it for specific reasons which you're sure of. 'They,' you say, for instance, are persecuting you because you are the only real Christian in the world. And all these elements are lacking from Phil's account. He doesn't know who did it or why they did it; all he knows is just what he saw when he opened the front door. The same thing the taxi driver saw: the house in ruins and windows smashed and the door smashed too."

I really appreciate Tessa saying this. So I think Paul, as a part of the counter-culture, does not regard the word "paranoia" the way I regard it. I regard it as a great insult. *(laughter) Somebody* zapped me, and I'd like to know who it was, y'know? And I really *don't* know who it was. And I'd like to kick their ass if I ever found out who it was. But I don't see this as paranoid, you see.

There was a paranoid part—and Paul understands this, and I think he made it clear in the article. The paranoid part was that before the hit on my house, I and my girlfriend, who was living with me, believed that this was going to happen. We believed that some people were going to hit the house, just burst in, destroy and take stuff, pillage...all this stuff. We believed it for about a week. And all our friends told us we were paranoid. But I got her out of the house, and the day after I got her out of the house, it happened...exactly as we both anticipated it happening.

This raises several curious questions. We were paranoid, in a sense, when you believe that unknown, invisible people are going to hit your house at any moment. I remember she and I huddling in the bedroom, and saying, "Well, I tell you what we'll do: we'll call the PG&E and tell them that our pilot lights have gone out, and they'll send out a truck and that means that they'll be out in the back yard for a while, and that'll give us a couple of hours." We were *so sure* that this was going to happen.

Apel: The dilemma you were in sounds like that old joke...you know: "Just because you're paranoid doesn't mean they *aren't* after you."

Dick: Yeah. She was the one that first said, "I think the house is gonna be hit." And she was completely crazy. She thought they were going to come in through the coils in the air conditioner. I had to get her out of there because she was breaking under the strain. I would take her out to a restaurant, and she would just sit there and look at the menu. She was unable to order. I'd have to order for her, like she was a child. But she was absolutely right. And I was sure enough of it to get her out of there.

I talked to people whose houses had been hit on drug busts—those no-knock drug busts where the cops come in through the doors and windows—and they'd say they had these strange sensations that they were being watched, and that this thing was in preparation, and then it would turn out to be true. It may be that paranoia is an atavistic sense system that we have left over from the days when we were hunted by fierce predators in the jungle.

Briggs: I think it's interesting that feelings like that come out especially in a counter-culture, and I think it may be partially due to exposure to a wide variety of drugs. I think people are more open to think about things like, "They're going to bust me; I can feel it." Most people would think that's an irrational feeling and dismiss it.

Dick: Well, if you're in a counter-culture and you've got contraband, they may find something. In the straight world, first of all, they're not holding. So what're they worried about? Anyway, they run the establishment anyway, so it's just a joke idea that they're going to be hit, since they're the master class. But in the counter-culture...well, it's like the "Fabulous Furry Freak Brothers" comics, you know; every time there's a knock on the door, they flush the stash. This feeling is part of being in the counter-culture. I remember every time a police car drove slowly up the street, we'd all run out in the back yard and throw the plants over in the neighbor's yard.

I remember one terrible time—just one ghastly incident—where...*heh heh.* Shit...where the goddamn police car stopped, and there was an unmarked cop car behind it, so we knew, y'know, that it was the moment of truth. So we had one plant, and we had a chain of instructions: "Throw the plant. Pull the plant and throw it." So I yanked this plant up, and I threw it over the fence. And I looked up, and standing on the other side of the fence were three of the largest black dudes I had ever seen in my life. *(laughter)* And they stand there, and they look at this plant at their feet, and one of them says, "We done seen the narc vehicle too." I couldn't think of anything to say, so I just went in the house. *(laughter)* So pretty soon—about an hour, like—there was a knock on the door. And I open the door, and there are these three black guys standing there. And I thought: *They are going to kill me. And I deserve it.* I wouldn't argue, y'know... But what they had done was they had roasted our plant in their oven, and manicured it and rolled it into joints, and they felt they should share the joints with us. So we all sat around and smoked it all up. And I thought, *Y'know, that's not how I would have handled it.* But I mean, y'know, if you've got something growing in your backyard, you're going to be paranoid all the days of your life, until you get the damn thing out of your yard.

So...what question did you wish to pursue next?

Briggs: One of the things that I'd be interested in is the relationship between you and your readership. One of the obvious differences between science fiction and other genres of literature is that the science fiction people all get together and wear funny clothes at conventions...

Apel: You're slanting the question already! *(general laughter)*

Dick: That is about as slanted as you'll ever hear... Can't improve on that.

Apel: This is the King of the Slanters here... We lived through lean times together, and he leaned so far he's slanted.

Dick: My conception of my readership was primarily entirely that of the editor who would read the story. I was writing for Tony Boucher, or Horace Gold or John W. Campbell. When I started writing, you know, I was writing stories, not novels, so everything I wrote I really wrote hoping that it would be bought by one of those three. I always wrote for one of the three major magazines. I was in Berkeley, but I didn't have any contact with fans. I went to my first convention in 1954, and I was mainly interested in talking to the writers. I was entranced to meet people like Jack Williamson and A.E. van Vogt. I couldn't believe I was actually meeting these people—they were gods to me. They still are. I was *a fan* of these giants.

I'm not sure I have a concept of my readership yet. I'm not sure it's ever progressed beyond the idea of an imaginary editor. To me it wasn't the reader who bought it, it was the editor who bought it; it was as simple as that. The big change came when I wrote *The Man in the High Castle,* because that book was *not* written for Donald Wollheim. I had sold *Time Out of Joint,* and had gotten the idea of selling a hardcover novel. With *Man in the High Castle,* I had no concept of an audience at all. I had no concept even of an editor. It was a pure relationship between me and the characters in the novel, and it stayed pretty much that way. So the big change in my novel writing was when I stopped selling to Ace entirely and began to sell to Doubleday, where I was not writing for Donald Wollheim, I was writing for Larry Ashmead.

Briggs: What was it like, working for Wollheim?

Dick: My first contact with Donald Wollheim was your typical disastrous contact between a sentient organism and something that grew on a rock on the planet Pluto. To avoid a libel suit, I won't say which was which. *(immense laughter)* First of all, Donald Wollheim said, "I will buy it if it is exactly 6,000 lines long. I did not say *60,000 words,* I said *6,000 lines.* I don't really care what's in it, as long as there are not too many characters and it's not too complicated." That was *Solar Lottery,* and he bought it. He would communicate through these harangues... He'd say, "I really think this book is the worst of them all." He really would say things like that. Such a tactful way of handling matters. Like, he said *The Man in the High Castle* was sick, dated, and not science fiction, and a lot of other things like that, which shows it was a good thing I was aiming for the hardcover market by then.

But mostly I wrote for the editor. I have no idea, even today, of who my readers are. If someone comes up to me and says, "I read your books, and all of my friends read your books," that doesn't tell me anything. Unless he's a very unusual person and has 150,000 friends, he's not a sampling I can extrapolate from. I don't want to sound cruel when I say this, but even if I could extrapolate from the people who come up to me, I would prefer not to. This isn't the right sampling. How shall I put this delicately? The worst thing that could happen to me would be to wake up some morning and find myself imprisoned on a planetoid with people who read my books and liked them. So many horrible, ghastly aspects would immediately be evident: First, they'd want to talk to me about my books, which I wouldn't want to do anyway.

Apel: *(to Briggs)* C'mon, let's go.

Dick: Sorry, guys. I make certain exceptions. That asteroid fantasy would be like an infinity of mirrors, reflecting back nothing.

Dick Lupoff put it very well: In 1964 he was at this party, and was discussing with somebody the meaning of the ending of *The Man in the High Castle*. And (he said) there was this guy, smoking a cigar, who kept trying to butt into the conversation and say what the ending meant. Finally, Lupoff turned to the guy and said, "Will you *please* not bother us; we're discussing the ending of *The Man in the High Castle.*" And the guy says, "Well, I'm Philip K. Dick, and I wrote it." *(laughter)* I can see myself standing at the periphery of a circle of my own fans, and they're all discussing some book of mine, and I'm saying, "Um...um...What *I* think he meant was..." and they turn to me and say, "Butt out, joker." It would either go that way, or they'd want to know what *I* thought, and that would be a drag.

Apel: *(to Briggs)* Let's go. *(laughter)*

Dick: My books don't turn me on all that much. *(laughter)* The only book I've ever written that I really like is *A Scanner Darkly*. Maybe that's just because it's my most recent book. I don't even like *Man in the High Castle*. I *do* like *Dr. Bloodmoney;* I reread that recently, and I really thought that part where Bill is swallowed by the owl and the owl barfs him up, and he's shouting, y'know, "Write letters of protest to President Johnson!" was one of the best scenes in science fiction I've ever read. I like the whole book.

So my concept of my readership is that they are my punishment for having written the books. The next worst thing to being stuck on an asteroid with people who read my books would be to be stuck on an asteroid with just the books. I see this scene where I die and when judgement is passed against me—which I hope it isn't—they say: "And your punishment is a very special one, because you've done a very special thing: You are going to have to read your own books *for the rest of eternity*...especially *Vulcan's Hammer!" (previous great hilarity looks mild in comparison to this)*

Actually, there is always the theoretical possibility that there are noble minds of high stature whose calm gaze and intelligent eyes are fastened with loving fascination on the deathless prose which I have produced...

Apel: Well, thank you.

Dick: ...but I think every single part of that sentence is wrong. My girlfriend Joan [Simpson] reads my books and remembers them pretty well, and she's cool; she's AOK.

Now there's a perfect example to illustrate my idea of my readership: I get this letter from her boyfriend which says, "My girlfriend has a complete collection of all your books and she would like to meet you," and gives a description. Even though the description was very favorable, I just imagined this...this *thing,* wearing Coke bottle bottoms for glasses, whose knuckles dragged along the ground when she walked. Something with parts falling off...definitely fungoidal. Something that Lanacaine would be appropriate for. *(laughter)* But, I thought, *Well, y'know, she wants to meet me.* If fans write me and give me their phone number, I always call them up. They always go crazy. It's such a trip to call them up. For three dollars I can completely freak out some guy in Norwalk...

Apel: And get a reader for life.

Dick: Yeah. Really. And they always scream *(in cracking falsetto) "Let me put on my tape recorder!" (laughter)* And Joan's number was included, so I called her up, and she behaved, like, "Naw, this isn't Philip K. Dick. You're lying! You're just some jerk. Get lost!"

(laughter) "He wouldn't have such a high-pitched, squeaky voice like you have, or stammer or mumble like you do." So I had to convince her it was really me, y'know. A dollar and a half's worth of phone call. So I had no idea what she'd be like until I saw her. Talking on the phone gave me no idea. The phone impression you get of people is *incredibly* misleading. Someday I'm gonna write a novel about it, because I think that what you hear over the phone is so different from what... It's amazing just how little a phone conveys.

Once I saw her, though, I was delighted. But how representative of my readership Joan is, I don't know. I'll never know. I have no concept of my readership.

The thing is, I'm going to write the best book I can write under any circumstances, no matter who the audience is. Like when I drive my car, I drive to the best of my ability. I just write the best I can; float the thing out. Like I make it into a paper airplane, and sail it out, and hope some money comes back and I can survive.

Apel: The fact that you have no idea of your readership might just work in your favor as an artist. You're not writing for anyone but yourself, so the vision is your own. You're not trying to please every member of some nebulous, multi-opinioned audience.

Dick: Yeah. It's like, if you were building a chair, you would build the best chair you could build.

Apel: And you wouldn't try to please everyone who was going to sit in it.

Dick: Yeah, right.

Apel: Good analogy.

Briggs: I think that attitude is terrific, but there seems to be some misunderstanding of it in the science fiction world. For years, they've been saying that that's what they want to have happen, to write the best book you can write. On the other hand, you write something like *The Man in the High Castle,* and it gets criticized right and left, because they say it's not science fiction.

Dick: Yeah. Even Tony Boucher, at first, would not accept *The Man in the High Castle* as science fiction. Really amazing. I was really surprised that a man of his caliber would say something like this. I heard him review it over KPFA, and he said it was really a mainstream novel. Which is what it really was; once you got through the first page, it was really a mainstream novel. Then I talked to him at a party, and he said, "That book was a breakthrough in science fiction." And I thought, *Gee, that just goes to show you the hangup we all have*...that if it's good, it's not science fiction, and so on.

Apel: Yeah. And since you and the book both carry the "science fiction" nametag, a fine mainstream novel like *The Man in the High Castle* gets no critical attention, little exposure, and a tenth of the revenue that, say, a Vonnegut book might bring in.

Dick: I was just going to bring that up. If Glenda the Good appeared to me and said, "I have wonderful news for you...You're going to go the route that Vonnegut went," I'd say, "Wait just a minute."

Apel: You'd balk.

Dick: I think if I have to choose, I'll stay with lurid covers... I don't want to end up writing *Breakfast of Champions*. I mean, Jesus Christ! Spare me being crowned Caesar, then becoming like Caligula and making my horse a senator. Nobody knows what the cover on the first edition of *The Rubaiyat* looked like. Or *Moby Dick*. I liked the early Vonnegut so much, and I *loathe* the late Vonnegut. Actually—this is a terrible thing to say, I suppose—but I've gone so far as to feel a personal loathing for Vonnegut, that he has conspired voluntarily and deliberately to do this. This is not something like "he's lost it," like a singer loses her voice and it's a tragedy, but I think he did this with malice aforethought. I hold him personally responsible. He has *debased his own talent,* and that's what St. Paul called *hubris.* I know what it is and I don't like it. I'd really rather go back to what Spinrad calls the "peeled eyeball" covers and be published by DAW and go my little way, carrying my little light through my little dark corridor and finally come to the end of that little dark corridor and have the light extinguished, rather than inflate myself like that hot air balloon during the Franco-Prussian War that was one hundred miles in diameter. I don't want to be remembered as the world's largest hot air balloon. I'd rather be back on Grub Street, like in the '50s.

They're two awful alternatives—stories appearing in *Imagination* magazine, or inflated, sententious, contentless stuff—but then again, I *don't* have to take one or the other. I've got other alternatives. I can just keep on truckin'.

Briggs: I was reading an article about John W. Campbell recently, and it included your name in a list of people who couldn't work for him, just because of the way he was, both personally and professionally. Was there some clash between you and Campbell?

Dick: Absolutely. Campbell once wrote in words that I was crazy. He said, "I can't print your stuff, and I'll tell you why: because you don't believe that the psionic talents really exist. Unless you will place them at the core of society, as the master talents ruling society, and not as peripheral, marginal and external to society, I will not print your stuff." And he says, "Psi"—he liked to use that term—"is a necessary premise for science fiction." And I thought, *Well, the same to your cat! (laughter)* He is going to tell me this is a "necessary premise" for science fiction? He said, not psi where it's somebody who gets stoned, like in *Slan,* but where psi is solemnly regarded as a lofty thing. That did it. After that I knew there was no quarter asked and none given between me and Campbell.

First of all, I didn't really believe at that time that psi talents existed. I honestly thought they were within the realm of the occult. I can't honestly say I've ever believed in psychic talents as real things. I've written about them, but I've never believed them. I'm still not willing to concede that they exist. I'm now willing to concede that they *may* exist. I certainly have not built, and will not build, my career around what he called a "necessary premise" to the exclusion of all other premises. I'll stick it in when I feel like it. I'll stick time travel in when I feel like it. If he had said, "Time travel is a necessary premise to science fiction," I would have had the same reaction. The man had simply gone mad, as far as I'm concerned. Fortunately, we had Tony Boucher and Horace Gold to turn to, plus the lesser magazines. Some of the lesser magazines may have been disreputable, but at least they didn't tell you that there was *one premise* for science fiction.

Campbell makes me think very much of J. Edgar Hoover, who

finally ossified in his office. It was a waste of time to submit to him. And I found *Analog* unreadable. I haven't read it since...shit, would you believe 1944?

Apel: Too bad Campbell didn't live long enough to see all the precognitive elements in your books. He had his writers writing about psi, while you were out doing it.

Dick: One of the things that is often brought up as a question, an issue, to the science fiction writer is the "futurist" issue; the idea of your books coming true. People are always saying, "You guys were ahead of your time. You particularly were ahead of your time. You wrote a book in which coffee was hard to get and very expensive, and you wrote it in the '50s; now here it is the '70s, and coffee is hard to get and expensive," and so on. I have always said that that is not the job of the science fiction writer, to be a futurist, to sit down and ask himself, "What do I think it *really will* be like in 1992?" I have never done it. I remember a kid's magazine wrote to me and asked me to contribute an article as to what I thought the world would be like in fifty years. And I didn't have the *slightest idea.* Never have! I have never asked myself, "What is the world gonna be like?"

Science fiction to me is a framework in which you place a novel of ideas, which you can sever from the concrete world you live in; where you're free to invent. You know, you say it's 1992, because if you say it's 1977, it reads kinda funny to have people having vidphones, and teleporting around, and cloning each other and fusing into a polyencephalic organism. *(laughter)* If you say it's 1977 and it's San Jose, California, somebody is apt to notice a discrepancy between your books and reality. But if you place it ahead twenty, thirty years, you're freed of all these things. You can have people walk around in laser holograms, and like that.

Apel: Yeah. One of the points that Robert Anton Wilson's great book *Illuminatus!* makes is that Orwell's *1984* is was not a fantasy of the future, but a parable of the present. This seems an apt description of much of your work. People and their interactions are still the same. The assignment of a date is almost arbitrary. If you look at the jacket *of A Scanner Darkly,* for instance, it says the novel takes place in 1988, but the book itself says the date is 1992.

Dick: Yeah.

Apel: It might as well be 1975. In 1992, they're still going down to the 7-11.

Dick: They still have carburetors rather than fuel injection, too. *Obviously* that book is not set in the real future. That's a perfect example; you're absolutely night.

I remember when Ballentine acquired the manuscript. Judy-Lynn Del Ray wanted me to revise it. She said, "Well, it's set in the future, and they're talking slang from the '60s. I want you to abolish"—as if by a wave of the hand—"*all* of the slang, throughout the *entire book,* and *manufacture,* from your own brain, an *entirely new slang.* I decree that you will do this." And I wrote back and I says, "Judy, you know *damn well* the book is about the '60's. It says so in the Author's Afterword." *(laughter)* "First of all, I'm not able to make up a whole new slang." And she says, "Well, they did it in *Clockwork Orange.* And if he can do it, why can't you do it?" And I says, "The book is *not* about the future. The book is about the *past,* as a matter of fact. You know it, because it says so." Not that I'm lazy... It's just that I'm trying to capture a milieu which is already perishing, and I'm setting it ahead, since this is a convention of my writing.

Apel: I know it's impossible to get an objective answer in asking you for an accounting of your best books, so I'm just going to ask you which ones you're proudest of...and which would get you through the least nights on your purgatory asteroid.

Dick: I want to qualify what I've said denouncing my own writing. Whenever I write a book, I really write as well as I can. That even includes *Vulcan's Hammer, Dr. Futurity,* and *The Unteleported Man.* It isn't that I say, "Well, I'm only being paid three cents a word; what the fuck; crummy pay, crummy book." I really try to write a good book, but they don't all come out good. The intent is not sufficient to guarantee a good result. Some of the worst books I've written—like *The Zap Gun*—are books which I've *labored* over. *Eye in the Sky,* which I think is a much better book, I wrote in two weeks.

Apel: I love that book. I read it about once a year; I think it's the funniest science fiction book ever written. If you can do that well in two weeks, you deserve to be complimented.

Dick: Sometimes it works and sometimes it doesn't. My agent says the harder it is to write a book the worse it is, usually; those that flow well are better.

Apel: It's interesting that Zelazny says just the opposite. He suspects books that are easily written.

Dick: That doesn't always hold true. I really like *A Scanner Darkly,* and I spent years on that. I really like *Ubik,* I really like *Dr. Bloodmoney, The Man in the High Castle, Game Players of Titan, Eye in the Sky.* I love *Clans of the Alphane Moon,* because the entire thing works up to this one funny scene where they call off the attack on the rocket ship and the robot hasn't been told and goes and hammers on the door.

Apel: I really love that book, too, for a number of reasons, not the least of which is the scene near the end where the relations among all the characters get so complex that the main character has to just sit down for about three pages and try to untangle who is on who's side. He finally realizes that it's an impossible equation to solve; there are just too many people doing too many illogical things, some *entirely on their own!*

Dick: That's a funny book in many ways. I like *The Simulacra;* I think it's a very fine book in some ways. It's incredibly complex. There's an incredible number of characters. I don't care for *Martian Time-Slip.*

Apel: That's talked about as one of your major works—

Dick: I know.

Apel: —but I'd have to agree with you. I didn't find it very original.

Dick: I think it's a *dull* book, too. I rather like *Now Wait for Last Year.* I finally decided that I liked the last part of *Flow My Tears,* but as a whole, I don't like it. I don't think it's totally satisfactory. My appreciation is directed now at *A Scanner Darkly.* One that I vacillate about is *Galactic Pot-Healer.* Sometimes it seems funny to me, sometimes it seems...stupid. Stupid. Nothing can be said for it. Another one I'm not sure of is *A Maze of Death.* I get different reactions when I read different parts. There's a part in there where the same whole conversation is repeated twice. It's long, and everybody's babbling away. But it's different—it's carefully rewoven so that the second time around it's not the same; it has a different meaning.

Apel: Did you ever see the film *Last Year at Marienbad?*

Dick: No. I've been told about it, though.

Apel: It's a beautiful film, and they use that device constantly. There is a whole "party conversation" built of snatches of sentences and ambiguous phrases that is repeated at different times, and as the action of the film progresses, the same words take on new and different significance every time they are repeated.

Dick: Somebody has told me I had to see that him. Anyway... I don't like *Do Androids Dream of Electric Sheep?* at all; I really loathe that book. *(Note: This was long before* Blade Runner, *which Phil admired greatly. One must also keep in mind that Phil's opinions of his own books tended to change from hour to hour, and seemed to depend in large part on to whom he was talking.)*

Briggs: Oh, good. I have to tell you I detest it.

Dick: Yeah, there are certain books of mine I wish I could shovel under, and that's one of them. An interesting one is *The Three Stigmata of Palmer Eldritch,* as far as I'm concerned. I have read that and had the distinct impression that it was an extraordinary book—so extraordinary that it may have no peer. It may be a unique book in the history of *writing. Nothing* was ever done like this. And then I've read it over and thought it was completely crazy, just insane; not *about* insanity, it *is* insanity. God, it's a weird book.

Briggs: If I were to pick a favorite from among your books, that would be it.

Apel: Right; same here. It is certainly in a class by itself. That's the book that should probably be pointed to as your major work.

Dick: I think if anything I write is to be retained within the cultural flow that *Three Stigmata* stands a very good chance. Either it will eventually be consigned to oblivion as a bizarre exercise in madness, or it will be considered a breakthrough book. I have a very strong feeling that *Ubik,* too, contains some important ideas.

(Note: During a break, we talk of the lives of career science fiction writers and how they end up; Heinlein in his cyclone-and-barbed-wire-fence-surrounded acreage, replete with flagpole and fallout shelter is contrasted with Leiber in his one-room, fifth-floor walk-up. Phil shakes his head sadly. "That's what a science fiction writer fears most. You ought to ask me that.")

DSA and Briggs: *(in unison)* So, tell us, Phil...what does a science fiction writer fear the most?

Dick: I can only speak for myself, but in 1964 I was driving along the MacArthur Freeway in Oakland, and I saw this horrible old, old hotel—"Rooms by the day or week"—and I said, "I'm gonna wind up in a little room in a horrible old, old hotel in the slums of Oakland. It could be tomorrow, or twenty years from now, but I feel it coming; I feel this horrible destiny."

Then I tried to think why that would be the case. Why would I wind up like that? A lot of it has to do with the financial situation that science fiction writers are in, except for the great ones, like Heinlein. Isolation and loneliness are what's so horrible.

Writing is a solitary occupation. A friend of mine had great ambitions to become a science fiction writer. While he was writing his second novel, his wife left him, and one of the reasons she left him was that he spent all his time writing. Even a year later he was still asking every day, "Is that the price you have to pay to be a science fiction writer?" He was aware of the great similarity with my life. On several occasions, the woman I was living with would leave me when I was right in the middle of the book, and in a very vulnerable position, psychologically. I had all my psychological energy tied up in the book. He said it almost seems like some kind of fate that overtakes science fiction writers. He didn't mention Leiber or Heinlein. Now he's afraid the same thing will happen again if he finds another woman and keeps on writing.

Apel: It takes a lot of personal fortitude to continue in the face of loneliness and low income; to know that day after day you are going to be alone at your typewriter with just your thoughts. But then, in another sense, I suppose that could facilitate the process of writing: if the outer world is so difficult, it's that much more of an incentive to plunge headlong into an inner world and find fantasies good enough to write about. By creating, thereby recreating your own life.

Dick: That's a good point. I was living that way in Santa Ana. It scared me that my first reaction to my current girlfriend moving out was one of relief and happiness. There's a certain attraction in being alone with my thoughts and working materials. For the first time in my life, I was ready to face that fate that in '64 looked so terrible. Actually, I had a good apartment, a car I liked, and so on. For the first time I could see the advantages of solitude to a writer.

When I met Joan, I had a certain fundamental decision I had to make: not, did I want to get involved with her as an individual, but did I want to get involved with *anybody*. I've been involved with so many women, but it always ended badly...at least it always ended, which to me is synonymous. I finally decided that whatever positive effect being alone would have on my writing, I would always be asking myself, "Why are you doing it?" if I was alone.

This brings in a point that I feel very strongly about in my work, which I really would like to say. I hope you use this in the final draft. I feel that when I write a fairly successful book I'm giving something. I'm not just a consumer, who enjoys the products of other people's work and ingenuity and creativity. I feel that I'm giving back something to the world, the universe, the cosmos, my society, other people. I've done a lot of books and stories, and I've given a lot back. And I want something in exchange, in return. What is it I want back, I ask myself, if satisfaction in writing is not sufficient to justify doing it? Well, I don't want admiration. I don't want recognition. Money, no. Well, you always want all those things *automatically,* because they're connected with the book. But what I want back from the universe is something that has nothing to do with the books. It has to do with my personal life. It's something that every human being is entitled to and every human being wants. And that is someone to love and be loved by, and to be with. Whether I wrote or not, I'd want that. If I think that I have given these books out of me and

I'm *not* getting an affectionate relationship back, I feel it's a gyp. This raises the issue that my writer friend raised. If he's going to lose his wife because he writes, he's lost the very thing that means the most to him.

Briggs: Funny how things almost always seem to work that way.

Apel: Perhaps it appears to work that way in order to make the thing *more* dear when you get it back. You have to die to be reborn. The one thing Richard Nixon ever said that I agree with, for instance, is that he didn't mind being thrown out of office, because only if you are capable of experiencing the depths can you appreciate the heights attainable.

Dick: Well, I never believed, like my friend did, in a direct connection between the writing and losing a relationship. They would have left anyway; it just happened that way.

This really raises the question of what a writer really gets out of writing, intrinsically, when money, recognition, admiration are stripped away, and you deal directly with the writer's relationship to the book. What does he get out of the book? I don't enjoy reading my writing; I get uncomfortable seeing my books around. I tend to give my books away, because I just don't like seeing them around.

The one thing that I get back from the writing that is really intrinsic to the writing is this: I have seen certain people do or say certain things that I feel should be preserved; that should not be the ephemer of the moment. I have gotten these people down, saying and doing these kind of things. And it's almost always the same kind of thing: it's a meager person, a person who we would normally not regard as exceptional in any particular way, who has momentarily transcended his meagerness—usually unbeknownst to himself—to strike at the heart of humanness; to encapsulate briefly the very core of human thought or feeling; to act in some way that can serve as an illustration to others because of its spontaneity and profundity.

This is why *Scanner* is important to me, I think. There, more than any other book, I was recording what actual people did and said which would have vanished into the ether otherwise. I was in a position that no one else was in. I was in a position to remember it and recapture it. These were, for the most part, illiterate people, so they'll never know. Some of them aren't even alive to know. The one thing that really means something to me is little braveries, little displays of strength and courage, and something more than competence.

Apel: This seems to harken back to our early conversation about small acts of kindness that separate humans from animals or androids.

Dick: Exactly. Once I saw this junkie, completely out of it, unable to move, who heard the jack slip while a junior high school kid was changing a tire on a car in our garage. The kid was yelling, while this 5,000 pound Pontiac started to roll backward onto him. And this poor burned-out junkie, this guy who thought he had bugs all over him, who had almost no brain circuits left, ran out of that living room, out into the garage, and knocked the kid out of the way of the car. At that instant, the jack gave and the car came down right where the kid had been standing. It could have broken his back. This all happened so fast that I was still trying to get the car door open to put on the car brakes when he hit the kid like a linebacker. But he knew that I would be too slow. I said, "Shit. I was too late, wasn't I?" And this burned-out creature—who's now dead—said, "Yeah. If it had been a convertible, I could have leapt in, but I knew there was no time for the brake." This burned-out brain had known what to do. Then he went back and sank into the incredible brain suffocation of heroin, and lived only another year. He not only *did* the right thing, but he knew *why* it was the right thing. How he did that was an unfathomable mystery to me.

And there was another element here: his caring; his concern for the kid. We're dealing here with the *debris* of the human race, the people that Shockley would sweep into the incinerator, you know? The heavy metal used to cut the heroin he used—lead or mercury, probably—formed deposits in his neuroreceptors which were irreversible, and eventually killed him. Yet he exhibited at different times tenderness, caring, and appropriate behavior in emergency situations. The falling car incident was not the only time; he saved my life on another occasion when the brakes failed on his car.

I really want you to use this part, to tie in with what we talked about before. In two emergency situations he exhibited appropriate behavior and could rationally explain why he had chosen that behavior. He was fucked up in ways—well, a lot of it is in *Scanner.* His problem was damage, not merely madness. This was damage to a delicate instrument, the human brain. And yet, on some highly important levels, that brain still functioned. He was still a human being, with the finest attributes a human being can display. I say this even though he was stealing everything I had because he was a junkie. I have no animosity towards him...I stand in wonderment. If *this* person could exhibit these fine human qualities, then what marvelous capabilities all of our brains must have.

It's like this: After having sent my ship of inquiry into the universe to discover the mysteries of the universe, the ship comes back finally, after 26 years, and says, "The greatest mystery in the universe is the human brain." And then I say, "And what is the answer to the mystery?" And it responds, "I just said, it's the greatest mystery, didn't I?"

So what I've learned in 26 years of thinking and writing about it all is *where* the greatest mystery of the universe is located. It's in between our left and right ears. It's an incredible thing. There are more possible neuronal interconnections in the human brain than there are stars in the universe, and that should tip you off right there.

If somebody asked me "What have you learned by asking 'What is reality?' for 26 years?" I'd say, "I've learned that I don't understand the human brain. But, man, do I admire it!"

Apel: Thank you very much, Philip K. Dick.

Phil K. Dick in Interview

PART II

Apel: We were thinking about the charge often leveled against you that your works are liberally spiced with precognitive bits. Your novel *We Can Build You,* for instance, with its Lincoln simulacrum, predated Disney's Mr. Lincoln robot by several years.
Briggs: And your occasional use of "Newsclowns" predated the "Happy News" television concept similarly.
Dick: That precognitive thing in my novels has really spooked me. It's really there. You can see how I would become aware of it in direct proportion to the number of books I wrote: if there was such a factor, the more I wrote, the more I'd begin to notice this.

Let's establish just for the record examples thereof. In the rough draft of *Flow My Tears, The Policeman Said,* there's a girl named Kathy. Her husband's name is Jack. She is nineteen years old. She appears to be working for the criminal underground, the anti-establishment thing, but actually—because she hopes to get her husband out of a forced labor camp through cooperation—she is working for the police. The policeman she is working with is on the Inspector level, which is unusual.

Now, that was written in 1970 and the first draft put aside. In December of 1970 I met a girl whose name was Kathy, who was nineteen years old, who appeared to be a dope dealer, who, it turned out much later—I didn't know this for *one year*—had been arrested and had made a deal to inform to the police if they'd drop the charges. Her boyfriend was named Jack, and the policeman she worked with was an Inspector. That's when the precognitive thing in my books really hit me. My novel was so close it was damn near actionable. I could just see an attorney listing all this stuff, you know. Precise details.

Apel: Any single one of those things could be accounted for by chance—everybody knows a Kathy and a Jack; everybody in the counter-culture knows a dope dealer, and so on—but when so many "coincidences" pile up, it exceeds the bounds of chance.

Dick: I have really spent a lot of time thinking about this stuff since I began to notice it. I mean, several people have said to me they thought there were precognitive elements in my books, but it didn't really strike me until this thing about *Flow My Tears.* God, I *met* the Inspector she was working with. That's how I found out about it. She and I went into a restaurant and she stopped dead and said, "We can't go in there; Inspector So-and-so is in there." And in my book, he wears a gray coat, or something like that, and there he was, sitting there in a gray coat. I really had to ask myself about this. And what I began to notice was that the precognitive material was coming to me in my sleep, in dream form. That was in 1972, and I began to pay real attention to my dreams from that standpoint. The more time passed the more I was forced to face the actuality of the precognitive elements. The irony was that my second novel, *The World Jones Made,* was about a precognitive. And it didn't do him a damn bit of good. He couldn't avert the event. It was hell for him. He had precognition for one year ahead. And when he got within the last year of his life, he had a precognition of being dead, so it really was not a talent that gave him any options.

Paul Williams doesn't believe it's possible to be precognitive. He and I have had a lot of discussions about this. He says since the future doesn't exist, how is it possible to have any knowledge of it? He says the future does not exist.

Apel: That's a supposition right there that can be refuted. The best theory I've heard about "the future" is very simple. You have a pretty good idea of what you're going to do tomorrow, and maybe for the next few weeks or even years. And so do I. *That's* the future: your own intention to make things happen. And when all those individual intentions of the future intermingle, you've got a general picture of "the future." Some of those intentions are mutually contradictory, and cancel out, or influence your intention.

That's what happens when things don't work out as you planned, when the future you've projected "doesn't come true." But if little happens to deflect you from the future you've constructed in your mind, in your *intention,* you can foresee just what's going to happen. It's not just "there"…you've got to *put* it there.

Dick: Yeah. There are many, many views of what the future consists of, including entirely mechanistic theories. I've read enough about time to know you really cannot say that events are not already there and just pop into the present like on a groove on an LP. The whole piece of music is there, and time just tracks along. Whether or not the future is "there" is a real question, and has never been answered.

Anyway, we were discussing the precognitive elements in *Flow My Tears.* Now, this is something I really would like to talk about. This is something you won't find your other writers saying. I'm gonna say something that I'm really gonna regret saying. But then again, that's a familiar experience. *(laughter)* Somebody told me once that I was more candid with interviewers than I was with my own wives. That I would tell them things I wouldn't tell my own wives, or my mother… Well, certainly not my mother; heaven forbid I tell her anything. *(laughter)*

OK…By the time I read over the final draft of *Flow My Tears* and realized that I had shown real precognitive elements, I had to accept something which I'm not really interested in, which is the ESP stuff. It's not really something which I particularly like. I mean, I don't get off on it. I've written books and stories where parapsychological talents were employed, you know, but I can't honestly say I've ever believed in them as real things.

But there was something about that book that really freaked me. There's a dream sequence…General Buckman's sister is dead, and he's flying home, and he's really grief-stricken. And he has this dream. His main feeling is hatred…the desire to kill Jason Tavener. Buckman has set up Jason Tavener to be busted. Tavener has actually committed no crime. And Buckman, in his psychotic grief at the death of his sister—which was purely accidental—has lost touch with reality. He's forgotten he's setting up an innocent man. He was looking for a collar on Tavener, then his sister dies in Tavener's proximity, and Buckman begins to talk about shooting Tavener, just as if he thought that Tavener had actually done it. So he makes this complete psychotic break. He's on his way home, and he's all screwed up about this. And he goes to sleep and has this dream. It's set in a rustic background, where Buckman lived as a child. He dreams of a posse of men on horseback, wearing helmets and multi-colored robes. There's one who looks like a wise old king...he has a snow-white beard, like wool. And there's a man whom the posse is going to kill, sealed up in a nearby building. The man cannot see them coming, but he hears them coming and lets out a great shriek of fear. At which point Buckman's psychotic rage—his desire to kill Tavener—is completely transmuted into grief for this man hiding in the building in the darkness; grief for this man who is going to be killed.

Buckman is brought back to sanity by this dream. He's brought out of psychotic anger at an innocent man—previously Buckman's been talking about taking a piss on Tavener's shoe; he takes it *that personally*—to an appropriate affect, which is grief. He comes out of the dream and he lands his vehicle at an all night gas station and he embraces the first human being he sees. It happens to be some black guy standing there while his tires are being rotated. He embraces a complete stranger.

So the dream brought Buckman back to sanity. That's the part that I rewrote very carefully. That's also the part—I've been told—for which the John W. Campbell Committee presented me with their award for that book; mainly for that specific episode.

I actually had that dream. There was a case where I consciously wrote something that I dreamt in my writing. But when the book came out, I had the curious feeling that I wrote more than I realized. I couldn't put my finger on exactly what it was. You know, you hear the phrase, "the author wrote more than he knew"...well, I had this feeling. Very, very strong feeling. I was waiting for feedback from my readers. I'm very, very responsive to reader criticism. Not so much professional critic criticism, but reader criticism. I thought someone might let me know what was going on.

Flow My Tears came out in 1974. Now this is where my head was at in February of 1974. This was a very stressful period for me. I was having wisdom teeth removed and receiving regular injections of sodium pentothal. Meanwhile, I was experimenting with Linus Pauling's orthomolecular vitamin program, and my thoughts began to go very fast. I had read that the orthomolecular vitamins, used with schizophrenics, produced more synchronous neural firing, but that it also speeded up neural firing. What occurred to me was, "Well, it can't hurt." *(laughter)* Evidently. That's the thing about water-soluble vitamins, y'know; they're not gonna leave traces of heavy metals in the neuroreceptor sites.

Also I had a lot of anxieties about...oh, I'll be candid about this...I had a lot of anxieties about some anti-war stuff that I did. A lot of anxiety about the authorities finally getting me for the anti-war stuff that I did. At that time I had a wife and a little child; when I did the anti-war stuff I had no wife and no child, and I said, "What the hell, y'know? I'm utterly wretched anyway; I might as well strike a blow for peace and human dignity." I'd engaged in some illegal anti-war stuff. Aren't I cool, saying this on tape during an interview? *(laughter)* I'm Joe Cool, man, sayin' this on tape... But the authorities know I did it, so it's not going to come as a surprise to them.

So, you see, a lot of heavy stuff was going on. Actually, my psycho-therapist—she was a really neat chick; I really believed in her—she told me that I would have to approach the government and discuss what I had done and try to work out some kind of détente with them. The war was legally over. So I was trying to get up the courage to write the government and say, "This is what I did, and that's the way it is. And this is where I live." I felt like a dissident in Russia.

So all these goddamn things were going on. Five different plot lines at once. And after taking the vitamins for a while, my thoughts began to go very fast. I wasn't physically manic, where I'd run around and do a lot. But my thoughts just simply moved faster and faster. It was like moving down a dark tunnel, and these colored lights started going.

Apel: I got the same thing when I started on an orthomolecular program. Too many B vitamins. They keep your mind awake.

Dick: My mind was awake.

Apel: All you do is talk to yourself in your head all night long.

Dick: All night long; yeah, man; I'm goin' rappity-rap-rap-rap... So I decided to recite a mantra. And I only knew one mantra; I was ignorant about mantras. So I recited "Om" over and over again. And it really worked; it cleared my head of all the thoughts, like, *Am I going to jail?* and so on.

Then one afternoon, after having a sodium pentothal injection, I came home and had a flash of memory. Now, this is really very hard for me to say, because there's no way I can say it without indicting my own probity by the very nature of what I'm going to say. Suddenly, for just a second, a curtain lifted and I remembered a past life. Just for a second, but I remembered the entire thing in that second. Just like when you remember a person's name, you remember the whole person, not just the name. Then the curtain dropped. It was so scary, and I was in so much pain, I was able to forget that I remembered. But from then on, I was living with only partial amnesia. The Greek word is *anamnesis:* not "remembrance," but *loss of forgetfulness.*

Then one night in March of 1974—I say this with a certain amount of reticence—my memories began to come back. Not just a brief flash, like lightning, but longer segments.

Apel: Deeper memories? Genetic memories?

Dick: Yeah. Gene pool memories. In fact, I talked to a guy who got a master's degree working with rats to prove gene pool memory, and he was able to produce it through large doses of—

All: *(in unison) Orthomolecular vitamins! (laughter)*

Dick: And I said to him, "Barry, I gotta tell you something...I was taking orthomolecular vitamins and I retrieved buried memories from a past existence." And he says, "For God's sake, don't *tell* anybody! I know it's true; I did my master's thesis on it with rats. But *God,* keep your *mouth* shut! Don't tell anybody in the mental health movement. We are the modern policemen in the world." Any one of them can throw you in the rubber room. He went on to tell me that tremendous stress activates these memories in rats. So I even got *that* right. And I remembered an existence in which the world described was the same as the world in *Flow My Tears.*

Apel: So...it wasn't a previous existence, but an *alternate* existence.

Dick: You got it. You got it. Exactly right. Only it took me three years to figure it out. For three years, I spent between four and eight hours a day doing research and trying to understand how I could have a previous existence in the *present.*

If I were to detail that world, it would be completely congruent with the world in *Flow My Tears.* Then I asked myself, *Does this explain where the corpus of my writing comes from?* And the answer is *Yes.* The entire corpus of my writing deals with *a landscape*...a kind of world which is somewhat like ours and somewhat different. And all my books interrelate. Ursula LeGuin pointed that out—that all my books seemed to take place on a particular alternate world. And in 1974, I actually remembered being in that world. Some of the technology was more advanced than ours, like in my books. They made great use of advanced hydraulics, for instance.

But it was a ghastly garrison state, with forced labor camps. And in that other world, I was an active political revolutionary. I was not just a passive opponent of the Establishment. I remember we blew up a big fortress, a big prison. Actually blew it open, like you'd blow open a safe. I remember being pursued by the authorities. The Establishment was just like it was shown to me in *Flow My Tears.* In that world, all civil rights movements had failed. Most amazing of all, Christianity was outlawed.

Apel: Had it always been outlawed?

Dick: That I don't know. I inferred that what happened was that in that world, Christianity had been completely absorbed by the Roman Empire and a Romanesque civilization, along those lines.

Apparently, I got zapped in that other world. We were Christians, but more in the political revolutionary sense; you know, blowing up prisons. Anarchistic. A lot of people were in prisons or forced labor camps.

Apel: How do you know you're not just changing minds with someone in Russia today? When he's awake, you're asleep, and vice versa. His realities become your dreams…

Dick: My first reaction to what you're saying is: I never thought of that. My second reaction is that this world resembled what Solzhenitsyn had written in *Gulag Archipelago*…which I had not read at that time. And there were Russian names…

All right… I'm going to be quite candid with you at this point. You can publish this and they'll come and get me. So I wrote to Leningrad and said: I would like to know if you people, by any chance, are making attempts to electronically boost telepathic signals. I want to know especially if you are using microwave boosts. No answer.

Apel: Microwaves don't carry much information, but they do carry it a long way. And it's been a theory of mine for some time now—which Cleve Backster's work with plants supports—that telepathy operates in the microwave band. The Russians have been beaming microwaves at the American Embassy in Moscow for fifteen years now for some purpose. There's a link between microwaves and cancer, and I thought there might be something there. But maybe they're trying to read the minds of the Embassy personnel.

Dick: What happened was that with these memories came a personality—it was a package deal. I discovered that I had been taken over by a distinct personality—a "not-me." He had a very distinct personality. He preferred beer and I preferred wine. It's those little things that were so indicative. He kept calling the dog "he" and the cat "she," and I knew perfectly well that the dog was "she" and the cat "he." He kept making that mistake. He would drive my car, but could never find the air vents, the placement of which is optional, not standard. He found the hot, dry weather of Orange County unbearable, while I like it.

Apel: Did you think it might be your two brain lobes interacting, trying to get into synchronization?

Dick: Yeah, I tried that. I tried each theory I could come up with for a while.

Apel: Did you try the Jungian standpoint, that this might be an autonomous complex, some unconscious personality constellation, crying for attention?

Dick: Yep. Tried that one. *(laughter)*

Apel: I like the Russian telepathy thing.

Dick: Listen, man, I was *convinced*—convinced is too mild a word—on that for a while. I just said to my therapist, "You can say whatever you want, but they are fooling around with microwave boosts of telepathic signals. And I happened to be in the right spot at the right time." There were just too many Soviet fragments mixed into the material for me to discount that possibility. Too many Russian names; scenes of Russian laboratories and equipment.

One of the few hard facts that I have that I can trot out is that there was a great deal of language being spoken that I could not understand, but which I would write out phonetically. It all turned out to be Greek. There were no exceptions.

The translations were revealing. My wife had taken a year of Greek and translated it correctly. I was reading one of Jung's books on the origin of the liturgy, and—holy smoke—the key phrases were the ones I had dreamed. Later I dreamed a continuation of the passage he quoted—fourteen lines ahead, according to the Greek/English Bible I looked it up in later. Nowhere in Jung's article did this passage appear.

But all this still didn't explain all the Russian elements. There were all these Russian technicians running around, with all these electronic things they were wiring up.

You want to hear worse? There's worse to come. You think *that's* bad…

Let's take the following proposition as the most probable hypothesis: My ego was descending into the collective unconscious, and as it did, it encountered progressively lower and more archaic strata. I did have that feeling. It gets lower, and older, and more archetypal. What I got as the payoff—when it reached its lowest point—and all this, remember, is happening in hypnagogic and hypnopompic states, or full dreaming sleep—was a figure which was humanoid, but quite different from us. The cranium was much more avocado-shaped, overhanging in the back. They were deaf and mute, within chambers that looked like bathyspheres, and communicated with me through electronic equipment. At one point the electronic transduction of sound from me failed, and two Russian technicians appeared and began fooling with wires.

But here is the part that to me is the most striking, that I will never forget as long as I live. They had a third eye right in the middle of their foreheads. But it was not a pupil-type eye; it was a lateral lens. It was definitely electronic, not organic, and was removable.

Briggs: Your description of the aliens is akin to several others' descriptions. Betty and Barney Hill, for example.

Dick: You'll have to take my word for it that I hadn't read their account when this happened to me. But when I saw their drawing of the eye on the stalk coming out, it was the same one I saw; it really was. Exactly.

I saw a woman and a man this way. The woman showed me how she could appear as a human being and told me... This part really appeals to me, I must say. It gave me a great feeling of joy, and still does. Did then; does now. She said, "We have seen the conspirators who killed the Kennedys, Dr. King, Bishop Pike and Malcolm X, and we are going to destroy them." And she showed herself sitting among a group of natty, East Coast Establishment types, and she turned the third eye on them and scanned them all and *saw* what they had done. This is *pre-Watergate* stuff.

Apel: Why were you witness to all this? Why were you singled out?

Dick: The answer to this, too, came to pass. They jammed me, like you would jam a radio signal. They jammed my personality out of motor control with this other personality. And this other personality was there for a purpose. This was March of 1974, and he knew something that was not known publicly then. He had a distinct and exact mission to perform.

It seems that Charles Wiggins of the House Judicial Committee—the committee which would be in charge of impeachment proceedings—had come from Fullerton. And he had a policy of personally reading and answering every letter that came from Fullerton. I was living in Fullerton; he was my Congressman.

And this personality sat me down and wrote Wiggins often, and once even wrote *The Wall Street Journal* a letter which they printed. His message was that the Nixon transcripts were forgeries; that the original tapes differed from the transcripts. The transcripts were not evidentiary but were self-serving, and that the tapes would not bear out what the transcripts showed. This personality continued to write Wiggins up until the day Nixon resigned, then left. When it left, it left a horrible vacuum, a terrible void, behind. Even my wife felt it. That's the one point she can testify to. She couldn't see what I saw; she couldn't experience what I experienced, but... Well, I sensed a kind of bioplasmic energy in the apartment, and she sensed it too. She was aware of it. And when it did leave, she was as aware of its passing as I was. That really unnerved her.

Apel: But if it's the Russians, what is their motive in removing Nixon from office?

Dick: No matter what theory I apply to this puzzle, there's a piece left over or one sticking out somewhere. This personality that took me over—I called it "Thomas," just to have something to call it— this "Thomas" would go out at night and sit for hours looking up at the sky, trying to locate a particular star.

Briggs: Ten to one it was Sirius. Crowley thought the intelligences that dictated through him were from Sirius. And [Robert Anton] Wilson thinks he might have had contact with Sirius in '73.

Apel: Yeah. Alan Vaughan, the psychic, thinks he might have been in contact with higher intelligences from Sirius in '73, too. *(Note: These stories are detailed in Robert Anton Wilson's* Cosmic Trigger.) Did "Thomas" ever locate his star?

Dick: He couldn't find it.

The other thing it—this "Thomas"—engaged in was medical information. My little year-and-a-half-year-old son had a serious birth defect which the doctor failed to notice. And this...*mind*...which took over diagnosed it and told my wife to take him to the doctor immediately and to tell the doctor what it was and to request immediate surgery. She did, and she came back and said, "They're scheduling him for immediate surgery. He does have that birth defect"...which could have proved fatal at any time.

Not only that, but it diagnosed a couple of complaints of mine. A lot of it passed unnoticed by me, because of the way it would continually lapse into Greek. It was an effort on its part to halt its flow of thought in Greek and switch back to English. English was an effort for him; it had to consciously think to do it. Medically, it was very hip. And very concerned about my little son.

The thing you were talking about, the microwave thing, was that our cat, our poor cat, who was in the apartment all the time, died of cancer soon after that. It kind of scared me when you said that, about cancer. I happened to be at the doctor's office for another reason, and the nurse took my blood pressure and she let out a scream. It was 278 over 243...stroke level. And they put me in the hospital. Maybe it was I was just extraordinarily freaked by these experiences. Or maybe...

I really have no theory which will wrap this up. The book I'm working on for Bantam, *VALIS,* is really an account of this, fictionalized. I assign the experiences to a nonexistent friend of mine, whom I call "Nicholas Brady." And in the book, I'm a character under my own name. And I know Nicholas Brady, and he's having all these weird experiences, and I keep ripping them off to put 'em in a novel. I'm completely cold-blooded about it, and I'm deceiving Nicholas Brady by using the experiences in my novel, and I'm deceiving my publisher, who wants a fictional work. *(laughter)*

(Some comments deleted by request)

Dick: Don't put that in the final. Please.

Apel: OK.

Dick: Promise?

Apel: Cross my heart. But that's pretty good. *(laughter)*

Dick: Anyway... I developed a composite theory, trying to keep Occam's Razor in mind: the simplest explanation that fits all the facts. I'm afraid that in this case, even being parsimonious leads to a fairly complicated theory. The theory I like best is this: I know for a fact that the Soviets have tried to contact extra-terrestrials telepathically. My theory—and it's just a theory—is that they found some way to boost their signals, and while they were fiddling around, they got an answer. Dr. Nikolai Kozyrev, Russia's leading astrophysicist, has stated publicly that they've already picked up signals from ETIs emanating from within our solar system. The U.S. Government has officially discounted this pronouncement; we say it's junk satellites floating around. But Kozyrev has been right before on major things; he has a very good reputation for being accurate. He predicted volcanic activity on Venus, for instance. Also, Kozyrev has a whole new theory on what *time* is. Time is energy poured into a material system, is how he defines it. He said Time is the only energy which propagates at an infinite rate of speed.

Apel: Because it's always the present.

Dick: Yeah. And it's always present. And an event in one place is transmitted through this energy field of Time simultaneously to another place. One of the main things the Russians are trying to do is figure out how to communicate with far-flung satellites so there's no time lag.

Well, I think… Let's say I was sitting in an office in Washington, D.C., and I had all the facts of my experience in front of me. Nicholas Brady walks in, hands me this stuff, then turns and walks out. So I have all this, just reported as raw data, you see. And I'm sitting there at this desk trying to figure out just what the hell does all this mean? And I say, "Aha! I've got it!" Kozyrev is in charge of this project of contacting ETIs for the Soviet Union. Kozyrev is involved in experiments with Time. He's actually performed experiments with Time.

Apel: Didn't they describe that in *Psychic Discoveries Behind the Iron Curtain?* Isn't he the one who stretched the time field at one end of a phenomenon and measured it actually shrinking at the other end?

Dick: That's right. In that book they said his paper was too difficult to paraphrase, and they gave the U.S. Government agency to write to for a copy of Kozyrev's monograph on Time. And I sent away for it, and got it, and read it.

OK. So Kozyrev is fooling around with Time, and he's fooling around with telepathy, and he's fooling around with trying to contact ETIs. And he gets it all together, and this thing goes *zappo!* out into space. I mean, the Russians will try anything. They're completely crazy. And Kozyrev is sitting there waiting for ETIs to answer.

Meanwhile, I'm sitting in Fullerton, doing nothing but listening to Kiki Dee tapes to find the hidden meaning. It's three A.M., and I can't sleep, so I'm listening to bubblegum rock. And what happens is there's an exchange of signals between the Russians and the ETIs. And I'm in the pathway of the signal and I pick it up. Somehow I pick the goddamn stuff up, involuntarily.

The one thing that adds weight to this possibility is that Kozyrev had said that the ability to "thicken" and "thin out" Time depends on whether it's winter or summer. So the first piece of hard evidence I have is the Greek words, since I know no Greek. The other piece of evidence I have is that this occurred *precisely* at the time of the Vernal Equinox. *Exactly* on the date of the Vernal Equinox.

Apel: Can you describe what it felt like?

Dick: Sure can. March 18, 1974. All of a sudden I began to experience incredible phosphene activity. Later I found out—from a Russian study—that phosphene activity can be stimulated by radiation. Our astronauts experienced this, and the cosmonauts as well. This lasted for eight to ten hours. And what I saw was abstract art. Thousands of abstract art paintings flashing by at incredible speed. One would permutate into the next. I saw all the Klees, then the Kandinskys, and so on. I used the experience in my novel *A Scanner Darkly*. This was before I dreamed any Russian dreams.

What this all seemed like to me was what I understood to be the contents of the Leningrad Art Museums, which have a *tremendous* number of modern abstract paintings. I leaped to the intuitive conclusion that what the Russians had decided to do was transmit pictures—all of humanity's artworks—off to the stars, with an emphasis on the abstracts, as these would be easiest to transmit and easiest for an alien mind to understand.

I'll be quite frank with you. I believed for months—and I'm

not sure I don't believe it still, if pressed—that what happened was this: The Soviets sent out some signals. They got an ETI response. Then they crank their machinery up to peak power and fire these pictures off at top speed. Every goddamn art piece in the Leningrad museums.

Apel: Computer to computer.

Dick: Exactly. They just poured this stuff because, for all they knew, they only had one shot. "The door opens and the door closes..." That was the subjective intuition I got.

They were works of art, with specific styles and definite idiosyncratic touches. They were not the kind of thing you see under acid or mescaline, and it wasn't the "buzzsaw" effect you get with belladonna and similar alkaloids. And these pictures ran in clusters. One artist's style, then another's. And this went on for *eight solid God damn hours!* I was scared out of my mind, but I said to myself, *Well, it's certainly strange, but it's so incredibly beautiful that I'll just groove with it.* My right hemisphere was picking up every one of these pictures. And by the time it was over with... *(long pause; then quietly but intensely)... Holy smoke! ...(long pause)... I just flashed on something...*

Apel: A new insight?

PKD *Yeah!* The next day... *(long pause)... Holy smoke!... (animatedly)* All right, I get up the next day, right? There's full daylight, I'm still experiencing phosphene activity... All of a sudden... *(long pause as Phil stares off into space intently)...* Man, I'm tellin' you, I could make a case for this theory now! *(laughter)* All of a sudden, it switched from graphic art to abstract cosmological concepts, in diagrammatic form. What I was zapped through was basic, cosmological premises, all the way back to Plato. Not only that, but the name "Plato" actually appeared.

Apel: That seems the logical followup to transmit: first, your artistic vision, and then how we arrived at that vision; what the philosophy behind it is. First the pictures, so the aliens know they're dealing with a creative intelligence, then the explanation of how it works. If I'm right, they'll work their way down to science and technology next: the application of our creative intelligence.

And at that point, they might be able to begin an exchange of knowledge...once the aliens know how to talk to us in words and concepts we'd understand.

Dick: You see the line of thought I'm pursuing... *OH!* Excuse me just a second! *Holy Christ! God damn!* Then, after a while, *engineering principles!*

Apel: Exactly!

Dick: Yeah! Right *on,* man! After a while, advanced engineering principles began to appear. Diagrams, and thousands of pages of written material at flash speed. I was barraged with written stuff. The written stuff stayed longer than the graphics. Like freeze frame. This is all coming back to me now! What are the chances... What are the chances that a transmission like this would come in this order—graphic abstract art, philosophic cosmological principles, engineering principles—and *not* be an attempt to contact and explain ourselves to ETs? Then there's those impressions of Russian technicians and three-eyed aliens.

Apel: I was talking about something like this recently with Alan Vaughan. He co-authored a book entitled *Dream Telepathy,* which describes experiments where—oh, you're gonna love this *(laughter)*—where their "senders" tried to telepathically transmit works of art to the "receivers."

Dick: As a matter of fact, I think I have read that. After these experiences, I bought well over a thousand dollars worth of books on these subjects, and just voraciously read and studied. I was fascinated to discover that art masterpieces were a good thing to use as a telepathic sender, because, man, I was at the art museum for eight hours. *(laughter)* And when I was finished, I really had my money's worth. I am so fascinated that this went from artwork to philosophy—basic philosophy—to engineering principles. But the funny thing is that you brought up right away this business about the Russians. I mean, this goddamn place that I remembered...it is *so* much like Russia... *Oh, God!* Hey, God, I'll really add weight to your theory, man! Things that I couldn't fit in—y'know, like I got this jar in my head of facts that don't fit any theory. You know, there's 3,000 theories, but the jar stays full with a constant amount of facts. Some get taken out, but every time one's taken out, another one's got to go back in.

This is another thing that made me think that the Soviet Union was involved: a part I haven't mentioned at all, but which provides a clue. The Greek is one clue. But the Greek *could* be scientific Greek mixed in with the Russian. My ex-wife pointed that out to me. And Kozyrev's theories and interests and his publicly stated pronouncements; that's another clue. But here's the other thing that made me think of the Soviet Union: There was this tremendous impression I had, in my dreams, of contemporary Russian classical music. I would dream of symphony orchestras playing Prokofiev, but it was not Prokofiev I was familiar with. And then I could describe the color of the album box, and it was a different kind of album box than we use. It was felt-covered. And I know in some parts of Europe they use a kind of felt-covered album. But they were long, Russian, modern compositions, which I'm not into. I'm not into that kind of music. I'm into classical music, but not those particular pieces. I remember saying to my wife, "I can see the color of the album box from which this Prokofiev I'm hearing was taken from." And I described it to her. But I have never owned such an album in my life. Yet I have this memory of owning it, taking the records out, playing them. All modern Russian stuff. Shostakovich and Prokofiev, predominantly.

There was one dream in which I was at some kind of Institute. It was like a school, where they had the doors marked, y'know, like B-l, B-2, B-3.

Apel: Like vitamins. *(laughter)*

Dick: Yeah. They were working on these transmitters, and showing how they were set up. What this particular Institute was doing was freighting FM music transmissions with extra information. The extra information was married in the transmission; buried subliminally. All sorts of dreams of this kind.

Apel: OK...let me see if I've got a handle on this: Somewhere in Russia, you've got a psychic twin...a "Corsican Brothers" type of mental twin. Like you, he was an FM radio disk jockey...only he'd be playing a lot of Russian classical music. And They—the KGB, or whoever—They get him to transmit subliminal messages in his broadcasts. This upsets him, and he goes renegade…he becomes an active political dissident, like you were a passive political dissident. So the police pick him up and throw him in the Gulag, or some other labor camp or asylum. And Kozyrev, who's mucking around with time, telepathy and alien contacts, runs some tests on some prisoners or inmates, and finds out this guy is a latent telepathic transmitter. So they strap him into this machine and boost his native powers, using microwaves. Or whatever. He becomes a living component of this telepathy transmitter. And if it kills him, well, he's only a dissident, and it's for the higher glory of the State anyway. And you—since you're already psychically in tune with him, linked with him, receiving him—you pick up all this transmitted stuff. They've boosted his sending power, and it overwhelms your receiving abilities. Plus you were in a vulnerable receptive mode anyway, what with the stress, and the vitamins and so on.

OK… So they contact the aliens and use this guy as a living telepathic translating machine. A communication link, with their electronic boosts, which would account for the technicians and labs and aliens and such. But the aliens, who use telepathy all the time, know about you being accidentally linked into this loop, which the Russian novices don't know. So the aliens use you in the Nixon thing. I mean, even *we* knew Nixon was a dangerous lunatic. And who knows *what* the aliens' mission here was. Maybe the Nixon thing was part of it.

Anyway… So they jam your personality with a doppelganger of one of their own people, or of the guy in Russia—who's probably living your life as *his* dreams *(laughter)*—or with some autonomous ego-complex they dredge up from one of your own past lives, as a Greek doctor or something. You did say you felt like you were descending into the collective unconscious. Or maybe they jammed you with a computer personality; an artificial intelligence program designed to think and act like a human being. And then, long after the aliens are gone, or your twin in Russia is burned out like an overloaded circuit, or stuck in an asylum somewhere, you might still be somewhat in tune with him, picking up his memories. Or maybe the guy is really insane, and what you're picking up is his hallucinations. Or maybe he's dead, but that telepathic blast transferred a lot of his memories, like a shotgun effect...and you're still dredging up his memories out of your unconscious. Those dreams of Russian music and stuff.

Does this make any sense at all?

Dick: Hell if I know. *(laughter)* It makes just as much sense as any theory I've been able to come up with.

Briggs: If things like this happen to you, your search for reality is over. You're writing about reality, because reality is like a Phil Dick novel.

Dick: How horrible.

Afterword

"Tell them the good part," Joan kept insisting throughout the end of this interview. "Tell them the *important* part!"

He finally gave in. "The important part," he said, "is that it was conveyed to me in these dreams that I would get a letter from a woman that I didn't know, and upon receiving the letter I must phone her. She had a Russian name. This was reiterated on and on and on and on.

"The letter finally arrived..." he continued.

"Dinner's ready!" called Joan

We ate and moved on to other topics, the recorder turned off. Little did we suspect that this mysterious missive was one of the major events in this strange history. We still do not know the full, true story of this letter, although the best fictionalized version of what it was, what it meant and what Phil did about it is probably contained in *Radio Free Albemuth* (pages 101-110). Comparing the other autobiographical events from this interview with Phil's fictionalized versions, in *VALIS* and *Radio Free Albemuth*, I feel fairly safe in assuming that the description of the events in the latter were close to what actually happened. Certainly future revelations and biographies about Philip K. Dick will cast more light on this mysterious Xeroxed letter than we have been able to do.

The dinner conversation did, however, retain the "Russian flavor," even though it branched out into other areas. Since none of this was taped, I have to rely on my (admittedly faulty) memory for the reconstructions of Phil's monologues.

One story does stick out in my memory, though. For whatever reason, Phil mentioned that he had once actually been invited to go to Russia.

"I got this letter, direct from Moscow," he told us, "signed by some fairly important scientists, who invited me to visit Russia so they could talk to me."

"What on earth for?" I asked.

"Well, it seems they had read *UBIK,* and had already formulated theories that the afterlife was remarkably close to what I had theorized in that novel," he explained. "They wanted me to come over so they could find out what I knew—and probably experiment on me to find out *how* I knew," he chuckled.

"You didn't go," I stated, prompting.

"I actually considered going for a while," he said. "I had an elaborate, just *elaborate,* code system worked out with a friend whereby I could communicate detailed information through seemingly innocuous words and phrases on postcards, to let him know if I was in trouble with the authorities.

"But I finally decided against it. The more I thought about it, the more I became convinced that if I went, I would not return. Tell you the truth, I was scared shitless that they'd get me over there and that's the last anyone would ever hear of Phil Dick.

"And so, instead, one day a few months later, this black limousine pulls up in front of my house. This was your archetypal sinister black limousine, with the shaded glass windows and so on. And three men in trench coats got out and came to the door. I was watching this from the window, and I was thinking, *Oh, shit. They've finally caught up with me.* I had, at that time, no idea about who 'They' were; I was just convinced that *someone* had caught up with me for whatever sins I might have committed. Or they thought I had committed.

"At any rate, it turns out that they were from the Russian Embassy. The scientists in Moscow had received my letter, in which I had fabricated some excuse for not visiting, add they had requested that the Embassy send a delegation to interview me in my own home. They were very nice and polite, and once they explained who they were and what they wanted, I let them in and we talked about *UBIK* for an hour or so. I didn't tell them nothin'. Just played stupid. Then they left, and I've never heard from them since."

One portion of this story was verified later. When I informed Phil in early 1979 that I was going to be traveling around South America for six months, he insisted I carry his address with me.

"If you should experience any difficulties with the authorities," he instructed me, "write me a postcard and include this line: *I'm running out of cigarettes.* Then I will know you're in trouble and can contact the proper authorities. Have you got that? *I'm running out of cigarettes.*"

I never had to use the code, but it was nice to know it was there.

On a more serious note, Phil's revelations about his "mystical experiences" in this interview were intended by him to be his first public disclosure of these events. As our interview book was never published, the general public first learned of this material through his short interview in Charles Platt's *Dream Makers* in 1980.

Platt may have been unconvinced about Phil's experiences— possibly because no short description can do them justice—but Briggs and I were sobered by the revelations. We had already spent enough time with Phil to know that he was as sane, as intelligent and as thoughtful as anyone either of us had ever met. We came away from his revelations shaken, feeling as though we had been swept through the portals of the Twilight Zone to become privy to—and an unwilling part of—some vast, cosmic conspiracy. We were convinced. We were, I now believe, more convinced than Phil was.

When, after calming down, we finally felt free to whisper of these matters, our initial question was *What do we do with this information?* That question remained unanswered until now…

Much later, our question became: *Is this how Philip Dick writes a book?* By creating a vast, living conspiracy—a belief-system based on his experiences, observations and conjectures—and then, at some point, deciding to separate it from the realm of "reality" to that of "fiction"? This could explain why he was able to impart such a high degree of verisimilitude into his writings. Like his characters, he had lived the plot.

Whatever the explanation, we feel this interview material is valuable for at least two reasons.

First, it is the fullest and most detailed account yet of the biographical basis for Phil's final fiction. Hopefully it will serve as a valuable guide for anyone intent on unraveling the separate threads of actual and fictional experience, dream and reality, and facts forming fiction in the "only apparently real" universe of Philip K. Dick.

Second, this interview and the story "Eye of the Sibyl," which follows, seem to fill in the gap between *Valisystem A/Radio Free Albemuth,* which Philip Dick had just completed, and *VALIS,* which he had not yet begun.

Some mystery still surrounds these works, however. According to Phil's "Exegesis," for instance, the religious explanation of his *VALIS* experiences was always his first choice and main line of thought. So why did he write the technological/political theory first, as *Radio Free Albemuth,* and why develop the complex Russian theory of this interview?

Even here, the final word may have come from Philip K. Dick himself: "No matter what theory I apply to this puzzle, there's a piece left over or one sticking out somewhere."

The Eye of Sibyl

INTRODUCTION

"The Eye of the Sibyl," by Philip K. Dick, was "written I think in 1978," according to Paul Williams, executor of the Dick estate, who supplied the story.

In addition to being an interesting piece of fiction in its own right, "Sibyl" provides a unique footnote to Philip Dick's "mystical experiences" which form the backbone of *VALIS* and *Radio Free Albemuth*. "Sibyl" is yet another attempt by Phil Dick to fictionalize his experiences, and might be considered a "missing link" between these two major works: one can detect in "Sibyl" the slow turning of Dick's public analysis of the events from the technological/political to the mystical/religious. The discerning reader will also note the first appearance of some of Dick's hypnopompic and hypnagogic phrases later incorporated into the "Tractates" of *VALIS* (excerpts 15 and 16).

Following "Eye of the Sibyl" is a letter from Philip Dick to his friend Dr. Patricia Warrick, dated 11 September 1978. This letter was also provided by Paul Williams; he felt—as do I—that it makes a fitting "afterward" to the story. It is printed here with the kind permission of Dr. Warrick.

I am greatly indebted to Paul for his cooperation in supplying me with this material, and to Russell Galen, Phil Dick's long-time agent and friend, for allowing me first American publication rights to "Eye of the Sibyl."

The Eye of Sibyl

Philip K. Dick

How is it that our ancient Roman Republic guards itself against those who would destroy it? We Romans, although only mortals like other mortals, draw on the help of beings enormously superior to ourselves. These wise and kind entities, who originate from worlds unknown to us, are ready to assist the Republic when it is in peril. When it is not in peril, they sink back out of sight—to return when we need them.

Take the case of the assassination of Julius Caesar: a case which apparently was closed when those who conspired to murder him were themselves murdered. But how did we Romans determine who had done this foul deed? And, more important, how did we bring these conspirators to justice? We had outside help; we had the assistance of the Cumean Sibyl who knows a thousand years ahead what will happen, and who gives us, in written form, her advice. All Romans are aware of the existence of the Sibylline Books. We open them whenever the need arises.

I myself, Philos Diktos of Tyana, have seen the Sibylline Books. Many leading Roman citizens, members of the Senate especially, have consulted them. But I have seen the Sibyl herself, and I of my own experience know something about her which few men know. Now that I am old—regretfully, but the necessity which binds all mortal men—I am willing to confess that once, quite by accident I suppose, I in the course of my priestly duties saw how the Sibyl is capable of seeing down the corridors of time; I know what permits her to do this, as she developed out of the prior Greek Sibyl at Delphi, in that so highly venerated land, Greece.

Few men know this, and perhaps the Sibyl, reaching out through time to strike at me for speaking aloud, will silence me forever. It is quite possible, therefore, that before I can finish this scroll I will be found dead, my head split open like one of those overripe melons from the Levant which we Romans prize so. In any case, being old, I will boldly say.

I had been quarreling with my wife that morning—I was not old then, and the dreadful murder of Julius Caesar had just taken place. At that time no one was sure who had done it. Treason against the State! Murder most ugly—a thousand knife wounds in the body of the man who had come to stabilize our quaking society...with the approval of the Sibyl, in her temple; we had seen the texts she had written to that effect. We knew that she had expected Caesar to bring his army across the river and into Rome, and to accept the crown of caesar.

"You witless fool," my wife was saying to me that morning. "If the Sibyl were so wise as you think, she would have anticipated this assassination."

"Maybe she did," I answered.

"I think she's a fake," my wife Xantipe said to me, grimacing in that way she has, which is so repulsive. She is—I should say was— of a higher social class than I, and always made me conscious of it. "You priests make up those texts; you write them yourselves—you say what you think in such a vague way that any interpretation can be made of it. You're bilking the citizens, especially the well-to-do." By that she meant her own family.

I said hotly, leaping up from the breakfast table, "She is inspired; she is a prophetess—she knows the future. Evidently there was no way the assassination of our great leader, whom the people loved so, could be averted."

"The Sibyl is a hoax," my wife said, and started buttering another roll, in her usual greedy fashion.

"I have seen the great books—"

"*How* does she know the future?" my wife demanded.

At that I had to admit I didn't know; I was crestfallen—I, a priest at Cumae, an employee of the Roman State. I felt humiliated.

"It's a money game," my wife was saying as I strode out the door.

Even though it was only dawn—fair Aurora, the goddess of dawn was showing that white light over the world, the light we regard as sacred, from which many of our inspired visions come—I made my way, on foot, to the lovely temple where I work.

No one else had arrived yet, except the armed guards loitering outside; they glanced at me in surprise to see me so early, then nodded as they recognized me. No one but a recognized priest of the temple at Cumae is allowed in; even Caesar himself must depend on us.

Entering, I passed by the great gas-filled vault in which the Sibyl's huge stone throne shone wetly in the half-gloom; only a few meager torches had been lit...

I halted and froze in silence, as I saw something never disclosed to me before. The Sibyl, her long black hair tied up in a tight knot, her arms covered, sat on her throne, leaning forward—and I saw, then, that she was not alone.

Two creatures stood before her, inside a round bubble. They resembled men but each of them had an additional—I am not sure even now what they had, but they were not mortals. They were gods. They had slits for eyes, without pupils. Instead of hands, they had claws like a crab has. Their mouths were only holes, and I realized that they, god forbid, were mute. They seemed to be talking to the Sibyl but over a long string, at each end of which was a box. One of the creatures held the box to the side of his head, and the Sibyl listened to the box at her end. The box had numbers on it and buttons, and the string was in rolls and heaps, so that it could be extended.

These were the Immortals. But we Romans, we mortals, had believed that all the Immortals had left the world, a long time ago. That was what we had been told. Evidently they had returned—at least for a short while, and to give information to the Sibyl.

The Sibyl turned toward me, and, incredibly, her head came across that whole gas-filled chamber until it was close to mine. She was smiling, but she had found me out. Now I could hear the conversation between her and the Immortals; she graciously made it audible to me.

"...only one of many," the larger of the two Immortals was saying. "More will follow, but not for some time. The darkness of ignorance is coming, after a golden period."

"There is no way it can be averted?" the Sibyl asked, in that melodious voice of hers which we treasure so.

"Augustus will reign well," the larger Immortal said, "but following him evil and deranged men will come."

The other Immortal said, "You must understand that a new cult will arise around a Light Creature. The cult will grow, but their true texts will be encoded, and the actual messages lost. We foresee failure for the mission of the Light Creature; he will be tortured and murdered, as was Julius. And after that—"

"Long after that," the larger Immortal said, "civilization will draw itself up out of the ignorance once more, after two thousand years, and then—"

The Sibyl gasped and said, "That long, Fathers?"

"That long. And then as they begin to question and to seek to learn their true origins, their divinity, the murders will begin again, the repression and cruelty, and another dark age will begin."

"It might be averted," the other Immortal said.

"Can I assist?" the Sibyl asked.

Gently, both Immortals said, "You will be dead by then."

"There will be no sibyl to take my place?"

"None. No one will guard the Republic two thousand years from now. And filthy men with small ideas will scamper and scrabble about like rats; their footprints will crisscross the world as they seek power and vie with one another for false honors." To the Sibyl both Immortals said, "You will not be able to help the people, then."

Abruptly both Immortals vanished, along with their rolls of string and the boxes with numbers which talked and were talked into, as if by mind alone. The Sibyl sat for a moment, and then lifted her hands so that by means of the mechanism which the Egyptians taught us, one of the blank pages lifted toward her, that she might write. But then she did a curious thing, and it is this which I tell you with fear, more fear than what I have told already.

Reaching into the folds of her robe she brought out an Eye. She placed the eye in the center of her forehead, and it was not an eye at all such as ours, with a pupil, but like that, the slit-eye of the Immortals, and yet not. It had sideways bands which moved toward one another, like rows... I have no words for this, being only a priest by formal training and class, but the Sibyl did turn toward me and look *past* me with that Eye, and she did then cry out so loud that it shook the walls of the temple; stones fell and the snakes far down in the slots of rock hissed. She cried in dismay and horror at what she saw, past me, and yet her strange third eye remained; she continued to look.

And then she fell, as if faint. I ran forward to lend a hand; I touched the Sibyl, my friend, that great lovely friend of the Republic as she fell faint and forward in dismay at what she saw ahead, down the tunnels and corridors of time. For it was this Eye by which the Sibyl saw what she needed to see, to instruct and warn us. And it was evident to me that sometimes she saw things too dreadful for her to bear, and for us to handle, try as we might.

As I held the Sibyl, a strange thing happened. I saw, amid the swirling gasses, forms take shape.

"You must not take them as real," the Sibyl said; I heard her voice, and yet although I understood her words I knew that the shapes were indeed real. I saw a giant ship, without sails or oars...I saw a city of thin, high buildings, crowded with vehicles unlike anything I had ever seen. And still I moved toward them and they toward me, until at last the shapes swirled behind me, cutting me off from the Sibyl. "I see this with the Gorgon's Eye," the Sibyl called after me. "It is the Eye which Medusa passed back and forth, the eye of the fates—you have fallen into—"

And then her words were gone.

• • • • •

I played in grass with a puppy, wondering about a broken Coca-Cola bottle which had been left in our back yard; I didn't know by whom.

"Philip, you come in for dinner!" my grandmother called from the back porch. I saw that the sun was setting.

"Okay!" I called back. But I continued to play. I had found a great spider web, and in it was a bee wrapped up in a web, stung by the spider. I began to unwrap it, and it stung me.

My next memory was reading the comic pages in the Berkeley Daily Gazette. I read about Brick Bradford and how he found lost civilizations from thousands of years ago.

"Hey, Mom," I said to my mother. "Look at this; it's swell. Brick walks down this ledge, see, and at the bottom—" I kept staring at the olden-times helmets the people wore, and a strange feeling filled me; I didn't know why.

"He certainly gets a lot out of the funnies," my grandfather said in a disgusted voice. "He should read something worthwhile. Those comics are garbage."

The next I remember I was in school, sitting watching a girl dance. Her name was Jill and she was from the grade above ours, the sixth; she wore a belly dancer's costume and her veil covered the bottom part of her face. But I could see lovely kind eyes, eyes filled with wisdom. They reminded me of someone else's eyes I had once known, but who has a kid ever known? Later Mrs. Redman had us write a composition, and I wrote about Jill. I wrote about strange lands where Jill lived where she danced with nothing on above her waist. Later, Mrs. Redman talked to my mother on the phone and I was bawled out, but in obscure terms that had to do with a bra or something. I never understood it then; there was a lot I didn't understand. I seemed to have memories, and yet they had nothing to do with growing up in Berkeley at the Hillside Grammar School, or my family, or the house we lived in...they had to do with snakes. I know now why I dreamed of snakes: wise snakes, not evil snakes but those which whisper wisdom.

Anyhow, my composition was considered very good by the principal of the school, Mr. Bill Gaines, *after* I wrote in that Jill wore something above her waist at all times, and later I decided to be a writer.

One night I had an odd dream. I was maybe in junior high school, getting ready to go to Berkeley High next year. I dreamed that in the deep of night—and it wasn't like a regular dream, it was really real—I saw this person from outer space behind glass in a satellite of some kind they'd come here in. And he couldn't talk; he just looked at me, with funny eyes.

Two weeks or so later I had to fill out what I wanted to be when I grew up and I thought of my dream about the man from another universe, so I wrote:

I AM GOING TO BE A SCIENCE FICTION WRITER.

That made my family mad, but then, see, when they got mad I got stubborn, and anyhow my girlfriend, Ysabel Lomax, told me I'd never be any good at it and it didn't earn any money anyhow and science fiction was dumb and only people with pimples read it. So I decided for sure to write it, because people with pimples should have someone writing for them; it's unfair otherwise, just to write for people with clear complexions. America is built on fairness; that is what Mr. Gaines taught us at Hillside Grammar School, and since he was able to fix my wristwatch that time when no one else could, I tend to admire him.

In high school I was a failure because I just sat writing and writing all day, and all my teachers screamed at me that I was a Communist because I didn't do what I was told.

"Oh, yeah?" I used to say. That got me sent up before the Dean of Boys. He told me off worse than my grandfather had, and warned me that if I didn't get better grades I'd be expelled.

That night I had another one of those vivid dreams. This time a woman was driving me in her car, only it was like an old-time Roman style chariot, and she was singing.

The next day when I had to go see Mr. Erlaud, the Dean of Boys, I wrote on his blackboard, in Latin:

UBI PECUNIA REGNET

When he came in he turned red in the face, since he teaches Latin and knows that means, "Where money rules."

"This is what a left-wing complainer would write," he said to me. So I wrote something else as he sat looking over my papers; I wrote:

UBI CUNNUS REGNET

That seemed to perplex him. "Where—did you learn that particular Latin word?" he asked.

"I don't know," I said. I wasn't sure, but it seemed to me that in my dreams they were talking to me in Latin. Maybe it was just my own brain doing reruns of my Latin 1-A beginners class, where I was really very good, surprisingly, because I didn't study.

The next vivid dream like that came two nights before that freak or those freaks killed President Kennedy. I saw the whole thing happening in my dream, *two nights before,* but more than anything else, even more vivid, I saw my girlfriend Ysabel Lomax watching the conspirators doing their evil deed, and Ysabel had a third eye.

My folks sent me to a psychologist later on, because after President Kennedy was assassinated I got really weird. I just sat and brooded and withdrew.

It was a neat lady they sent me to, a Carol Heims. She was very pretty and she didn't say I was nuts; she said I should get away from my family, drop out of school—she said that the school system insulates you from reality and keeps you from learning techniques to handle actual situations—and for me to write science fiction.

I did so. I worked at a TV sales shop sweeping up and uncrating and setting up the new TV sets. I kept thinking that each set was like a huge eye, though; it bothered me. I told Carol Heims my dream that I had been having all my life, about the space people, and being in Latin, and that I thought I'd had a lot more I'd never remembered when I woke up.

"Dreams aren't fully understood," Ms. Heims told me. I was sitting there wondering how she would look in a belly dancer costume, nude above the waist; I found that made the therapy hour go faster. "There's a new theory that it's part of your collective unconscious, reaching back perhaps thousands of years...and in dreams you get in touch with it. So, if that's true, dreams are valid and very valuable."

I was busy imagining her hips moving suggestively from side to side, but I did listen to what she said; it was something about the wise kindness of her eyes. Always I thought of those wise snakes, for some reason.

"I've been dreaming about books," I told her. "Open books, held up before me. Huge books, very valuable. Even holy, like the Bible."

"That has to do with your career as a writer," Ms. Heims said.

"These are old. Thousands of years old. And they're warning us about something. A dreadful murder, a lot of murders. And cops putting people into prison for their ideas, but doing it secretly—framing people. And I keep seeing this woman who looks like you but seated on a vast stone throne."

Later on Ms. Heims was transferred to another part of the county and I couldn't see her anymore. I felt really bad, and buried myself in my writing. I sold a story to a magazine called *Invigorating Science Fact,* which told about superior races who had landed on Earth and were directing our affairs secretly. They never paid me.

I am old now, and I risk telling this, because what do I have to lose? One day I got a request to write a small article for *Love-Planet Adventure Yarns,* and they gave me a plot they wanted written up, and a black-and-white photo of the cover. I kept staring at the photo; it showed a Roman or Greek—anyhow he wore a toga—and he had on his wrist a caduceus, which is the medical sign: two coiled snakes, only actually it was olive branches originally.

"How do you know that's called a 'caduceus'?" Ysabel asked me (we were living together now, and she was always telling me to make more money and to be like her family, which was well-to-do and classy).

"I don't know," I said, and I felt funny. And then I began to see violently agitated colored phosphene activity in both my eyes, like those modern abstract graphics which Paul Klee and others draw—in vivid color, and flash-cut duration: very fast. "What's the date?" I yelled at Ysabel, who was sitting drying her hair and reading the *Harvard Lampoon.*

"The date? It's March 16," she said.

"The year!" I yelled. "Pulchra puella, tempus—" And then I broke off, because she was staring at me. And, worse, I couldn't recall her name or who she was.

"It is 1974," she answered.

"The tyranny is in power, then, if it is only 1974," I said.

"What?" she answered, astonished, staring at me.

At once two beings appeared on each side of her, encapsulated in their inter-system vessels, two globes which hovered and maintained their atmosphere and temperature. "Don't say a further statement to her," one of them warned me. "We will erase her memory; she will think she fell asleep and had a dream."

"I remember," I said, pressing my hands to my head. Anamnesis had taken place; I remembered that I was from ancient times, and, before that, from the star Albemuth, as were these two Immortals. "Why are you back?" I said. "To—"

"We shall work entirely through ordinary mortals," J'Annis said. He was the wiser of the two Immortals. "There is no Sibyl now, to help, to give advice to the Republic. In dreams we are inspiring people here and there to *wake up;* they are beginning to understand that the Price of Release is being paid by us to free them from the Liar, who rules them."

"They're not aware of you?" I said.

"They suspect. They see holograms of us projected in the sky, which we employ to divert them; they imagine that we are floating about there."

I knew that these Immortals were in the minds of men, not in the skies of Earth, that by diverting attention outward they were free once more to help inward, as they had always helped: the inner Word.

"We will bring the springtime to this winter world," F'fr'am said, smiling. "We will raise the gates which imprison these people, who groan under a tyranny they dimly see. *Did* you see? Did you know of the comings-and-goings of the secret police, the quasi-military teams which destroyed all freedom of speech, all those who dissented?"

Now, in my old age, I set forth this account for you, my Roman friends, here at Cumae, where the Sibyl lives. I passed either by chance or by design into the far future, into a world of tyranny, of winter, which you cannot imagine. And I saw the Immortals which assist us also assist those two thousand years from now! Although those mortals in the future are—listen to me—*blind.* Their sight has been taken away by a thousand years of repression; they have been tormented and limited, the way we limit animals. But the Immortals are waking them up—*will* wake them up, I should say, in time to save them. And then the two thousand years of winter will end; they will open their eyes, because of dreams and secret inspirations, they will know—but I have told you all this, in my ancient, rambling fashion.

Let me finish with this verse by our great poet Virgil, a good friend of the Sibyl, and you will know from it what lies ahead, for the Sibyl has said that although it will not apply to our time here in Rome, it will apply to those two thousand years from us, ahead in time, bringing them promise of relief:

"Ultima Cumaei venit iam carminis aetas;
magnus ab integro saeclorum nascitur ordo.
Iam redit et Virgo, redeunt Saturnia regna;
iam nova progenies, caelo demittitur alto.

Tu mode nascenti puero, quo ferrea primum
desinet, ac toto surgent gens aurea mundo,
casta fave Lucina; tuus iam regnat Apollo."

I will set this in the strange English language which I learned to speak during my time in the future, before the Immortals and the Sibyl drew me back here, my work there at that time done:

"At last the Final Time announced by the Sibyl will arrive:
The procession of ages turns to its origin.
The Virgin returns and Saturn reigns as before;
A new race from heaven on high descends.

Goddess of Birth, smile on the new-born baby,
In whose time the Iron Prison will fall to ruin
And a golden race arises everywhere.
Apollo, the rightful king, is restored!"

Alas, you my dear Roman friends will not live to see this. But far along the corridors of time, in the United States (I use here words foreign to you) evil will fall, and this little prophecy of Virgil, which the Sibyl inspired in him, will come true.

The springtime is reborn!

September 11, 1978

Dear Pat,

After talking to you tonight I remembered that the first hypnagogic images which I saw after my 3-1974 anamnesis consisted of the Cumean Sibyl with a third or ajna eye, telling me that she had seen the conspirators who had killed the Kennedys, Dr. King and my friend Bishop Pike, and that the conspirators would be destroyed. She showed me a brief occluded glimpse of them, and they all wore eastern-establishment expensive business suits. Later, I came to realize that she was speaking about Nixon and his crowd.

I will go into this fully when I see you. But I do want to present to you this Eclogue of Virgil (his Fourth) which I firmly believe pertains to these matters (the translation is mine):

Ultima Cumaei venit iam carminis aetas;
magnus ab integro saeclorum nascitur ordo.
Iam redit et Virgo, redeunt Saturnia regna;
iam nova progenies, caelo demittitur alto.
Tu modo nascenti puero, quo ferrea primum
desinet, ac toto surgent gens aurea mundo,
casta fave Lucina; tuus iam regnat Apollo.

At last the Final Time announced by the Sibyl will arrive:
the procession of ages turns to its origin.
The Virgin returns and Saturn reigns as before;
a new race from heaven on high descends.
Goddess of Birth, smile on the new-born baby,
in whose time the Iron Prison will fall to ruin
and a golden race arises everywhere.
Apollo, the rightful king, is restored!

In my opinion, this prophetic eclogue refers to our own time. The other night during a hypnagogic state, I heard this sentence: "The head Apollo is about to return." Previously, over the years, I was told, "St. Sophia will be born again, she was not acceptable before." And, "The Buddha is in the park." And I dreamed of a great book divided into two parts; the first had ended, in which Siddhartha was sleeping, and now he would be awakening. To me, all these sentences refer to the same thing: the incarnation among us once more of the Immortal King who will rule—the Golden Age which the Romans, through the Sibyl, looked forward to and which apostolic Christianity so deeply anticipated, but anticipated, alas, too soon; it was not to come during their time.

Thus the direction of my thoughts takes a mystical and prophetic turn, with a sense of the imminent Parousia, in which I fully (in fact totally) believe. Although I tend to see it in Christian terms, I believe the Savior who is either about to be born or who is in fact already born extends beyond the scope of any one religion, that Zoroastrian expectations as well as those of other religious systems will be fulfilled.

The dream in *Flow My Tears* refers to this coming event; it was an actual dream that I had, and I knew to put it in the novel. In the novel the words "Felix" and "king" are placed together—at the time I wrote it, I thought Felix was just a name...I did not realize that I had written "the Happy King," who is indeed the king we have waited for.

This letter is a private communication between the two of us; I do not want to state openly my expectations. But, I think, every day the fulfillment of the prophecy of Virgil comes closer. Of course, many people in history have believed this, which is why I don't want to talk about it publicly. I urge you to see the film "The Man Who Fell To Earth" starring David Bowie; it is a very beautiful study of this whole situation. K.W. [Jeter] goes to see it again and again, gaining more meaning from it each time.

I admit I may be a fool or a lunatic, but in my secret mind I honestly feel such longing for this, and such a sense of its imminence: I believe that the Iron Prison has already fallen—the fall of Nixon and his police tyranny—and that in truth, in very truth, Apollo (whoever that may mean; call him Christ, Apollo, Buddha, St. Sophia, Siddhartha, anything) the rightful king is restored—not a thousand years from now or even a year from now...but that at this moment as we go through the routine of our daily lives, they are smuggling him across the water into (I have occult reason to believe) England, a new-born baby who is not human but transhuman, ultrahuman, however you wish to put it: the Immortal Man. This is what keeps me alive, this eager expectation. "Die Zeit ist da!" as Klingsor says in "Parsifal." "The time has come!" I feel the celestial forces stirring in their own excitement, which I feel I mirror. Well, if I'm wrong, it's at least kept me going through some very sad years.

Phil

A Dream of Amerasia

INTRODUCTION

Ray Faraday Nelson, perhaps best known in science fiction circles for his novels *Blake's Progress* and *Then Beggars Could Ride* (among many others), was a long-time friend and confidant of Philip K. Dick. In the early days of their careers, they met frequently as part of an informal "writer's round table"; some of the ideas developed by them eventually culminated in a novel *The Ganymede Takeover,* a Dick/Nelson collaboration.

When planning this volume, I contacted Ray to query him on the possibility of doing a short essay on this collaboration. I deduced that, as the only writer ever to personally collaborate with Phil *(Deus Irae* with Roger Zelazny was done mostly through the mail), Ray might have some insight into the workings of Phil's mind.

Ray responded with this essay, "A Dream of Amerasia," which was more than I could ever have hoped for. This touching piece reveals much about Philip Dick—as a writer, as a friend…and as a man.

I wish to express my deep appreciation to Ray Nelson for allowing this essay to be published here.

A Dream of Amerasia

Ray Faraday Nelson

Phil Dick spoke to me in a dream last night.

He clutched my arm and said, "Don't give it to them."

"Give what to who?" I asked. Phil was in that intense phase I had come to know and dread when he was alive.

"Don't give the outline and notes for the sequel to *Man in the High Castle* to the Philip K. Dick Society."

"Why not?"

"Because then it will never be written."

"But even if I keep the notes and outline, who will write it?"

"You will."

In the dream I remembered the brainstorming sessions I had had with Phil and the many other members of the San Francisco Bay Area science fiction community on those long lazy Sunday afternoons in East Oakland. Three outlines for novels had been developed during these sessions during which everyone threw ideas into the common pool, and I had gone home to put the resulting chaos into some sort of order. Only the first, *The Ganymede Takeover,* was actually written and published. (It has since been repeatedly published in the USA, England, France, Italy and Germany.) The second, *The Whalemouth Colony,* was later recycled by Phil in part. The third and best, *The Ring of Fire,* remains to this day little more than an outline and a lot of scribbles on odd bits of paper…and perhaps, if I haven't erased it, a tape recording of a brainstorming session.

Ring of Fire was intended to be a sequel to *The Man in the High Castle,* Phil's Hugo-winning tale of an alternate timestream in which the United States and her allies lost the Second World War. The "ring of fire" refers to the ring of volcanoes and earthquake faults around the edge of the North Pacific Ocean which corresponds to the Japanese Empire as it exists at the end of *Man in the High Castle.*

Phil had originally intended *High Castle* to be the first in a trilogy of alternate-timestream stories beginning after the defeat of the Allies, continuing through the gradual falling-out between Germany and Japan, and ending with the Third World War, fought between the former Axis powers with the kind of super weapons which we know in fact the Nazis had on the drawing boards. *Ring of Fire* covered the period of the falling-out, during which a remarkably creative society called Amerasia came into being, produced a few immortal works of art combining Eastern and Western influences, then was destroyed along with all but one of its artists, writers and musicians on the first day of World War III, which ends *Ring.*

The third book, *Fuji in Winter,* described the brief and apocalyptic war that almost exterminated humanity, but ended in a note of hope as a new religion, uniting the best elements of all the previous religions, arises in the ruins.

The whole "Amerasian Trilogy," as we called it, was to be told, not from the viewpoint of the generals, presidents, emperors and other big shots, but from the viewpoints of the "little guys"; the ordinary men and women who, by their choices in difficult and dangerous conditions, make society possible. Their stories were to be interwoven in such a way that the larger events of history would be more implied than reported. Phil particularly wanted to write the separate strands of narrative first as short stories, then weave them together into the novels, but not in strict chronological order—as in Bradbury's *The Martian Chronicles* or Asimov's *Foundation* series—but in bits, jumping from one strand of narrative to another; from one viewpoint to another, within a single chapter.

Phil and I were both impressed by the artistic accomplishments of the Japanese during the Edo Period, when Japan was closed to the West. Phil felt that if someone like Basho could write real poetry under the repressive conditions of the Tokagowa Shoganates, the human spirit would have found a way to survive even if the Nazis and Imperial Japanese had conquered us. He felt, however, that the Nazis were the greater of two evils, though he was empathetic enough to be able, at least for the purposes of story writing, to see things from the Nazi point of view...which sometimes put off other members of our little Sunday afternoon brainstorming club, particularly Jewish Avram Davidson. The Japanese, Phil felt, were redeemed by their almost instinctive love of beauty, of nature, of family life. Like all peoples at war, they might commit an occasional atrocity, but they would never adopt genocide as an accepted government policy. Thus the Japanese, in the Amerasian Trilogy, emerged as more or less the "Good Guys," and the Nazis as the "Bad Guys."

At the time of the plotting, sessions, neither Phil nor I felt ready to write *Ring of Fire.* We wanted to do a lot more research, a lot more brainstorming. I think I should honestly mention that Phil at that time was suffering from a bad writer's block from which he sometimes felt he would never recover, and that these brainstorming sessions and proposed collaborations were seen by him as ways to either get his own creative juices flowing again, or to recruit others to carry on projects dear to his heart that he felt he would not be able to complete himself.

So, in the spirit of doing a kind of preliminary sketch for *Ring of Fire,* we set to work on what eventually became *The Ganymede Takeover.* The Japanese occupation of the United States west of the Rockies was represented as an occupation by "worms" from Ganymede, and we used this as a comic metaphor for the Japanese Imperial Court, Two characters originally intended for *Ring of Fire* actually debuted in *Takeover:* Joan Hiashi, the Amerasian girl, and Dr. Balkani, the sadistic German psychiatrist. Percy X, the Black militant guerrilla, was also based on a more minor character originally intended for the other book. The general shape of the plot—that of a buildup to an apocalypse—was also a reflection of *Ring,* as were some of the incidents.

The fact is, we wanted to write *Ring,* but we had to write something, so we wrote *Takeover.*

Since we were "only practicing" for "the big one," we wrote the book we did in a spirit of almost hysterical hilarity, enclosing weird newspaper clippings and Beatle bubblegum cards in the installments of the ongoing story we mailed back and forth. When we met—first at his place in East Oakland and later at his other place in Marin County near the water, we often spent more time smoking grass, dropping acid and flirting with each others' wives than working. Not for nothing is *Takeover* dedicated to both Kirsten and Nancy. Joan Hiashi is a composite, in many ways, of these two remarkable women, and many of the concepts and plot twists were contributed by them in the nonstop brainstorming that always formed a part of our relationship. We never actually "swapped wives" or "swung," yet the emotional involvement of this foursome went far beyond what normally passes for friendship between two married couples.

It seems to me most commentators of Phil's life and work vastly underestimate the influence women had on him; not only the women he married, but the women with whom he practiced a latterday version of courtly love. One secret of his great charm was that he actually listened to women; actually took seriously what women said. Few men do. And I think it was Nancy who started Phil in the direction of the ecstatic mysticism that dominated his final books; Nancy who actually had a guru, while the rest of us only talked about having one; Nancy who actually had visions. Nancy who in her whole approach to life personified the kind of gentleness and love that would equally express true Christianity or true Buddhism.

It would not be going too far to say that the living reality of Nancy Dick was what convinced Phil and I that the religion we saw arising after World War III was humanly possible.

I have since met another one of his wives, Anne Dick, who is writing what will probably be the only really insightful biography of the man, and found her equally remarkable in another way. I strongly suspect it was she who contributed to Phil's worldview the great emphasis he placed on the importance of the arts, even such seemingly minor arts as jewelry making. Phil always attacked the idea that there were "fine" arts and "commercial" arts; "high" arts and "low" arts. From him beauty could express itself anywhere, in any genre. Until I heard Anne Dick hold forth on the exact same topic in the exact same words, I didn't know where Phil had picked up the notion…and it is Anne who has devoted her life to the creation of beautiful things.

I will never forget one particular sun-drenched afternoon.

I had recently dropped acid and was about a day into a slow, gentle re-entry. I lay on my belly in T-shirt and jeans on the old, rickety dock out back of Phil's place in Marin County and watched the sunlight dance on the water like electric flame. Sometimes a fish or two would dart swiftly below me. Sometimes a seagull would cry out above me as it wheeled in the sky. I lay there a long time. It seemed like about five centuries. I was happy.

Nancy came and knelt beside me.

"What are you doing?" she murmured.

"Watching the fire on the water."

"Do you like bright sparkling things?"

"Yes."

I heard her leave but I didn't look up.

Soon she returned.

She slipped something around my neck. I saw it was a crystal necklace, full of little rainbows.

"Your necklace…" I began.

"Yours now," she corrected me.

I still have it, but I don't wear it in public anymore. Pretty things don't send the same signals now as they did then.

But last night, as I say, I dreamed of Phil.

And he told me to write *Ring of Fire*.

I will have to dig through my manuscript boxes from that period. I'm sure the outline and notes are there, and with luck also the tape. And—as Phil requested—I will not surrender these items to the Philip K. Dick Society. All this time that book had been quietly simmering in my mind. Now it is ready at last to serve. Without really knowing what I was doing, except perhaps subconsciously, I have been researching it all these years, storing up information, scribbling ideas on little pieces of paper and 3 X 5 cards, trying out ideas in my writings. What neither of us could do then, I now think I am ready to do.

In the dream we were in that alternate reality where Japan won the Second World War, but in that reality, Phil is still alive. The particular stresses that, in our home reality, destroyed him, in that reality were replaced by other stresses…equally challenging, but not so directly harmful physically.

He lives in the Edo district of Tokyo, in what is called "The Floating World" —a kind of Disneyland recreation of the Japanese "Bohemia" of the early 19th Century, before Japan was opened up to the West. He watches Kabuki and No plays. He sips sake with beautiful Geisha girls and expounds his views on dream and reality to a circle of devoted followers, who nod and smile and ask respectful questions.

And last night he gave me my assignment.

But in the dream I was not the only one there. We were in a teahouse, sitting on pillows on the floor around low teakwood tables, and with us were a select group of Bay Area science fiction writers. Phil turned to the others, who had been throwing in ideas for the common pool—just like in the old East Oakland days—and said, "Amerasia is not just for Ray and I. It is for all of you. All of you have been reaching for Amerasia in your writings, in your dreams. All of you have visited me here again and again. You and many others. You may all write stories set in Amerasia. You may all help to bring Amerasia into reality in your own time-stream. You may all play a role in the creation of the final religion, whose symbol will be the Golden Sundisk; the true catholicism that embraces the truths of both East and West; the religion we have all been blindly groping towards in both our work and our lives. You all have something to contribute, and I will help you all; guide you in your dreams, give unity to the many voices in which you will speak."

I looked around and these are some of the faces I recognized:

Adrienne Martine-Barnes, Grania Davis, Dick and Pat Lupoff, Terry and Carol Carr, Carol Robia, Robert Silverberg, Roselore Fox, Ernest Callenbach, Anne Rice, Marion Zimmer Bradley, Diana Paxon, Jon DeCles, Kirsten Nelson and Stan Koyama. There were others, but I don't recall them now.

Dreams fade in the daylight unless you do something to preserve them.

What I will do is begin work on *The Ring of Fire*.

Philip K. Dick: The Dream Connection
D. Scott Apel

I tell you these things for what they are worth.
They are true things; they happened.
—VALIS

I

"Maybe your destiny lies directly at the center of Disneyland."
—Radio Free Albemuth

Philip K. Dick died on March 2, 1982, of circulatory collapse brought about by several massive strokes.

I got the news by phone from Kevin Briggs. His account was sketchy in its details, but the vital point was clear: Phil was dead. I was more baffled than shocked, at that point. After all, Phil was young, comparatively. Fifty-three year old men don't die of strokes.

Briggs and I planned to attend whatever services might be held, if we could find them. But in those days, we were not part of the PKD "circle." We had no idea who to call for details. I tried Ted Sturgeon, but he knew little more than we did. And while we were searching for a Los Angeles contact, a quiet memorial service was being held just up the coast from us in Marin, where Phil had lived for several years. In what was to be the first in a series of bizarre coincidences, I found out months later that a co-worker of mine, Rik Thompson, attended the service (and later wrote a summary of it for the "Phil Dick Appreciations" in *Locus)*. My best contact was only a few yards away from my desk, and I never knew it.

Phil's death was upsetting to me, but not terribly so. I had had friends die before. Doug Kenney, for instance; co-founder of the *National Lampoon,* co-writer of *Animal House,* and co-writer and producer of *Caddyshack.* After Doug's tragic death, I even began a short story in which the spirit of a dead humorist inspired the writing of a small-time comic in Los Gatos.

Another dead friend was Leigh Brackett, with whom Briggs and I did a wonderful, laughter-filled interview the week before George Lucas asked her to script *The Empire Strikes Back.* She went into seclusion to work on the screenplay, and died of cancer the week after finishing her first draft.

What intrigued me was that these three people were the only contacts I have ever had with major motion pictures, and they all died soon after promising to help me get started in Hollywood.

Once is incidence, they say; twice is coincidence; three times, conspiracy... or synchronicity. Strange synchronicity.

Phil's death, though, bothered me in two ways. First there was the obvious tragedy involved in seeing a major writer cut down in his prime. His latest books were masterworks; he was finally getting the recognition he so richly deserved; he had many great books left in him.

Second was the more personal aspect. I'd catch myself reading a book or seeing a movie and thinking, "I bet Phil would really enjoy this. I'd better call him and...oh." No Phil to share with; no Phil to bring up to the house; no Phil to show *Last Year At Marienbad* to...and there never would be. He was alive in my mind. But I had to remind myself of the facts. I had to content myself with rereading *UBIK,* searching for clues he might have left about his own afterlife.

The October, 1983, issue of *Locus* (which arrived in early September) contained a tiny item which startled me. It seems that one David Alcott, a staff writer for the Oakland, California *Tribune,* wrote a piece questioning whether Phil was actually dead. Due to certain "oddities" surrounding Phil's hospitalization and death, Alcott advanced the theory that the whole thing might have been a hoax, enabling Phil to begin a new, anonymous life.

This theory had a profound effect on me emotionally. Could it possibly be true? Could my dead friend still be alive? Or was this reporter just a scoop-seeking paranoid?

Cautiously, I queried Alcott. He sent me a copy of his article of August 28, 1983, along with a letter of his own speculations.

"You should know," he wrote, "that since the publication of the story, I have consulted the *I Ching* three times on the issue and got startling results—

"#1-Q: Will I investigate further?

"Ans: Clarity within makes it possible to investigate the facts exactly. When a man meets his destined ruler, they can be together ten days.

"#2-Q: Is Dick alive?

"Ans: A man must hide his light in a time of darkness. The injury is not fatal. Feigned insanity. (Hex. 22 & 36)

"#3-Q. Is the contact from Apel a sign Dick is trying to reach me?

"Ans: He flutters down, not boasting of his wealth, together with his neighbor. The approach is made quite spontaneously because it is based on inner conviction. The flying bird brings the message. (Hex. 11 & 62)"

Alcott concluded by admitting he had no idea why Phil might have perpetrated this hoax.

But I did. I knew. I dug out of my files a copy of a letter Phil had sent me in September, 1981: the now-famous "Tagore" letter *(see Appendix III)*.

In this letter, Phil described a vision he had had—a vision of a "new Savior," living in Sri Lanka. That's where he was headed: to search out Tagore, as Horselover Fat had done in *VALIS*. Fat's madness was complete, now. He had possessed Phil.

But what could I do about it? Fly to Sri Lanka to search for Phil? I had had no vision. If I was wrong, I'd not only be insane but in debt as well.

There was one thing I could do, however: I could write about it. And so, in September of 1983, I began work on my fourth detective novel, entitled *Tagore*. In this book, Richard K. Philips—a science fiction writer who played a major role in my first detective novel, *The Coincidence Caper*—fakes his own death, then surreptitiously contacts my detective character to act as his bodyguard on his search for "the new Savior."

I began making furious notes: outlines, plot twists, snatches of dialog, themes. But working on this book was painful, like swimming underwater in a suit of armor. The more I worked on it, the more depressed I became. It got to the point where I couldn't even bear looking through my notes. Inertia would overtake and paralyze me; I'd sit staring at the pile of notes, then sullenly collect them and shut them back in my desk drawer.

One day in October the fantasy collapsed. Who was I kidding? The third, unwritten sequel to a yet unpublished novel? No one would ever read this book. No one would care. I'd be wrenching my own guts only to get them wrenched again when the book ended up unpublished, unpublishable.

And what about Phil? Was he dead or alive? Was there some hope I'd hear from him, or was the "hoax" theory itself just a cruel hoax? I had to know and I couldn't know.

And worst of all—the most crushing blow—was the revelation that no matter how much I wrote about Phil, I could not write him back to life. *Why bother with any of it?* I kept asking myself in endless repetition. *What's the fucking use? Why bother at all?*

I ended up on the bed that day, crying uncontrollably. I hadn't felt such grief, such despair, such utter futile hopelessness, since my first love affair ended, nearly a decade earlier. Emotions I never knew I had, in an intensity I'd only experienced once before, vomited to the surface of my consciousness. My hopeless motive was exposed; my irrational fantasy of writing Phil alive was revealed as pure Aesculapian idiocy.

My girlfriend, Margie Bowers, tried to console me. She held me and talked to me and comforted me. I had no idea what she said, except, "People are thrown together for a reason." *"Thrown together…"* curious phrasing. But the same words Jung used to define "archetype"…

When the storm cleared, I realized that there was indeed a way to ascertain the truth: an odd way, but the only way available for such otherworldly circumstances.

And so, on October 31, 1983, I sent a letter to Alan Vaughan. Mr. Vaughan is well-known in the field of parapsychology, partly for his books *Dream Telepathy* (1973; co-authored with Stanley

Krippner and Montague Ullman), *Patterns of Prophecy* (1973), *Incredible Coincidence* (1979), and *The Edge of Tomorrow* (1982). But he is a man blessed with twin gifts: as well as being a fine writer, he is also a gifted psychic. He was tested, for example, at the Stanford Research Institute, and was able to reproduce every effect the more sensational psychic Uri Gelled claimed to be able to produce: changing the temperature of metal in a vacuum, reading messages in locked boxes, and so on. He has successfully predicted numerous details of the space program, as well as the Watergate scandal and the assassination of Robert Kennedy. The Central Premonitions Registry lists Vaughan as "the world's most accurate psychic predictor." He holds an honorary Ph.D. in Parapsychology and has appeared on many national television programs, including *Nova* and *20/20*. He makes his living off his considerable skill, writing, lecturing, consulting and teaching seminars in psychic development.

Alan Vaughan had one additional qualification which made him uniquely suited to aid in my quest: he was a personal friend. We had known each other for years, since his tenure as editor of the San Francisco-based *Psychic* magazine in the mid-'70s. We began corresponding about synchronicity in 1975, and met informally several times throughout the following years. I knew him to be a warm, gentle, intelligent man with a quiet but pronounced sense of humor. And I knew with personal certainty the reality of his psychic abilities and his sincerity in their use. If anyone could discern the whereabouts of Philip K. Dick—whether in this world or the next— it would be Alan Vaughan.

I outlined for him what I've outlined here, and asked for his help. A taped reply of his psychic reading arrived in mid-November.

His conclusions were striking. "You ask about Phil Dick, the writer," he began. "Someone believes he is still alive, and you wonder if that's true or not… Well, I just had the oddest feeling that, yes, he is, by conventional standards, dead…but that he'll be in contact with you."

I sat bolt upright in my chair, staring at the tape turning in the machine.

"It seems he had several books or story ideas left over, and he might try to channel one or two of them to you. Somehow he will be able to inspire some of your writing," Vaughan continued. "Not automatic writing, but it's like you're channeling him or tuning into him. I feel that he can, in a sense, inspire some of your writing—if you'll let him. There seems to be a colorful quality, a wild humor, that will be engaged in your creativity that I might put down to his influence.

"But more important than the writing will be your experiences with getting in touch with Philip K. Dick, shall we say, psychically."

I played the tape back again to make sure I had heard it correctly. Like a dutiful servant, it played back precisely the same message. Alan Vaughan had even correctly picked up that Phil's body had been cremated.

I had asked Vaughan a few other questions as well, including whether or not he could give statistical odds as to the likelihood of his predictions occurring. "As a matter of fact, I can sometimes do that," he said, whereupon he proceeded to do so. Fifty-fifty chance for this; 85 percent chance for that... "And as for the Phil Dick thing...It's gonna happen." He was that sure? He was that sure.

Following my initial shock, my native skepticism returned.

OK, I told myself; *maybe it will and maybe it won't.* I've done too much research and had too many personal experiences to dismiss life after death. But the dead contacting the living? Save it for *UBIK.*

The next few months were life at its most mundane: doing things I didn't want to do to get things I didn't need to have. Going to my comfortable but boring job every day; working through boring required courses at night; trying to catch some sleep and maintain a relationship on weekends.

All that began to change in March of 1984. I began dreaming of Disneyland.

Now wait just a damn minute, I can hear you thinking. *Just what the hell does dreaming of Disneyland have to do with anything?* Well...bear with me. We've reached here a limitation of literature: trying to force a holographic event into a linear transcript. This piece of the puzzle does harmonize with the others, when viewed in the proper context.

Disneyland, for instance. I love it. Always have. A key event in my life—one of those epiphanic, imprinting experiences that forever defines or reveals one's destiny—was sitting spellbound before the television set at age three, watching the first episode of *Disneyland,* which chronicled the building of the park. I've made my pilgrimage to Anaheim nearly one hundred times in the past quarter century, and I still haven't had enough.

Or dreams. For the past eighteen years I have kept a nightly record of my dreams. If I were to list the top ten experiences in my life, at least half of them would be dreams. I have read everything on the subject from Zolar to Jung (with a strong preference for the latter). And I've had too much personal experience to dismiss dreams as "random fragments of the unconscious," or "wish fulfillments of the id." Any activity which one undertakes for several hours each day deserves more attention than these glib dismissals. Saying dreams are "the mind's way of integrating sensory experience" is like saying "food is fuel for the body." An analysis like this overlooks taste, texture, aroma, gourmet meals, banquets and parties, and on and on. Some dreams are junk food, to be sure. But some are ambrosia: the food of the gods.

On March 15, 1984, I dreamt of Disneyland in two separate dreams. The following night I was there again. This time I went into a different version of Disneyland's Haunted Mansion; this one built as an old suburban house. I got out of the ride car in the kitchen to see how all the 3D hologram "ghosts" were created.

Two weeks later I had a similar dream: I was back in the Disneyland Haunted Mansion again. But I was the only one on the ride, so the ride operator stopped it to let me look around. He came out to tell me that the park was closed and I would have to walk out. I asked for a tour, and he took me into a well-lighted "backstage" area which was like a small old house. In order to gain access to this area, I had to pass a guard station; I did this by telling the guard I was looking for my friend Chrissi (who will appear later in this narrative). My guide then took me to another part of the ride; a huge warehouse where a party was in progress: a celebration party in honor of Philip K. Dick.

I saw many of my friends in the room, including Robert Anton Wilson (a real-life friend) and Orson Welles (who, at that time, was alive, but whom I did not know). And on a video monitor set up to photograph and amuse the guests, I saw Phil. Excitedly, I told everyone: even if we couldn't see him, he was here "in spirit." He was enjoying the party, walking among us and wearing a bright yellow shirt and a smile. We clustered around the monitor while he explained that he would contact us using what he called a "calendar code": a matrix of letters and numbers which looked like a calendar. He also "transmitted" many individual words and several phrases to us in Latin.

I woke after this, in the middle of the night, with a pleasant sense of well-being, and the sentence "He's happy and among friends" echoing in my mind. My next thought was simply: *"Phil's coming through."*

Daylight returned my skepticism, although not as strongly this time. The emotional content of the dream lingered and had meaning, enough that I pondered over a few of the dream elements. Alan Vaughan had said Phil would bring me several qualities in his contact. A "wild humor" was one; what better joke than for a ghost to reveal himself in a haunted house? (Phil lived very close to Disneyland during the last years of his life, as well.) He'd bring a "colorful" quality to my writing...was that indicated by the bright yellow shirt? He'd "channel" through me, and I'd "tune in" to him...was that the TV "channel" we were "tuning into" at the party? Phil knew Latin. He'd dreamed in Latin. I don't and never had.

But what the hell was that "calendar code"? That baffled me...until I realized that the dream had occurred during the wee hours of April first: April Fool's Day. Back to the wild humor again. I nearly dropped my notebook laughing.

Maybe Phil Dick really did contact me, I thought. Or maybe I'm the April Fool. Whatever the explanation, for the first time in months I felt at peace about his fate. If it was a real contact, it was certainly a "practical" joke. Contact or not, I had the feeling I should shut up about it. It just won't do to go around in waking society blabbing off about your dream conversations with the dead. Bad form.

On June 8, 1984, I had a dream which lasted the entire night, and consisted of one single element: me reading a short story. In the dream, I read page after page after page of typewritten material, for hours on end. But when I woke, I couldn't recall the story—just the reading.

The following night, June 9th, I dreamed of reading a magazine interview with Orson Welles done by Robert Anton Wilson. I also read a long list of words and later wrote page after page and read many, many pages. In a later dream that same night, I was back at Disneyland, behind the scenes of the Alice in Wonderland ride.

Curiouser and curiouser. Welles and Wilson were at Phil's "April Fool's" party, which took place behind the scenes of a Disneyland ride. And Alice's adventures were all a dream. Once again, I had entered Wonderland. Mostly I wondered what was going on.

June 10th: Another night filled entirely with dreams of reading, writing, reading, writing. I was waking up exhausted, as though I had worked all night. Three nights running, and I still couldn't remember what I was reading and writing.

On June 11th, I was at it again. This time, though, there was a difference: Philip K. Dick was there with me. We were collaborating on a story. We sat together at a bare card table illuminated by a single overhead light bulb, shaded as though it were lighting a poker table. Surrounding us outside this cone of light was...nothing. Just darkness, as if we were floating in starless space. We wrote and read and handed pages back and forth all night long. We had no time for conversation; we were hard at work.

I dreamed this single scene for eight solid hours. And when I woke exhausted after our night's labor—I *still* could not remember a single sentence of the story.

The collaboration became clearer on the night of June 12th. Phil and I were back in the same scene as the previous night, still working on the same story. It was a very "Twilight Zone" type of story, but I did not like the downbeat ending or the internal "gimmick." Something happened in the story between the 23rd and 25th of one April, and a second event occurred the 18th of the following April. But since the people in the story were using only one calendar, it appeared to them as though the second event had occurred first. A cheap gimmick, I thought; a dream gimmick, not a story twist.

That was the last dream in that series. Maybe Phil got pissed off at me over artistic differences and left.

I still had no idea what the story was about. But on June 20th, I hit upon the idea that possibly the story material was being "programmed" into my unconscious—like people do with sleep-learning and hypnosis tapes—and that it would rise to the surface when the time was right to write it. I decided to be patient.

That night, I dreamed I was reading a book of contest-winning science fiction short stories. Among other things, the Introduction said not to appeal to the judges' sentimentality by dedicating stories to dead science fiction authors. This introduction went on to discuss several of Philip K. Dick's main themes, including "accidental interdimensional travel," whatever that might be. It took me months to realize that this is what Mr. Tagomi does in *The Man in the High Castle.*

Eventually, the story did become apparent. I sat down and wrote it out, easily, within a few days. I'd had the initial idea for years, but with no satisfactory middle or end. Now it just flowed, with almost no work on my part. It concerned a man who discovered that the great works of literature of the ages were systematically disappearing from the shelves of bookstores and libraries and from the consciousness of Humankind. My character was the only one to remember Homer, Twain, Shakespeare and a dozen others. And when he tried to recreate these masterpieces, all he got was rejections and insults from publishers. I called the story "Last Writes," and gave it a very "Twilight Zone"-type twist ending.

When I gave the finished piece to a couple of friends for review, I was in for some surprises. One commented on the "Phil Dick" influence, for instance... without, of course, knowing anything at all about the previous events. The other—a Ph.D. in Mathematical Linguistics—analyzed it more completely, finding in it a deeper level of meaning than I had ever consciously intended. She found a parable about using those influences one admires to help develop one's self, but eventually having to outgrow them, give them up, transcend them. And I thought it was just a funny little Twilight Zone story.

What's odd about this…a writer writing? Two things. First, I don't write short stories. I write novels. I've written ten books in the past decade, and only one other short story. Second, as a novelist, I retain strict control over the many levels of material that go into my writing. No one, in ten years of writing, has yet been able to tell me of a theme in one of my books that I didn't consciously manipulate in there. Another indication that this was material rising from the unconscious. Mine, or…

One more oddity: I called my main character "George Valentine." No matter what other name I tried, "Valentine" seemed to be the only one that "fit." Later I found out that Phil claimed his basic philosophy was "Valentinian."

But where did the "calendar code" fit in here? Why did my story-conference dream make a point of the April dates? I still don't know for sure, but I do have a couple of intriguingly coincidental clues. One whole section of the story consists of George Valentine's jumbled recreation of Hamlet, built entirely from Shakespeare's most-quoted lines from his entire canon; April 23, of course, is Shakespeare's birthday. And in my clipping/research files I stumbled later across two Jack Anderson columns about government psychic research dated April 23 and 24, 1984; followups to a 1981 column of his which I had my PKD character quote in my first detective novel.

Since these were dreams, I also checked back through my dream logs for activity on these dates. On April 18, 1983, I had a dream about a surgeon who cloned himself so he could die and return to explain the nature of life after death. And my dreams of the 25th and 26th of April '83 were both precognitive of minor events...the only precognitive dreams of that year (I usually average four or five a year).

I remembered no dreams on April 18, 1984, but on April 24th, I dreamt about two people: my friend Chrissi—who I told the Disneyland guard I was seeking in the first dream—and Alan Vaughan.

Coincidences. But coincidences enough to crease my brow.

Phil was no stranger to dreams himself, especially not meaningful dreams. Much of his dream activity is discussed firsthand in Part II of the interview in this book. But the main points bear condensing for our present purposes. First, there was the precognitive material which Phil realized in 1972 was coming to him in his dreams. Second was his dream written into *Flow My Tears;* the healing dream which he claims won him the Campbell Award. Third, there was the whole nexus of events involving dreams of Greek and Latin he did not know, and of "aliens" who he believed were using him. Fourth, there were the dream fragments and hypnagogic and hypnopompic imagery which he considered meaningful enough to work into the cosmology developed in his Exegesis and the "Tractates" of *VALIS.* Additionally, there is Phil's confession in his essay "Man, Android and Machine" that he'd written so many dream experiences into his novel *The Martian Time-Slip* that he couldn't separate them, when he read the book.

Finally, according to Paul Williams' November, 1975 *Rolling Stone* article on Dick, Phil began dreaming scenes for a *UBIK* film six months before he was ever asked to write a screenplay.

Even from these few examples, we can see that Phil attended to his own dreams very carefully, and placed much stock in their value and meaning. He told Gregg Rickman as much in *The Last Testament:* that he was basically a Jungian when it came to dreams, and that the more one attended them, the more rewarding they became.

My own dream experience subsided after this first "contact," although the next six months included frequent recurrences of some of the prominent symbols clustering around my experience: Disneyland; screening a PKD interview film; and many, many dreams of just reading material which seemed vaguely related to the subject. In addition, I began to remember almost all of my dream activity. For nearly seventeen years of attending to and training myself to remember my dreams, I was content to recall fragments three or four times a week. Now, with no further training or prompting, I was recalling all my dream activity; three or four full dreams every night. I felt—and still do—that this was a major breakthrough in establishing communication with my own unconscious. And this ability persists.

Still I told no one, not even my girlfriend. She lay asleep beside me throughout these nights, unaware of my dream life.

What neither of us knew was that the dream was about to come to day.

II

Although we remain unaware of supernatural entities
they guide and direct us.
—The Exegesis

In late September, 1984, Andy Watson, editor of the Philip K. Dick Society Newsletter, wrote me to ask permission to reprint portions of Briggs' and my interview with Phil. He had found Phil's copy in the estate's files and was interested. I wrote back on October 1, granting him permission, gratis. But the request started me thinking. If 600 subscribers were interested in reading excerpts from the interview, why didn't I publish a small-press edition of the entire transcript? We had eight hours worth of tapes, after all, plus a few extra anecdotes...

A week later, PKDS Newsletter #4 arrived in the mail. I read it cover to cover and came away crushed. Not only did it contain an essay by Tim Powers on how he and K.W. Jeter were "David and Kevin" in *VALIS*—roles Briggs and I thought we played—but it also contained the first mention I had seen of Gregg Rickman's *three volumes* of interviews with Philip K. Dick. And here was I—the world's most famous unknown writer—sitting in obscurity in San Jose, unable to compete with or even answer these stars of the Phil Dick universe. *We* were David and Kevin; Phil *told* us so. *We* had the best Phil Dick interview; he told us that, too. *I* was supposed to have done that interview book—Phil and his agent and I had discussed it years earlier. And *I* was getting this new material from Phil. Maybe. And, Goddamn it, that last part was just too personal and too bizarre to even talk about, let alone publish.

Depression climbed to frustration and finally to outright rage. *All right,* I told myself. *I can play that game, too. Nobody gets anywhere by sitting around feeling sorry for himself or by basking in his own obscurity.*

Too often in the last ten years I'd seen my own good ideas made successful by someone else. This time I was ready to do something about it. Win, lose, or called-on-account-of-rain, I'd publish my own book and tell my own story of my friendship with Philip K. Dick.

But I would *never* mention the dreams.

I began work, rallying my friends for favors. I wrote Robert Anton Wilson, then living in Ireland, outlining my plan and asking for an introduction. I wrote Ted Sturgeon, sending him a copy of the pages of the interview Briggs and I did with him where he talks about Phil's philosophy *(see Appendix II)*, asking him to expand on their long Octocon discussion about it. I wrote Paul Williams, asking if he could dig up some unpublished piece by PKD for inclusion. And I wrote Ray Faraday Nelson, asking if he'd consent to contribute a short essay on collaborating with Phil on *The Ganymede Takeover.*

With these mailings, the floodgates of synchronicity burst wide open. Phase II of this strange history had begun.

The first sign came back almost immediately. *One day* after Ray Nelson received my request, he mailed me his finished essay, "A Dream of Amerasia" (included in this volume). I nearly dropped it when I read the first line: "Phil Dick spoke to me in a dream last night."

Him too?

I called him soon afterwards to acknowledge receipt and to thank him. How was he able to respond so quickly?, I asked. "Oh, I've been working on that essay for the last week or so," he replied. "It wasn't intended for publication; it was just something I wanted to put down on paper."

And the dream of Phil? The dream which showed him inspiring writers from his "kind of Disneyland recreation" of a Japanese setting? Was that just a literary device to frame the piece?

"Oh, no!" the usually laconic Nelson replied with uncharacteristic vehemence. "That was a real dream; I actually had that dream. And I intend to follow its advice and write the sequel to *The Man in the High Castle.*"

There it was: another writer, receiving writing guidance from his dead friend in his dreams. And being told, in the dream, that others would receive this guidance, too. Ray had no clue I was included, and had experienced this already, myself. Not strangely, I heard the *Twilight Zone* theme begin playing in the back of my mind.

How many others might also have been touched by this madness, I wondered. There was one resource to check: past issues of the PKDS Newsletter. I dug them out and combed them.

In Issue #4, I found a curious essay entitled "Phil Dick Lives," by science fiction author Rudy Rucker. In it, Rucker tells a story about meeting a man he felt was Phil Dick: "...in walked Phil Dick. He didn't *say* he was Phil Dick, but he looked to be wearing his circa-1974 body...hell, *I* don't know what Phil Dick 'really' looks/looked like, but I knew *this was the guy...*" This "meeting" took place at a party which Rucker attended with a friend named Henry Vaughn. My "contact" also took place at a party...and was predicted by a friend named Vaughan. Further, Rucker states that while writing one novel, "every day, starting out, I'd pray to Phil Dick and ask him for guidance." Coincidentally, Rucker won the Philip K. Dick Award in 1983 for his novel, *Software.* Ray Nelson spoke at the acceptance awards.

In Issue #3 I found another clue: an essay by Paul Williams' ex-wife Sachiko, entitled "To The Spirit of PKD," reprinted from the science fiction fanzine *Trap Door.* "Since PKD's death he is always with me when I need help. I start calling him in my mind and I feel he is with me and giving me help and support somehow," Sachiko wrote. Later, she continued: "When I first dreamed about Phil...I heard his voice coming from the ceiling..."

Finally, David Alcott's letter to me made mention of the novel Tessa Dick—Phil's wife during his "mystical experience" days—was working on. Phil had helped her in its writing, she told him, and since his passing, she still felt his presence and guidance when working on it. Tessa's novel was to be titled *The Darkening of the Light*—curiously, a variation of the *I Ching* hexagram Alcott had thrown when asking "Is Dick alive?": "A man must hide his light in a time of darkness."

Just what the hell was going on here? Five people, independently of one another, receiving career guidance from a dead friend? Three through dreams, one through prayer. One shown that the contacts would be occurring; one told in advance by a reputable psychic; all partly attributing their plans or successes to this inspiration; all woven together by a web of synchronicities within synchronicities. Just what the hell was going on here?

Several years ago, in conversation, Robert Anton Wilson told me he found himself flying around the country lecturing on space migration and similar topics, and he realized he was "living in a novel": Heinlein's *The Man Who Sold The Moon*. I now found myself a character in some larger plot, too. But what kind of book was I living in? A ghost story? An essay by Jung? A detective novel as written by H.P. Lovecraft? My own short story about Doug Kenney? *The Cosmic Trigger? VALIS? UBIK?* Or worse...*The Three Stigmata of Palmer Eldritch,* starring Philip K. Dick as a benign demigod, invading the dreams of those he was close to? I saw a clear pattern emerging, but remained determined to deploy my skepticism to avoid being swept into a web of credulousness. I needed more evidence to build a case; I needed more information to determine what this pattern meant. I resolved to take a step backwards and view my experiences objectively. This is difficult to do without tripping.

My resolution was put to the test the very next day. October 23rd's mail included a letter from Paul Williams and the piece he had chosen for this volume. This story, "The Eye of the Sibyl," is based on Phil's "mystical experiences" of February and March, 1974...experiences which (to my knowledge) were known only to a few close friends, and were described fully in only two other places:

Phil's own novel *VALIS,* and Briggs' and my 1977 interview. But I had never even transcribed that portion of our interview; it just didn't fit the body of our original book. Only half a dozen of our friends—including Alan Vaughan and Robert Anton Wilson—even knew of its existence. And it was on the strength, length and interest of this material that I was going to base this book-length expansion of our original interview. There is no possible way Williams could have known about any of these points, and yet he had sent me a story which perfectly dovetailed with my material and plans...a story which contained this curious line of dialog from one of the "Immortals": "In dreams we are inspiring people here and there..."

The *Twilight Zone* theme began assailing my mind's ear...

So what did I have, after less than two weeks of work on this book? A unique, extensive interview with Phil Dick about his psychic experiences; a short story by Phil Dick based on and expanding this same material, offered serendipitously; an essay involving dream experiences paralleling my own; and a nexus of coincidences too meaningful to ignore. The book had assumed a life of its own, pointing me toward what it demanded to be: not a simple interview and essay collection, but a chronicle of Philip K. Dick's psychic life.

I had the eerie feeling that I was indeed living in a benevolent version of *The Three Stigmata;* that Phil himself was manipulating these coincidences from some other realm, guiding me with psychic nudges into expressing his peculiar message.

But I needed more evidence to support a conclusion of this outrageous nature. (There is never enough evidence for a skeptic; that's the rule.) Once again, there was only one person I knew capable of answering the question of what was going on. So once again, I determined to write Alan Vaughan. This time, however, my scheme was more bold: What I proposed was a direct contact with Philip K. Dick, in order that he himself might answer my questions about the motives and means behind his dream connection.

III

"Have you dreamed about the Anarch since?...
We're told that in his previous life the Anarch occasionally
communicated with his followers through their dreams."
—Counter-Clock World

My decision to contact a professional medium began Phase III of this curious history.

But before you dismiss me as a prime candidate for the Home for Hopeless Lip-Diddlers, be warned: this history gets better. Or worse, depending on your point of view.

I was getting into this. I had gathered enough clues to piece together a theory. I had done what detective work I could, and was prepared to take that existential plunge into the belief-system I had created—or which had been created for me. As William Blake said in his poem "To God":

If you have formed a circle to go into
Go into it yourself, and see how you would do.

My rationale was simple. The dreams were a purely personal, internal phenomenon. I could relate them, but I could not share them. The synchronicities were physical events, observable by others, but still had to be tied together or explained by personal meaning—my meaning. The next step in this outward push toward external objectivity would have to be to remove as much of this personal element as possible. The use of a medium—the only instrumentality available—if successful, would provide a slightly more objective event than those that merely "happened" to me. A successful contact—a "close encounter of the third kind"—would be a *real event:* one that could be recorded, analyzed, checked, validated...and shared.

As I stated earlier, I have no problem with the concept of spiritual survival after physical death. The only major problem I had to grapple with was that I might be on the receiving end of the evidence...the fly trapped in the center of the web of synchronicity.

But really, what was I worried about? If my theory wasn't true, at very least I had a "stranger than fiction" series of synchronicities to spark my sense of wonder. And if it *was* true, all indications pointed to it being benign guidance. If it was true, I was perhaps the only one who could follow up on it, who could play detective in this ultimate "missing person case"; who would risk appearing a public fool for the chance to solve this mystery. And if I could get some external validation for the truth of my theory—perhaps even from Phil himself, through a reputable medium—I might be able to understand what was going on, which would benefit Phil Dick's following as well as me. Perhaps I could even find out *how* he was doing this, which could be a valuable contribution to parapsychology. And perhaps—maybe; just *maybe*—I could talk once again with my absent companion.

I decided to set aside the question of sanity and pursue the theory, until it collapsed or was proven. I was in such high, positive spirits (no pun intended) that I decided to attempt a contact with Phil myself. It was all a game, after all; I figured that as long as I had decided to play it, I might as well have some fun with it. If Phil Dick had so little trouble contacting his friends, maybe he was accessible to receiving them, too. I'd go right to the source, and ask him psyche to psyche if he'd like to attempt a medium-link contact.

I had no real idea how to go about this, but I did have a plan. On the night of October 24, 1984, I went off to bed to test my plan. Rather than mentally mumbling over the events of the day or those planned for the next while falling asleep, I created in my mind's eye a very vivid picture of myself in Disneyland. I pictured the park at night, empty save for me. I walked myself through the streets of this image, calling out Phil's name. I wandered over to the Haunted Mansion and got on the ride, still calling for Phil. I fell asleep.

I found myself in a large, lovely cabin, high in the mountains between Los Gatos and Santa Cruz—just a few miles away. Now, the hallmark of most dreams is the acceptance of the most outrageous situations as normal, and not questioning them with one's waking-world critical intelligence. But I was looking around this cabin, puzzled. What was I doing here? Then—in the dream—I remembered that this was the same location I had had my PKD character living in my detective novel, *The Coincidence Caper*.

No one was around in this archetypal dream home, so I lay down on a couch and fell asleep. Some time later I was awakened by my friend Chrissi (who was linked in this dream nexus twice earlier). Once again I was puzzled—this time to find myself in the same location as before I fell asleep within a sleeping dream.

At this point Phil entered the cabin. I was shocked to see his face so vividly. I asked him how he knew Chrissi, but he wouldn't answer. I wondered if he knew he was dead, and why she didn't tell him.

Phil just sat on the couch scowling at me with the same intense stare he had in life. I was uncomfortable; his look made me start. This was no ordinary dream: it was far too vivid, far too intense. Events in a normal dream flow, and the dreamer flows with them. This dream had movements which surprised me; motions which startled me. I knew I had something important to ask him.

But Phil spoke first. "Do you love me?" he demanded intensely.

"Completely and unconditionally," I replied without a moment's hesitation. "But don't get me wrong," I continued. "It's not a sexual thing. You and I made different choices in that area long ago: we both worship women. But I feel as close to you as two men can get; closer even than brothers." By this time I had quite forgotten my question.

Phil listened intently. He smiled; he seemed pleased.

A gray fog came rolling through the door and began to swirl around our feet as we stood there. The cabin—the "set"—began disappearing into the mist.

I was shocked. I was awake, wide awake and still in the dream. I knew what was going on, although I could hardly believe it.

"You..." I accused him, "you created this whole set, didn't you! The mountains, the cabin; everything! And now you're taking it away! *You've been in control of this whole dream, right from the start, haven't you!"* He just smiled a Cheshire cat smile and disappeared into the mist.

I started walking, following him through the thick fog. I found myself walking down a gray, fog-filled tunnel. Eventually I saw a rectangular opening at the end. A jet plane was flying slowly by—a 747; red and white. And there on the tail was Phil, holding on with one hand, and waving to me with the other. I stood at the end of the tunnel watching this, laughing.

"So long, bud," I yelled after him. "Come back soon."

I woke up laughing. Was it that easy to find him?

I never did get to ask him my question. But I got what I felt was another legitimate contact. Maybe that was the meaning of Alcott's third *I Ching* reading, the one in which he made reference to me: "The flying bird brings the message" ...and takes away the messenger.

That dream made up my mind: I'd write to Alan Vaughan and go ahead with my "high-flying" plan.

So here I was in Phase III, still getting phenomena from Phase I: the dream contacts.

The Phase II events—the synchronicities—continued as well.

On October 26, I wrote Russ Galen, Phil's longtime friend and agent, now agent for his estate, about purchasing the Dick story Paul Williams had sent me. Since we had not had any contact for over five years, I reintroduced myself, just to be safe.

On November 2nd, I received his reply. "I do remember you," he wrote, "to prove which I enclose a copy of a recent letter to Paul Williams which might interest you."

This letter from Galen to Williams (reprinted in its entirety in PKDS Newsletter #5) told the story of how PKD first came to Galen's attention: through our 1977 interview. "That interview," he wrote, "...had an extraordinary impact on Dick's work, and was also the key event in my own career as a literary agent...It was, and still is, the single most exciting first encounter I've ever had with the mind of another person."

(Galen's enthusiastic praise to Phil about his work, it seems, broke Phil's writer's block and enabled him to thoroughly rewrite the completed *Valisystem A (Radio Free Albemuth)* into an entirely new novel, *VALIS*—in which Briggs and I played a role as characters in Sonoma. Another circle had been closed.)

This letter went on to describe the development of Galen's association with Phil Dick, both professionally and personally, over the years. It ended with his stories of taking on K.W. Jeter and Tim Powers—Briggs' and my "alter egos" from *VALIS*—as clients.

What prompted Galen—seven years after he had read the interview—to write such an account on the very day I was busy writing my re-introductory letter to him?

The following day I received Alan Vaughan's reply. "How fascinating to read your letter about the Philip Dick project," he wrote. "It sounds like it's organizing itself.

"You ask me about my participation. I regret that I don't work as a medium to contact various spirit entities at will...I would advise that you contact a bona fide medium who does regularly contact the 'other side'—Shirley Black, who heads the Temple Foundation in Campbell..."

(Note: These names have been changed for reasons that will become apparent later in this narrative. I originally thought this change a clever rearrangement of the actual names: same initials, same sounding name, and the obvious joke built into Shirley "Temple" Black. Yet even this inspiration eventually fell into the realm of synchronicity:

(I spent eight hours on December 13, 1985, writing the following section on "Shirley Black," then drove out to the local newspaper, the San Jose Mercury News, *to deliver a freelance*

article. While waiting for my editor, I picked up a section of the day's paper in the lobby. Since it was Friday the 13th, they ran an article on superstitions, which included the line: "Psychic S—B— shares a superstition with former child star and ambassador Shirley Temple Black."

(Over a year later, my cleverness had caught up with me.)

Shirley Black... the name rang a bell. Then I remembered where I'd heard it: only a week or two earlier, while flipping through the TV channels at random one evening, a program caught my interest and I began watching it. It was a local documentary about Shirley Black on Alcatraz Island, hunting ghosts and picking up psychic impressions from the prison. "I was thinking about [Shirley] today before your letter arrived," Vaughan ended, "and now I know why."

I took a chance and looked up Shirley Black's Temple Foundation in the phone book. Strangely, I recognized the address. It was not, as Vaughan believed, in Campbell, a few miles away. It was, almost literally, right around the corner from my house.

The "Twilight Zone" theme began playing in my head again. I was getting used to it.

On November 7, I wrote Ms. Black a three-page letter outlining the previous events and suggesting the contact be attempted through her if she was willing. I typed the letter at home, but forgot to type an envelope. When I asked one of our departmental secretaries at work to type it as a favor, she recognized the name. "I took a class from her a couple years ago," she said.

"What a coincidence," I smiled in reply.

On November 13, my girlfriend stayed home sick from work. Not unusual; we each get a dozen sick days a year and usually use them. Most often, we sleep in; this particular morning, however, she got up and tuned in a San Francisco-based TV talk show, *People Are Talking.* Neither of us had ever watched the show before. Their guest that day: Shirley Black. Margie called later to tell me she'd videotaped it for me. I thanked her, and got up from my desk to go somewhere. As I passed the secretary who'd typed my envelope, she hailed me. "Someone told me Shirley Black is going to be on *People Are Talking* this morning." she said. "Too bad you can't watch it." I just smiled.

I came home about five o'clock that evening and put on the tape. While I was watching Shirley "read" for people in the audience, we got a phone call. It was some unknown man wanting to know if this was the Temple Foundation. *Twilight Zone* theme again, please.

Later I realized that this coincidence could be calculated mathematically. The Temple Foundation phone number has the same prefix as our home, but an entirely different number—all four digits are different, and only a single numeral was common to both. The chances of reaching us as a random wrong number would be one in 10,000. Sure, more people would be calling after a TV appearance, but Shirley Black is on local television regularly, and we'd never before—and not since—had this particular mistaken call. And what are the odds that a wrong number like this would be dialed while I was watching a tape-delayed replay of the very person the caller wanted?

We spent November 22nd, Thanksgiving, with Margie's parents. After a huge meal we retired to the den to watch a movie on videotape. Two hours later, when we turned off the VCR and the television image came on...there was Shirley Black on the screen, holding a seance on Alcatraz, in a rebroadcast of the show I had seen a few weeks earlier.

Somehow, Shirley Black was already linked into this nexus of events.

The following day, while searching the movie listings of the local paper, I stumbled across a small ad: Psychic Shirley Black Lecture, November 28. The address was the conference room of a local shopping mall. Since I had not heard from her in over two weeks, Margie and I determined to go to the lecture and hand-deliver a copy of my letter.

When I arrived home from work the afternoon of the lecture, there was a call waiting for me on my phone answering machine. It was Shirley Black's secretary, calling to inform me that Shirley wanted to talk to me. There was no indication whether or not she was interested in the project. By that time the Temple Foundation was closed, so Margie and I went to the lecture and looked up the man who had called. He knew little about the matter, but set up an appointment for Monday, December 3rd.

That night I told Margie the whole story. She has studied metaphysics herself, so she had little trouble accepting my experiences or my speculations —particularly since she witnessed the synchronicities involved in the creation of the book multiply almost daily.

That night I fell into a dead sleep; literally the first dreamless night in months. On arising, the first thing Margie asked was, "What were you dreaming about last night?"

"Nothing," I said.

"Oh yes you were. You were talking in your sleep. You woke me up."

"That's crazy," I said. "I never talk in my sleep." I never had, either.

"You were talking to Phil," she said.

"What?"

"Actually, you were just answering. I couldn't hear him, of course. But you kept saying, 'Yes, Phil… No, Phil… I know, Phil… Wait a minute, Phil; slow down...' and like that. You woke me up and I listened for a while, but I decided you were talking to someone you knew, so I wouldn't interrupt you."

I was baffled, and still am. All I know is that my sleep pattern was different that night—a solid six hours before waking, instead of the usual four—and that I was (so to speak) dead to the world for those six hours. And all I remember after that was an early-morning dream—a dream about *Blade Runner*. Were these more pieces of the puzzle? And if so...*what was he telling me?*

One other interesting coincidence occurred around that time. I had spent much of my free time in November transcribing and typing up the full eight hours of interview tapes for this book. When I finally finished, I pulled out my calculator to approximate the word count. My best-guess estimate: 30,594 words. Half the length of a short novel; not bad. I put the sheaf of papers in my desk and walked out to my car to go to lunch. I glanced down at the odometer and smiled. My exact mileage: 30,594.

IV

"This situation is very complex, Joe.
It doesn't admit to simple answers."
—UBIK

On Monday, December 3ʳᵈ, 1984, I met with Shirley Black at the Temple Foundation in Saratoga. A big, husky woman who towered above me, she exuded warmth and friendliness, smiling and laughing and holding my shoulder as if we'd been best friends for years. She took me back into her office, a tiny, dimly lit space crammed full of imitation Egyptian relics.

"So..." she said when we settled in, "how can I help you on this?"

I reminded her of my letter, outlining the highlights of the predictions, dreams, synchronicities and research. I asked if she was familiar with Philip K. Dick.

"No," she said, "but that's in my favor. This way anything I can tell you would be news to both of us. Things you can check out and verify. For instance—it wasn't the strokes that killed him, it was cardiovascular collapse." No mention had been made of the strokes. "That's something I can check out," I said.

"Please do," she insisted. "That's what this is all about." It wasn't until months later I found out she was correct.

She went on to tell me how intrigued she was with the amount and type of coincidences, which is why she decided to see me. "I get thousands of letters a week, but yours was brought to my attention," she said. "If you knew how difficult it is to get in to see me, you'd think it was a miracle that you're sitting here now. Of course, I won't charge you a penny for any of this. Don't spread it around, though." she chuckled. "As for the psychic contact, there's nothing about this that can ever hurt you. It can scare you, but it can't hurt you. People hurt you, not spirits."

We chatted briefly about Phil Dick's philosophical orientation, and how—because of this and because he was a writer—he might be able to give us a detailed description of the afterlife. He wrote about life after death before, I mentioned, describing his novel *UBIK*. She listened and nodded.

"That's very similar to what my guide has told me," she said. "'You are all dead and we're alive from our point of view,' she said. 'You're the ghosts in our world. We don't know we're dead. The only way we know we're dead is that we get reciprocation from the living.' So what Phil was trying to do was put forth that whole concept and do it in a reality format.

"You know his life was terribly unhappy," she continued without pause. "Terribly alone. Never found a real love in his life, my guide said. He had a very alienated childhood. Absence of both parental figures. If they were around, he wasn't aware of it. There was a maternal grandfather that he knew."

I said I didn't know that much about his childhood. But I believed his parents were divorced when he was very young, and that—if his story "Eye of the Sibyl" was truly as autobiographical as it sounded—his maternal grandfather did live with them.

"He was terribly afraid of violence," she continued. "Almost obsessive about it. Nothing about Phil was menacing. As a matter of fact, he was almost ultra-sensitive and soft."

This sounded like Phil to me. And she had tuned into a couple of things she couldn't possibly have known—the strokes; the family dynamics. I asked if she were picking this stuff up directly. "I have a guide that I reciprocate with," she explained. "She's talked to him to get proof positive of who he is."

"So he's still being interviewed, even on the other side," I laughed. "That's a wonderful thought."

"She can get contact from him, but I'd like to hear him in his own words," she said. "She's not as cut and dried as he would be, since he's lived here recently.

"She says he's sorry he didn't go into more medical. I don't know what that means. But he had a *very* strong thrust toward healing—wanting to heal; wanting to make better.

"He's got three books he wants out," she continued. I thought even then I knew the three books: mine, Ray Nelson's and the one Alcott informed me his ex-wife Tessa was writing. And all three of us felt we were getting guidance from Phil.

"Yours," she continued, "—not just 'cause you're sitting here, because that wouldn't help me one way or the other, or you, to tell you a story to make you feel better—but yours is the best. Because you're getting the direct reciprocation. I think you'll really skyrocket with this. And he'll become a cult figure."

I had one more question: Why me? Why was I chosen for this contact? Phil had several friends closer to him than me.

"No," she stated emphatically. "There were very few people he liked. There were a lot of people he tolerated. He was genuinely fond of you. The others were tainted by his own philosophy. He wanted someone more open-minded. He chose an untainted one...a novitiate in his cult group."

Well...the personal stuff was arguable, but there was no denying that she knew what she knew about Phil.

So: Would she be interested in performing a seance? Absolutely. "The multiple contacts, the numerous synchronicities, the quality of the reciprocation... This really entrances me," she laughed. "Literally."

We checked the calendar. December 16th was Phil's birthday, and it was a Sunday when we were both free. "That's great for me," she said. "Bring a tape recorder." And how much tape? "It could last a good couple hours," she said.

We shook hands and joked about the whole thing on the way out. "If you see Phil before I do," she laughed, "tell him Shirley says 'Hi'."

I drove home giddily. After all this time I was finally going to get some answers—and in less than two weeks. I marveled at the manner in which I had been nudged through this maze. And now I was just about to taste the cheese at the end.

Margie was as excited as I was, and planned to come along. The evening before our appointment, she called me from the bedroom to the living room.

"You ought to come see this," she said. Her five-year-old daughter was camped in front of the TV set, watching a *Laverne and Shirley* rerun.

"I hate this show," I protested.

"Just watch," she said.

The plot concerned the girls discovering their house was haunted, and holding a seance to contact the ghost. "Good sign, huh?" she smiled.

"Heavy ju-ju," I replied. "Shirley gets her ghost."

• • • • •

Sunday, December 16th, 1984—the 56th anniversary of the birth of Philip K. Dick—was gray, gloomy and heavily overcast. The streets, the trees, the lawn, the car—everything was slick from the occasional burst of cold rain. I packed a tape recorder, some blank tapes and my list of questions into my briefcase, and we bundled up and left. I kept thinking of that movie, *Seance on a Wet Afternoon*, and giggling nervously.

We arrived ten minutes early. The Temple Foundation was locked tight. No lights were on inside. I rapped at the glass door, in case Shirley Black was in one of the back rooms. No answer. I went around front to the main offices. Locked. No lights, no movement. Well, we were early. I went back to the car to wait.

Two o'clock, and no one arrived. Two-fifteen; still silent.

"Maybe she's just late," Margie suggested.

I checked around again, peering in and rapping on windows. Two-thirty. "Maybe she had an earlier appointment and it ran overtime," Margie tried.

I popped a note that we'd be right back in through the mail slot, and we got some coffee and warmth from a little restaurant in the building complex.

Two-forty-five: I checked again. The note lay untouched on the floor. "Maybe she forgot," Margie whispered.

Three o'clock. Quiet and still as a graveyard. Margie just looked at me and shrugged.

"Maybe she's dead," I said.

Time to go home—wet, cold, dejected. I left a last note: we waited over an hour; here's our phone number if you get in; we can be here in five minutes.

Nobody called.

I phoned her secretary Monday afternoon to find out what happened.

"I have no record of an appointment with you on Sunday," he said. "And Shirley *never* works Sundays." When I spelled out the details—including that I had a tape of our meeting and the setting of the date—he suddenly remembered that they had talked "briefly" about this earlier that day. "She just forgot," he said. "She has *so* much on her mind. And now she's *so* busy, I don't see much hope of rescheduling you." He sounded *so* sweet, *so* sympathetic—that kind of secretarial sympathy that's as shallow and cardboard as a dimestore get well card.

I tried explaining the emotional wringer I was being put through. I tried to explain how important this meeting was to finishing my book. I praised Shirley's compassion and abilities, and subtly hinted that most people would go out of their way to make up for the inconvenience of a forgotten appointment.

Supercilious sympathy was all I got. No, Shirley's fully booked for months. No, I'm afraid you can't talk to her directly. But you're more than welcome to pay $400 and attend an "open trance" session, where you'll be allowed to ask three questions.

Phil Dick sprang to mind again: I was talking to the door in Joe Chip's conapt in *UBIK;* the one that wouldn't let him out without paying a nickel. I was talking to an android.

But this was between Shirley and me. And if this, this *secretary,* insisted on wedging his way between us, I'd go to her directly.

I wrote a short letter that evening, cautiously expressing my disappointment. She *was* doing this for free, after all. And I didn't want to piss her off; I had no other leads.

I drove a copy of my letter out to her office Tuesday afternoon, assuming that if I mailed it, it would be intercepted by the secretary and she'd never see it. My timing was perfect; Shirley was just leaving the building as I drove in the parking lot. I rolled down the window as she walked by.

"I am *so* sorry about Sunday," she said without preamble.

"Well, that's OK," I said. "We all forget things."

"Oh, no, I didn't forget. I was in bed all day with food poisoning. But don't you worry—I'm still very interested in doing it. Just call my secretary and we'll reschedule."

Back to square zero. I already had his reply. But I tried once again, detailing my chat with Shirley. I might as well have taped his first response and played it back.

I wanted to cry. I wanted to punch something. I wanted to rush out to his office, slap him silly and shove ectoplasm up his nose.

And so, in the waning days of December, I had reached a dead end, with only frustration and anguish to show for my mad race through this macabre maze. I was left out standing in the cold rain— stood up, knocked down, worn out. And all I could see was the darkening of the light at the end of the tunnel.

•　•　•　•　•

1985 began as upbeat as 1984 was miserable. Margie and I vacationed in Rio de Janeiro—my first vacation in four years—and stopped at Disneyland on the way back, spending a day in the park with Alan Vaughan and his family. Over the next six weeks I arranged to write a feature article a month on home video for two different major newspapers; the *San Jose Mercury News* appointed me their video critic, with a weekly column; and I arranged with the local PBS television station to host my favorite series, Patrick McGoohan's *The Prisoner*. My writing career was picking up at a rapid clip—although hardly in the manner which I expected.

Just before I returned, Shirley Black had left on a three-week "psychic safari" in Kenya, and was therefore unavailable until late January. My own vacation and her absence, however, did tend to calm me down and soothe my grating impatience and ferocious frustration.

I got back in contact with her in late January. We had missed Phil's birthday, I wrote, but would she be available March 2nd—the third anniversary of his death?

Receiving no response after three weeks, I dropped her another short note in mid-February, once again querying the March 2nd date, and suggesting that if she'd lost interest, she might refer me to another reputable medium. And I returned to my other projects, waiting patiently for a reply.

Margie, however, was not so patient. She was part of this now, and decided on March first—and on a whim—to stop by an occult bookstore on her route home from work, in an attempt to ferret out some other reliable psychics.

When she arrived home, there was a message on the phone answering machine to call the Temple Foundation. Shirley Black had called while Margie was out looking for alternates.

Maybe this is it, I hoped against hope. The last-minute call to bring me in on March 2nd and finish the book.

When I called back, I got the secretary again. He explained that Shirley was swamped with work. She wanted to do the contact, but she also wished to wait until it could be done right, instead of on schedule. I reluctantly agreed, remembering as I did Phil's reply to the publisher who expected *VALIS* in ninety days: "Do you want the best possible book or the fastest possible book?" And I suspected, even as I agreed, that I was falling into the same trap in which Phil had placed his publisher.

In his case, however, he did intend to finish the book.

March 2nd came and went with no séance. On April 9th, I received a short letter from Shirley Black's secretary. "I know you stated you needed Shirley's input to complete your book," he wrote, "but at this time, that appears impossible. Also regarding another creditable medium to assist you in your endeavors, this is not possible. We have not heard of any other reputable trance medium...who could do this type of contact.

"At this moment, Shirley's schedule just doesn't permit any involvement with items outside of the Temple's needs."

We were literally down to the bottom line now; "the bottom line" being a business term for the accounting of money. I wrote back on April 11th with an alternate suggestion: book me as a scheduled, paying customer. "This seems a fair solution to both our problems," I wrote. "I could get the information I need at a specific time, and you could schedule me as a regular client rather than an outside project." This way, "we would both be supporting the Temple by generating extra revenue."

A month later, I received his reply. "Shirley finds it impossible to devote time to your endeavor...[she] feels it is only fair, to you, to be able to properly give sufficient time to do the project justice. And this she does not have.

"Please understand Shirley feels it is not the right time for her to be involved in your project..."

Totally stonewalled. Time may be money, but even my money couldn't buy her time. I was wasting my time.

In the meanwhile, my manuscript sat on the shelf collecting dust. Without a final chapter, I couldn't be sure that either the tone or the direction of the book was correct. With a slam-bang grand finale, the events could be written up to point inexorably in its direction. At the other end of the scale, with no further incidents, the project could be dropped entirely—written off as an incomplete quest, my own reverse paranoia and psychosis kept private. But, writing as I went along, the book could only be a disjointed journal: an archaeological collection of old bones, cataloged without the benefit of knowing how the skeleton was constructed.

Sadly, reluctantly, I closed the chapter on Shirley Black.

But even before she was through with me, I realized that in order to carry on at all, the time was right for exploring other avenues.

• • • • •

(Note: The reader interested only in narrative flow has permission to skip the rest of this chapter, while the author despondently ponders unanswerable philosophical questions.)

The whole Shirley Black affair was disheartening, at best. Not only was I left without a major medium, but I was stuck with a number of unanswered questions and philosophical anomalies. Why did she suddenly do an about-face, for instance? She rushed me in before dozens of other—paying—clients; she acted genuinely intrigued about the events and sincerely excited about the contact; she volunteered her efforts and her own free time. Why the 180 degree turn in interest and contact?

Several theories present themselves. The most obvious is fraud. Maybe she couldn't do it, and I'd know it. And write about it. But that didn't jibe. She'd proven her talents over two decades of mediumship—and had walls full of framed letters from writers and scientists and law officials attesting to her accuracy and thanking her for her help. I'd seen her in action myself, and she did OK. And what she told me about Phil sounded good. So that theory wouldn't hold too much water.

Maybe she had received some psychic warning to "drop the case." Maybe Phil's benign guidance did not include her. But there had never been any indication of this, in her initial contact, in our initial meeting, or in the later correspondence. Psychic contact "can scare you," she'd said, "but it can't hurt you."

There is always the cynical view. Shirley Black, from all accounts, always has the time to appear as a last-minute guest on local television programs, yet she didn't have two hours to spare for me. But my book was a tiny project, not likely to spread her publicity very far, nor to the right crowd. She could help me, but chose not to...because I couldn't help her. I hate this theory—not only because I liked her...but because it has happened so often in the past.

Maybe she really was home in bed with food poisoning that day, which would harmonize with my most likely theory: her secretary was blocking me. If she was actually sick, he had lied to me. And the longer he could keep me from her, the less likely she'd be to remember. Her interest would wane, or if she didn't hear from me she'd think my interest had waned. But once again, the question became: Why? Why was he blocking this contact? If it was to extort money from me, he'd had his chance—and passed it by. Maybe he thought he was just doing his job, screening people away from her—whether she wanted him to or not—and protecting her from overextending herself. All I knew for sure was that one of the two of them had lied to me about why she failed to appear.

For some reason, Shirley Black—or her secretary—or both— just did not want me around.

On the other hand, maybe the intensity of my intention and the obnoxiousness of the secretary were blinding me to the reality of the situation. Perhaps Shirley Black and he were, in fact, telling the truth: Shirley was willing and able...but not ready. Only time would reveal the answer.

Months later, another psychic suggested another possibility. He explained that there was a group of "narrow-minded scientists"—

including prestigious names like Carl Sagan and Isaac Asimov—who sought to pick up where Houdini left off, exposing fraudulent psychic and mediums. These self-styled "ghostbusters"—consumer advocates for the Aquarian Age—would plant clients with mediums, asking them to contact the spirits of nonexistent "loved ones" who had passed from this veil of tears. Perhaps, this psychic suggested, my case sounded too much like a set-up—after all, I *did* write science fiction—and the naive medium was cautioned against the contact by her staff.

We were back to fraud again—only in this scenario, the tapping-tables were turned: they'd think it was *me.*

Whatever the reason, the whole affair did seem suited to a work on Philip K. Dick: multiple theories; no final answers. And—after pondering the situation at length—I don't believe we can discount the information Shirley Black *did* provide merely because of her later flakiness. Some differentiation can be made between the two realms in which she operates: her strengths lie in the psychic world; her weaknesses in this one.

What bothered me even more than Shirley Black's erratic behavior, however, was the question of the synchronicities. So many had occurred pointing to her being the right person to make the contact: her proximity, the coincidental television appearances, the curiously-timed phone calls—all, I believed, led me right into her office. But the trail was a dead end; a red herring. Where, then, was the meaning in these meaningful coincidences? Or were they merely an end in themselves, rather than signposts? A year later, I still have no satisfying answer.

One possible answer to the first question was suggested by the psychic who clued me in on the "ghostbusters" group. "It seems as though the *quest* is the thing." he said. "Had you just waltzed into a séance and gotten a reading, you might not have been able to communicate the emotional intensity of the events as well as if you're put through some trials yourself. This could easily be a 'trial by fire,' to test your resolve and persistence—and to prepare you for expressing your emotions in a manner convincing to your readers."

What he said made sense, and harmonized with a point Alan Vaughan had made in his initial reading: "...more important than the writing [of stories inspired by PKD] will be your experiences with getting in touch with Philip K. Dick, shall we say...psychically." Hearing this from two independent sources made this theory a little more real, as distasteful as it was to me personally. But I was dealing with transpersonal events, which always involve some pain and frustration. And I was dealing with paranormal events, which always involve some mystery.

Whether or not his theory was valid, however, would depend on two things, neither within my direct control: the eventual outcome of these events, and the reaction of the reader to this history.

V

The time you have waited for has come. The work is complete;
the final world is here. He has been transplanted and is alive.
  —"Mysterious voice in the night"
  from The Divine Invasion

As I have already mentioned, on March first, 1985, Margie stopped in at a local occult bookstore attempting to ferret out a reliable psychic. She discovered that the owner's husband had himself been a trance medium before his death, and so she took an active interest in the field. She gave Margie a list of local psychics and mediums, who used the store as a meeting place, resource center and "bulletin board" to advertise their services.

Margie came away with three names. And, that same day, when Shirley Black's secretary informed us Shirley would be unable to perform a séance on Phil Dick's birthday, we resolved to try them out—while continuing to attempt to convince Shirley to participate.

Early in March, we called a young woman who had reportedly accomplished some trance channeling of her own deceased relatives. She was a novice, however, and had never attempted contacting anyone outside her family.

She had no luck in reaching Phil. She did contact an "entity" who she thought was Philip Dick, but was literally shocked out of her trance by him/it barking "No!" at her.

The only peculiar thing that happened that evening was that our mantle clock stopped while she was in her trance. I had wound it only hours before.

Our second attempt was made the evening of March 10th by Michael Bebeck, who represents himself as a "psychic counselor." Bebeck has established a creditable record for himself among the psychic community of Monterey and Santa Cruz, California, the area south of my own home, Silicon Valley. He gives readings, hosts his own radio show and teaches classes in psychic skills. Some of the classes he teaches are held in the bookstore where we first heard of him.

Bebeck was not the typical image of the ethereal, spaced-out psychic or the frail, pale medium. He turned out to be a robust young man with dark hair and a well-groomed beard, active eyes and a wide smile. He was expansive in his gestures and quick with his wit and laughter. Margie and I both took an immediate liking to him, and he seemed right at home in our living room.

I gave him a very brief and purposefully sketchy outline of the major strange events chronicled in this narrative. He knew nothing of Philip K. Dick.

When he felt ready to begin, he tested his tape recorder—only to find out that the batteries were dead.

"That's really odd," he said. "I just put in fresh batteries yesterday, and I haven't used it since."

I brought out my trusty recorder and plugged it into the wall socket. Now we were ready.

He explained a little about how he worked and what we could expect. He also had Margie and me do some meditative exercises under his guidance—visualizations which he claimed would relax us, put us in a perceptive mood, and at the same time "raise the energy level" of the room to enhance the possibility of a contact. They worked, and well. I was excited, and had a very strong positive feeling about the possibility of a contact. And the room itself seemed charged with electricity—not the metaphorical energy of enthusiasm, but actual, spark-discharging electricity. I could feel it flow from my palms, even when they were separated by two feet. Margie felt it as well.

Bebeck was ready to begin. He closed his eyes, rested his head and went into his trance.

The following is a transcript of the recorded reading.

(Note: In order to differentiate between Michael Bebeck talking and the entities channeling through him talking, I have used the convention of placing in quotation marks that portion of the dialog belonging to "Spirit" rather than to the medium. My own thoughts,

notes and background, added later, appear italicized and in parentheses.)

(Explanation of the "garbled" sections of the tape will be found following the reading.)

● ● ● ● ●

MICHAEL BEBECK READING
March 10, 1985

MB: What is your intent with your friend? What is it in your heart that you know you want to do?

DSA: He died at a young age; I have a feeling that his work was not completed on this plane. Plus the fact that my research suggests he has been in contact with other people, mostly through their dreams, giving them career guidance. So I'd like to find out what he's left unfinished, how he's accomplishing these contacts, and to what end.

MB: I'm hearing something else, too. I heard two voices, this one talking here and one behind it saying, "I want more of it. And I also want to be able to ask for what I get."

DSA: Yeah.

MB: It feels like there's no control. And it also feels like not everybody is understanding the information.

DSA: That's correct. I think I may be the only one at this point.

MB: And yet he doesn't give you as much as the others.

DSA: I don't know.

MB: It feels like people who need more, he's giving more to. He figures that you've got it more together...*(silence)*

I went in to ask him a question, and all I got was "No!"

(Curiously, this was exactly the same response that the previous attempt had elicited, only a week earlier. In that case, however, the strength of the objection knocked the novice right out of her trance state.)

(MB goes into a deeper trance.)

"I intend to illuminate my concepts with ideas I am formulating from this place. I come to work with people who are formulating creative pursuits of their own. My ideas were founded in thought. I wish to illuminate them with higher consciousness energy. So my work is to participate in that energy at the same time that I bring the concepts that I learned on this plane to them. My words are music, the sound of the melody of my enlightenment. I seek enlightenment that I may enlighten. Do unto those who inform others."

He was talking and I was repeating it. I don't know if the information came from him, though...

(At this point, one of Bebeck's other guides came through, speaking in an Indian accent.)

"There are several ways to experience what it is you are seeking. My suggestion would be to experiment. Be very playful and loving, and most of all very experimental. It does not matter which method you use. The process, the seeking, is what is important. Experience the process, and refine. Be very free form..."

All right, I've released that entity. He sometimes comes through with suggestions like that, but I didn't know he was going to come through with this. Let me try something a little different...I ask for information that suits the occasion. *(silence)*

The image that I got was you might push out a lot in the beginning. The first stuff might sound better to you, but the good stuff will come later. It feels like the process itself has to be very free-form. Then you go in and edit it in the way that feels best as well as sounds best. You could get lost in the phenomena. Let's face it, this whole phenomena is very interesting.

Do you have any questions about what we've gone over so far?

DSA: I guess my basic question is, Are we going to be able to contact Philip Dick?

MB: Yeah...for what he wants to answer. When I started out there, he was real stubborn. He's gonna answer exactly what he wants to. He's not real attached to telling you things. The key to this work is to ask, with loving intent from the heart. Always ask for love and knowledge. He's learning to bring the light to the word. That's what he basically was telling me. He's doing a spiritual schooling on that side, and his intellectual schooling on this side.

How about answering your questions now? You're gonna get a *lot* more information than you need. You're gonna get *so* much more that it's gonna be more editing than it ever is writing.

DSA: OK. First of all I'd like—

MB: He says right away, "I'll answer what I want to." I want to ask him something... Why are you so stubborn? *(pause)* This is really weird. "I want my privacy!" he said.

DSA: Ask him this: Am I on the wrong track—

MB: No. He comes through even before you finish and says "No."

DSA: Well then, couldn't he be a little more cooperative?

MB: "I am not here to cooperate. I am here to share. I choose the ones that hear the best; I choose who hears the trumpet."

DSA: Doesn't he want a chance to speak directly?

MB: "I am not concerned with words. I seek knowledge."

DSA: That's what I'm seeking, too. I want to explain to his friends what he's doing. Can we find out if it's really Philip K. Dick?

MB: "Yes. I am a multidimensional being and may impart my cosmos in many ways."

DSA: Can he describe the first contact dream he had with me?

MB: "It was the color you are wearing and came through your mind."

(I was wearing a bright yellow shirt, just as I saw Phil wearing in that dream. This was not intentional, merely comfortable.)

DSA: That's exactly right.

MB: I see the image of an airplane. Maybe a biplane?

(At the end of the October dream, where I first attempted to contact PKD on my own, I saw him fly away on the tail of an airplane. Thus, perhaps he was picking up both "first contact" dreams—him to me, and me to him.)

DSA: He and I have a hobby in common, too. Can he tell me about it?

MB: The image came through of a picture of a ball. I didn't recognize it. There were words on the ball.

(After the reading, I offered Bebeck some snuff, which comes in

a flat, round container about the size of a silver dollar. The words "Dean Swift Snuff" are printed on the front of the circle. "That's it," Bebeck said in response to my offer—and sneaky test. "That's what I saw when you mentioned your hobby."

(I had guessed this when Bebeck described the "ball." By this point, the "PKD entity" had scored direct hits for both my "identification" questions...and had even volunteered extra information based on a question I never expected was vague enough to yield two answers...both correct.

(I was pretty well convinced)

MB: *(continuing)* He said, "Don't concern yourself with my habits. Seek my knowledge."

DSA: I just want to make sure it's Phil.

MB: Ask him more specifics. He says, "Don't doubt the physical expression. It is the way that the information feels that is important. Do not focus on detail, but rather on energy. If your minds want satisfaction, I will give you that at a later date, both through yourself and others."

DSA: Can he tell me the message of my recent dream about him?

MB: The message, in essence, was of the urgency of your career. How to get it together. Sort of like guidance counseling.

(This was the exact idea and words I had been using to describe my theory of what I had discovered of PKD's contacts with other writers, delineated earlier.)

DSA: What is his goal in contacting his friends?

MB: To share his heart with them, in the only way he knows how, which is work.

DSA: How does he accomplish this?

MB: A direct channel through the intellect when the conscious mind is *(resting? Much is lost here on the garbled tape.)* He would energize their own concepts, so they'd think quicker. So a lot of what they got was their own stuff, energized by his impetus.

DSA: That seems to be true for the cases I've uncovered. I had the idea for my story for years, for instance, but never had a good middle or end. Then it all fell into place, almost overnight. Why does he choose to do this in their dreams?

MB: "It is the only state where you let your intellect down."

DSA: Are these contacts made because of unfinished business on this plane? Is it part of the overall blueprint of his life?

MB: No. *(Two sentences garbled)*

DSA: Who else has he contacted?

MB: A woman. Someone dear to him. A wife, or his daughter.

(Bebeck did not know that PKD had any children, or that he had multiple wives: "a" wife, he said; not "his wife.")

DSA: Any other writers?

MB: "Many that are here; many that are incarnate."

DSA: How do we appear to him?

MB: "As loving friends. No matter what the state of the body, we are still friends."

DSA: Does he see us; have images of us?

MB: "I have only vibration."

DSA: Has he manipulated the synchronicities?

MB: "I am not as potent as you think. I am merely an advisor. Do not make me a god."

DSA: It seems you've had great success climbing into people's dreams—

MB: "Many people climb into your dreams. You just see them as your own. Many contribute to *(garbled)* It is only that you know my vibration that you can identify me."

DSA: Well, you're welcome anytime.

MB: "I know that, or I would not come."

DSA: Do these contacts strengthen or weaken you?

MB: "They alter some parts and make them die to create others. It is like the process of plant growth. It is also like cellular growth, where certain cells join to create *(garbled)*.

DSA: Phil, you wrote about the afterlife as you imagined it in your book *UBIK*—

MB: "It is different than I imagined. I concentrated too much on the visual experience and not the vibrations. It was important for me to describe it and not feel it."

DSA: Are there any parts of *UBIK* which you feel are still valid?

MB: "Many. But there are many that I didn't know, many that I just suspected, and many that I only thought were true."

DSA: What's the closest existing philosophy you know of that would describe your current—

MB: "Gurdjieff."

DSA: Do you have any further insights into your experiences of March, 1974?

MB: "It was a primary experience to a wider field. I experienced the portals of my own passing on."

DSA: Which parts of *VALIS* and of your Exegesis seem most valid to you now?

MB: "The spaces between the words. The silent cadence in between the heavy overtones."

DSA: Do you have any further information regarding the birth of the new Savior, Tagore, or of his message?

MB: "He lacked the female balance."

DSA: Is he still in existence?

MB: "He was a composite of many *(garbled)*. He changes according to *(garbled)*.

DSA: Were you correct in your assumption that this person exists?

MB: "All things exist."

DSA: On the earth plane.

MB: "When we draw from the pollens of life, it fertilizes a blossom of many forms."

DSA: Phil, you're getting obscure now.

MB: "Obscurity is the space in between the words. Pollinization is the *(garbled)* and the blossoming. You need the parts of the seeds of what is alive to create new growth."

DSA: How long will you be around to inspire us?

MB: "I am changing forms from my persona on the earth plane to a higher consciousness. That that you seek will not be in existence much longer. I am refining and *(garbled)*."

DSA: How can we contact you, like you've contacted us?

MB: "By love, and requests with sincerity."

(Here we talked about who he has communicated with on the "other side": Bishop Pike, Jung, his sister and others.)

DSA: Can you describe your passing over?

MB: "It was the same as birth, in reverse."

DSA: When did you first realize that you were physically dead?

MB: "Before I died."

DSA: Was that part of your plan, to finish your work on this plane, then leave?

MB: "It was flexible till the end."

DSA: Was there a point where you could have chosen to stay alive and continue?

MB: "I may always choose. I always have freedom. I always will have freedom."

DSA: What would you have accomplished had you chosen to stay here?

MB: *(strongly)* *"More books!"*

DSA: You had plans for more?

MB: "I never planned to stop!"

DSA: Are you passing some of these plans on to your friends now?

MB: "They pass their own plans. I merely suggest."

DSA: I'd like to know why you chose me as one of the people you'd contact.

MB: "You're a receptor."

DSA: Is there anything else you want me to do for you?

MB: "Live in love. Purify your thought. And educate others."

DSA: Is there anything you want me to do for you personally?

MB: "I have no personal desires."

DSA: Do you have any insight as to why you appear to me so closely in conjunction with Disneyland and symbols like that?

MB: "The child in you is the most educated."

DSA: Can you give me any information that would convince others that this is a legitimate contact, and not a hoax or a delusion?

MB: *(garbled)* "...again to try to convince, we are in argument. When we let our hearts find it, we are in agreement."

DSA: Are you happy?

MB: "Emotions I do not experience as on the Earth. I merely flow, vibration and expansion."

DSA: Is that pleasurable for you?

MB: "Pleasure is not my goal. The light is my goal."

DSA: Anything else you want to say?

MB: "Intelligently approach your heart. Let the boy mature, but do not let the man hold back the boy."

DSA: That's about all, except I would like to talk to you again, if you agree.

MB: "Soak in a bathtub of this energy. Assimilate the information in this tape. When you feel you have felt it in its entirety and are satisfied, then seek the next level."

DSA: OK. I just want to let you know that I love you, and we all miss you very much.

MB: "This is not the end of the tape."

DSA: Am I right in assuming I'm a detective on this case, and I'm trying to track you down to find out where you went and what you had left to say to us?

MB: "You are a detective, you're a seer, and you're a curious little boy."

DSA: Will you help guide me with this book about you?

MB: "What else am I doing?"

DSA: *(laughs)* You're absolutely correct, and thank you. I feel your presence, and I enjoy it tremendously. I wish to continue it.

MB: "That's up to you to choose. But do not be impetuous."

DSA: I've thought this through, and you're welcome any time, in any form.

MB: "Alright."

DSA: And I'm not making a god out of you.

MB: "Yes, we were just going to say that...I have many forms, and many ways in which to communicate. Do not intellectualize my vibration...feel it."

DSA: The main reason I'm so interested in getting hard data and facts is to put it in this book.

MB: "You will get what you need. It is the vibration that convinces, not the word. Write from your heart, from your intuitive, creative knowledge. Then write to enlighten. Write from the tunnel of light. Follow the light in the tunnel."

DSA: And what will I find at the end?

MB: "Endlessness."

(As Michael Bebeck opened his eyes, ending the trance and the session, the tape clicked off.)

VI

There is no route out of the maze.
The Maze shifts as you move through it, because it is alive.
—VALIS

We chatted with Bebeck a while over tea after the reading, as he came out of the "jet lag" he said always followed his trances. And while we were sitting around relaxing, I tried playing back the tape.

Something had gone wrong. Somehow the tape had recorded at a slower-than-normal speed, even though the recorder only runs at one speed. When played back at normal speed, all the voices sounded like a coked-up Mickey Mouse. This has never happened before or since with this machine. Even Bebeck was perplexed.

"First my batteries go dead, then your machine slows down..." he mused.

"It couldn't have been my batteries," I said. "I had it plugged in the wall socket."

"We *all* felt that electricity in the room," he continued. "And the tape ran out exactly as my trance broke. It's almost as if the tape had to run slower to get the whole message on it..."

March 10th, the day of the reading, was a Sunday. Bebeck left about eight in the evening; Margie and I sat around for a while discussing the contact and the "electrical coincidences," then decided to watch some TV to relax before bed. Neither of us was in the habit of watching Sunday night television, so I just turned on the set to watch whatever was on.

The first thing that appeared on the screen was the black and white image of a Rod Serling imitator, part of a commercial *Twilight Zone* parody. And the first thing I heard was the familiar strains of the *Twilight Zone* theme. Somehow fitting, I thought.

The next show that came on, *Crazy Like A Fox,* had a plot that took the San Francisco-based characters up to Sonoma—where Phil had lived when I interviewed him—and opened with a totally gratuitous shot of a red biplane winging through the skies. (By gratuitous, I mean the plane did not appear again in that show and played no part in the plot. No explanation or further mention followed its appearance; it seemed to be there solely for "local color.") Once again, I thought of the *I Ching* reading: "The flying bird brings the message." And I was reminded of the "identification" answer from the reading involving the airplane.

During this show, a commercial break enticed viewers to stay tuned for the next program, *Trapper John, M.D.,* with this synopsis: "Messages from a deceased surgeon help Trapper John perform a delicate operation."

So there were three more synchronicities lining up within half an hour of one another. I thought back to the *Laverne and Shirley* episode Margie called my attention to the evening before my aborted seance with Shirley Black, and I began to get an inkling of how Phil might become convinced that he was getting messages from bubblegum rock: Here was I, tuning randomly into garbage TV and also receiving coincidentally meaningful messages.

(Now here's another interesting coincidence: I finished writing this section on Bebeck on a Friday in December, 1985. That evening, I was watching the new *Twilight Zone* program, which included a commercial advertising the next episode of *Crazy Like A Fox*...with Jack Warden dressed up in a surgical gown, cap and mask. I might never have realized that here was a variation on the same theme—similar images reshuffled into a new constellation—had I not reviewed this material that very day.

(Aside from this "clustering" aspect, this incident can almost be seen as a meaningfully coincidental echo, or as a synchronicity stripped of its original meaning. The significant content of the first cluster was missing entirely from this one: I *chose* to turn on *The Twilight Zone* this time, for instance; I did not have it thrust upon me; the series *Crazy Like A Fox* was, in itself, meaningless; the key point in the first cluster was the shot of the biplane; and the surgeon garb was irrelevant; the "message" lay in the phrase "messages from a deceased surgeon..." The cluster's *structure* had reappeared, but devoid of its vital *substance.)*

Yes, I am hedging and stalling, hemming and hawing, trying to avoid committing myself to the important point, the reading itself. And the answer to your question is: *Yes,* I sincerely believe that Michael Bebeck made an actual contact with the spirit of Philip K. Dick.

Most of my intellectual reasons for thinking this true are contained in my notes within the reading. The description of *UBIK,* the accurate mention of Phil's family, the initial stubborn rejection, exactly duplicating our first attempt to channel him—all give credence to the idea that this was indeed Philip Dick. Most convincing to me, however, was the fact that my "identification" questions were answered correctly. The airplane of my first contact with him, and the bright yellow shirt of his first contact with me...the spirit of Philip K. Dick passed my identification test with (dare I say it?) "flying colors."

But there was another side to this contact as well: the emotional side. Near the end, for instance, our tones were almost conversational: comfortable, communicative, friendly. The analysis of my own personality struck deep and resonant chords of correctness within me: "The child in you is the most developed." And a touch of Phil Dick humor shone through as well. "Soak in a bathtub of this energy," he said, prompting me to recall the bathroom graffiti of *UBIK:* "Jump in the urinal and stand on your head/I'm the one that's alive. You're all dead."

The new information—the information I never expected—was intriguing as well. The idea of playful, free-form experimentation was quite appealing, for instance, and served to alleviate much of the tension I had felt concerning this whole affair. This was *fun.* It was *supposed* to be fun! I was a detective, as I suspected, a seer, as I was attempting...and a curious little child. I was going to dig into this psychic mystery playfully. Only by being myself could the affair come to a satisfactory resolution. Maybe, just *maybe,* that's why I was "called" in the first place.

The new information was hopeful, too—"You will get what you need"—although not in the manner in which I expected: "It is the vibration that convinces, not the word."

Finally, the idea of Philip Dick energizing *our own* concepts—the already existent ideas of his contacts—explained a lot. My own story fell into this category, as did Sachiko's music and the novels of Nelson, Rucker and Tessa Dick. It was a pattern I had overlooked before, possibly because it slightly amended Alan Vaughan's initial theory that Phil would be "channeling" book or story ideas to us. "It's more like he's giving your own ideas a 'turboboost'," Bebeck said. This was *new data*—something which I had never considered, but something which fit the data—and something which Michael Bebeck had no physical way of knowing.

My belief that this was indeed an actual contact grew each time I reviewed the transcript. The more critically I reviewed it, the deeper my appreciation for the details became.

I became, eventually, about ninety-eight percent convinced. One percent was native skepticism, combined with a "wait and see what else happens" attitude. The other one percent was based on a lack of actual knowledge of the mechanics of this psychic realm. After all, since no one has ever really been able to present a coherent theory of psychic phenomena—a "unified field theory" of the mind—there may very well be some other explanation heretofore undiscovered. But in the absence of any such theory—and applying Occam's Razor to what I *did* have—the only valid conclusion I could draw was that the event was precisely what it appeared to have been: a medium-link with the entity known as Philip K. Dick.

Occam's Razor was one scientific principle I applied to this reading. But there was another principle of experimentation I could also apply: repeatability.

Thus began the further search: the search for a second medium and a second contact, in the grand hope of verifying the first.

The first stop was, once again, Alan Vaughan. In April, 1985, we exchanged letters. His reply to me was dated 18 April—and, curiously, I received a second, unexpected letter from him the next week, dated 24 April. Both, I recalled, were "dream story" dates, and the second, the date of a dream about Vaughan a year earlier. "In Santa Barbara there is a famous British trance medium, George Daisley," Vaughan wrote. "You may recall that he gave several successful sittings to Bishop Pike... I can also recommend that you contact the British trance [medium] Douglas Johnson... [he] did some excellent sittings for me."

Soon afterward I wrote them both.

George Daisley was not a familiar name to me, but Bishop Pike was. I knew that Phil had been a good friend of his; indeed, Pike was the model for Phil's "Bishop Archer" in his final novel *The Transmigration of Timothy Archer.* I had myself, years earlier, read Pike's book *The Other Side*—a fascinating chronicle of Pike's attempts to contact his deceased son, whom he had reason to believe was "haunting" him. Further, I knew that Phil had sat in on several of Pike's seances; perhaps even one of Daisley's sessions, I thought.

Daisley dropped me a card with his phone number and suggested I call, which I did on May 21st. He was very friendly, speaking loudly with a distinct British accent. But he was only vaguely helpful. No, he didn't know Philip K. Dick. No, Philip Dick never sat in on any of his sittings with Bishop Pike. "I'm sorry I can't help you on this," he continued, "but I feel that I'm not the one to make this contact. However, I know that they are listening from the other side, and are aware of your seeking. The message I get is that you should be patient and they will send the proper channel when the time is right."

Another false lead; another dead end. But at least a dead end with a signpost, pointing a way back through the maze.

Douglas Johnson's reply arrived the following day. "I certainly believe that on occasions one can communicate with the so-called 'dead' by 'dreams'," he wrote. "These may well not be dreams, but out of the body experiences that are recalled when you are awake… I would be happy to give you a reading although you must realize that I cannot guarantee to contact your friend. Sadly, we cannot call up the next world. I will try…I only hope it is successful."

I sent him a blank tape cassette, my list of questions—the same one I used with Bebeck—and a check a few weeks later. And at the end of July, I received his reply: a letter with my uncashed check enclosed.

"I regret that I have not been able to contact your friend," he wrote. "I think you will find it impossible to get clear answers to your list of questions. Communication is alas, not like that, seldom 'cut and dried,' and so much is given in symbolic form (rather like dreams)…I certainly wish you success in your quest but doubt if *any* psychic would be able with certainty to get more than a vague approximation of what you hope."

Well…Johnson was partially right, in my estimation, but partially wrong as well. Bebeck did get through, I believe, but much of what he got was in symbolic form. Another dead end.

In August, Margie and I spent a "get away from it all" weekend in Capitola, a small town between Santa Cruz and Monterey. And who should walk into the little cafe in which we were having Sunday brunch but Michael Bebeck. We reintroduced ourselves and he remembered our seance. "It was very interesting," he said. "But I don't think I'd want to try it again." I was getting dead end rejections without even asking!

Two things kept me from being discouraged, though. The first was another interesting coincidence that occurred on July 6th. The mail that day brought me two items. One was a copy of *Video Review* magazine which carried my first published magazine article—the peak of my career as a writer at that time. The other item: a copy of *UBIK: The Screenplay,* by Philip K. Dick—his book about life after death. If Bebeck was correct about Phil giving a "turboboost" to my career, this synchronicity seemed little less than a major wink from Philip Dick.

The second encouraging item was that there was a hallway in this maze I had yet to travel. The third name on the list of psychics that Margie had obtained in March was that of Kevin Ryerson, who split his time between Santa Barbara and San Francisco. Ryerson is best known for the role he played in Shirley MacLaine's best-selling "spiritual autobiographies," *Out on a Limb* and *Dancing in the Light.* He describes himself as a "trance channel in the tradition of Edgar Cayce and Jane Roberts," with over a dozen years of experience as a psychic. Unfortunately, because of the publicity he'd received from MacLaine's books, he was much in demand. I had phoned his message machine on April first and had been put on a waiting list. Months later, I still had not heard from him. I had no recourse, though, other than to be patient and hope for the best.

Early in October, Paul Williams, founder of the PKD Society, and Andy Watson, editor of the PKDS Newsletter, spent the afternoon at my house stuffing Newsletter #8 into envelopes. Joining us was Jim Purviance, who was there to include in each mailing an ad for a small-press book he was publishing, Richard Lupoff's *The Digital Wristwatch of Philip K. Dick.*

"Sounds interesting," I said, recognizing Lupoff as among those writers Ray Nelson saw Phil inspiring in his dream. "What's it about?"

"Well, Lupoff got this idea that when you die, your consciousness can transfer to the nearest object with an electronic chip in it, like a digital watch, and live on for a while," Purviance explained. "So his story is about Phil's life after death."

"Oh," I said.

I didn't get around to actually reading Newsletter #8 (Sept. '85) until a week later. In it was a list of stories which dealt with Phil Dick's afterlife—enough that Philip Jose Farmer labeled this "a new genre." There was also an offhand reference to Briggs and me in an interview, and another irritating mention that Tim Powers is "widely acknowledged" to have been the model for the character "David" in *VALIS*.

I had this strange feeling of *deja vu*. Wasn't it exactly a year ago that I came away devastated from Newsletter #4? Just a year ago that I first read of Powers' claim to be "David"? That I resolved to write my own book? And now, a full year later, Philip Dick afterlife stories were becoming "a new genre," Powers was being "widely acknowledged" as "David"...and I was still lost in the maze, banging my head against the dead ends; still doing research on events that could permanently modify viewpoints of both these opinions.

If the events of the previous October were echoing—repeating in a weaker form—so were the emotions of that time. I went to bed that night with the same feelings of futility and frustration as those of a year earlier. The solution then seemed to be starting this book. The solution now seemed to be finishing it. I was running out of patience.

The following day—six months and two weeks after my initial request—I got a call from Kevin Ryerson's secretary to set up an appointment.

VII

*"I got through to you—all of you—every chance I could, every way
I could. I did everything that I had the capacity to bring about.
Damn little. Almost nothing."*
—UBIK

I was happy to be back in business again. But for some reason I found myself unable to get excited about the appointment. I tried, but there was just nothing there. I might as well have been going to a job interview for all the enthusiasm I could muster.

November 22nd—the day of my appointment, and the 22nd anniversary of the assassination of John F. Kennedy—was a true San Francisco winter day. A cold, bitter wind swept through the streets; overhead, gray clouds were slowly turning black, threatening rain at any time. I was a few minutes early for the 2:30 meeting, but I rang the "Ryerson" buzzer outside the locked gate of the apartment building anyway. There was no reply. Well, maybe he's still with his earlier appointment, I thought. I tried again. Still no answer. Maybe he's just out, and will show up on time, I thought. Yeah, that's it. This won't turn out like Shirley Black.

Forty minutes later, I was still blowing on my hands to keep warm and pressing a cold, callused finger to the buzzer every five minutes, in case he was asleep, or had entered through some back entrance. It was a long drive from San Jose, and I determined to persist. I did not relish the thought of driving back empty-handed. About this time a neighbor came along and opened the gate. I explained my situation, and, while she would not let me in, she agreed to check Ryerson's apartment. Maybe the buzzer was broken; sure, that's it. She buzzed down on the intercom: no answer, no noise, no lights. He's not home, and don't bother me again.

I tried one last-ditch attempt, phoning the apartment from a payphone in the hospital around the corner. No reply. I drove home, determined to do my own exposé of flaky psychics.

Actually, since I had no great expectations, I couldn't feel too much disappointment. Mostly I wondered just how often this was going to happen. Two major psychics, two broken dates. Soaked and frozen.

I called Ryerson's Santa Barbara number the next day. "What happened?" I asked.

"Well," his secretary said, sounding a bit embarrassed, "he says that by his watch, he was there on time." A wide range of possible retorts came to mind: Christmas is coming soon, maybe he could use a new watch; I'm operating on PST, Pacific Standard Time, but he seems to be operating on WPT: Weird People's Time; and so on. But I bit my tongue.

"He does this occasionally," she explained. "He'll go out for lunch and lose track of time. You know how psychics are. They only live about halfway in this world." I said I really didn't know how psychics are, but that I was learning—the hard way. And what were we going to do about it? "Well, we've had a cancellation," she said. "Can you make it at 9 a.m. on December 9th?" I said I could and we confirmed it.

On Sunday, December 8th—the day before my rescheduled reading—I spent the morning, as usual, over coffee and the Sunday paper. The local magazine section of the paper ran an interview that day with Shirley MacLaine—the woman who had boosted Ryerson to national recognition. And I learned that her birthday was April 24th, which, curiously, was a key date in the dream-state story I believe I collaborated on with Philip Dick.

Later that afternoon, standing in line at the supermarket, the headline of a tabloid newspaper caught my eye: "Family Videotapes Dead Mom's Ghost." This immediately reminded me of my first contact dream: I saw Phil on the monitor of a closed-circuit video camera set up to entertain the guests at the memorial gathering. These printed coincidences gave me a little more hope that Ryerson would be helpful—or would at least show up.

On December 9th, at 9 a.m., I rang Ryerson's buzzer. He buzzed me through the locked gate and greeted me at the door of his second floor apartment.

He wasn't what I expected from reading MacLaine's books. He reminded me of myself, actually: mid-30's, a bit overweight and in need of a haircut. He had a big smile and a friendly, casual attitude. We chatted about the weather, and he took me into his "work room": a smallish room with bare wood floors, furnished only with a china pantry, a naked table and two folding wooden chairs.

Ryerson's readings last two hours. The second hour is his trance reading, and in the first hour he discusses with his clients how he works and reviews their specific questions and interests. He said I should go first, and I spent about fifteen minutes filling him in on the background of my experiences—cautiously avoiding mentioning anything for which I wanted trance answers.

He was intrigued. "This really calls for some free-form experimentation, I think," he said; the same idea—and the same words—Bebeck's guide had used. I was getting intrigued as well.

"I know you speak through a guide," I said, "but do you think we could get through directly to Phil Dick? Channel him directly?"

He was unsure. "I *do* do that sort of thing," he said, "but I don't advertise it. In this case, though, it definitely warrants a try. I can't guarantee anything. It may take me more than one session. Our best bet is for you to ask my guide directly when I'm in trance."

We filled up the hour talking about related subjects, only occasionally tying them to Phil Dick. We established that he was only a few months younger than I, and that we had both begun our interest in psychic phenomena in high school. I had originally intended to go into parapsychology, and had graduated from college with a BS in psychology—just about the time I got side-tracked into writing. Now the two careers were intersecting in a manner I could never have predicted.

Once we established that I knew something of the subject, we were free to speak a little more deeply about it. I was fascinated by some of Ryerson's theories on astrology, telepathy, mediumship and hypersentience, many of which he had obtained from his trance guides. I was excited about talking to an intelligent, insightful and knowledgeable thinker and listened carefully, occasionally sharing my own theories and opinions. He seemed pleased that I was capable of grasping some of his more esoteric ideas.

About 10 a.m. Ryerson decided it was time to go into his trance. We turned on and tested the tape recorder, and he began, closing his eyes and shuddering slightly.

Although Ryerson was himself interesting to talk to, his reading was far from satisfactory. What I desired was a channel for Philip K. Dick; this he could not provide. Instead, I spent the best part of an hour talking to Ryerson's guide, "Tom MacPherson," an amiable 16th century Englishman (he claimed) who spoke in a raw, robust British dialect with heavy emphasis—and volume—given to the end of each sentence.

MacPherson could only claim a "rudimentary" contact with PKD, but suggested that another attempt "on some future date" could be successful. Unfortunately, he was unable to answer any of my "identity questions" posed to PKD—the same questions Michael Bebeck had answered with uncanny accuracy—so I had no real evidence that he was even in "rudimentary" contact with Phil.

I can't, of course, blame or fault Ryerson; seeing him was a longshot in my estimation, and I attended the sitting hoping only to get some "psychic insight" into my experiences, and Phil's. It was disappointing, though, to get so little of what I expected, and to find out that he had the ability to channel discarnate entities, but was unable to do so with Phil. The reading is worth digesting into a few highlights, however.

MacPherson agreed that PKD was "most definitely" contacting people through their dreams, in an effort to "stir up his old friends" and "provide much of the inspiration that they wish to have in their works."

"The network of individuals whom he is carefully pulling together," MacPherson continued, "will prove to be more than just writers and authors. They will be *doers*... I do believe your Philip Dick [has] ambitions of hoping to see some of the concepts and world view that he had in his works actually come to fruition in the social order." (This is an interesting comment to compare with Ray Nelson's similar sentiments in his essay "A Dream of Amerasia," and with Phil's final public message, the "Tagore" letter—for which, see Appendix III.)

On the matter of further contacts, MacPherson said that I should "look for one more direct evidential contact," although I am not sure whether he was suggesting or predicting the next step in my quest.

At one point I expressed concern over my present dilemma: Should I publish my book now, or hold off, waiting for a second contact, or a more concretely evidential event—which might never occur?

"Quite frankly," MacPherson said, "I would publish the work now. Mr. Dick would like the work published—even in the form it's currently in. The work is one of keen interest.

"I highly doubt you're going to receive ironclad evidence," he continued. "Mr. Dick took care of that in advance. For instance, there was some talk of a hoax surrounding his physical passing." (I had discussed this with Ryerson before the reading.) "The key thing is that this was brought off so you would not get too hung up on evidential issues yourself, in the sense that with the hoax of that rumor, even if you were to produce a materialization of Mr. Dick before the President, Congress, the Pope, the Queen and Carl Sagan, they would merely accuse Mr. Dick of having faked his own physical passing, as rumor had it.

"It's almost a contradiction in terms to look for concrete evidence in something that's a phenomenon of energy...The key thing is that you already have the concrete knowledge. The weak point is the so-called concrete evidence.

"There was a certain audience for this material already, and [your book] will give that audience reinforcement as to the experiences you are now having. And you have had bags of experiences. [Accepting them] depends on one's standards of evidence."

As to Phil's "mystical experiences," MacPherson advanced the theory that they were, in part, influenced by a "collective" of discarnate writers—among them Verne, Welles, Dickens and Bacon—who were "in many ways [trying] to stimulate him into applying his well-developed authorship skills into the realm of the paranormal and the collective effect on the social order. He was realizing that the so-called hard, physical sciences had been exhausted as a subject material for his fiction. This interest in the more mystical realm was an attempt to interface the so-called psychic experience with the realm of speculative fiction, with the purpose of seeing how the psychic sciences or mystical experiences could enter into his works and eventually act as a blueprint of the social order. Not unlike the works of Jules Verne, leading to direct inspirations of flight, submarines and so on." This "writer's collective" theory is one that— to my knowledge—Phil never developed, nor does there seem any evidence in his experiences that this was the case. But it did sound a bit like Alcott's *I Ching* reading: "He flutters down...together with his neighbor." And if this theory was somehow correct, then Phil is now just doing unto others what had already been done to him!

Most of the rest of the reading was either too vague to be of use, or was just a rehashing or reiteration by MacPherson of what Ryerson and I had discussed prior to the reading. In closing, MacPherson discouraged me from attempting my own contacts with Phil, as "the intellectual effort hinders" contact. (This may or may not be correct, but—as will be seen shortly—was certainly relevant.)

The Ryerson reading was also accompanied by a few unusual occurrences. Before they can be fit into the context of the narrative, however, it is necessary to backtrack a bit.

Once my first appointment with Ryerson was broken, I resolved to attempt another contact with Phil Dick on my own. I began—as I had over a year earlier—"programming" my dreams before sleep, hoping for a contact similar to the previous one.

I started on the 29th of November. After three nights of trials with no results, on December 2nd I dreamed of being in a haunted house. I took this as an encouraging sign; that's how it had all started before, after all.

The following night, I remembered two separate dreams—both of which took place in the same mountain cabin as my original self-initiated contact dream. In two nights I had digested months of earlier work. Surely I was on the right track...and yet, there was no sign of Phil. I determined to continue...to take the next step.

The following night, December 4th, I dreamed I was a detective, on the trail of a serial killer. I found a body in the hallway of an apartment building, and entered the apartment. Inside were stacks of bright yellow magazines, much like *National Geographic*. The spines were marked like *National Geographics* as well, all reading "United British Isles Kingdom" in bright red letters. A radio announced the name of the serial killer (not PKD), and this was followed by aerial shots of a huge skyscraper, glowing orange through the windows; glass walls illuminated by sun and fire. Even within the dream this reminded me of the skyscraper shots in *Blade Runner*. Inside this building, Phil Dick was revealed as the killer, dressed as a doctor prepared for surgery, in a light green mask, cap and gown. He was preparing to do an autopsy on a body—my body.

I woke up just before he touched the scalpel to my face. I lay there in the dark, vacillating between panic and triumph. It was all right there: me as a detective (even investigating post-death events); the bright yellow magazines with the acronym "U.B.I.K" on the spines; the *Blade Runner* references (based on the novel *Do Androids* Dream...); and, finally, the vision of Phil, glowering at me as intently as he had in my earlier contact.

On the other hand, there were all those sinister elements: the serial killer, the fire in the building, the impending autopsy. Maybe I was being scared off, I thought. Maybe I wasn't supposed to get through now.

I went back to bed and had two more dreams. In one, I was on a secret mission: I had been hit with a "pink beam" of light giving me instructions, and I went to a graveyard to disinter some person. I was also convinced that Kevin Briggs—my partner in the Phil Dick interview—was trying to kill me. In the second, I was frustrated because I couldn't get into Disneyland. Even when I won a handful of bright yellow entry passes, it only led to a fight with Margie.

So there were most of the rest of the dream symbols (Disneyland, the bright yellow color), combined with new Phil Dick-related images (the "pink beam" of VALIS), and carrying over the deathly and sinister imagery of the previous dream. And maybe there was the message: I couldn't get into Disneyland, where my first contact took place.

What intrigued me most was the "payoff" of the first dream—the glimpse of Phil at the end, dressed as a surgeon. It finally dawned on me that this "surgeon" image was a recurring symbol, one closely connected with these Phil Dick occurrences. There was that odd series of coincidences following the Bebeck reading, for instance, which included the commercial promo about receiving "messages from a deceased surgeon." And in my initial attempt to decipher the "calendar code" by matching dates to dreams, there was that dream of April 18, 1983 about a surgeon who cloned himself to die, return and explain the afterlife. Now it further became clear that this "surgeon" was indeed Phil himself— something that harkened back to Shirley Black's comments, "He's sorry he didn't go into more medical...He had a *very* strong thrust toward healing."

What this surgeon symbol "meant" I did not know. Maybe it had something to do with the fact that the original novel *Blade Runner,* by Alan E. Nourse—from which the PKD film borrowed the name—was about a surgeon. Or maybe a clue lies in this quote from *VALIS:*

"VALIS had fired healing information at us, medical information. VALIS approached us in the form of the physician..." Or maybe not.

On a similar note, what did the three appearances of "Chrissi" in this dream nexus "mean"? Even though in two dreams she heralded Phil's appearance, her presence seems inexplicable—irrelevant but for the seriality, the meaningful repetition. Maybe this had something to do with the fact that Phil had a son named "Chris"— who was the subject of the "medical information" fired at him by "VALIS" in his mystical experiences.

Or maybe these images didn't "mean" *anything* in themselves, I thought; maybe the important thing was that *any* set of symbols recurred so synchronistically. Perhaps they were merely a structure, denoting that there was meaningful content to be found wherever they clustered. The images are not the message, just as in a book, the words are not the emotions to be conveyed.

The Ryerson reading was five days later. When we were finished, I drove back to Sunnyvale to work—just in time for lunch. After I ate, I pulled out a paperback I was reading, a few pages a day, on my lunch break: John D. MacDonald's *One Fearful Yellow Eye*. I was reading my way through MacDonald's "Travis McGee" detective novels, in no particular order, during those months, and had started this one a few days earlier.

I began where I had left off, on page 128. On page 131, MacDonald mentioned Kurt Vonnegut. Odd, I thought; Vonnegut never really became popular and "hip" until a couple years after this book—written in 1966—was published. Ryerson and I had talked briefly about Vonnegut, as well—as had Phil and I in our interview. Too bad there's no message for me, I chuckled.

The last line of the next paragraph was this: "O speak to us from beyond, Great Surgeon."

Very funny, I thought. But not worth mentioning—even in a novel with "yellow" in the title. "You'd see any coincidence as synchronicity in this state," I told myself. "You're just fishing for material."

A couple pages later, when McGee launched into a monologue about hypersentience—as Ryerson and I had discussed a while earlier—I had to remind myself of this again. "Your mind is drifting," I told myself. "You're just fishing." Five pages later—just when I decided to stop reading and go back to avoiding work—this line caught my eye: "Once, long ago, I went drift fishing with friends..."

Maybe I was fishing for coincidences. But five in less than twenty pages? In a book which contained no others, before or after that section? In a series of novels in which I had never found one before? And in the small slice of the book I read immediately following the Ryerson reading—and only days after I discovered the "surgeon" symbol? Maybe I was fishing. But I had hooked a big one. Or maybe I was the fish, getting hooked.

A few days later, I spent all morning working on the Ryerson transcript, still puzzling over all this material. I wandered out to my car to go to lunch, but was blocked at the first intersection by a huge red and white truck. My first thought was that it was a Coca-Cola truck. My second thought was of the plane in my Phil Dick dream. As I pulled closer, I could see the white in the red was a word, a single word painted on the side of the truck: RYERSON.

VIII

"...I don't hold the same relationship to the regressed world that the rest of you do; you're absolutely right: I know too much. It's because I enter it from outside, Joe."

"Manifestations," Joe said.

"Yes. Thrust down into this world here and there. At strategic points and times..."

—UBIK

Like tides rising and falling, the Phil Dick activity subsided for about three months. In late March of 1986, it began to pick up again.

On the night of March 23rd I had two dreams. In one, I was working on a truck which belonged to Harrison Ford, star of *Blade Runner*. I broke a door mechanism, but realized this was a dream and I could change the events in it.

In the second, I picked up a *National Geographic*. On the cover was a sepia-toned photo of Joanna Cassidy (also in *Blade Runner),* surrounded by jungle cats, and the headline for an article on *Blade Runner*.

The three *Blade Runner* references reminded me of Phil, naturally, but the *National Geographics* reinforced the connection. *National Geographics* played a role in the 4 December 1985 PKD dreams. And later, when checking out other dream activity, I discovered I had dreamt of a *National Geographic* on 15 December 1984—the night before my aborted reading with Shirley Black. The presence of these *Geographics* might be meaningless if, say, I dreamed of the magazine regularly anyway. But the fact—based on perusal of over eighteen years worth of dream journals—is that *these were the only times* that *National Geographics* had ever appeared in my dreams. And all three appearances were in the immediate proximity of PKD activity. Here was another image like the "Chrissi" and "surgeon" images: meaningless in itself, but meaningful in its contiguity to Phil Dick material.

The week of 5-11 April, 1986, was rife with PKD activity.

On 5 April, I dreamed I was "hanging out" in a suburban house with Phil. We were having a fun time, laughing and joking. We sat down at a kitchen table and grabbed each others' wrists in a gesture of solid friendship. I told him how happy I was to see him, and asked if he'd heard the rumors that his death had been a hoax. He got a good laugh out of that. *"Hear* about 'em?" he said. "I *started* 'em!"

On 7 April, I had two long dreams with no real plots, but each involving Alan Vaughan, Shirley Black and Robert Anton Wilson. Vaughan and Black had discovered something monumental, which I read about in the newspaper. Vaughan was my boss and ordered me to print up some books. Later they sent me to a library, where I picked up a book entitled *The Man of Gold.*

On the night of 11 April, I had five dreams. By dream research standards, I remembered virtually all of my unconscious imagery for that night. One was brief and irrelevant, but the four which followed were long, vivid and interrelated.

Very briefly, in the first I was at a farmhouse with a group of people who thought I was dead. I had written my own obituary, and when these people read it and asked if it was correct, I said, yeah, I wrote it myself, and they laughed. So I knew they were just pretending I was dead by ignoring me. I saw a message from PKD written on a wall: "Dear Scott: AOUR," it began, then spelled out some sentence about telling others, or thanking them for listening. I knew it was a message from Phil that I could pick up only because I was in the *UBIK*-like "half-life" of being considered dead. I thought, within the dream, that "AOUR" was perhaps a misspelling of some word, or a combination of words, and that AU and OR might be closer to the real message.

In the second, I was in a school which looked like a huge indoor shopping mall. I climbed a narrow square-spiral staircase; from the top, I spotted Phil Dick below—dressed as Santa Claus, complete with a sack of presents slung over his back. I pointed him out to a friend, who agreed it was Phil.

In the third, I met a man from Sacramento who was having the same kind of PKD experiences I was having. He gave me a piece of paper on which he had written a message from Phil Dick he'd gotten in a dream the previous night. Within the dream, I knew that I had gotten the same message on the same night. Now we had some external validation, I thought excitedly…but I forgot the message.

In the final dream, I was looking through the bookshelves in a store and found a reissue of an old paperback by Philip Dick. I had never heard of it before, but grabbed it and knew there was a message in it for me—it said so in writing on the cover. The cover itself was colorful, streaked with glowing blue and pink like melting pastels on a TV screen. The title of the book was a short word which I could not quite make out: *AULIS, VAULIA* (like *VALIS?*), *AULIA, AURIA,* or something similar. The capital "AU" stuck out, though.

Common elements clearly emerge. In three of the four dreams, I received a written message from Philip Dick. And in all four, I had "external validation" of PKD and his messages.

It was during this same week that the synchronicities began again, too—sometimes overlapping the dreams.

Two days after the above dreams, for instance, Margie asked me to move some furniture. When I did, I discovered a book I had thought lost for over a year; an English paperback edition of *The Hitchhiker's Guide.* Although the title is different, the color cover was the same as I had seen; a unique wash of blue and pink melted pastels with a background pattern as if it were a photo from a TV screen.

Another instance of synchronicity revolved around the third recurrent detail of this dream series: the combination of letters "AU." Although within these dreams and on waking analysis I could not remember the messages from Phil, this forgotten content seemed far less important than the idea that I was getting a written message at all. But this "AU" combination stood out in two of the three written message dreams—and was implicit in the "Santa Cl-AU-s" image. Anything appearing this often, I felt, must be something important. I considered it might be "AV"; these are Alan Vaughan's initials, and transposing them on the dream-book title might yield *"VALIS."* But I didn't want to stretch what I *did* know far enough to distort it. The synchronicities were organizing themselves quite nicely without my conscious intervention, and there is, to my mind, a vast difference between interpretation and manipulation. The former could be detached from an accurate accounting of these phenomena; the latter would invalidate this very accuracy, and had to be avoided.

The only other association with "AU" I could come up with was that it is the chemical symbol for gold. (Curiously, the leftover letters from the first "AU" dream—OR—also mean "gold," in French.) That rang a bell in my mind: only four nights before these dreams, I had dreamt of another book with "gold" in the title: *The Man of Gold.* Could this be a reference—or two—to Philip Dick's short story collection, *The Golden Man*? I dug out my copy to check. Although years ago I had been inspired by Phil's introduction to the book, I found nothing in that piece relating to these current events. So I turned to the story entitled "The Golden Man," and read it for the first time. The title character was named "Cris"—and had the ability to see into the future.

So here was a fourth repetition—at least in permutation—of the "Chrissi" image, combined with prediction: Alan Vaughan's major talent. These two people had connected before, as well: in my dream of 24 April 1984—which was itself a key date in the story Phil Dick "inspired" in the June, 1984 dreams. (As if this isn't enough of a coincidence, the other dream connected to a "dream story" date—that of a surgeon cloning himself in order to die, return and explain the nature of life after death, on 18 April 1983—was preceded that night by two other dreams. One concerned a detective; in the other, I was watching a total eclipse of the full moon. When the dark disk passed, the moon had been transformed, I wrote in my dream journal the following day, into a "beautiful glowing gold.")

This image of a "golden man" we have already come across in this volume, too: as the "golden race" of Apollo mentioned in the closing poem in "The Eye of the Sibyl." This poem, a translation of Virgil's *Fourth Eclogue,* further plays a significant role in *The Transmigration of Timothy Archer*—as evidence of Bishop Archer's "transmigration" after death into the mind of another person.

The web was still weaving symmetrically, I thought—and may finally be yielding some meaning. I was once again assuming the role of the detective, tracing these clues back first through my associations, and then through Philip Dick's.

(In early July, long after all this was written, I was reading a book entitled *The Art and Practice of Clairvoyance* by Edward C. "Ophiel" Peach, a Los Angeles-based magician. In it he discusses the occult nature of the "light" which appeared when the God of Genesis spoke the words "Let there be light"; a discussion which includes this line (the emphasis is his): "This light, whose Hebrew name is AOUR, is the living, fluidic GOLD of Hermetic Philosophy."

(This was the very word I had dreamed, and all in capital letters, just as I had dreamed it. *AOUR:* a word in a language I never knew, and a word which itself means gold—the metaphoric gold of the alchemy—appearing along with other dreams also full of gold symbology.

(My experiences now were paralleling Philip Dick's, to a minor degree: more than just dreams and meaningful coincidences, I now had *real data that I did not know, either consciously or unconsciously,* entering my sleeping mind. It seems somehow fitting, too, that this word means "light," given the numerous coincidental repetitions of the "light" metaphor in this material, as in the frequent appearance of the phrase "the darkening of the light," and PKD's insistence in the Bebeck reading that "I seek the light."

Two other instances of synchronicity occurred during that same April week.

On the evening of the 11th—the night of the four PKD dreams—Margie had me collect for her every photo of Phil I could find, so she could choose one to use as a model for her dustjacket. She chose one from an old PKD Society Newsletter issue, and I agreed it was the best one for our purpose. Surrounding the photo was an excerpt from Phil's massive "Exegesis"; when I read it, I discovered three iterations of images from these events. "Although we remain unaware of supernatural entities they guide and direct us," read one quote. Another commented that "we live as children and choose as children," reminding me of Michael Bebeck's reading, in which he called my quest that of "a curious little boy." The excerpt ended by saying that trying to find the "real purpose of life" is "a dream and a guess and a search among mists" echoing my search for him among the mists in my dream of October, 1984. Not every one-page excerpt of Philip Dick's works speaks directly to me three times. And the dreams that night *were* about receiving a written message... Perhaps this quote acted in some sense as a "disinhibiting stimulus"—a term which Phil used often in writing about his own experiences—initiating the dreams.

The other interesting coincidence occurred on April 7th. While driving home from work, I saw a new sign at a local junior college announcing an upcoming lecture by Shirley Black. And when I arrived home, the day's mail included a copy of the Canyon Press chapbook "The Digital Wristwatch of Philip K. Dick"—Richard Lupoff's tale of Phil's life after death. (In it, Lupoff writes a clever ending in which PKD plays a joke on him by writing the story under Lupoff's name. The irony here—to me, at least—may be that although Lupoff thought he was writing fiction, the joke may be just as he wrote it: if Vaughan's original predictions and Ray Nelson's dream are any indication, PKD may have indeed inspired the story. Curious, too, that in our interview Phil based one comic vision of his own afterlife on an experience he'd had with Lupoff...

(Later, near the end of June, just as I was finishing writing this essay, I obtained a copy of the other "PKD afterlife" story, "The Transmigration of Philip K.," by Michael Swanwick, published in the February, 1985, issue of *Isaac Asimov's Science Fiction Magazine*. Throughout much of the story, a "gray fog" creeps and lingers at the fringes of "reality"—as in my October, 1984, lucid dream where the "set" disappeared into a gray fog. One scene of this story has a businessman activating a clone of himself, similar to my 18 April 1983, dream of a surgeon cloning himself; and at the end of the story, "Phil" tells the central character "you came through with flying colors"...the same phrase I used a year earlier to jokingly refer to my correctly-answered identification questions after the Bebeck reading. Add here another thread to the web.

(In addition, the May, 1986, issue of *Locus* contained an item that writer Michael Bishop had sold a novel entitled *Philip K. Dick Is Dead;* a novel in which PKD is called a "pivotal character." By the time this is published we can *all* compare my experiences to his fiction to see if there is any overlap. And readers of this volume may very well read Bishop's book in a new light...)

As early as January of 1986 I received a few meaningfully coincidental "written messages" from PKD—in a sense. January saw the publication of *Radio Free Albemuth*—the alleged "first draft" of *VALIS,* but a radically different novel, and the most recent novel that PKD had completed when Briggs and I interviewed him. In addition to the quotes I've used to preface parts of this article—quotes tailor-made for these experiences—I found some other curious parallels between 1977's *Radio Free Albemuth* and my own novel *The Coincidence Caper,* written in 1981—a novel in which Philip Dick plays a role as a major character.

At the end *of Albemuth,* for instance, the first book written by the "evil empire" for the Phil Dick character to endorse is called *The Mind Screwers;* in my *Coincidence Caper,* much of the plot revolves around a book entitled *Operation Mindfuck. In Caper,* I have my Philip Dick character writing a book about subliminal transmissions from satellites to televisions—something discussed in *Albemuth*. Also, the idea of the government influencing propaganda through novels is common to both books.

None of these things are in *VALIS,* the rewritten *Radio Free Albemuth*—and this early draft was not available for reading. I couldn't have read these ideas and stolen them; likewise, Phil never saw my *Coincidence Caper*. These were independently developed ideas, undiscovered by me until nearly a decade after Phil wrote *Radio Free Albemuth*...a project originally titled, appropriately enough, *To Scare The Dead*. Did I "tune in" to Phil's *Radio* through *Coincidence?*

Uncovering these things in January spurred in me the strong desire to finish this book—to wrap it up and release it.

To accomplish this, I redoubled my efforts to obtain a second evidential contact. And just as the dreams and synchronicities overlapped, so did the synchronicities once again overlap this outward push to find a medium.

I wrote Kevin Ryerson, putting my name on his waiting list, for instance. When I didn't hear from him in nearly four months, I called his San Francisco number on April 24th. A recorded announcement said, "This machine is on announce-only from April 24th through May 18th..." Missed him by one day—a dream story/"calendar code" date. I called him on this date because it was significant to me. I never expected it to be important to him as well. But it meant he was in Santa Barbara, out of my touch for several weeks. Judging by the time schedule on which we first met, I realized that it would be at least two months—and possibly much longer—before I could get with him again, far too long to wait for the timely completion of this manuscript. Strike one.

In February, I wrote to Shirley Black again. Perhaps after a year, I thought, her schedule had loosened up, or she'd changed secretaries. It was a long shot in the dark, but who knew? As Dr. Brown says in *Back to the Future,* "I figure… what the hell."

I received her reply in early May. She remembered my situation and our meeting, but reiterated that she was "presently committed to my own goals and until they come to fruition, I must delay other considerations."

Strike two. But this was basically what I had expected, based on past performance, so I wasn't too disappointed. Mostly I was just trying to tie up loose ends. I already had several other lines of inquiry going, including one brand new one.

In early March, while looking through some old PKD Society Newsletters for a piece of information, I chanced across a reference to a woman named Francie Steiger, the wife of writer Brad Steiger, who writes books on the paranormal. She was also a friend of Phil's and is herself psychic. According to this Newsletter entry, she was evidently the psychic who phoned Phil to warn him about his health upon her receipt of a copy of the "Tagore" letter (as related by Phil in Rickman's *The Last Testament)*. I thought that, as a friend of his, she might be interested in these experiences, and that, as a psychic, she might be more open than most to considering them seriously. My main motives in writing her, though, were to query whether she or her husband might be able to put me in touch with mediums Alan Vaughan was unfamiliar with, and to ascertain whether she, as a psychic, had experienced any of the dreams, synchronicities or other Phil Dick-related phenomena that I—and others—had experienced. (Interestingly, Ryerson had, months earlier, recommended writing the Steigers on this first point—even though neither of us was aware at that time of this personal link between Francie and Phil.)

I called Vaughan to see if he knew her address; he did, and insisted on giving me her phone number as well. Although in a different state, she has the same three-digit prefix as I do (and Shirley Black does). Once again in my mind's ear I heard the familiar strains of the *Twilight Zone* theme.

Following this, I dug up a brochure for a psychic seminar that Vaughan had sent me a couple years earlier; I recalled she had been in attendance, and wanted to check the correct spelling of her name.

The pamphlet also contained her picture—side-by-side with Alan Vaughan's. I was glad that I didn't have to pay royalties every time I heard that tune.

Later that same evening I opened the *UBIK* screenplay book to the point where I had, months earlier, left off reading: page 104. On the very next page, the character "Francy Spanish" tells her "UBIK dream." I had to laugh. Here was Phil's fictional "Francy S." relating a dream about life after death—while I was attempting to contact Phil's real-life friend "Francie S." to query her about my dreams of his alleged life after death. And this only seven pages after Joe Chip took his ride in another recurring image: a "red and white Curtiss biplane."

As of August, however, I had received no reply from Ms. Steiger. Strike three.

But I wasn't out of the ballgame yet. By the time of most of these rejections, I had moved into an entirely new inning.

My fourth and final effort also began in March. Once again I wrote Alan Vaughan, requesting a reading about these events. Although he had stated early on that direct contact with discarnate entities was outside the scope of his abilities, I thought I might put to use his long suit, prediction, to determine whether or not there was to be another evidential contact, in what form it might arrive and how long I might have to wait for it. Such information, I felt, could aid my decision about when to publish this history.

His taped reply arrived on April 18th—a significant "calendar code" date... and a day on which I was in Disneyland, yet another recurring thematic image.

The tape contained one of the most hopeful turns of events yet. "You're concerned about a second Dick contact," he began. "Quite possibly my guide, Li Sung, might be able to do that. He recently has had some success in doing this sort of thing. We'll see what we can do there."

On April 24th I sent Vaughan a package of material that he requested to aid in his contact attempt: a photo of Phil, an autograph and a signed letter, and my list of questions. The night before I mailed this package I had a curious dream, one more concerned with thinking than with action. I dreamed I had just returned home from Disneyland, and sat down and read two stories about Philip Dick's life after death. Lupoff's was one; in the other, Phil had discovered a cure for death. While he was thankful for being able to discover this, he was also saddened that he could not share it with more people.

I wandered down a hall of this dream house to the bathroom, thinking about how to write the final pages of my essay. Mentally, within the dream, I worked on a paragraph which, in its final form, read like this; "Do I believe I actually had contact with Philip K. Dick? Yes. But can I expect—or even ask—others to believe my experiences? Sadly, the answer must be no. I can here only report my own experiences and express my personal interpretations. But without any hard factual evidence, I will understand if you remain unconvinced." The dream ended with me thinking about writing Alan Vaughan to have his guide Li Sung channel PKD (a decision I had already made in waking life).

The significances in this dream gradually became apparent to me. The "written message" of the second story, for instance, seems clear: if my chronicle is convincing, Philip Dick has indeed found a symbolic "cure for death": evidence that we live on past our physical demise...although presented to a limited audience.

The awareness of a more subtle significance of these recent dreams dawned on me as well. The first foreshadowings or "preverberations" indicating the first dream contact with PKD were the dreams of mid-March, 1984, where the Disneyland Haunted Mansion was built as a suburban house and I went through the kitchen. Seventeen days later came the first contact, in the Disneyland Haunted Mansion. And now here I was, after two years, leaving Disneyland—both symbolically, in the dream, and literally, only days before—and returning to the kitchen of a suburban home, to discuss with Phil the death hoax that triggered these events in the first place...and—seventeen days later—wandering through this house, writing in my dream the conclusion to this chronicle. The events—and even the time schedules—were recurring in mirror image. I had come full circle. I was walking back through Alice's looking glass into the "real" world; I was, symbolically, "bringing it home." An end was near.

The only question that remained to be answered was whether this interpretation was correct. Would Alan Vaughan be able to get through?

IX

"I came back to this world.
From the next world. Out of compassion."
—The Transmigration of Timothy Archer

This idea of coming full circle with these experiences—symbolically, in the dreams, and possibly in real life, if Vaughan, who predicted them, could contact Phil—was driven home by a dream on May 3rd. In this dream, I was sitting in a dimly-lit bedroom of a rural house, writing down a very important dream in the failing light. This dream-within-a-dream concerned having to take a written test to get into Disneyland. I dated this internal dream "3/23/86"; it seemed vitally important to get that date on there and remember it, and I traced over the numbers until they were thick and dark and deeply inscribed on the page. When the "darkening of the light" of the room was finally complete, I went downstairs and out of the house, where I ran into Margot Kidder. She told me she had been living with Harrison Ford since October, and then went off to milk some cows, illustrating to me the proper method to do so. In a later dream that night, Joanna Cassidy appeared briefly.

Cassidy and Ford were, of course, both in *Blade Runner.* And my final contact with Phil Dick before his death concerned his new love for Margot Kidder. *(See "Phil As I Knew Him" in this volume.)* When I had a chance, I went back to my dream journal and looked up March 23, 1986. As described earlier in this narrative, my dreams of that date contained similar imagery: Harrison Ford and a reference to dreams within dreams in the first; Joanna Cassidy appearing later on. The wheels within wheels were still spinning; the circularity was becoming explicit—and, once again, I was dreaming of a written message of great importance...this time, my own dream.

(Please do not get the mistaken impression that I see anything psychic or mystical in the process of remembering my own previous dreams within a dream. My unconscious memory may have worked better here than the conscious process—I had to look up the dreams of this date when I awoke before I consciously realized the parallels—but memory is still just memory. The significance seemed to be the reference to PKD material in a dream with similar imagery; a "reminder," reinforcing the idea of a closing circle—and the idea that this material was important enough to require repetition. As we shall soon see, this turned out to be the case.)

This "feeling concept" of an end drawing near—of the circle of experience closing—was also indicated in a dream of May 11th. In it I was watching a surgeon perform a brain transplant. When he finished, he said to me, "That closes the crystal ring." Here was yet another appearance of this "dream surgeon," now finishing his operation—the same operation he had started on me on 4 December 1985?—and gravely pronouncing the closing of the circle. Was he perhaps transplanting *ideas* from one "brain" or mind to another?

On May 17th I dreamed it was Christmas Eve. I was gathered with friends and family and everyone was in good spirits. On June 3rd—seventeen days later—I dreamed it was Christmas Day. I was at my family's old house, and found numerous presents under my bed. The following night, I dreamed once again that it was Christmas. Once again, I was celebrating with family and friends, and this dream ended with us starting to open our presents.

The following day, June 5th, Vaughan's reading arrived in the mail. *This,* I realized, was my present...a present from the Santa-garbed Phil Dick of my 11 April dream; the only glimpse of Phil I'd caught in a night rife with written message/external validation dreams about him. I had dreamed of celebration parties, as in the first contact dream; I had found my presents under the bed in which I sleep and dream; I had seen a red and white suited Santa who carried on the color scheme of airplane dream, *UBIK* biplane synchronicity and more (and doesn't Santa, too, fly through the sky?); I had seen a secular Santa symbolizing a religious holiday of the birth of one who would eventually be resurrected. My present had arrived...I hoped.

I flicked on the TV and sat down to open Vaughan's package. On the screen appeared an old rerun of *WKRP;* an episode centered around newsman Les Nessman's adventures as an aerial traffic reporter—flying in an old red biplane. I opened the package and looked at the tape. The label gave the date of the sitting: May 31— the same day I had received Robert Anton Wilson's afterward to this volume in the mail.

Dreams, symbols, synchronicities, readings...they were indeed all coming together, occurring virtually simultaneously. I had achieved, within one day, an overlap of all three categories of material...*if* Vaughan's reading could give evidence that he had in fact channeled Phil.

It is you, dear reader, who must be the judge of that—to yourself, at least.

•　•　•　•　•

ALAN VAUGHAN READING
May 31, 1986

The following transcript is an edited version of the Vaughan sitting, which totals about sixty minutes of tape. Some material has been deleted for space considerations; this consists mostly of repetition, personal comments directed to me and vague flowery prose with no relevant content.

I was not present at this sitting; Vaughan worked from a prepared list of questions read to him by an assistant. I could not, therefore—as with the Bebeck and Ryerson readings—pursue any new or different lines of thought, nor get clarification on what was said.

In his trance channeling, Vaughan acts as a vehicle to allow his oriental guide, Li Sung, to speak through him. Occasionally some words were indistinct; I have filled in these small gaps as best I could interpret from the sound and the sense surrounding them. These interpretations are indicated in the transcript as italicized words in parentheses, as are my own comments.

*As in the Bebeck reading, this is not Philip Dick "speaking through" the medium. In Bebeck's case, the channeled entity spoke to him and he repeated what he heard; in this case, Li Sung is doing the listening, repeating and interpreting. However, as with the Bebeck transcript, when Li Sung is directly quoting what he hears from this entity, I have enclosed the words in quotation marks. The questions read by Vaughan's assistant are denoted **Q:**; the answers from Li Sung/Vaughan are denoted **A:**.*

And now, as Rod Serling might say, "Presented for your approval..."

This is Alan Vaughan, doing a trance channeling for Scott on the case of Phil Dick. Soon my friend Li Sung should be coming through, we hope, and he will attempt to make contact. *(silence; in Asian accent)* Good afternoon! We are pleased to be joined by your presence once more. And what may we do today?
Q: I have a list of questions for Philip K. Dick.
A: Let us first see if we may find Philip K. Dick. *(silence)* Well, he is going to be evasive today, because this is a test.
(This is the same response we received with every channeling attempt.)
Let me see if we may bring some pictures from him to you, hm? *(silence)* He sits; he is dressed in a most casual way. He fashions clothes much as he wore on earth. And he draws sentences somewhat. He writes, "Scott, I'm really excited that you're doing this project." He has a little bet going on, you know? With those who stated that it would be very difficult to do. But he is trying to prove point.

Well perhaps now we may begin, for although there is not perfect alignment, there is presence of his energy here and we will try to utilize that energy in response to your questions. Please, what is first question?
Q: Can you describe the habit we had in common?

A: Well—little joke here: "breathing too much," hm? Let us see...he writes little note here; let us try to see if we may read it...Well, this is another of his jokes. He says, "Going to the bathroom by yourself." *(chiding)* Mr. Dick, please, we are trying to be serious here, hm? *(silence)* We see little metal object... *(I would like to think that the combination of the "little metal object" and "breathing too much" combine to implicate a snuff tin and the strong inhalation necessary for ingestion, but I'm afraid that might be stretching these images a little too far.)*

Well, we are not certain at all that you are to receive here the response that you wished. Perhaps later more will come of these questions.

Question next, please.

Q: Can you describe the dream I had in which you first contacted me?

A: We hear a cry of protest: "Please do not let him go on like this; this is like interrogation!" Nevertheless...there is Mickey Mouse laughing. He says, "Remember Jiminy Cricket's song..."

(Here is some Disney imagery, though not specifically Disneyland, as in that dream. But the song? "When you wish upon a star, your dreams come true.")

Well, there is some confusion here about why this transmission. Mr. Dick indicates that it is a little like trying to send a code by shaking an oak tree, hm? To see how many acorns fall off.

Question next, please.

Q: What is your goal in contacting us?

A: "My friends," he says, "you have been chosen to relegate authority and information about the status of the coming changes. For this happening is to be recorded in the annals of your writings that no man shall go with eyes darkened when he should see the light."

(Another permutated echo of the "darkening of the light" image which has dogged the footsteps of these experiences from the very beginning.)

"It is, we fear, a difficult thing to believe that our world can be in contact with yours. Many persons will dislike intensely the idea that we of our dimension could appear to them or in any way influence them. Scares them shitless, hm? Well, that is of little interest to us. However, you should realize that the prophecies of the changes were made in earnest, and do, we believe, reflect the future state of your physical world. *In memorium* is a phrase we would have used for those who do not pay attention, hm?

"Currently there is a fire which burns dangerously on the earth and is harbinger of more disasters of atomic fire. The nuclear fallout can be destructive to many. There may be in the near future three more such disasters and they will presage the brushfires of war, of Armageddon. Yet we pause in our communication to remind you that the purpose of prophecy is to prevent such things from happening."

(This reading took place during the days when the meltdown of the Russian Chernobyl nuclear reactor was much in the news. And yet, it was this same subject—the nuclear insanity of our times— that occupied Philip Dick's thoughts during the final days of his life. The "Tagore" letter (see Appendix III), Phil's description of a vision of the new savior, "his body wounded by radiation as a living symbol of the nuclear ravishing of the planet," indicates this clearly.

(Even though Philip Dick denied the role of science fiction writer as prophet, the two instances in which he violated this principle are curiously relevant here. The "Tagore" letter is one example; the other can be found in The Book of Predictions, *published in 1980 by David Wallechinsky, Amy Wallace and Irving Wallace. In this collection of predictions from celebrities and psychics (including Alan Vaughan) PKD wrote about the year 1985: "By or before this date there will be a titanic nuclear accident either in the USSR or in the US..." — missing the actual instance by only a few months, six years in advance.*

(Current events regardless, the message of this reading clearly echoes PKD's final public message: a prophecy of the dangers of nuclear madness.)

Question next, please.

Q: What enables you to make these dream contacts? Do you have some special energy or knowledge that makes this possible?

A: That is easy! In your mind, it is like a great ocean with fish swimming about. So we merely have to lure the fish in our direction. We do not have to create the fish. So we blend with that wild energy of yours and bring influence to what is already going on. You must understand that when we appear in your dreams we are utilizing *your* vehicle; it is not one totally of our own construction. So we come and we go and we hope the message is heard, but it is because of you, and because of the open energy that you provide, that we are able to penetrate somewhat. There are expressed within your consciousness symbolic meanings which perhaps interfere a bit with our intention, but they are nonetheless *(like ripples in the water)*, an unavoidable problem.

(Here is perhaps an explanation for the meaningless but recurrent images —Chrissi, surgeon, etc.: they were contents of my own mind which gravitated toward these "contacts" as iron filings cluster and pattern around a magnet. Inferring that a contact had been made by looking at these clusters of symbology would thus be akin to deducing a boat had passed by looking at its wake.)

And question next, please.

Q: Are you manipulating the synchronicities too?

A: Perhaps we have not answered the question before in the way you might have wished, so let us proceed then to this process of communication. I am somewhat offended by your use of the word "manipulation," for that is not the case at all, but rather Dick, in conjunction with other spiritual beings, form a group, which together fashion a plan of life through—and with the cooperation of—your group. And so we are partners in the enterprise, not manipulators. We are a collection of *(souls connected)* by spiritual means—like a spider web, you know? And so it is in your world also. These collections are made so that each person is in the right place to carry forth his part of the plan. You are like the strangers who have come together on a cold night and warm their hands before the fire. They all share the fire, but none has manipulated it.

Question next, please,

Q: Can you describe your current state? Specifically, how does it compare to the afterlife in *UBIK?*

A: *UBIK*…a nondescript kind of place, but had a few features of the physical world. But now Mr. Dick realizes that there is an infinity of beauties, of joys, emotions and, indeed, of choices. *(This is expanded upon at length.)* Or sometimes he thinks, "Twinkle, twinkle, little star—where the hell are we?" That is because there is no "place" here, see?

What is question next, please?

Q: What is the closest existing book or philosophy you came across that would describe or explain your current state?

A: "Well," he says, "I fondly read and reread *The Bible,* trying to make sense of that mad scheme; trying to taste the texture of the holy words. But I found only tears *(and gall).* There was so little hope. The Book of Revelations appeared more like a vulture about to land on the *(carcass)* of civilization. That was not philosophy that I wanted in my heart. I wanted a braver world that would be beyond the ordinary, that sought information from highest sources, and that painted with words the wisdom of the ancients that blossomed into flowers of glory. Oh, I should have been a poet, you know!"

Q: Do you have any further insights into your experiences of March, 1974? Specifically, which parts of *VALIS* and of your "Exegesis" seem most correct to you from your new viewpoint?

A: Try to understand how human consciousness functions in a multidimensional way. It is necessary to realize that the senses confine our *(perceptions).* If you had full senses and full sensations, you'd probably explode! Too much information!

In March of '74 there was a period of dramatic and impassioned insight; of opening the valves of the senses beyond the physical. Mighty perceptions, strung together in telegraphic wire of perception. Oh, yes, sometimes we were accused of being somewhat out of our minds, hm? Well, we were not out of our minds at all—we were in another mind, in another universe. We side-stepped into the strata of higher becoming and being, and so we were able to appreciate all things at one seeming glance; pulsating messages, telepathically beamed.

(This does remind me of Phil's experiences as detailed in our interview. The "other mind" of "Thomas"; the flash-cut artworks appreciated all "at one seeming glance"; his theory that these were "telepathic transmissions" by Russian scientists or "higher being" aliens.)

The writings were merely reflections of sense perceptions and not perceptions of the self. Are these writings worthy as we look upon them now? The writings are...cockroach heaps, you know? They are worthy, but they are not the answer. They seem somewhat puny. But nonetheless, we are pleased to think that they are as good as any written by those in the flesh on this topic.

Question next, please.

Q: Do you have any information regarding your concept of the new savior or of his message?

A: Just a moment...Mr. Dick has smile on his face. He says, "When I got here, the first thing I did was ask, 'Where's Christ?'"

(Now that sounds like Phil!)

"And everywhere I looked there was Christ. Each person seemed to be a mirror of Christ. But then I realized that perhaps there are a whole universe of Christ spirits incarnating. The savior is a hope; a spirit that exists in potential in every human heart."

Q: How long will you be inspiring us? Are you planning any more revelations?

A: That's a laugh! He has been attempting to get through to some very beautiful but very thick heads. He chuckles with long drawl, "This is fucking hard work!" But he says he is up for it, for getting through the difficulties. He is being trained somewhat to do this communication. It may take him a while before this process is perfected. But he will see you, Scott, as you sit with lady medium, and you will be able yourself to sense his presence, his energy. In the coming fall there will be appointment in which you will be making this contact, as will he. There should be three contacts in all, for the purposes of this first little test plan. You see, this is sort of a test project.

Question next, please.

Q: What insight or information could you relate to me to convince others that our dreams of you are legitimate contacts, not a hoax or a delusion?

A: Just a minute; Mr. Dick is writing another note... "Remember to tell him about the bathysphere." Some instrument for going down to deep depths of water. Like being observer; one who cannot interfere in the ocean but one who is merely looking about the great depths of water.

(*"...it is like we are underwater: not in a dream...but in a tank, being observed" thinks Angel Archer while pondering Tim Archer's transmigration.*)

Oh, this is like great depths of the mind. We sense—rather, his energy indicates—that so it is with him; that he cannot interfere with your personal destiny, but that he is keeping an eye on you from this bathysphere and trying to help you understand.

Question more?

Q: How can we contact you as you've contacted us?

A: As we have indicated (*in an earlier, deleted portion of the tape*), if you will be open to letting our energy flow through your being and to write, that we will come. For you know, when you open to us it is like a light that we see that draws us to you and guides us to you. Then we can hover near for a time. But it is still like person in bathysphere trying to tell the fish things, hm? So it takes a while to blend these energies. (*Here instructions are given for channeling.*) It is not only Mr. Dick, you see; there are several others joined with him who wish this method to be attempted.

(*This reminded me of Ryerson's similar statement. Even though I had been quiet while listening to the tape, during a silence at this point I started talking back to the tape recorder. "Who?" I demanded. "Verne? Dickens?" Following my outburst, the next line on the tape was this:)*

Also he says if you'll shut up for a time, you'll be able to listen a little better. Just listen.

("CHIP: You know I'm here. Does that mean you can hear and see me?

("RUNCITER: Of course I can't see and hear you. This commercial message is on videotape; I recorded it two weeks ago..."

(From UBIK: The Screenplay*)*

So it is that the first endeavors will be somewhat modest, but you should also be aware that there are a great many powerful influences in the universe which can come through that opening. You are like person sneaking up to milk a cow, and you find there are hundreds of cattle stampeding towards you. So milk the cow very gently, hm?, and don't disturb the others.

Is there more, please?

Q: Is there anything more you wish to pass on to us?

A: There is one more note coming... "Tell him about dinosaurs. Dinosaurs and ducks." Why are they alike? They both know how to go underwater, to find their food. And they both know how to smile. Well, it is not exactly smile, it is more like strange grin. If you can keep in your brain a duck and a dinosaur, grinning at you, then you have the understanding of what the world is about. It is something of a joke, yes? Keep your sense of humor intact, and that will guide you through the perils you encounter.

(A cute image, if somewhat confusing. But as I sat listening to the tape, pondering this image, Margie smiled and pointed at my chest. I was wearing a Donald Duck T-shirt.)

X

"What if I believe you?" I said. "What then?"

"Then," Bill said, "you are happy because your old friend is not dead."

"And that's the point of this?"

He nodded. "Yes."

"It would seem to me," I said carefully, "that there would be a larger point involved. This would be a miracle of staggering importance, to the entire world. It is something that scientists should investigate. It proves there is eternal life, that a next world does exist... Don't you agree? "

"Yes. I suppose so. That's what Tim is thinking; he thinks that a lot. He wants me to write a book..."

—The Transmigration of Timothy Archer

The quality of the material in Alan Vaughan's reading seems impressive to me. The prophecy of nuclear pollution and the analysis of Dick's March, 1974 experiences both echoed and duplicated Phil's own descriptions of these major concerns and dominant influences of his final years. The image, too, that this entity was communicating with the medium and guide through "written notes" echoed my own recent recurring dreams of PKD providing me with "written messages."

And—once again—synchronicities were clustering about the reading. The idea that—just as in the Bebeck reading—the shirt I had on was somehow relevant to the reading (as well as to the "first contact" dream); the specific message to "shut up" after my only verbal outburst while listening to the tape; an interruption while listening to the reading by a phone call from my credit union, informing me that my loan to publish this book had been approved.

The "written message" image was an interesting correlation between dream and reading material, but another such correspondence seems even more significant. Li Sung's final message to me was, "You are like person sneaking up to milk a cow... So milk the cow very gently, hm?" And my dream of May 3rd ended with Margot Kidder, Phil's last love, demonstrating to me the proper method of milking a cow. (This was a dream, therefore, that not only referenced past PKD connotations—a previous dream filled with similar imagery—but also foreshadowed future PKD activity.) And like the "written message" overlap, the internal dream and the external reading repeating this single picture created an occurrence of synchronicity, the psychic bridge between these worlds.

Yet even though these two images did tie PKD material of all three major categories of phenomena together, this could not be taken as identification of Philip Dick. And regardless of the number of fitting images and synchronicities, the validity of this material, to my mind, hinged upon this question of identity. The answers to my "identification questions" within the reading were—at best—near misses. The reading would hardly be evidential without some specific and unequivocal identification.

This, too, was provided.

The penultimate "note" coming directly from this channeled entity was this: "Remember to tell him about the bathysphere." *So what?,* you ask. How could this word, this image, possibly identify the entity as Philip K. Dick?

I invite you to turn back to Part II of the interview in this book, where Phil describes the "payoff" of his vision—"when it reached its lowest point": alien figures "within chambers that looked like bathyspheres..."

I further invite you to turn back to the story "The Eye of the Sibyl" in this volume, where PKD fictionalized this vision by writing about "creatures... inside a round bubble"; the ancient Roman character's description of the same modern device.

"The part that to me is the most striking" about his vision of these aliens, Phil continues in the interview, "that I will never forget as long as I live," was their third eye. In "Sibyl," "it was this Eye by which the Sibyl saw what she needed to see, to instruct and warn us." Phil's message from Vaughan's reading: "he is keeping an eye on you from this bathysphere and trying to help you understand."

It is not the *appearance* of this word, however—as unusual as it is—that lends evidence of identification, but the *implications of the image* based on Philip Dick's own associations with it. In a symbolic sense, these "aliens" or "Immortals" were Phil's science fiction metaphor for an unseen influence that guides our destiny; a crystallized image of an otherworldly, autonomous consciousness expanded beyond our own. By now envisioning himself within that "alien bathysphere," he is thereby implying that he, too, is no longer of this earth: *he has become the Immortal* of his own visionary experience; he has become one of those who "In dreams...are inspiring people here and there."

This one word, traced through the author's unique associations, in material *unique to this book,* thus becomes a code word, speaking volumes. Not only is this one word, then, a unique identification in answer to a specific question, but it also freights a symbolic message along with it. It is a message built from images personally meaningful to Philip Dick and only to Philip Dick. And it is the message of this book: the spirit of Philip Kindred Dick lives on...not symbolically, through his writings, but *literally.* The "payoff" of his vision thus becomes the payoff of his post-mortem proof; the image he'd remember *as long as he lived* thus resurfaces to evidence his continued survival.

If this seems too much to ask of a single word, it was still much more than I had ever demanded. My own identification questions would have been satisfied by the correct one-word responses: "snuff" for one; "Disneyland" or "party" for the other.

And, I recalled, I had had a similar experience just weeks earlier, in tracing the "golden man" image from my dream back through material unique to this book, to Phil's final use of the image: as evidence that the spirit of Timothy Archer had returned from the "other side." Was this experience a "trial run," perhaps? To teach me the procedure and allow me to practice it—or to lend more weight, more validity, to this objective repetition?

I had hoped for identification; I'd even counted on it, owing to the ease and accuracy with which Michael Bebeck channeled answers to my test questions. (There, too, I got more identification than I had asked for or expected, and was told, "If your minds want satisfaction, I will give you that at a later date.") What I could never have counted on—and certainly never foresaw—was the *dramatic harmony* created by this second evidential sitting.

I see this dramatic harmony operating in at least three major ways in these experiences, wrapping the themes and "plot lines" up in an awesome grand finale and making this book take on a structure almost as if it were a plotted novel. Consider this as an outline, for instance: A man has unusual and meaningful dreams of a dead friend. He begins to notice synchronicities and similar testimony from other people, all pointing to the influence of that friend. He holds a séance and gathers evidence. He attempts to validate this data with a second séance. And, after great difficulties, he receives as the final message a unique form of identification, replete with a symbolic message of the fate of his friend. The best material was saved for last; the suspense built page by page, finally resolving in an astonishing denouement.

Or consider this skeletal plot: A unique interview segment about a dead writer's psychic visions inspires a man to publish the interview in book form. An unpublished story based on these experiences is offered as the capstone to a series of interrelated synchronicities; the arrival of this story is what convinces the man his book should be a "psychic history" of the writer. Once set off on this course, the man receives, in a séance, an exact reference to a unique, specific and personal image common only to the interview segment and the story—material to which only he has access, and material which, twice before, has guided him in making major decisions concerning his history.

Or consider this scenario: A world-renowned and reputable psychic informs a man that he will be contacted by a dead friend. After experiencing a number of seemingly important dreams and meaningful coincidences involving this friend, the man takes an existential plunge into a belief-system that these are real messages and that the deceased is trying to communicate with him and with others. He contacts the psychic in an attempt to channel the dead friend; the psychic, however, does not have this ability, and recommends several other mediums. After a 17-month quest filled with half a dozen mediums, numerous failures and rejections and only one evidential contact, the man writes the psychic who originally predicted this event. Incredibly enough, during that same 17-month period, the psychic has developed the very skill necessary to complete the task. And in the final phrases of the final reading, the discarnate entity reveals his identity, thus validating the bulk of the phenomena.

Dramatic harmony was well-served by the unfolding of these events, and dramatic unity as well, in the yoked associations—the braiding of unique imagery from earlier material—and in the circularity implicit in this and in Alan Vaughan's integral role in the drama. The final reading fixed a symmetrical framework within which the smaller cycles of image and experience constellated—the final dreams, for instance, which mirrored the first. This integrity of experience, this "bookending" of first and last events, might best be expressed in T.S. Eliot's lines, "In my end is my beginning/In my beginning is my end." Yet even though the events appear circular, a better metaphor is that of an upturning or tightening spiral. My quest may have led me back to where it had begun, but the events could now be viewed from a new perspective: a higher level—or greater depth—of knowledge and appreciation, owing to the weight of the experiences...and to their final outcome.

Again, Eliot said it better than I can:

We shall not cease from exploration
And the end of all our exploring
Will be to arrive where we started
And know the place for the first time.

XI

Francesa said sharply, "It wasn't a dream; it was an authentic
visitation. I can distinguish the difference."
"Sure you can Francy," Don Denny said. He winked at Joe.
—UBIK

Taken as a whole, these experiences have a distinctly *UBIK*-like
flavor. In that odd novel, the allegedly dead Glen Runciter
repeatedly intruded into the world of the "living"—Joe Chip and
company. Although the main revelation of the novel was that these
two categories of existence were directly reversed, the point of view
of the characters throughout most of the book was that the deceased
Runciter was desperately attempting to contact his surviving staff.
He did so using a tape recorder, a television, a telephone, graffiti on
bathroom walls, a skywriting biplane (in the screenplay) and written
notes in many forms.

In my own experiences, the intrusions into the land of the living
took the form of dreams and synchronicities—synchronicities
revolving around a tape recorder (the Bebeck tape speed difficulties
and the Vaughan tape "talking back" to me), television clips (the
surgeon messages and Shirley Black appearances), telephone calls
(several Shirley Black calls, among others)—as well as dream graffiti
and bathroom references in the readings (Bebeck's "Soak in a bathtub
of this energy"; Vaughan's "Going to the bathroom by yourself"; my
dream of writing the end of this book while walking back and forth to
the bathroom).

The synchronicities also appeared in written form in letters,
newsletters, tabloid papers, stories and novels. And the lucid dream of
October, 1984—in which I accused PKD of "creating the set" in
which we met—is curiously akin to Jory's imagined "pseudo-worlds"
of *UBIK,* created for the half-lifers to inhabit.

Even the recurring "airplane" image reads like a *UBIK* object.
Although in my dream PKD rode a modern red and white jet, all

subsequent synchronicities revolved around a red *biplane.* Like the modern airplane in *UBIK* which degenerated into a "red and white Curtiss biplane," this seems to illustrate, per *UBIK,* the degeneration of symbolic forms between our "real" world and Phil's new "imaginary" world—only here, it works in reverse: the forms or images originating in this other realm degenerate when translated to our material world.

Seen from this perspective, the dream story dates might indeed be a "calendar code." The gimmick of that story was that a second event appeared to occur before a first event. This could be interpreted as precognition (and bring us back to Vaughan—who appeared in a dream on one of those dates, *two months before* the dream story dates appeared), or it could indicate the regression of time, as the half-lifers experienced in *UBIK.* Here again, though, the degeneration of objects is witnessed *not* in the after-death realm, but in *our* world. The message of the code, then, would be complex but clear: that assumed as the "real" world is in fact the false world of Maya, of illusion; that taken as the "imaginary" world—the land beyond death—is actually the realm of timeless and immortal forms, of which our material world is but a pale shadow...an idea that mystics and religious figures have been advancing for millennia.

In this interpretation, Philip Dick's message is clear: There is a realm where essence transcends death...*and it is far more "real" than the world of mere materiality.* And his method of illustrating this is by providing examples which can be held in comparison with his own writings on the subject. "I intend to illuminate my concepts with ideas I am formulating from this place," we were told in the Bebeck reading. "My ideas were founded in thought. I wish to illuminate them with higher consciousness energy. So my work is to...bring the concepts that I learned on this plane to them."

This is one way of looking at these experiences; another scenario like those presented in the previous section. There are certainly many ways of analyzing these events; many interpretations and conclusions. I have one; Robert Anton Wilson—as delineated in his "Afterwards"—has another point of view and therefore another interpretation; you will undoubtedly have your own, one perhaps different from either of these.

My own approach to the material has been decidedly dual-edged. On the one hand, my attitude mimicked Phil Dick's approach to his own unusual experiences. For Phil, each and every theory was believed true—at least for a while—and was extended until it collapsed under the weight of its own illogic. Enough events occurred to convince me to *assume the position of belief* that these were actual contacts by PKD in order to follow up on them, in an attempt to see just how far the "belief-system" could be stretched. On the other hand, my attempt to "make-believe" this theory was tempered by the attitude of Robert Anton Wilson: *believe nothing.* My goal in setting these events on paper has been to present them as objectively as possible—no easy task, as so much of the material is subjective in nature—so the reader might draw his or her own conclusions.

To clarify this, I will state once again that the idea that the consciousness of Philip K. Dick lives beyond death and is communicating with living individuals is a *theory,* in the scientific sense: a hypothesis assumed for the sake of investigation. The experiences previously presented are the evidence to support this theory, but *proof* of this theory is—at best—an individual judgment, reserved for those who weigh the evidence. All I have to offer is a tightly-woven tapestry of circumstantial evidence—inadmissible in a court of law, but hopefully evidential to the intuition. How one interprets and accepts this evidence will determine the relative validity of the theory—*but only to the interpreter.*

My methods for approaching these odd phenomena may have been the same as those of Philip Dick and Robert Anton Wilson, but the results I obtained were radically different than the outcomes they were, or are, used to deriving. Each succeeding incident served not to demolish my theory but instead to support it. Each new turn of events, each string of dreams and synchronicities and each new reading, did not collapse, but reinforced, the structure.

As to why I was chosen to receive this material...I still have no real clue. But I will state this, and very bluntly: I'm not crazy and I'm not stupid—although I have pondered both those assertions numerous times in the last two and a half years. "Not crazy" is—like my hypothesis—an individual judgment, and certainly not one that can be proven. Indeed, the evidence might indicate the opposite conclusion if considered superficially. It would be very easy to dismiss my experiences with a psychobabble scenario such as this: "Rather than accepting the inevitability of death and assimilating this into a mature reality-view, the subject's grief over the loss of his friend caused a reversion to a childlike (autistic) level of mentality, one ripe for his enturbulated unconscious to seize upon the 'escape clause' provided by the alleged psychic: the irrational notion that the deceased would be in contact with him. This erroneous, wish-fulfilling premise, fueled by coincidences in which the significances were overvalued and among which the connections were at best tenuous, thus sprang into a full-blown obsessive neurotic fantasy: an attempt by the subject's unconscious not only to relieve the boredom of a mundane life, but also to recompense himself for the 'loss of status' and attention his ego had allegedly suffered at the hands of people closer than he to the deceased."

I don't intend to waste your time or mine, however, in defending my alleged sanity. Suffice it to say that those who don't occasionally question whether or not they are sane usually aren't (and vice versa)—and the louder one proclaims his sanity the more people look at him through narrowed eyes.

"Not stupid"—or in this sense, "not gullible"—however, is a claim I've worked hard to defend: by maintaining a skeptical attitude and a sense of humor, by withholding judgment on these events until I had developed and tested a workable theory—and by not blindly accepting *anything* at face value. (I actively refrained, for instance, from engaging in the "automatic writing" which was suggested by several psychics, as even a positive result would yield only "inadmissible evidence." What a field day the rational analysts would have with this material had I included some idea like, *"Of course* I'm channeling Philip Dick: this sentence I wrote says so, and that proves it!"*)

Additionally, I endeavored to be "not stupid" by applying scientific principles of experimentation to these events. Repeatability was one such attempt. Although I had little control over the majority of the dream material, when I did attempt to initiate a contact, the result was apparently successful—immediately. And, a year later, when I attempted this again, the result, once again, seemed successful. This may easily be seen as a form of "wish fulfillment," but the particular numinous quality of these dreams is not something I have ever—before or since—been able to "program" on demand into my dreams, although I have tried repeatedly.

This repeatability holds true for the readings as well. The first, however evidential, needed the verification of a second—and, by my standards, obtained it.

Another principle I kept in mind was Occam's Razor, the scientific and philosophic rule that "categories of explanation should not be multiplied unnecessarily." This principle of parsimony, according to Webster's Dictionary, has two interpretations.

The first is that the simplest of competing theories that accounts for all observed phenomena is preferable to the more complex. The theory I developed fulfills this requirement. It is a simple theory, grounded soundly in philosophy and religion and with millennia of history behind it, and uncluttered by such baroque inventions as "aliens from Sirius," "other minds" or "Russian microwave telepathy." The phenomena consisted of a limited number of recurring images, all weaving into a symmetrical web, and all indicating the same central source and message. There are no loose ends, no puzzle pieces—as Phil put it—"left over or...sticking out somewhere." The internal integrity of the constellation of events is uninfringed by inconsistencies.

There were failures, though; I can't deny that. I felt compelled to test the dream material in the real world, but to little avail. Although I've tried at least a dozen different date-to-letter methods of breaking the "calendar code" to find a message, for instance, the results are only gibberish. And searching out a copy of *National Geographic* for the date given on the cover of the "Cassidy and cats" dream issue yielded nothing even remotely connected with this material.

(Curiously enough, though, as I was sitting at work writing the description of that dream, a co-worker came in with a stack of *Geographics* she had cleaned out of her house and was passing around the office. She handed me the latest issue, dated June, 1986; on the cover was a sepia-toned photo of a jungle cat, as in my dream, and inside—in *two* separate articles—were photos of people dressed up as Santa Claus, as in my 11 April dream of PKD. I can't even seem to discount my own experiences without getting feedback invalidating the denial.)

I'm not surprised that there is little physical correspondence between the dreams and the real world. But, as Wilson points out in his "Afterwards," this dream material can be true *on its own level.* The extension of this idea would be that lack of connection between these levels does not detract from the validity of the message *on its own level.* The dreams may not have given me "real" data about the "waking world," but this should not diminish the importance of their message, *which does not concern the waking world.*

On the other hand, if the synchronicities are considered at least partially as uninfluenced physical events (which is inherent in the definition of "synchronicity") rather than entirely as projections of my own unconscious biases, there was indeed some overlap, some penetration into the material world by this "message." The numerous peculiarities surrounding April 23rd and 24th are but one example: the dream story dates and "calendar code" intruding into the waking world.

Another failure is inherent in the use of Occam's Razor. The second interpretation of this principle is that explanations of unknown phenomena should be sought first in terms of known quantities...which brings us back to—if not "crazy"—then at least the "material rising from the collective unconscious" type of theory that Wilson advances in his "Afterwards." (Technically, "crazy" is not a "known," or even a valid explanation. It is a logical fallacy, the *argumentum ad hominem:* argument against the man, rather than against the data. Even if I *am* crazy, the explanation might still be true.)

Or does it? It is important to note that the same "Occam's Razor" analysis would yield similar results if applied to the "collective unconscious"—*which is itself just a theory.* It is a sound philosophical hypothesis, but with little scientific research behind it and no physical proof of its existence. By its nature, it defies physical proof. Evidence exists...but it is the same type of evidence I am using to support my theory: the recurring dreams of individuals, and the recurring myths of cultures: the collective dreams of a people.

So perhaps, with this material, we are not dealing with "known quantities" after all. Even applying Occam's Razor, we are brought right back to...the unknown.

The observation that these two *equally valid* interpretations of this principle cancel each other out when applied to this material could indicate that it might not be applicable. "Questions about the origin of transpersonal experiences, or the migration of ideas," Wilson writes in his "Afterwards", "do not belong in quite the same category as questions about how many jelly beans are in a given bottle. Most of the errors of philosophers, as Wittgenstein demonstrated, result from treating questions on one level of discourse as if they were questions on another level of discourse." Perhaps we are applying logic where logic does not apply; seeking scientific certainty—the existence of objective proof—where the most that can be expected is some form of certitude: faith in something not needing or—specifically in this case—*not capable* of proof.

In this respect, these two competing ideas—material rising from the collective unconscious and contact from the "other side"—are similar entities: equally valid, equally unprovable. The choice of one as "better suited" to explain this material is just that: a choice, not proof.

This battle of competing philosophies may be the result of the lack of physical evidence. I do not have any physical evidence: no ectoplasm, no videotaped manifestations of hologram ghosts, no cans of UBIK spray, no "Joe Chip money." Unlike Philip Dick, I dreamed no book passages in languages I never knew; unlike Bishop Pike, I had no clocks stop at the hour of death. But even these objective phenomena didn't help those who experienced them advance their theories. Inductive reasoning is suspect, as Phil himself repeatedly pointed out in those books written after his own "mystical experiences" and attempts at analysis.

There are worse fates than a lack of physical evidence, however. At very least there is in all these events *perceptual evidence* and a philosophical framework from which we may develop theories. But consider as a counterpoint such Fortean phenomena as a rain of toads. There is massive physical evidence that the event *did* occur—loads of toads in the road—but no logical, rational or even philosophical explanation for why or how it happened *or could happen*. Which experience, then, is more "real": the perceptual, explainable event, or the physical, but unexplainable, one?

Because any judgment on this material is solely a matter of choice, I can't dismiss Wilson's theory out of hand. I myself accept the collective unconscious as a working hypothesis in my dream research and analysis, and, near the end of these PKD experiences, new, archetypal material has occasionally been freighted along with the Phil Dick images in dream form. Their content is irrelevant to the PKD material, but their presence may not be. Just as, concomitant with the beginning of these experiences, I found myself—almost overnight—able to recall virtually all of my dreams, so was the resolution of these experiences presaged by discovering the verge of another major breakthrough in my relationship with the unconscious. Perhaps Bebeck was right: my unconscious has been given a "turboboost" by agency or agencies...not unknown, but unprovable.

The bottom line in this debate between theories is that *they are not mutually exclusive*. Few have explored this realm of the collective unconscious; fewer still have returned with maps. And no one has yet discovered how deep this underground river of consciousness runs, nor what tributaries converge into it, nor its source, its wellspring. It is in these theories that science and metaphysics meet face to face...or face to mirror.

To borrow phrasing from Wilson, in the model *I* currently find useful, consciousness or personality, in some form, survives physical death. One could hardly expect this surviving consciousness to be identical to that of the person while alive, however—just as one would not expect a living person at age three or twenty-three to communicate in the same manner, or hold the same opinions, as he would at age fifty-three...or even on any given day in his life, if queried once while sober and later while drunk or on LSD.

To me, the numinous quality of these experiences is not that Philip K. Dick's consciousness survived death, and not necessarily that some vestiges of his ego apparently survived intact. What is awesome is that this coherence of identity was able to repeatedly insinuate itself into our world: a whisper in a hurricane, perhaps...but a whisper heard by those who would listen.

("Insinuate," I think now, is a more proper term than my original "invade." *Invade* is defined, after all, as "to enter for conquest"; *insinuate* as "to introduce smoothly, subtly or gradually, or to communicate with artful references; to enter gently or slowly." Over the course of more than two years, these intriguing web-threads were spun gradually, communicated artfully and transmitted gently enough to eliminate any sense of invasion or entrapment by them or their spinner. The experience was not a "divine invasion," but instead a *mystic insinuation.*)

And so, until enough "contradictory material uncensored by consciousness" appears, or until a better model is offered—one which accounts for all the data in a more succinct form—this will be the model of my choice...but only insofar as it does not blind me to other possibilities, physical or metaphysical. It is a theory I am entertaining...and one which is entertaining me.

No, I'm not crazy and I'm not stupid. I am also not putting you on. This is no hoax, no fabricated fantasy. Perhaps I should have used the Phil Dick method, and written these experiences up as a novel, letting those who can read between the lines do so. But that would not be fair to anybody—and would (let's face it) make for a pretty dull novel. My experiences are pretty run-of-the-mill "contact from the Other Side" experiences when compared to the many other accounts of this nature—including Bishop Pike's—that exist in print. I could imagine and create far better fiction; what makes this material fascinating (to me, at least), is that it *is* fact—and far stranger as fact than any imaginative fantasy could ever be.

Maybe it will indicate some honesty in the reporting of these experiences by knowing that, once I made the decision to write them up, I wrote them up as I went along, never knowing the final outcome. A full eighty percent of the manuscript was already *typeset* before I received the final Vaughan reading—so I really had no way of knowing what was important to leave in and what should be edited out of these recurring dreams and images; I simply put in everything that seemed important and hoped that—somehow—some of the threads would eventually weave into a pattern that might yield some meaning.

The experiences happened as they are written, and were written as they happened. That they did indeed resolve into a coherent, internally consistent pattern due to the form of the final experiences is...what? Fate? An unconscious template? The random forces of the material universe which we just perceive as a meaningful pattern? Or part of some grander plan of unfolding experience? I don't know. All I know is that the web threads were clearly threads, but the form and magnitude of the web itself became apparent only over time.

I am also *not obsessed* with these events. You won't find me starting a new church with Philip Dick as its lord and savior—and I'm not about to write a million and a half words about these experiences, running them through every philosophy, religion and system of belief known to Humankind, to see what conclusions emerge in the output bin of each "belief machine." Even this small essay chapter is just a few random fragments strung together rather than a full analysis; a hopefully not too superficial discussion of a few points which crossed my mind; a small attempt at an objective analysis on reentry from the belief system I assumed for experimentation's sake.

In general, my position is that I was commissioned to perform a certain, specific task: to record, relate and validate, to the best of my abilities, these experiences. After two full years of dreams and synchronicities and two evidential readings, I feel I have fulfilled the responsibilities with which I was charged. I have completed my assignment, at the personal risk of losing friends and gaining the reputation as a gullible madman.

But to what end? Why is it so damned important to release this material, at the risk of public ridicule? What exactly is the message or intent behind these experiences?

To borrow Wilson's phrasing once again, I considered a variety of models for this data, some contradictory and some refinements of earlier hypotheses. The idea that PKD was channeling fiction, for instance, gave way to the theory that he was providing career guidance to his friends, which in turn developed into the consideration that our own thoughts were being "turboboosted." Running parallel to this chain of thought was the idea that PKD was attempting to communicate to settle unfinished business, which evolved into the thought that this "mystic history" constituted the bulk of that unfinished business, which in turn expanded into the more profound notion that he had an important message to deliver.

As to the first chain, only concurrence from others can validate its plausibility. And as for the second, if there is an important message anywhere to be found in this material, it would most likely be found in the readings: the direct evidential contacts. And yet the readings, while providing clear, definite and nonconflicting messages of a type which echo Philip Dick's final concerns, do not *repeat* the same message—nor the same explanations for the experiences. Some of this can be attributed to the use of different mediums (as in Vaughan/Li Sung's statement "we are using *your* vehicle; it is not one of our own construction"); the medium is, then—at least in part—the message. But that still leaves us without a clear message.

There are clues, however, as to what this message might be. The one thing consistent between readings, for instance—as well as among the dreams—is the *identity* of Philip K. Dick. And the overall point of the 11 April series of dreams was that the messages I was receiving from him were less important than the idea that I was getting a message at all. Vaughan had predicted this aspect in the very first exposure to this material: "More important than the writing (of fiction channeled by PKD) will be your experiences in getting in touch with Philip K. Dick, shall we say…psychically." So perhaps I was on the wrong track in theorizing that PKD had something of vital importance to transmit. The "message of vital importance" might be *that he can communicate anything at all.*

Yet even this does not fully answer my question *Why is it so important to release this material?*

Well…hell. I've come this far. I can't get into any more trouble with a little more speculation.

It is a widely-held observation that paying attention to the phenomenon of synchronicity increases the perception of its incidence. Almost everyone who has seriously studied the experience of synchronicity develops the same conclusion; I include here people like Vaughan, Wilson, John Lilly—and Jung himself, the originator of the concept and the term. This is the same conclusion that most people who study dreams eventually reach as well: that paying attention to them increases their frequency and meaning. Jung understood this; Phil knew it too.

Repeatedly in this material I experienced the overlapping of categories of events. Synchronicities followed dreams; dream imagery blended with reading material; readings were accompanied by clusters of synchronicities. So perhaps—just perhaps—this "depth on attendance" idea also lapses over into "contacts" such as I've experienced; contacts possibly originating from—and certainly present in—unconscious processes. If this is the case, the reference to these contacts as a "test project" in the Vaughan reading might well make sense: the whole point of this book would be to spread the idea of the possibility of these contacts to a number of other, like-minded—and open-minded—individuals, thereby increasing Philip Dick's chances to communicate. My sole role in this larger theory, then, would not be as the bearer of any transcendent message, but as the finger on this "cosmic trigger."

To use a gentler metaphor, my role might be the opposite of the legendary little Dutch boy at the dyke: I have been requested to *remove* my finger from this barrier between worlds, allowing Phil's little trickle to spout into a fountain.

Some will ignore my wet finger; they will deny that there is any water at all, or claim that the world ends at the wall. Others will claim that the dam is unbreachable. And some will sense a coming flood, and rage against the imminent destruction.

But if my role is the opposite of the Dutch boy's, so too is the goal: the levee of death needs not protection, but dissolution. And so, too, is the message: not a cry of dire disaster, but a joyous note of hope. Those privy to the fount may choose to drink from the fount, and will find their thirst for evidence quenched. They will take to the flow like a duck takes to water: grinning all the way.

Thus Philip Dick, who wrote so many of his own dreams into his fiction... Philip Dick, who lived—both before and after the writing—so many scenes from his own novels... Philip Dick will have achieved a position as strange as the strangest he'd created—as a Runciter, waking us from the sleepwalking "half-life" of "reality"—and one as benign in its similar effect as his most sinister fictional character: as a redeemed Palmer Eldritch, author (at least collaboratively) of our own—increasingly bizarre—realities.

And so—to echo "Shirley Black's" comment to me—if you see Phil before I do...tell him Scott says "Hi."

XII

The search, perhaps, was the goal.
—Radio Free Albemuth

A Parable:
THE FINAL SECRET OF DISNEYLAND
(Transcript of a dream of 19 November 1977)

"You might compare life to an amusement park," Angel Annette suggested to Walt on his first tour of Heaven. "Strapping yourself into a ride is like strapping your consciousness into a body, after which you get a series of pre-programmed experiences...the ride track, in the analogy, or your genetic, cultural and karmic programming for experiencing real events, in life's case. And when the ride's over, you just shed the vehicle."

"And what's outside the ride?" Walt asked.

"The park," she replied

"And what's outside the park?"

"Walt," the angel explained patiently, "we are the park."

• • • • •

Death, we all know, is final. We of the 20th century are far too enlightened, far too scientific, to place any stock at all in bizarre dreams, mysterious occurrences and occult nonsense like mediums.

"These random events," as Philip Dick's Angel Archer said, "are not manifestations of the dead—that couldn't be, for obvious reasons. One knows this instinctively; one does not debate this; one perceives this as absolute fact: it cannot happen."

Death—we all know—is final. Death immediately and terminally severs all contact, all communication, all hope. These occurrences of which we have written are not the behavior of death.

They are, however, the behavior of life. Friends do not just step out of our lives, disappearing into the mists; they make an effort to say goodbye; to explain where they had to go, and why. Planes do not disappear upon takeoff; we stand on the tarmac, waving our farewells, until a speck disappears in the sky.

I am humbled and awed to think that this friend, at the inevitable end of his human journey, took time to wave back in return. Such a wave conveys his undying affection; it comforts us and signifies that all is well. It informs us that his suffering is over, and was not pointless. It avows that his journey has, in fact, only just begun.

Do I believe I actually had contact with Philip K. Dick? Yes. But can I expect—or even ask—others to believe my experiences? Sadly, the answer must be no. I can here only report my own experiences and express my personal interpretations. But without any hard, factual evidence, I will understand if you remain unconvinced.

Perhaps I, too, will be accused—as Jay Kinney accused Philip Dick of his "Exegesis"—of "long-winded (and rather crazed) attempts to derive cosmic generalities from dream fragments, hypnagogic phrases and coincidental occurrences." My only answer is to reiterate, in this new context, the notation Phil himself made to me on his "Tagore" letter: "Make of this what you will. It is sincere."

If, however, I have succeeded in expressing my incredible experiences with more credibility than credulousness, then my final comments are addressed to the open-minded reader.

What have you gotten in exchange for the time spent reading this book? Not just a new insight into Philip K. Dick...but also *evidence of a life beyond death.* Phil's final message is clear: We all live; we all seek and suffer; we all die. *And we all live on.* In his life and in his death, as in his novels, Philip Dick willed us more than any of us had ever bargained for—more than any of us had any right, or even hope, to expect.

Perhaps, if this history is convincing, it might repay him in some small measure by retroactively lending some credence to his own revelatory dreams, voices and visions.

And if my experiences are dismissed as merely an infection of the Philip Dick form of insanity...well, I could be in far worse company.

> *Each of us, then, partakes of the cosmos—*
> *if he is willing to listen to his dreams.*
> —"Man, Android and Machine"

Addendum
To the 2014 edition

Coincidence or Synchronicity?
October, 2011

Twenty-seven years after my initial series of synchronicities orbiting around PKD, what should turn up but another one?

The background: I refer to an anecdote from this book (1999 quality paperback edition, p.117) detailing the second series of dreams about PKD in 1984 (extraneous details removed via ellipsis):

On June 8, 1984, I had a dream which lasted the entire night, and consisted of one single element: me reading a short story. In the dream, I read page after page after page of typewritten material, for hours on end. But when woke, I couldn't recall the story—just the reading.

The following night, June 9th, I dreamed of reading a magazine interview... I also read a long list of words and wrote page after page and read many, many pages...

June 10th: Another night filled entirely with dreams of reading, writing, reading, writing. I was waking up exhausted, as though I had worked all night...

On June 11th, I was at it again. This time, though, there was a difference: Philip K. Dick was there with me. We were collaborating on a story... We wrote and read and handed pages back and forth all night long. We had no time for conversation; we were hard at work.

I dreamed this single scene for eight solid hours. And when I woke exhausted after our night's labor—I still could not remember a single sentence of the story.

The collaboration became clearer on the night of June 12th. Phil and I were back in the same scene as the previous night, still working on the same story...

That was the last dream in that series.

The followup: the October 2011 issue of *Playboy* magazine ran an excerpt from the upcoming book *The Exegesis of Philip K. Dick*, edited by author Jonathan Letham. After a brief introduction, the excerpt consisted of a letter written by PKD to literary critic Peter Fitting, dated June 28, 1974.

From the letter (after detailing his experiments with megavitamins and other things):

"I was hoping only for increased neural efficiency. I got more: actual information about the future, for during the next three months, almost each night, during sleep I was receiving information in the form of printouts: words and sentences, letters and names and numbers—sometimes whole pages, sometimes in the form of writing paper and holographic writing...and finally galley proofs held up for me to read...and during the last two weeks a huge book, again and again, with page after page of printed lines."

June, 1974, was only a few months after PKD's mystical experiences, and three years before I met him. He never mentioned this dream-reading during our interview or, indeed, in any other description of his experiences that I've come across since. This letter was buried away in his files, in his manuscript for The Exegesis, disclosed here for the first time, to the extent of my knowledge. (It was not, for example, included in Lawrence Sutin's 1991 book, *In Pursuit of VALIS: Selections from The Exegesis*.)

The punch line to this latest coincidence—and the detail that elevates it to the realm of synchronicity in my estimation—is the cartoon that accompanied the final page of the *Playboy* article. A dead man (comically indicated to be deceased by X's over his eyes) lies in a hospital bed, while a doctor says, "The monitors all show that you're dead...but to be sure, we'll need to run some more tests." One of the recurring images in my dream sequences clustering around PKD was that of a doctor or surgeon—and the whole point of the "Dream Connection" essay was to question if dead is really dead. In the words of the cartoon caption, the "Dream Connection" essay is a record of me "running some more tests."

•　•　•　•　•

November, 2013

My essay "The Dream Connection" begins with an anecdote about how I'd had friends die, including Doug Kenney, a co-founder of the *National Lampoon* magazine, who had died before I could query him about contacts in Hollywood. "After Doug's tragic death" in 1980, I wrote, "I even began a short story in which the spirit of a dead humorist inspired the writing of a small-time comic..."

In November, 2013, I read the 2006 book *A Futile and Stupid Gesture: How Doug Kenney and the National Lampoon Changed Comedy Forever* by Josh Karp, a detailed history of *The National Lampoon* in general and Kenney in particular. The Epilogue closes with this story (extraneous details removed via ellipsis):

"In the immediate aftermath of his death and long thereafter, numerous subjects interviewed for this book told stories of being visited by Doug Kenney in their dreams..."

For me, the idea was fiction. But Kenney's friends had had the same experience that Phil's friends had had. None of them would ever follow up by consulting a medium, however...

"More than twenty years after Doug's death [the anecdote continued], Chevy Chase's wife asked him to accompany her on a visit to a psychic medium who worked from her small home in New York State. Reluctantly, Chase went along. A nonbeliever in such phenomena, he sat by as his wife tried to make contact with a deceased relative. Achieving no results, the woman asked Chase if there was anyone he wanted to contact. Chase mentioned that he had a deceased friend he often thought about.

" 'He's here,' the psychic said ... She explained how the visitor said that he'd left his glasses on the cliff and that his death was both stupid and embarrassing. Chase had provided her with no information. It was clear that she didn't know, nor could she have known, anything about Doug and his death.

" 'He's very funny, isn't he?' she said."

"Afterwards"

INTRODUCTION

Robert Anton Wilson is a well-known figure in the world of science fiction. His *Illuminatus!* trilogy (co-authored with Robert Shea) is a classic blend of science fiction and fantasy, politics and magick, adventure and philosophy, conspiracy theory and consciousness expansion...and just about everything else under the sun, all cleverly calculated to annihilate the artificial distinctions between "high" and "low" art.

Wilson, like Phil Dick, is one of the few recent writers to incorporate the findings of modern physics into his fictional framework—not just as ideas discussed or extrapolated, but as determinants of reality, integral to the structure of the novel itself. His *Schrödinger's Cat* trilogy, for instance, postulates the type of worlds we'd inhabit (and how we might respond to them) if each of the conflicting theories of relativity and quantum mechanics were translated from microcosmic speculations to macrocosmic—and human-scale—realities.

Wilson is also justly known for his philosophical forays into futurism and consciousness expansion. *Cosmic Trigger,* his book-length essay on mysticism, synchronicity and his own occult experiences (among a million other things) is, in fact, so close to what I was trying to accomplish (on a lesser scale) with my own "Dream Connection" essay that I asked Bob to comment on my experiences in his unique analytical style.

The result is this "Afterwards," a thought-provoking and humorous essay.

Although it was my pleasure, along with Kevin Briggs, to introduce Wilson and Dick in 1977, distance prevented them from any depth of contact outside of an occasional exchange of letters. My story of their initial meeting can be found in the essay "Phil As I Knew Him," earlier in this volume. Although when I wrote this essay I thought that was the extent of their contact, Wilson's cover letter accompanying his "Afterwards" expands on what I knew: "Incidentally," he wrote, "on the occasion when Phil and I first met, we did not merely gaze at bellydancers. An hour or so later, he called me on the phone, invited me over to his room and spent a considerable time asking me probing questions about my 'Sirius' experiences. He referred to his own 'VALIS' experiences only briefly and evasively; he wanted to know about my beyond-the-veil journey. I speculate in retrospect that he was trying to figure out how 'crazy' I was, to get an outside perspective on how 'crazy' he himself was."

"Afterwards"

Robert Anton Wilson

I

I am most happy to have this opportunity to comment on the Philip K. Dick controversy, which has (quite properly) concerned all intelligent Americans quite as much as the de Selby enigma concerns all of us on the cisatlantic side of the pond.

(De Selby himself, incidentally, is spending the week as a guest here in my Gothic castle on Howth Hill, Dublin, and insists that I should include in this exegesis his own bizarre theorizing on the classic 1930s film *King Kong,* and how it relates to current American foreign policy and Phil Dick's visions. I have suggested, gently, that he should take a walk and sample the excellent Guinness at our local pub, leaving me in peace to organize my own thoughts.) (1)

First of all, I would like to state unambiguously, for the record, that Scott Apel is not crazy. You can be quite sure of that because Phil Dick himself assured me that *I* am not crazy, and in that case I ought to know who's crazy and who isn't. If you have any doubts about Phil Dick, Scott Apel testifies that Phil wasn't crazy. In short, we all vouch for each other. You can't ask for a stronger chain of expert testimony than that.

Of course, the fact that I don't think Scott Apel is crazy does not mean that I believe any of his theorizing. I don't believe anything. I regard belief as the suicide of intellect.

As I explained in my *Prometheus Rising,* the human brain processes 10,000,000 signals per minute, and at least 99.5 percent of them are edited out—rejected as unimportant or irrelevant to our survival and status drives—before we form any conscious *Gestalt* or reality-tunnel of what is going on around us at the moment. This editing is extremely rapid, efficient and invisible to the conscious ego. Therefore, if we permit *belief* (or certitude, or dogma, or ideology) to take root in us, almost everything inconsistent with that program will be edited out, without our conscious awareness; only occasionally will something inconsistent with the belief program be *persistent* or *redundant* enough to come to the attention of the ego and require a conscious banishing ritual such as "Oh, that's really not important enough to think about" or "I couldn't have seen that. It must have been an optical illusion." Belief, therefore, functions in the individual exactly as censorship functions in a social system: it blocks signals, decreases awareness, lessens sensitivity and drastically lowers I.Q. This is true of Fundamentalist Materialists like Carl Sagan as surely as it is of Fundamentalist Christians like Jerry Falwell.

As a psychologist-philosopher, I dread belief as much as an epidemiologist dreads plague bacteria. In fact, I suspect that it is belief, not "neuroses," that accounts for the singular and terrifying fact that most people spend most of their time making themselves and other people miserable. They make each other miserable because they are editing out so many signals that they literally do not know who they are, where they are, or what they are doing to one another. They think they are in either Grand Opera or Soap Opera, and each imagines he or she is the protagonist of the action, with everybody else playing supporting roles. (2)

Of course, it is not easy to rid oneself of beliefs and dogmas. Neurologically, there is no sharp line of division, no Iron Curtain, between *perception, feeling* and *thought:* all three are part of one very rapid process. Most of our entrenched dogmas do not even appear to us as "ideas," much less as "beliefs"; they intermingle with, and color, our feelings and perceptions. *The world we see, normally, is made up of nothing but our fixed ideas.*

This synergetic interlock of thought-feeling-perception—this projection outward of beliefs, and mistaking them for people, places and events—makes up what the ancient Greeks called *nokos,* the veil, and Buddhists call *maya,* the illusion. Gurdjieff more bluntly called it "sleepwalking."

De Selby, who is thinking of converting to Rastifari—a sect he encountered in Liverpool during the years when the Irish government declared him *persona non grata*—believes, or claims to believe, that marijuana is the miraculous herb mentioned in *Revelations* 22-2 for "the healing of the nations." I regard this as highly imaginative, but I do not think it is "crazy." After all, an estimated 300,000 Rastafarians in England, and another 500,000 worldwide, believe the same exegesis on that text. As Charlie Chaplin said (in a morbid context), "Numbers sanctify." When more than a few people believe something it is not crazy anymore; it is a "minority viewpoint" which, in a democracy, must be respected. When the majority comes to believe it, it is officially beyond question, and you become "crazy" only if you then dispute it.

The Ayatollah Khoumeni says that if a man habitually sodomizes camels, that does not give his wife the right to a divorce, because "God" (with whom the Ayatollah is on intimate terms) disapproves of divorce in virtually all cases. However, a woman who discovers that her husband habitually sodomizes her brother may obtain a divorce, according to the Ayatollah. Is that more or less "crazy" than the dogma of the Pope (who is also on intimate terms with "God") forbidding divorce in *all* cases, which includes even cases of brother-in-law buggery? Andrea Dworkin, a leading spokesentity (I am avoiding the human chauvinism of writing "spokesperson") for Radical Feminism, says that heterosexual intercourse is exploitative of women, except when the man doesn't have an erection. Is she "crazier" than the Ayatollah and the Pope, just because she has (at present) less disciples? I doubt it.

Fundamentalist Protestants of the Falwell variety believe that the approximately 12 percent of persons in all societies who are homosexual have been cursed by God and, as if that isn't enough of a disadvantage, deserve to be persecuted by society, too; but they do not make the same claim about the 12 percent of deviants in all societies who are left-handed. Fundamentalist Materialists of the Sagan variety believe that their own brains were produced by 11 billion years of physical accidents followed by four billion years of biological "copying errors," but that these brains nonetheless are not as clumsy as those of the Pope and the Ayatollah (or Phil Dick, or me). Roman Catholics believe that after a piece of bread has an incantation intoned over it by an ordained priest, it changes into the flesh of a Jew who died 2000 years ago, and that devouring this flesh cannibalistically is not evil or disgusting but divine and wonderful.

A rather stentorian but intelligent American tourist I met at the pub yesterday, called J.R. "Bob" Dobbs, put it this way: "Hell, it's even more relative than Einstein imagined!"

II

In 1973, in Basel, Switzerland, was published *Les Dessous d'une ambition politique,* by journalist Matthieu Paoli. This book claims, with good documentation, that a secret society of French aristocrats, the Priory of Sion, had infiltrated the highest ranks of the French government and was conspiring to restore monarchy in France. Paoli also alleged that the Priory of Sion was allied with the Grand Loge Alpina, the Freemasonic lodge which controls Swiss banking. In passing, he prints a cover of one edition of *Circuit,* the Priory's internal news magazine; this cover depicts a map of France with a Jewish Star of David superimposed on it and what looks like a spaceship hovering above.

Also in 1973, in Paris, Gerard de Sede published *La Race fabuluese,* which also deals with the Priory of Sion. De Sede claims that the Priory is made up of aristocrats descended from the Merovingian kings of the early dark ages, that it has no political ambitions and that it is concerned only with passing on certain "occult" knowledge to those who are ready to receive such wisdom. At the end, abruptly, de Sede reveals that a member has disclosed to him the inner secret of the Priory of Sion: the Merovingian kings and the members of the Priory are descended from matings between the ancient Hebrews and extraterrestrials from Sirius. (3)

De Sede spends a large part of his book in examining the mysterious murder of the last Merovingian king, Dagobert II, who was stabbed in the Ardennes forest on 23 December 689 AD.

Also in 1973, I was engaged in what I called "neurological research" and others might call shamanism or even Jungian self-analysis. Full details are given in my book, *Cosmic Trigger*. Briefly, here, it can be said that I used yoga, ritual and psychedelics. The results were a web of dreams-and-synchronicities similar to those reported by Scott earlier in this book, together with an access in hypnogogic trance ("waking dream") to various "entities" who may or may not have been inside my head but were definitely outside my conscious ego. The synchronicities revolved endlessly around the number 23, although I did not then connect them with the murder of Dagobert II on 23 December 689 and did not, in fact, read de Sede's book until many years later. The principle "entity" contacted—the head honcho, as it were—claimed to be an extraterrestrial from Sirius.

Like Phil Dick after his "VALIS" experiences (which began the following year, 1974), I entertained a variety of hypotheses about these experiences—or, in my preferred metaphor, I considered a variety of models for the data. Like Phil, I considered that real extraterrestrials were involved, that I was simply going nuts, and that I had triggered an opening through which vast floods of data were pouring into my left brain hemisphere from the usually "silent" right brain hemisphere. I also consulted, informally, with three psychiatrists that I knew, who told me I was not psychotic and that many writers and other artists have such explosions of "unconscious" or "right-brain" material at one or more times in their lives. More amusingly, I consulted two psychics, one of whom told me I was receiving messages from an ancient Chinese Taoist-alchemist, and the other of whom told me I was receiving messages from a medieval Irish bard.

Around the time of my "Sirius" experiences and Phil Dick's "VALIS" experiences, I was given, by a chain of coincidences, a book called *Aleister Crowley and the Hidden God,* by Kenneth Grant. Mr. Grant, the Outer Head of the Ordo Templi Orientis in London (of which Crowley was previous Outer head) claims that Crowley was in telepathic communication with an extraterrestrial from Sirius.

The Ordo Templi Orientis claims descent from the Knights Templar of the middle ages. So does the Priory of Sion, according to de Sede. The Knights Templar had a fortification in Rennes-le-Chateau, about which we shall hear more later.

In 1976 appeared *The Sirius Mystery,* by Robert K.G. Temple. This book alleges that extraterrestrials from Sirius landed on Earth around 4500 BC in the Near East. Mr. Temple supports this thesis with ingenious decodings of the myths of the Sumerians and Egyptians, and explicit details from a North African tribe, the Dogon, who describe the Sirians as fish-people.

When Phil Dick wrote up a fictionalized account of his "VALIS" experiences in the novel of that same name, published in 1981, he included the Dogon fish-people, although he does not mention them in the interview with Scott Apel and Kevin Briggs in this book.

In 1982 appeared *The Sirian Experiments* by the distinguished Doris Lessing, a novel in which extraterrestrials from Sirius have been intervening in affairs on Earth for many millenniums. In the introduction, Ms. Lessing denies believing her story literally, but asks why Sirius plays such a large role in mythology and says, "I would not be at all surprised to learn that this earth had been used for purposes of experiment by more advanced creatures..." (The suggestive dots are her own, not mine.)

One explanation of this data is that extraterrestrials from Sirius were busy beaming "telepathic" imagery and/or ideas toward Earth in the last 13 years. Another model would hold that Phil Dick and

Ms. Lessing and Mr. Temple and the rest of us got together and hatched all this as a conscious fraud, just to annoy the Committee for Scientific Investigation of Claims of the Paranormal. A third model might suggest vaguely that some physical "energy" of some sort from Sirius was especially active in the '70s and influenced a lot of minds. A fourth model would be that, in Jungian jargon, a shift in the constellation of archetypes is occurring in the collective unconscious.

I don't believe any of these theories, since it is against my neurological principles to allow belief to get in the way of perception. I try to keep an open mind.

Questions about the origins of transpersonal experiences, or the migration of ideas, do not belong in quite the same category as questions about how many jellybeans are in a given bottle. Most of the errors of philosophers, as Wittgenstein demonstrated, result from treating questions on one level of discourse as if they were questions on another level of discourse. Questions of the numeration of jellybeans can be answered by counting, and that's that. Questions about visions and synchronicities require more subtle modes of analysis, I think.

According to the equations of quantum mechanics, an electron is in *every possible state* when we are not looking at it and only temporarily constrains itself into one state when we are looking. As Schrödinger said, in effect—I am paraphrasing a longish passage from *Mind and Matter*—it is hard to see how the little buggers can defy that Aristotelian Law of Contradiction when we aren't looking, but even harder to see how they can suddenly sober up and accept Law and Order again just because we start looking, when they don't even "know" we are looking. The Copenhagen Interpretation of Niels Bohr and his associates gets rid of this metaphysical *katzenjammer* by merely denying that the electron is in *any* state when we aren't looking because it is not defined or constrained until we look. That is to say, in popular terms, the grass isn't green until an eye that registers green looks at it.

As even schoolchildren and Jay Kinney know by now, Einstein refused to accept the Copenhagen view and insisted the bloody electron must be in *some* state whether we are looking or not. He argued this with Bohr for nearly 30 years in various physics journals, and the consensus of physicists is that Bohr won every round. Einstein's position is refuted one more time by Dr. N.D. Mermin in "Is The Moon There When Nobody Looks?", *Physics Today,* April 1985. Dr. Mermin demonstrates that nothing is there— nothing is defined or separated from everything else—until somebody looks. This view is deeply repugnant to common sense, but as Einstein himself said in another context, "Common sense is what tells us the Earth is flat."

III

Before I could develop my thesis any further than that point, de Selby returned from the pub with the quiet and thoughtful American tourist, J.R. "Bob" Dobbs. (It is now "holy hour," when the Irish pubs close.) I suspect that they both have "taken a drop," as the Irish say, which in American idiom means they drank enough to float the Royal Navy. De Selby insists that this is the point where I should consider the size of King Kong's penis, which is like an electron in quantum theory—he says—in that *the very fact that it is unobserved* causes us to speculate about it. When I asked J.R. "Bob" Dobbs if including Kong's penis in this philosophical commentary might intensify hostility in those who can already be expected to be paranoid and suspicious—I was thinking of the Committee for Scientific Investigation of Claims of the Paranormal—he said, "Fuck them, if they can't take a joke."

De Selby says that Einstein's obsession about what unobserved electrons are doing (4) is psychologically parallel to an audience's *unconscious* preoccupation with King Kong's penis, which is also conspicuously not available for examination. He has gone up to his room to get an essay on this point—an essay by a French film critic which, de Selby says, is "definitive."

J.R. "Bob" Dobbs, while de Selby was upstairs, started explaining to me that the Earth is hollow. That reminds me of Blavatsky, who made the same claim in *The Secret Doctrine,* written entirely while she was stoned on hashish, which she claimed "clarified the spiritual mind." (5) J.R. "Bob" Dobbs says H.P.B. smoked too much hash and got unclarified at a few critical points. He says the hollow Earth is not occupied by H.P.B.'s *boddhisattvas* but by "Nazi Hell Creatures." He showed me a book—*Jules Verne: Initiate et Initiateur,* by one Michael Lamy (Paris, 1984)—which avers that Verne was a high-ranking initiate of both the Illuminati and the Priory of Sion (funny coincidence that *they* should pop up again) and was permitted to explore one of the tunnels to inner Earth, at Rennes-le-Chateau.

That's damned odd, you know. It was at Rennes-le-Chateau that the Merovingian kings ruled and it was also there, in the 1890's, that the eccentric priest, Father Sauniere, built a temple to Mary Magdalene which included some very bizarre variations on the Stations of the Cross—one showed a Scotsman in full kilts at the Crucifixion of Jesus, and another showed Jesus being covertly carried out of the tomb during the night by conspirators obviously intent on faking a Resurrection. The whimsical Father Sauniere inscribed over the door of this temple the words, "THIS PLACE IS TERRIBLE." (6)

De Selby is back, with his "definitive" essay. It is called "King Kong: A Meditation," and is by one Kenneth Bernard. The opening pages demonstrate that, according to comparative anatomy, just as a six-foot-tall man usually has a six-inch-long penis (in erection, and whether Andrea Dworkin approves or not), a 24-foot-tall gorilla would have a 24-inch-long penis in erection. Bernard rejects this scientific logic after stating it, on the grounds that Kong is not a creature in science but in myth. Kong, he claims, is of the family of such ithyphallic gods as Dionysos or Osiris. His penis therefore would not be "normal" for his size but, like that of Dionysos or Osiris, *three times* what one would expect. Therefore, since logic and anatomy lead one to expect Kong to have 24 inches or two feet, he must actually have three times that, or six feet. It is this, Bernard argues, that creates the unprecedented panic in New York when Kong is on the loose and searching for his bride, she who was given to him by his worshipers but stolen back by the treacherous white imperialists. A gorilla in heat, even a 24-foot-tall gorilla with a two-foot penis, is merely frightening; the terror of Kong goes beyond ordinary fear and ordinary logic. A 24-foot-tall gorilla with a six-foot penis inspires Panic, in the etymological meaning. He is Pan Ithyphallos, right out of the collective unconscious.

I think Phil Dick's Blakean visions and Prophetic Books inspire the same kind of Panic, and for the same reason; they are explosions of image and energy from the collective unconscious. They are as "barbarous" and "unbelievable" as a giant gorilla with a six-foot whang climbing up the side of your building. The Rastafarians, similarly, wear their distinctive head-dress—"dreadlocks," they are called—precisely because they know this style looks bizarre, primitive and threatening ("savage") to the average White person. It is, to them, an affirmation of the African heritage stolen when their ancestors, like Kong, were enslaved and brought to White civilization to be used as "natural resources." (7)

A parable may be helpful at this point. A group of people agree to meet at a certain place and time to make noise. Another group arranges to be there and listen. The noise happens as scheduled, and everybody then leaves and returns to everyday affairs.

According to one kind of sociology, that is all one can say scientifically about a certain kind of event that occurs regularly in all large cities. According to another kind of sociology, such an analysis applies the tools of physical science to an area of discourse, like King Kong's penis, that requires other kinds of analysis. If the noise was Beethoven's Ninth Symphony, we must make an effort to participate before we understand the "meaning" of what is happening.

De Selby adds in this connection that Rastafarians never say "we." They say "I and I." This is because "I" has a special meaning for them, signifying the "essential Self" or "God within." To a Rastafarian, every "I" is equally divine. Saying "I and I" is acknowledging the divinity of both participants in an interaction. Disciples of Vico and Whorf would remark that this simple example shows how linguistic grids mold *thought, feeling and (apparent) perception.*

Similarly, Buckminster Fuller, following Wittgenstein's criticism of language, attempted to abolish from his vocabulary all words that do not refer to experience. Fuller soon abolished "existence" and "non-existence," since they do not refer to experience. To replace these operationally meaningless terms, Fuller then said "the tuned-in" and "the not tuned-in," which do refer to experience. In this revised semantics, the paradoxes of quantum mechanics become self-evidently simple. The not-tuned-in is not-tuned-in, and that's that. Curiously, some physicists claim that's what the Copenhagen Interpretation always meant.

De Selby interjects that while Ireland has no ithyphallic emblems similar to those of Dionysos and Osiris, we did have *shiela-na-gigs.* These were to be found in hundreds of rural churches until the 19th Century, when they were removed and mostly destroyed; a few are preserved in the National Museum. They are female nudes, holding their genitalia open with both hands, rather like *Hustler* centerfolds: (8) an earlier, more stark version of the Anima energy of the Black Virgin. These are generally considered "survivals of paganism" but Robert Quinn, an expert on them, claims they are Gnostic. Quinn says the first Christians in Ireland were all Gnostics, who had been driven out of Southern Europe by Roman Catholic persecution. (9) He claims the *shiela-na-gigs* were used for meditation purposes, to raise the *kundalini* energy.

It is curious that the *shiela-na-gigs* are stored in the *basement* of the National Museum and one needs special permission to view them. Nobody knows what *shiela-na-gig* means; it is not even a Gaelic word. The Gnostics were exterminated almost entirely and survive only in fugitive secret societies: the Illuminati, the Priory of Sion, the B.P.O.E.

In 1974, in a hypnogogic vision, Phil Dick saw (beneath the surface of our civilization) the Roman Empire in its prime. In *VALIS* he explicates this vision in a magnificent science fiction allegory: the last 2000 years never happened. What we think of as 2000 years of history is a false memory planted in our brains by the Empire itself, to keep us from realizing who rules us and what is happening to us every day. *"The Empire never ended"* becomes a Wagnerian refrain, like the voice of a super-Gurdjieff trying to wake us from our group hypnosis.

I accept Phil's vision as true, on the *mythic level,* as I accept that in the collective unconscious King Kong with his mythically necessary six-foot penis consummates his love every night with Fay Wray opening herself in the shameless eroticism of a *shiela-na-gig.* It may be biologically impossible, but that doesn't matter in the dreamworld. (10)

On the *sociological level* I once heard the same insight—"The Empire never ended"—from philosopher Alan Watts. As well as I recall Alan's words after 20 years, he said, "The greatest error of professional historians is the idea that the Roman Empire 'fell.' It never did. It still controls the Western world through the Vatican and the Mafia." (11)

J.R. "Bob" Dobbs interrupted at this point (he had been reading over my shoulder) and said, "Yeah, man, tell them. Our rulers do *not* mean well, and they are *not* stupid." But I guess he had too much to drink, because then he went on about the "Nazi Hell Creatures" inside the hollow Earth, and the Intergalactic Bankers and Lovecraft's "Elder Gods" and some gibberish about sex mutilators and cattle educators.

De Selby who, as an Irishman, holds his malt better, showed me another deeply disturbing passage from Bernard's "King Kong: A Meditation"—a passage which is "the whole key to Ronald Reagan," de Selby insists. Bernard argues that for Americans, "rats and cockroaches and bedbugs (vermin) are the living presence of the dark-skinned hordes." He tells of a panic on Park Avenue when roaches were discovered in some fine old mansions and a worse panic when "welfare people (epi-vermin) were found living in the Waldorf Astoria (something like finding a rat using your toothbrush)." Bernard insists that in the unconscious Kong not only deflowers Fay Wray, like the acid-head going through the keyhole, but leads an army of *millions and millions* of rats against the White House. Somehow this powerful surrealist image leads Bernard to the further insight that city-dwellers do not know where the plumbing in their bathroom goes because they are *afraid* to know: afraid to contemplate darkness and vermin and everything below the pure, hygienic surface of "White Christian civilization." (12) He cuts close to the bone here, I think. He must be considered with great gravity when he concludes that no white male can ever sit on a toilet to move his bowels without an unconscious anxiety that a *HUGE BLACK HAND* might reach up through the plumbing and *grab him by the testicles.* De Selby admits to a nervous premonition that Ronald Reagan might disconnect his paranoia from Nicaragua and Libya to start bombing the "heathen" Rastafarian hordes in Liverpool, and I must confess, at this point, a terrible image of Andrea Dworkin leading 10,000 Fat Ladies from circuses in an assault on our National Museum to destroy the last *shiela-na-gigs* and abolish the last trace of Gnostic subversion, finishing the Vatican's job for them.

Jung, as is well known, came to the same sort of insight, and first posited the "collective unconscious," after a dream in which he found beneath his basement an earlier strata containing Roman architecture, and below that, Egyptian ruins, and so on down, and down, to a Stone Age level with flint axes. The same symbolism appears in Lovecraft's "The Rats in the Walls"—*rats* again!—in which the hero finds, below his English mansion, a Roman cellar, and below that, a Druid temple, and so on, down to the Stone Age again; in the process of exploration, the hero himself regresses in time and ends up a cannibal.

Bernard says, with Gallic irony, "Our behaviorists meanwhile allay our fears by telling us rats can be taught to drink tea. They literally have rats on the brain. Behavioral psychology is the last refuge of the imperialist."

IV

"Holy hour," *dank' Gott,* is over; de Selby and J.R. "Bob" Dobbs have gone back to the pub, weaving a bit and singing "Mister Wong Has the Biggest Tong in Chinatown." I think I can now get this philosophical exegesis somewhat better organized.

Since Phil Dick often referred to *Finnegans Wake,* a book which impressed him greatly, it is profitable to note certain parallels between Joyce's masterpiece and Phil's own masterpiece, *VALIS.* This can be demonstrated by the use of a handy notation which Joyce invented and used in his notebooks.

Joyce employed four major symbols for the four major strata of the human psyche: E, **M**, **3** and Ш.

E, or Ego, is the only part of consciousness normally tuned-in by us. It is what is left over after the editing mentioned earlier, in which 10,000,000 signals per minute are scrutinized by the lower brain and a few dozen are admitted to awareness. In *Finnegans Wake,* it is one Humphrey Chimpden Earwicker, a publican, in Chapelizod, Dublin; in *VALIS,* it is Philip K. Dick, a science fiction writer, on an odyssey through Northern and Southern California. E is neither "real" nor "unreal"; it is, to quote de Selby, "a necessary part of our mental furniture." E's *appearance* of "reality" is like the "appearance" of "solidity" of chairs and tables; E dissolves into a series of moves in a social game, on inspection, just as chairs and tables dissolve into waves of energy under close inspection by physicists.

M is E in a repressed position; Joyce used this symbol, I suspect, because it suggests the bars of a jail. **M** is the personal unconscious of Freud; it often *seems,* like E, to be organized into a "solid" personality in opposition to E (cf. *Dr. Jekyll and Mr. Hyde*), but it can become a whole phalanx of opposed "personalities" as in *The Three Faces of Eve* and similar cases. In *Finnegans Wake,* **M** is, at first, Hosty, the murky figure who pursues and persecutes Earwicker, and later an interminable series of pursuers and persecutors; in *VALIS,* **M** is Horselover Fat, the psychotic, who is continually trying to lure or cajole Phil Dick to abandon his skepticism and enter the world of dream, myth and madness.

Unlike Joyce and Dick, most humans remain unaware of M within themselves and project it onto others. You can get a rather specific and highly detailed view of your own **M** —if you can stand the shock—by making a list of people who annoy you, frighten you, or make you uncontrollably angry. They are all external isomorphs of your internal **M**.

3 represents a rotation in space-time of the E/ **M** complex, and experience of it inevitably leads to speculations similar to Phil Dick's "orthagonal time," the "serial time" of J.W. Dunne, the "circular time" of *Finnegans Wake* (and Nietzsche and Ouspensky), or the "Eternal Now" of most mystics. **3** is also the "collective unconscious" of Jung, the "Akashic records" of Theosophy, the *aliyavijnana* ("treasury unconscious") of Buddhism, and in some sense the Life Force of Bergson and the "morphogenetic field" of the English biologist, Sheldrake.

Because **3** is transpersonal, it "is" both inside and outside at the same time; inside one's genes as information, and outside one's mind and lifespan as vast sociobiological forces manifesting over aeons of geological time. **3** has no "personality," even relatively: it sometimes appears as fourfold (Buddhist mandalas, the Four Old

Men in *Finnegans Wake)* or twelvefold (the Zodiac, the apostles of Jesus, the jurors in *Finnegans Wake)* but is more often an infinite series (Neitzsche's "Eternal Recurrence") or a series which appears to be infinite because the last term links back to connect with the first (as in the structure of *Finnegans Wake).* In *VALIS,* 3 is a series of Jungian archetypes including the Head Apollo, the Buddha in the park, Sophia the female messiah (c.f. the Black Virgins earlier) and the Wise Old Man who gives Horselover Fat the magic herb (see again *Revelations* 22:2).

3 has the characteristics of the One Mind when one is "in dream-time" as the Australian aborigines say; in ordinary time, it appears, in multiple cross-sections, as all the individual E's or egos of all sentient beings. (13)

If 3 seems like One Mind, Ш usually seems like No Mind, which is why the Taoists call it *wu-hsin* ("no mind"). Zen Buddhists more tersely call it *wu* ("nothing"). Just as 3 is not organized into a "personality" in the human sense, Ш is not organized into "existence" or "non-existence," "real" or "unreal." In one quantum metaphor, Ш contains both the "real" (measured) and the "potential" (unmeasured) in Heisenberg's model. In another quantum model, Ш is the non-local hidden variable of David Bohm, having "mind-like" and "matter-like" manifestations, but essentially neither "mind" nor "matter." It is on the Ш level that Schrödinger's cat is both dead and alive, in the famous quantum paradox, and on the Ш level that Joyce's Finnegan is also both dead and alive. Ш cannot be discussed except in *contradictions,* because it is not a thing but a context of all possibilities. In *Finnegans Wake,* Ш is the narrator who sees all and knows all because s/he *is* all; in *VALIS,* Ш is VALIS itself: a *V*ast *A*ctive *L*iving *I*nformation *S*ystem.

Do I believe Scott Apel's dreams and synchronicities tuned-in Phil Dick after his death? Yes and no. I do not believe anything. In the model I currently find useful—Joyce's model—E or Ego does not survive death; but then, as Buddha and Hume noted, it does not even "survive" a ten-minute walk to the mailbox to post a letter. Did Scott tune in the **3** and **Ш** levels that communicated through Phil? This seems undeniable to me, and no more mysterious after Phil's death than it is that William Blake, among others, tuned in **3** and **Ш** long before Phil's birth.

Anybody, anywhere, anywhen, can tune in **3** and **Ш**. That's the meaning of Phil's koan, "The Buddha is in the park."

V

De Selby and J.R. "Bob" Dobbs have returned from the pub, even more elated than earlier. De Selby is explaining that while Fay Wray was brunette in her other films and in real life, she was deliberately dyed blonde in *King Kong* to make her more "white," i.e., more "pure." (The natives offered only maidens to Kong, remember.) J.R. "Bob" Dobbs says that the Mitchell Brothers showed "bulldada genius" (whatever that is) in casting Marilyn Chambers in *Behind the Green Door*. Ms. Chambers, he explains, was not only blonde but previously a model for Ivory Soap, symbolizing their mystique of being "99 and 44/100ths percent pure"; this was offering a form of detergent baptism, or purgation of "Original Sin" (mammalian genes), suitable for America's partly-secular, partly Christian culture. Ms. Chambers, in *Green Door,* is kidnapped, as Fay Wray was in *Kong;* Ms. Chambers is then "given" to a Black super-stud of ithyphallic endowment (by White standards) and a bone in his nose (to symbolize "savagery"), just as Fay Wray was "given" to be "the bride of Kong." He insists that *Green Door* is the explicit version of all that was implicit in *Kong.* "Pornography," J.R. "Bob" Dobbs summarizes "is the unconscious escaping into daylight, and that's why it inspires terror. Read Freud on the *unheimlich*." I recall the essay to which he refers—"Uber die

Unheimlich," 1914. Freud there investigates the kind of eerie coincidences that Jung later named synchronicities, and asks not why they happen (a question which he admits baffles him) but why they provoke sensations of dread and awe. His conclusion is that *we recognize them as material from our own unconscious*, and are stunned that they are escaping from the night-world of dreams into day-time and public view—as if the *shiela-na-gigs* broke out of the basement where the National Museum hides them and cavorted on the floor of the *Dail hEriann* (the Irish Parliament).

So I see a revised version of *King Kong,* without the mawkish sentimentality of Dino de Laurentis' remake: this time with the desperate honesty of early surrealism, Kong's six-foot penis would frankly be shown on screen; he would not recapture his bride, but, after breaking out of the theatre, would be overwhelmed by Andrea Dworkin and the 10,000 Fat Ladies from the circus I imagined earlier, who swarm over him and *emasculate* him in gory detail right before our eyes; the offending organ is then thrown in the Hudson River, weighted down so it will never rise to the surface again. The Pope flies in by jet, to canonize Ms. Dworkin on the spot. Representatives of the Committee for Scientific Investigation of Claims of the Paranormal—James Randi, Robert Schaeffer and Martin Gardner, preferably—then appear on screen to assure us that gorillas do not grow that big, that the eye-witnesses were hysterical and hallucinating, and that the damage inflicted on New York is "more scientifically and economically explained" by positing the fall of a meteor.

De Selby has gone up to his room again and brought back an amazing book called *East-West/North-South* by Peter Okera. Mr. Okera, a Black man born and raised in Africa, studied physics in England, and concluded that he was becoming schizophrenic. *East-West/North-South* is an attempt to cure himself, by explaining the split in his psyche; it is in the form of a dialogue-or-trialogue (that is the question) involving Mr. Okera himself, an enlightened and liberal English housewife, and an extraterrestrial from Algol. The whole point of the book seems to be that *asking if the extraterrestrial is "real" or "only" a "metaphor"* immediately places one in a White reality-tunnel and makes it impossible to understand African modes of thought-feeling-perception. (14)

De Selby, of course, insists that the extraterrestrial was "encountered and endured" by Mr. Okera, and that *theories* about this are not specifically White, but just a function of "the instinct to gossip." In my version of Joyce's notation, I would say the extraterrestrial is tuned-in on the Ш level and to ask if the same extraterrestrial can be tuned-in also on the E level is like trying to drink the word "water" instead of the stuff that comes out of the faucet in the kitchen.

One thing Phil Dick understood clearly, which most of his commentators have failed to grasp, is that in the same sense that the Empire never ended and Earth is full of "Nazi Hell Creatures," it is necessary to state certain information in paradox, poetry, allegory and even philosophical metathesis, so that the authorities will not suspect exactly how subversive and dangerous you are. In that sense, and only in that sense, it is good that certain types spend a lot of time and energy arguing about whether the extraterrestrial is "really there," or whether a gorilla with a six-foot penis is a poetic symbol or just a crazed fantasy. The message gets through, for those who are ready, *between the lines.*

Reggae, the music of Ras Tafari, resounds from a hundred thousand ghetto-blasters...inner-city America increasingly looks like Ridley Scott's *Blade Runner,* taken from one of Phil's novels...The Reagan androids, who brag of being "mean as a junkyard dog," bomb anything that is non-white and looks, like Kong, as if it hasn't been "tamed" and emasculated yet...The Junkyard Dog peers from a rusted Model T Ford, growling like Lon Chaney, Jr., in the transformation of Man into Beast...A Black voice cries in the twilight, "White boy, we gonna get yo' mama!"

De Selby tells me he once knew a young man with a Ph.D. in Literature from Oxford who spent seven years wandering the villages of Wales, looking for the church described in Dylan

Thomas' famous poem, where the anchor crashed through the floor and revealed, below, a "moon-chained and water-wound metropolis of fishes." After seven years of fruitless search, the young man returned to Oxford to write a book denouncing poets as liars. Then, one night, he went *down to his basement* to change a fuse and heard a strange gurgling, sloshing sound. He turned around and saw—

But you *know* what he saw, don't you? We all know, although we keep forgetting. The purpose of writing commentaries is to make things complicated enough that we can forget what we know.

Howth Hill, Dublin, 23 May 1986

FOOTNOTES

[1] As du Garbandier has written in his provocative *De Selby et L'Or de Rennes,* "Le supreme charme qu'on trouve a lire une page de de Selby est qu'elle vous conduit inexorablement a l'heuresse certitude que des sets vous n'etes pas le plus grand."

[2] As de Selby says *(Golden Hours,* II, i), "Experience is the sum total of consciously apprehended states that have been encountered and endured. The narratives we tell ourselves, making ourselves the heroes of each episode, are the internalization of the *instinct to gossip.*" The "instinct to gossip" plays the same panchrestonal role in de Selby's system as the "will to power" in Nietzsche or "nausea" in Sartre.

[3] It should be mentioned at once that in *Holy Blood, Holy Grail* (to be discussed later), Biagent, Leigh and Lincoln claim that de Sede is not a neutral observer in any sense but a "front-man" or propagandist for the Priory of Sion.

[4] Heisenberg, who agreed with Bohr and Mermin on this point, said even raising the question of what the unobserved thing is doing is equivalent to the medieval debate about how many angels can dance on the head of a pin. (Quoted by Mermin, *op. cit.)*

[5] This same belief is held by the Rastafarians. Their religious meetings, called "head-restings," consist of smoking cannabis drugs and then searching the Bible for pro-phecies. Naturally, the more they smoke, the more prophecies they find.

[6] The story of Father Sauniere is told in *Holy Blood, Holy Grail,* by Baigent, Leigh and Lincoln. They conclude, after examining other mysteries of Rennes-le-Chateau and the nearby Knights Templar fortification, that the Merovingian kings were descended, not from extraterrestrials as de Sede alleged, but from Jesus Christ and Mary Magdalene.

[7] One thinks in this connection of the Black Virgins who are such a mystery to archeologists and a huge embarrassment to the Vatican. There are over 450 of these Black female ikons in European churches; the very city where this is being written, Dublin, has as

its patron—"Our Lady of Dublin"—a Black Virgin in Whitefriar's Church. According to *The Cult of the Black Virgin,* by Eon Begg, a Jungian therapist and former Dominican monk, these mysterious idols were introduced to Europe by the Knights Templar and have been perpetuated by the shadowy Priory of Sion. Oddly, Begg seems to think this idol represents not Mary, the mother of Christ, but Mary Magdalene; he even hints at the Rastafarian doctrine that Jesus, his family, his friends and all the ancient Israelites were, by modern definition, Black or negroid.

[8] J.R. "Bob" Dobbs says that the difference between the centerfolds in *Playboy, Penthouse* and *Hustler* is this: the women in *Playboy* look as if they want you to make love to them, the ones in *Penthouse* look as if they can't wait and have started making love to themselves, and the ones in *Hustler* look as if they are having a gynecological examination.

[9] Dagobert II, the last Merovingian king, curiously left France as soon as he was crowned, went to Ireland, and remained there for over a decade. This has never been explained. When Dagobert II returned to France and took up his kingly duties, he was murdered as noted earlier. The authors of *Holy Blood, Holy Grail* claim the Vatican killed Dagobert. It gives one furiously to think, as the French say.

[10] An old Sufi parable from the 1960's: a drunk, a pot-head and an acid-tripper returned to the house they shared and found they had lost their keys. "Let's knock the damned door down," said the drunk aggressively. "Let's just sleep on the grass," said the pot-head serenely. "Why not float through the key-hole?" asked the acid-tripper radiantly.

[11] On Mafia-Vatican links, see Richard Hammer's *The Vatican Connection.* On Mafia-Vatican-US banking links, see Penny Lernoux's *In Banks We Trust.* On Mafia-CIA links, see Lernoux again and Carl Oglsby's *The Yankee and Cowboy War.* On CIA-Vatican links, see David Yallop's *In God's Name.* "It is all one seamless web," to quote Alan Watts again.

[12] One thinks intuitively of the *shiela-na-gigs* hidden in the *basement* of the National Museum of Ireland, and of the meaning of the hollow Earth archetype.

[13] This is why Rastafarians say "I and I" for "we."

[14] This somehow reminds me of an old Zen story. "What is the Buddha?" asks the predictably naive monk. "The one in the hall," says the Master. "But the one in the hall is a statue—a piece of wood," says the monk. "Yes," says the Master. "Then what is the Buddha?" the monk persists. "The one in the hall," says the Master.

Appendices

Appendix I
A Letter from Philip K. Dick to D. Scott Apel

INTRODUCTION

The following letter, from Philip Dick to me, is included for several reasons.

First, it is a typical example of Phil Dick correspondence: detailed, intelligent, chatty. Note, for instance, how fluidly he switches gears from a detailed essay on quantum mechanics and Schopenhauer's Will to the weather in L.A.

Second, it contains an interesting summary of an unwritten novel and some humorous descriptions of and insights into *VALIS* and *The Divine Invasion,* as well as other works (and deals) in progress.

Third, it is a nice capsule description of his late years: working hard, playing with his "writer's group," and being ill—but, he repeatedly claims, happy.

The "Linda Ronstadt pirated record" he refers to was a gift I had sent him; during our post-interview conversations about music, etc., he confided that he had always been in love with her. "I saw her perform live years before she ever became popular," he told us, "and I knew she was something special. I seriously considered contacting her and asking to manage her career. God knows mine wasn't going anywhere. It would have been the high point of my life if I could have said, 'I discovered Linda Ronstadt.' I would even have liked that carved on my tombstone."

One short paragraph, dealing with familial matters, has been deleted on request of the estate, dealing as it does with people still living who "might be hurt" by Phil's sarcasm. So be it.

Notes in parentheses are Phil's; those in brackets and italics are mine.

The envelope is postmarked August 8, 1980, and contains the return address, all in lower case: "philip k. dick, famous mystic."

A Letter from Philip K. Dick to D. Scott Apel

August 6, 1980

Dear Scott,

Forgive me for not answering you sooner; originally I had hoped to get a phonecall from you when you were down here, and then later on—well, all kinds of things: I've had to get together nine permissions to quote for VALIS, passages from very highbrow reference and scholarly books...and I've been ill—am ill now, and taking antibiotics. Tomorrow I see the doctor again. My friends say I've got the catclap from emptying the catbox. Also I am working in great haste on my new novel. I just learned that the sequel to VALIS, which is VALIS REGAINED *[later retitled* The Divine Invasion*]*, will be published hardback by Simon and Shuster, for which I get an extra $2,500, bringing my total payment up to $17,500. It took me only twelve days to write the novel which is a study of Judaism. I did two years of research. VALIS, meanwhile, will come out in February of next year; the cover is holding it up. I've read the galleys and really liked it, although I found I had not written the novel I thought I had. It is a study of a man's passage into acute mental illness, his brief return to sanity, only to pass back into mental illness again, and his courage in facing the fact of his defeat. I thought it had to do with extraterrestrials.

Now, about the Linda Ronstadt pirated record. I am so delighted as to be unable to express myself. However, I must admit that in my world (my fantasy world) Linda does not talk about blowing her nose on the microphone. This fits in with sections in VALIS REGAINED where there is a female vocalist named Linda Fox, galaxy-famous, who the protagonist is in love with (from a safe distance). He finally meets her and when he hits on her she says, "Sorry; it's my time of the month." He is crushed. His fantasy collapses. However, the real Linda Fox is superior to his fantasy so it is all right, the message being that reality is preferable to fantasy, although it does include such things as the female monthly curse. David Hartwell at Simon and Shuster says he thinks it's my best novel. Personally, I think VALIS is better, but less a genuine SF novel, it being so autobiographical. VALIS REGAINED is an account of YHWH's secret return to earth, in the womb of the protagonist's wife. The novel depicts YHWH growing up with impaired memories of his own identity (shades of van Vogt) until finally a disinhibiting stimulus triggers off anamnesis (loss of amnesia). He then kicks the shit out of Belial (Satan); well, actually, the novel ends with the beginning of the final war between YHWH and his antagonist, so we don't know the outcome.

Also, I sold a story to *Playboy* (for $2,000) which is a very good story, but, after buying it, they wanted massive changes. The whole story revolves around a Gilbert Shelton Fat Freddy Says poster, and *Playboy* in their infinite wisdom wanted the poster excised from the story and a *Playboy* illustration used instead. Also they wanted sex put into a scene involving a four-year-old boy, and the main character made into what they call an "A-head" which I presume is acid-head. I told them no, and they bought the story anyhow, much to our surprise. I donated the two thousand dollars to Cambodia famine relief. And I sold a very short story to *Omni,* so I am going great guns.

My novel-in-progress is about a planet that undergoes strange changes. Turns out it is a computer that has three modes of ratiocination, modes corresponding to the three realms of Dante's COMMEDIA. Whereas Dante started at the bottom and worked up, I start at the top and work down. The protagonist, a spy from Earth, is baffled by the sudden periodic transformations in the planet, in its landscape, people and way of thinking. There is a superhuman mode of thinking, then human, then subhuman or android. I am basing the superhuman mode on quantum mechanics.

Speaking of quantum mechanics, I am currently (for the time being, anyhow) persuaded that the key to explaining my mysterious mystical-religious experiences in 1974 lies in quantum mechanics; this theory was presented to me by Professor Patricia Warrick who read my MS of VALIS and who knows a lot about modern physics. She feels that I am the first fiction writer in the world to write from a post Newtonian standpoint, and this will be put forth in the book she is doing on me (I recall that I told you about her; she tells me what I am up to in my writing, not me her). Apparently, I somehow perturbed the reality field in 1974 and saw—well, I don't know what I saw, but in my opinion there is one step lacking in the thinking of the theoreticians in quantum mechanics and that is a recognition of Schopenhauer's Will. When they take that into account they will have it. My theory is that our Will (which lies outside our consciousness) creates a field that becomes part of the external reality field to form a single seamless field, and it is this field that we experience when we experience reality; viz: our Will is a component which cannot be excluded. If we can gain conscious awareness and control of our Will we can influence our "external" reality by a direct application of our own mind—setting up just the kind of perturbation that I experienced in 1974. Our center of consciousness must expand to fill the volume of the field of our Will—the ultimate in consciousness expansion. At this point we become what the ancients called Adam Kadmon, the Primal Man, who filled the entire universe. This is the great goal of the secret societies, in my opinion, and it can be understood in terms of the observer-participant universe of quantum mechanics (which in my own writings I have called the *idios kosmos,* after Heraclitus.)

The weather down here has been terrible and it has been terribly hard to work, which is another reason I haven't promptly responded. Yesterday the underground comic artist Spain dropped by visit me, a real treat. I am thinking about going back up to the Bay Area to visit Joan *[Simpson],* about whom I think constantly. It now seems to me that I made a dreadful mistake in breaking up with her, but I must admit that I am quite happy these days, being as I am involved with my writing and doing quite well at it. The SF book club picked up The Golden Man, doing a handsome cover on it; I am getting an enormous amount of feedback from the introduction I wrote for it; Gary Panter the punk artist got in touch with me and is coming down here; we've talked on the phone repeatedly and he seems like a wonderful guy. And then there are my MOVIE DEALS, all four of them: on Second Variety, We Can Remember It For You Wholesale, Do Androids Dream of Electric Sheep, and a French interest in Confessions of a Crap Artist (it's too hot to type in caps, so forgive me). I can't really complain of anything. The new little movie company making the film Claw based on Second Variety paid me the purchase price, $17,500, and that took care of my taxes. I probably mentioned this to you, but I bought my conapt outright, for $51,474, so my expenses are quite low.

[Some comments deleted by request.]

We have a sort of little circle of writers down here, five of us who are selling (including me, but I always sell). It's a nice life; we get together once a week, smoke cigars and drink Wild Turkey bourbon and talk dirty and shop. I have no complaints, except that I miss Joan. The girl I met in France phoned me and said she realizes she's in love with me and would I come back to Metz to be with her? but I don't think I will; I'm too lazy and she is too nuts.

Well, thank you, again, for the outta sight Ronstadt record. I'm glad the intro *[to* The Golden Man*]* got to you; I really meant it when I wrote it, and I read it over now and then and draw strength from it myself. Keep in touch and say hello to everyone from me.

With affection,

Phil

Appendix II
Theodore Sturgeon on Philip K. Dick

INTRODUCTION

The following short excerpt is taken from an interview with Theodore Sturgeon conducted by Kevin C. Briggs and me in October, 1977.

While preparing this volume, I wrote repeatedly to Sturgeon, asking if he would care to comment in detail on his private "philosophical discussion" with Philip Dick at the Octocon science fiction convention. I received no reply. Later, I discovered the reason why: Ted himself was in ill health, and soon afterward passed away.

All that is left written about their relationship, then, is this excerpt. I have chosen to include it for the simple reason that, although brief, it is illuminating.

Theodore Sturgeon on Philip K. Dick

Apel: I couldn't help overhearing—because I was eavesdropping—just a snatch of conversation between you and Phil Dick this afternoon. You were saying something like, "I've waited fifteen years to have this conversation with you," and proceeded to talk with him for half an hour or so...

Sturgeon: That conversation had been holding fire, building up in me, for a good long time. It was a fascinating experience, when you three [Phil, Briggs and myself] walked in here and I launched into this, precisely like one of those kids diving off the cliffs at Acapulco, without any preliminaries. Off we went. There are a lot of things that I have been very sure about for a long time that I feel Phil has been bumbling into and out of, into and out of, for a long time, without any clear delineation of what it is. I think Phil recognizes that I knew what it was, too. It's a whole universal concept which I don't think I'll go into in great length right now. I'm too curious to see what Phil is going to do with it. But it has to do with my whole idea of the cosmos and intelligence, that is to say *entity* intelligence...

Apel: If you *want* to go into it in great detail, that's what we're here for...

Sturgeon: Well, as I say, it's complex, and I don't want to use up the entire interview time with this; it's too large. But it was a fascinating experience, to be able to talk with him about this. I've really only gotten together with him twice before. Once when I lectured in Fullerton, but I couldn't spend too much time with him. Another time he came up to the house; he just blew in like a northwest gale, surrounded by flying icicles and withered leaves; he roared in and roared out, and that was that. *[Sturgeon said of this meeting to Paul Williams, "I felt as if I'd been through a hurricane that night."]*

On the other hand, I've read a lot of what he's written and am profoundly impressed by it. He is one of the great talents around. It's a wild talent, but there's a reason for that, too. I think he's on the very verge now of confronting who he really is.

The kind of thing that Phil Dick does reaches very deeply into his readers, and actually dictates their actions and their thoughts to a great degree. And Phil is willing to take responsibility for that. He wants more than anything else to be free to write, and life keeps piling things on him, making him afraid, making him wary, and sometimes making him aggressive. When he drives away devils, sometimes the devils are there...but sometimes they're not, and he drives them away anyway, which makes it a little rough on his surroundings. A writer like Phil ought to be a writer who writes.

Appendix III
The "Tagore" Letter

INTRODUCTION

In September of 1981—just six months before his death—Philip K. Dick experienced the capstone of his "mystical visions": a vision of a "new savior," incarnated once again to illustrate to Humankind the fatal folly of its ways.

This vision was apparently so overwhelming to Dick that he wrote the following letter, dated September 23, 1981, to Ed Meskys, the editor of *Niekas,* a small science fiction magazine, in hopes of getting the word disseminated. In addition, he mailed out something on the order of 85 copies of this letter, apparently (according to Paul Williams) to nearly everyone in his address file.

It would be very interesting to find out just what kind of response he obtained. One response is detailed by Phil himself in Rickman's *The Last Testament;* although not mentioned by name, the psychic/writer Francis Steiger took this vision as a projection of PKD's own ill health—at least as Phil interpreted her response.

Robert Anton Wilson, in a letter to me dated 23 May 1986, had this to say: "Phil sent me the Tagore letter at the same time he sent it to the other 70 or 80 people who got it. I wrote back; in general, I said all visions are true in some sense but one should not take them as necessarily true in the how-many-jelly-beans-in-the-jar sense."

I was at a loss as to what to say concerning such a delicate matter, and honestly don't remember whether my response was a short call or a short letter—or what I had to say. Nothing of great importance, obviously.

Some enterprising scholar could probably have a field day tracing PKD's "Elijah complex" from his "other mind" experiences detailed in the interview in this volume and though his intimation in *The Last Testament* that this "other mind" was the biblical prophet "Elijah," through the use of "Elijah" in his novel *The Divine*

Invasion, to this letter, in which he fulfills this—real or imaginary—role as a "new Elijah" heralding the "new savior."

Some have pointed to this letter as an indication of Philip Dick's "mental illness"; these individuals have obviously overlooked the self-mocking humor, the carefully constructed emotional impact of an essay by a writer at the peak of his powers, and the ethical correctness of this intense message. This is no construction of a sick mind, either in form or in content. The means by which the message was obtained—by vision, intuition or logic; through a true, spurious or future "Tagore"—should not diminish the wisdom of its content.

The copy which was sent to me came with this marginal notation: "Scott: Make of this what you will. It is sincere."

This letter was, to the best of my knowledge, Philip K. Dick's final public message.

The "Tagore" Letter

September 23, 1981
Dear Ed,

All the people who read my recent novel VALIS know that I have an alter ego named Horselover Fat who experiences divine revelations (or so he thinks; they could be merely hallucinations, as Fat's friends believe). VALIS ends with Fat searching the world for the new savior who, he has been told by a mysterious voice, is about to be born. He got me to write this letter as a way of telling the world—the readership of *Niekas,* more precisely—about it. Poor Fat! His madness is complete, now, for he supposes that in his vision he actually *saw* the new savior.

I asked Fat if he was sure he wanted to talk about this, since he would only be proving the pathology of his condition. He replied, "No, Phil; they'll think it's you." Damn you, Fat, for putting me in this double-bind. Okay; your vision, if true, is overwhelmingly important; if spurious, well, what the hell. I will say about it that it has a curiously practical ring; it does not deal with another world but this world, and extreme is its message—extreme in the sense that if true, we are faced with a grave and urgent situation. So let 'er rip, Fat.

The new savior was born in—or now lives in—Ceylon (Sri Lanka). He is darkskinned and either a Buddhist or Hindu. He works in the rural countryside with an organization or institute practicing high-technology veterinarian medicine, mainly with large animals such as cattle (most of the staff are white). His name is Tagore something; Fat could not catch the last name: it is very long. Although Tagore is the second incarnation of Christ he is taken to be Lord Krishna by the local population. Tagore is burned and crippled; he cannot walk but must be carried. As near as Fat could make out, Tagore is dying, but he is dying voluntarily: Tagore has taken upon himself mankind's sins against the ecosphere. Most of all it is the dumping of toxic wastes into the oceans of the world that shows up on Tagore's body as serious burns. Tagore's *kerygma,* which is the Third Dispensation (following the Mosaic and Christian), is: the ecosphere is holy and must be preserved, protected, venerated and cherished—*as a unity:* not the life of individual men or individual animals but the ecosphere as a single indivisible unitary whole, a life-chain that is being destroyed, and not just temporarily but for all time. The demonic trinity which Tagore speaks against—and which is wounding and killing him—consists of nuclear wastes, nuclear weapons and nuclear power (reactors); they constitute the enemy which not only may destroy the ecosphere but already, as toxic wastes, are destroying it now. So again Christ acts out his role of vicarious atonement; he takes upon himself man's sins but these sins are real, not doctrine sins. Tagore teaches that if we destroy the ecosphere much more, Holy Wisdom, the Wisdom of God (represented by Tagore himself) will abandon man to his fate, and that fate is doom.

Tagore teaches that when the ecosphere is burned, God himself is burned, for the Christ has invaded the ecosphere and invisibly assimilated it to himself through transubstantiation—which is the great vision Horselover Fat has in my novel VALIS. Thus Christ and the ecosphere are either one or rapidly becoming one—much as Teilhard de Chardin describes in THE PHENOMENON OF MAN. The ecosphere does not evolve into the Cosmic Christ, however; Christ penetrates it, which is exactly what Fat saw and which so amazed him. Thus Christ now speaks out—not just for the salvation of mankind or certain men, "the elect"—but for the ecosphere as a whole, from the snail darter on up. This is a systems concept and was beyond their vocabulary in apostolic times; it has to do with the indivisibility of all life on this planet, as if the planet itself were alive. And Christ is both the *soma* (body) and the *psyche* (the head) of that collective life. Hence the ultimate statement by Tagore— expressed by his voluntary passion and death—is, *He who wounds the ecosphere literally wounds God.* Thus a macro-crucifixion is taking place now, in and as our world, but we do not see it; Tagore, the new incarnation in human form of the Logos, tells us this in order to appeal to us to stop. If we continue we will lose God's Presence and, finally, we will lose our own physical lives. The oceans especially are menaced; Tagore speaks of this most urgently. When each canister of radioactive wastes is dumped into the ocean, a new stigma appears on Tagore's terribly burned, seared legs. Fat was horrified by the sight of these burns, the legs of the savior drawn up in pain. Fat did not see Tagore's face, only his tragically burned body, and yet (Fat tells me) there was an ineffable sweetness about Tagore "like music and perfume and colors," as Fat phrased it to me. Burned as he is, wounded and dying as he is, Tagore nonetheless emits only loving beauty, absolute beauty, not relative beauty. It was a sight that Fat will never forget. I wish I could have shared it, but I had better things to do: watch TV and play electronic computer games. All that good stuff by which we fritter away our lives, while the ecosphere, wounded and in pain and in mortal danger, cries out for our help.

Cordially,

Philip K. Dick

Coming soon from Atomic Drop Press

The Infinite Mistress
by D. Scott Apel

An Alec Smart Mystery (#2)

"Fans of Donald E. Westlake's comic crime novels will love
The Infinite Mistress."
—ComiCaper.

When a bubble-headed North Beach topless dancer hires a young Silicon Valley private eye to investigate the authenticity of her "past life memories," little does he suspect that he's about to become entangled in a plot that has repeated itself through several lifetimes—and always ends tragically for the dancer.

Or is it all just coincidence? The real question is, can he piece together the past-life clues he uncovers in time to dodge the juggernaut of karma and avoid the fated fatal finale? It's taken several lifetimes, but this time around, time is running out. A fast, funny, and original twist on the mystery novel.

Now available as an ebook wherever fine ebooks are sold.

Coming soon from Atomic Drop Press

Killer B's:
The 237 Best Movies on Video
You've (Probably) Never Seen
by D. Scott Apel

The iTunes Movie Guru (Emeritus) shares his selection of the best unknown movies available on demand.

From the Introduction to Killer B's:

We live in an age of unprecedented access to movies. Too bad most of them suck.

Netflix, iTunes, Amazon, Vudu, Hulu Plus... Thousands and thousands of movies are available at your fingertips. But with so many titles, the big question remains *How do you find a* good *movie?*

The answer: *Killer B's: The 237 Best Movies on Video You've (Probably) Never Seen. Killer B's* makes full use of the on-demand advantage: easy access to lesser-known films. It's just as easy to find a hidden gem as a recent blockbuster...if you know what you're looking for. *Killer B's* lets you know what to look for.

Whatever you call them—buried treasures, sleepers, word of mouth movies, or "killer" B movies—these are great little films that never got the publicity, distribution or attention they needed to allow their audience to find them. Killer B's are terrific but little-known films, designed with a general audience in mind—no "cult classics," no "forgotten favorites," no "so bad they're good" flicks, just the delight of discovery.

Life's too short to watch bad films. Don't be stung by bad movies—put *Killer B's* to work for you, and find a few good movies you've (possibly) never heard of and (probably) never seen!

Now available as an ebook wherever fine ebooks are sold.

Coming soon from Atomic Drop Press

Mein Summer Kampf

Or, Everything I've Ever Written That Was Funny, Almost
by D. Scott Apel

The most common response I get to that title is: "You think that's funny?" The answer I'd really like to give you is the Joe Pesci answer: "Funny how? I mean, funny like I'm a clown, I amuse you?" But the answer I will give you (and Joe) is: Yes, I do, or I wouldn't have made it the title of this collection of short humorous essays, ludicrous lists, satirical stories and even (shudder) a couple parodic poems. Yes, the answer is Yes.

There is only one other word I'd like to say about this collection: *subtle*. And that is the last time you will ever hear that word used in connection with this material. An ex-girlfriend once told me that I was like a 1,000 watt light bulb: very bright, but a little obnoxious. And I've been informed that my humor has a certain "*je ne sais merde*." I prefer to believe, however, that, like the blind man whose other senses are heightened to compensate for his lack of sight, my total lack of common sense or any sense of common decency has allowed my sense of to humor expand...occasionally so far as to exceed the boundaries of comprehension or appreciation of those poor souls born without a humor gland.

Of course that is not you, despite what they all say about you behind your back. So, what the hell. Take a chance. Prove them wrong. You might just LYAO. I mean, it's FREE, for chrissake.

(Except on Amazon. They *won't let me give it away free*. WTF?) What have you got to lose? I'll answer that question, too: You know that old adage, "You get what you pay for"? This book proves it wrong: Even though it's free, and you're still getting far less than you paid for.

Hm. That hardly sounds like a successful sales pitch, now does it? OK, try this old adage: "Ya pays yer money and ya takes yer chances." Well, you're not paying anything, so there's a chance you might just get some laughs out of this collection. As a matter of fact, I *guarantee* you will, or your money will be cheerfully refunded. As long as you got the free version, anyway. If they made you pay 99 cents for this, then we'll have to fall back on the new adage for internet commerce: "99 cents is the new free."

Now available as an ebook wherever fine ebooks are sold.

www.ingramcontent.com/pod-product-compliance
Lightning Source LLC
Chambersburg PA
CBHW070656180626
46817CB00006B/2390